DAUGHTERS OF WARSAW

Maria Frances was born in London and grew up in the UK and Germany. She holds an MA in Creative Writing from Lancaster University and a PhD in Psychology from the University of Durham. She works as a writer and translator and lives with her husband and four children in Berlin. She is the author of five novels which she writes under her real name, Juliet Conlin. Her first German-language novel is also publishing in 2023. *Daughters of Warsaw* is her debut novel with Avon.

DAUGHTERS
of
WARSAW

MARIA FRANCES

avon.

Published by AVON
A division of HarperCollins*Publishers*
1 London Bridge Street
London SE1 9GF

www.harpercollins.co.uk

HarperCollins*Publishers*
Macken House, 39/40 Mayor Street Upper
Dublin 1
D01 C9W8

A Paperback Original 2024

23 24 25 26 27 LBC 6 5 4 3 2

First published in Great Britain by HarperCollins*Publishers* 2024

A catalogue copy of this book is available from the British Library.

ISBN: 978-0-00-859524-1

Typeset in Bembo Std by HarperCollins*Publishers* India
Printed and bound in the United States

To C.K.L.

Author's note

While DAUGHTERS OF WARSAW is a work of fiction, the novel is inspired by the actions of Żegota, a resistance group operating in Poland during the Second World War, and in particular by one of the group's leaders, Irena Sendler. Irena was a Catholic nurse and social worker who saved the lives of thousands of Jewish children from being murdered by the Nazis by smuggling them out of the Warsaw Ghetto. She kept meticulous records of the children's names and aliases, which she buried beneath an apple tree. She was recognised as Righteous Among the Nations by Israel in 1965, although she continued to resist being called a 'hero' until her death in 2008.

Irena Sendler is the only 'real' character in the novel; the others are all fictional, but they represent the heroic actions undertaken by Polish citizens who would not stand by and passively bear witness to the genocide of the Jewish population.

For me, writing historical fiction brings with it a huge responsibility, as it draws on real human lives – the joys, the tragedies and everything in between. As part of my extensive research for DAUGHTERS OF WARSAW, I travelled to the city and visited the remains of the Warsaw Ghetto, described by those who were incarcerated there as a true 'hell on earth', where survival was only possible through ingenuity, industriousness, solidarity and – perhaps most importantly – hope. Most of the ghetto was destroyed at the end of the Second World War, but its remains have since been put into a meaningful and respectful context and are well worth visiting.

However, good historical fiction is much more than a simple retelling of a particular historic period. It is not enough just to get the 'facts' right – the timescales, the settings, even the fashion of the day. Historical fiction should also capture something essential about human lives, and, if done well, provide some insight that is ultimately timeless. What stands out to me is the breathtaking bravery of those such as Irena Sendler, apparently ordinary people who risked their lives and those of their loved ones to stand up and fight against inhumanity. Setting a book during this particular slice of history is a tricky endeavour, as there is much a writer can get wrong, but it can also provide a unique perspective on the present and enable phrases like 'Never again' to become truly meaningful. In this regard, I hope I have done justice to Irena Sendler and her fellow Żegota members.

1

Seattle, Present Day

Lizzie stepped into her old bedroom, surprised by the familiarity of the smell – that slightly sweet, fruity scent of teenage perfume and hair spray. Her single bed was still covered by the patchwork blanket her grandmother had made for her when she was a child, and was pushed up against the back wall to make room for a sewing table, swathes of fabric, and a dressmaker's dummy.

She felt tears pricking her eyes yet again. She took a deep breath and dug her nails into the palms of her hands to stop them coming. She'd cried non-stop on her way here to her parents' house and already felt completely wrung out.

Outside, the wind rattled the shutters; it was late June but there was a storm on the way and the light was dim and grainy. She crossed to the far wall and switched on the small pink lamp. *At least it isn't cold*, she thought, and immediately her friends' well-meaning words – words she'd heard so many times over the past few years – echoed inside her head.

'At least you're still young.'

'At least you *know* you can get pregnant.'

'At least it wasn't fully formed yet.'

Lizzie didn't want to hear any more comments that started with the words 'at least'. All she wanted was for someone to take her in their arms and acknowledge that her pain – her grief – was real. The first time, four years ago, had been more of a surprise than anything, but it had happened just before the magical twelve-week mark, when the chances of miscarriage were highest, and she and her husband Alex hadn't told anyone. She cried for a couple of days, then thought: *best not to dwell on it*. She was pregnant again within four months. That one lasted a little longer – fourteen weeks. The size of a peach. People started making 'at least' comments.

Number three – a fig – was gone just as the morning sickness had subsided. She received a couple of text messages from friends, sent from a safe distance, telling her how sorry they were. How amazingly brave she was.

And this last one, the one she'd lost a month ago, was barely the size of a blueberry. It had felt so much bigger than that, and Lizzie wondered guiltily if she had put too much expectation on this little life – all her hopes and dreams – and whether her baby had struggled under the weight of it all.

People had stopped making any sort of comment; no one knew what to say.

In Alex's defence, he had never made an 'at least' comment. But after a while, he stopped hugging her. Eventually, he told her he couldn't speak without fear of saying the wrong thing.

'Tell me what to say, Lizzie,' he'd said, 'and I'll say it.'

But what *was* there to say? Grief was like that. It snatched and clawed at your heart, made you passionate with rage one

2

minute, and dumb-struck with sadness the next. When she and Alex could no longer stand the sight of each other, Lizzie had fled back to her childhood home, before one of them said or did something that might damage their relationship for good.

And here she now stood, in the bedroom she'd grown up in. She looked over to the window, recalling how, years ago, Alex had tossed little pebbles against the glass, late at night, to let her know he was there. They'd met at senior high school, some twenty years ago. High school sweethearts – it was a cliché they both joked about, but they had fallen in love as seventeen-year-olds and the only time they'd spent apart since then was when Alex went to med school and Lizzie was doing her bachelor's degree in teaching. They got married when Alex graduated, and started trying for a baby once they were both established in their respective careers. Lizzie began working part-time when they started trying to conceive. She wanted four kids, he wanted two, and they'd jokingly settled on three. They were young and excited, and it had seemed so straightforward at the time. She could never have anticipated the level of heartache it had caused over the past four years.

They had seen all the specialists, done all the tests, yet no one could tell them what was wrong. 'Just relax,' the doctors would say. 'Go on vacation, distract yourselves. It'll happen when it happens.'

But Lizzie's body, her *stupid, useless* body, couldn't hold on to a baby. *I'm a failure*, she thought, *a massive failure.* In her darker moments, she knew she wouldn't blame Alex if he left her for someone who could give him the children he so longed for. He had been working longer and longer hours lately, even though she needed him more than ever. And that's why she had been shutting him out. To make it less painful when he inevitably left her. She thought she'd cried enough to last a lifetime, but there always seemed to be more tears, and so she stood there, sobbing her heart out once more. It was no use. There was no stopping the tears; she was trapped inside her grief.

The door behind her opened and her mother came in.

'Oh, honey.' She came over to Lizzie and hugged her. 'Oh, honey,' she said again. 'You know how much we love having you here, but seeing you like this – it breaks my heart.'

She waited a moment until Lizzie's tears had subsided and then took her hand and squeezed it gently. 'Let's get you through the summer vacation, hmm? Then, when school starts again, you'll feel much better. You love your kids, right? It'll distract you from all this, I'm sure.'

'I'm not going back,' Lizzie said quietly.

'What do you mean?'

'I'm handing in my notice. I … I just can't bear it, Mom. Being around the kids. They're so sweet and I love them so much, but knowing I might never have one of my own, it's just too painful.'

'And Alex?'

Lizzie sighed. 'I'm too tired to talk about it, Mom. Tomorrow, maybe.'

Her mother gave her a sad smile and stroked one of Lizzie's dark curls behind her ear. 'We'll take it one day at a time,' she said. 'And you can stay as long as you want, *kochanie*. But as you can see,' she continued, gesturing around the small space, 'I've turned this into a sewing room, so unless you want to sleep alongside my patterns and fabric samples, you'll have to take some of this stuff up to the attic.'

4

The attic room was nicer than the name suggested, Lizzie thought as she stood there a couple of days later, looking around. It wasn't a dark and dusty space beneath the rafters; rather, it was a cosy den where she and her younger sister Hannah had sat and played with their dolls' house for hours, until their mom yelled, 'If you don't come down right now for your dinner, I'm throwing it in the trash!'

It had taken Lizzie two days to summon the energy to clear out her room, but having stubbed her toe painfully last night on her mother's sewing table for the umpteenth time, she decided she would have to make some space and tidy up. The attic room was small, but it had a quaint slanted ceiling and a mullioned window that let in the morning light. And if she stood on tiptoes and craned her neck just so, looking past the chestnut trees, she could just about make out the Pacific Ocean.

After she and Hannah had moved out, this room had become a storage area, stuffed full of things her parents no longer needed but to which they had become too attached to throw out: her and Hannah's yearbooks; her purple cheerleading pompoms; old photo albums; broken Christmas ornaments; romper suits worn first by her, then by Hannah. Their very first baby shoes.

She and Alex had bought baby shoes for their best friends, Susie and Geoff, when Susie gave birth to their first child a week before Lizzie's first miscarriage. Alex had wanted to buy a second set of the shoes – made of soft white suede, impossibly tiny at three-and-a-half-inches – for their own child, but Lizzie had said it was bad luck to buy things before the baby was born. Turned out it didn't matter.

Susie and Geoff had had another baby a couple of years later, shortly after Lizzie's third miscarriage. When Lizzie went to visit her in hospital, Susie had told Lizzie how bad she felt for her, but she was unable to hide the delight she felt for the newborn she cradled in her arms. Lizzie didn't blame her, of course she didn't, but it had become exhausting to suppress her own feelings of anguish and bitterness, and the creeping feeling of isolation as more and more of her friends and colleagues started having their own families.

She shook her head to dispel the memory and looked around the small, cluttered attic room. Where to begin? She had promised her mom that she'd recreate a sewing area up here and she'd have to make space for the table. Left of the window were six cardboard boxes and an ancient-looking leather trunk. She picked up the first box. It was heavy, but she didn't have to worry about lifting heavy things anymore. She no longer needed to worry about so many things: remembering to take her prenatal vitamins, going without her beloved sushi, drinking decaf in the mornings although she was tired all the time. She'd also be able to enjoy a glass – or three – of Cabernet Sauvignon with her mom tonight.

She bit her lip to stop the tears. None of that was any comfort.

She placed the box near the door to carry down later and did the same with the others. They would find a new home in the basement.

She grabbed a handle of the trunk to slide it to the door, but it was virtually immovable. She tried again, grunting with the effort, but it was too heavy. She'd probably have to empty it. Getting down onto her knees, she opened the clasps and swung open the lid. A Singer sewing machine, shiny black with the logo in curly golden letters. Lizzie knew where the mahogany base was; it had been repurposed as a sideboard that sat in her parent's bedroom. Beneath the machine were dozens of old leather-bound books – *Encyklopedye Polskie* – a Polish encyclopaedia, that may or may not be worth something. Lizzie would have a word with her parents about putting it on Craigslist. She lifted the books out, two at a time, sneezing as the decades-old dust travelled up her nostrils.

She got to her feet. There, now she should be able to move the trunk. Bending down to take the handle, she saw that there was something – a slip of paper? – stuck between the fabric lining and the side of the trunk. She teased it out gently. It was an envelope, yellowed and dried with age. Curious, Lizzie opened it and pulled out some photographs. The light was too dim to see them properly, so she crossed to the small window and sat down on an old wicker chair that creaked worryingly under her weight. There were three photographs in total; all old, black-and-white, and with crinkled edges.

The first photograph showed a young woman with dark hair piled up in a braided updo, sitting on a bench outdoors somewhere, with four children around her. One of them, a toddler, was sitting on her lap. Lizzie squinted in the poor light to take a closer look. She'd seen the woman before, in other family photographs. It was her *prababcia*, her great-grandmother Zofia. It was a flattering picture; her full dark hair, the high cheekbones, the star-burst creases around her smiling eyes. But who were the children? Lizzie checked the back of the photograph, but there was nothing written there. She knew that her great-grandmother had had a single daughter – Lizzie's grandma Magda – but she didn't know much of her family history beyond the fact that her family went back generations in Seattle.

The second picture was young Zofia again, this time with a group of women, some older, some Zofia's age. Her colleagues, perhaps? But they were wearing nurses' uniforms, which Lizzie thought odd, because she'd know if her great-grandmother had been a nurse, surely? Zofia was standing on the left of the group, a shy smile on her face.

In the third photograph, her great-grandmother sat beside another woman who had a young girl on her lap. They were sitting outside, a brick wall behind them. There looked to be frost on the ground, but the light was bright. Zofia and the woman were smiling into the camera, squinting slightly into the sun. The smile of the woman beside Zofia appeared strained though, and she was dreadfully thin. Lizzie thought she looked almost ill. The child, by contrast, appeared full of life. She was about five or six, head back in a laugh and judging from the out-of-focus fuzziness, was squirming to jump off the woman's lap. Lizzie turned the photograph over and let out a delighted gasp. There was something written on the back: *Warsaw 1942*, and beneath that the name *Szczęsny*, which Lizzie knew was the original Polish spelling of *Chesney*, the surname by which she had known her great-grandmother. Lots of Eastern Europeans had anglicised their names when they came to the States. Below that was another name: *Zielińska*. Lizzie had never heard that name before, but she presumed it belonged to the woman and the child.

She got to her feet, frowning. She should probably stick the pictures in one of the family albums for safekeeping, but something about the first photograph tugged at her, the one with her great-grandmother and the children. She took a last look at it. There was a natural intimacy between Zofia and the children that suggested a deep and tender relationship. Something beyond the affection you might have for a friend's children. She looked at Zofia more closely. Yes, the way she looked up at the boy near her shoulder was undoubtedly maternal. The toddler on her lap was snuggled into her chest, and one of the girls beside her, who must have been eight or nine years old, was looking at her with huge adoring eyes.

Could they be Zofia's own children? But if so, why had Lizzie never been told about them? Puzzled, she wiped her hands on her jeans and headed downstairs.

'Mom?' she called as she descended the narrow staircase to the second floor. 'Why did you never tell me *Prababcia* had other kids?'

2

Warsaw, September 1942

Zofia was hunched over the filing cabinet, glad the working week was nearly over. Her stomach rumbled audibly and she looked around, embarrassed that someone might have heard. At the far end of the large office, two colleagues were typing away furiously, but Lina, at the desk beside Zofia's, looked up and grinned.

'Hungry?' she said with a wink.

Zofia rolled her eyes. 'Always.'

She'd had a margarine sandwich for lunch and looked forward to a home-cooked meal of *gołąbki*, cabbage rolls stuffed with minced pork, mushroom, and onions. Lately, though, Zofia's mother had started adding more and more vegetables to the filling as meat was becoming increasingly expensive. Her father was a local business owner with a small workshop, manufacturing leather goods – belts, bags, wallets, suitcases – and although he worked very long hours to provide for his family, the war was taking its toll on businesses all over the city. Zofia's family were surviving, and there were many others who were worse off, but her younger sister

Zuzanna had been born with a weak heart and suffered from recurring bouts of sickness There were days when she was too pale and breathless to even get out of bed. The doctor's bills and medicines she needed to stay alive were more than they could afford on their father's income alone. The wages Zofia earned at the Social Welfare Department weren't grand, but it was a steady income and she enjoyed coming to work every morning.

Once she'd finished filing, she sat back down at her desk and tried to focus on the case file in front of her rather than her rumbling stomach. The office was filled the clackety-clack of Elżbieta's typewriter, the third woman Zofia and Lina shared the office with. Elżbieta was friendly, but rather prim and proper, and kept to herself most of the time.

Beside Zofia, Lina lit a cigarette. She claimed she smoked to help keep her figure slim, but that was plainly ridiculous, given her naturally petite, slender frame. Zofia thought it far more likely that she smoked to curb her appetite because there was never really enough to eat. She'd tried smoking herself, in an attempt not to feel so bloody hungry all the time, but she found the taste of tobacco quite disgusting.

'Only half an hour to go, girls!' Lina chirped. 'Let's—'

She was interrupted by the sound of a shout and a door being slammed outside in the corridor. Zofia looked up. It must be Mr Wójcik, the head of department, who had his office across the corridor from theirs. There were more muffled shouts, and the sound of a chair scraping across the floor.

Lina opened the door a crack and peered out.

'It's them,' she said in a low voice. 'The damn Nazis.'

Elżbieta tutted loudly but didn't say anything. From outside, they heard the stomping of boots and the bark of orders.

'Lina,' Zofia whispered, 'come away from the door before they see you!'

Lina's views on the German occupiers were well-known, and Zofia was constantly worried she might say the wrong thing too loudly. The Germans were notoriously thin-skinned and quick to dole out punishments on a whim – issuing fines and confiscating ration books, and worse.

A few weeks ago, Zofia had picked up one of Lina's files accidentally, thinking it was one of her own cases. She noticed her mistake as soon as she opened it, but something caught her eye and she began leafing through. It was the case file for the Abramowicz family, a Jewish couple who lived in the ghetto. Zofia was puzzled to note that the file said the couple had four children. She knew from the birth register that the couple only had three children, and indeed, when she checked, she found copies of the birth certificates for Aaron, eight, and his younger sisters Esther, six, and Frieda, five. In Lina's case file, there was mention of a fourth child, three-year-old Jonatan, meaning the Abramovicz family was receiving additional financial support.

Lina had returned to the office at that moment and Zofia had hastily replaced the file, but since then, she had occasionally snuck a look at some of Lina's other cases and found a similar 'tweaking' of statistics: making children a year or two younger, old people older, claiming living spaces were smaller than they actually were so Jewish families qualified for higher housing benefits. The whole thing made her uncomfortable. She liked Lina very much, and they were more friends than colleagues, spending evenings at each other's houses in the colder months, and going on picnics in the warm weather. Lina came from a large, tight-knit family with three brothers and two sisters, who liked nothing better than to play practical jokes on one another.

As a result, it had never crossed Zofia's mind to share her suspicions with anyone, least of all the head of department, Mr Wójcik. It would have felt like a betrayal. But as much as she hated being under German occupation, she worried about the trouble her friend might get into if her 'tweaks' were ever discovered. Zofia thought it was best to keep her head down and wait until this blasted war ended.

There was a sudden echo of quick, determined footsteps coming from the corridor outside and Lina rushed back to her desk. The door swung open and Mr Wójcik came in huffing and puffing. He was a large, portly man – *he must be getting extra food rations from somewhere*, Zofia thought.

Elżbieta's typewriter fell silent and the three women looked at him expectantly.

'Ladies,' he said, his chest wheezing audibly, 'some news. I've just had a visit from the Governor General's adjutant.'

Lina scoffed.

'I'll thank you to keep your opinions to yourself, Miss Dmowska,' Wójcik scolded. 'Now, according to the new regulations, this department shall no longer be providing assistance to the Jews. Effective immediately.'

'But—' Lina began, getting to her feet. 'But they need us! When was the last time you were inside the ghetto? The conditions are dreadful. So many people are sick, and those who aren't are starving. They can't just—'

'That's quite enough, Miss Dmowska!' Wójcik interrupted, raising his voice. 'Now sit down. I haven't finished.'

Lina remained standing for a few seconds, trembling, but finally sat back down. She pressed her lips together tightly and her face took on an expression Zofia couldn't read.

'From now on, soup kitchens are for Polish citizens only; the soup kitchens within the Jewish quarter walls shall be closed down,' Wójcik continued. 'Pensions and benefits – that includes financial support for young children and funds for housing support – shall be discontinued. Infection controls, however, shall remain in place.' He pulled a face. 'With the incidence of typhus among the Jews, it is perhaps not such a bad thing that the quarter has been sealed.'

Zofia had heard this justification for why the Nazis had sealed the ghetto countless times: it was allegedly to prevent the Jews from spreading typhus and other diseases. She bit her lower lip unhappily. She'd never set foot inside the ghetto, but she had heard about the squalid conditions from Lina. It was hardly surprising, given the poor conditions and lack of hygiene, that illness was rampant there.

'So to be clear,' Wójcik said, 'no further assistance for the Jews.'

'I'd like to see them stop me,' Lina mumbled quietly, but not quietly enough.

Wójcik took a few steps towards her and leaned over her desk, his moustache quivering. 'You are walking a very fine tightrope, young lady,' he snarled. 'If you would like your leaving papers, just say the word.'

Lina's eyes flashed and for a worrying moment, Zofia thought she was actually going to say something that would get her fired, but instead she just swallowed and angrily crushed out her cigarette in the ashtray.

An hour later, Zofia and Lina were pushing their bicycles down Karolkowa Street. The pavements were busy with people rushing to get home, weary after a day's work. Above them, the sky was a dreary dark grey and an unpleasantly chilly wind buffeted them from behind. It was early September, but they'd had a miserable autumn so far, with too many rainy days to count. Summer seemed a very distant memory now, and winter was yet to come. But still, it was nice being out of the stuffy office.

Lina lit a cigarette. 'You know,' she said, exhaling a thin stream of blue smoke, 'it took all I had to not get up and punch him in the face.'

'Who, Wójcik?'

Lina curled her hand into a fist and jabbed the air in front of her. 'Just like that. Right on the nose!'

The movement looked so comical, Zofia had to smile.

Lina sighed and they resumed their walk. 'It wouldn't have done any good, of course,' she said. 'Though he would have thoroughly deserved it.'

'Do you really think he doesn't care?' Zofia asked. 'I mean, he's been a social worker for so long, surely he wants to help those in need.'

'I'm not sure,' Lina said. 'I think he's quite comfortable with the notion of Jews as sub-humans. Oh, he'd give a needy man the shirt off his back, I'm sure. But only if that man were Aryan.'

Zofia thought back to Wójcik's comment about the Jews spreading typhus. He wasn't the only one to hold less than favourable opinions of Polish Jews; many of Zofia's neighbours hadn't bothered hiding their delight when Jews were forced out of their homes into the ghetto, and happily took over the large apartments they left behind, some of them still fully furnished. Zofia's own father, by contrast, had declined the offer to buy up his Jewish competitor's business at a knock-down price two years ago, when new laws came into effect that prohibited Jews from owning businesses. Others had not been so benevolent, and now her father was not only being undercut in terms of prices, he was also struggling to get his hands on the hides and skins he needed for the production process. Not for the first time, Zofia was grateful she was able to help contribute towards the family income. It had been her idea to train as a social worker when she left school – her parents had wanted her to look for a husband, get married and settle down, but since the war began and her country had been occupied by the Germans to the west and the Soviets to the east, these were extraordinary circumstances. There had been a good many arguments at home, but Zofia, who had inherited her father's pride – as well as his stubbornness – had finally managed to grind her parents down. Besides, the war had changed all the rules.

She had been working at the Social Welfare Department in central Warsaw for just over a year now and loved her work, even though the German occupiers were constantly introducing new rules and regulations, hampering the Department's efforts at every turn. Her main task was processing the paperwork from the Civil Register, ascertaining which families required financial assistance and social work support. She was still too new to have been assigned home visits, but she hoped she would be doing that in the new year. Working with real people, not just their paperwork, was why she had become a social worker in the first place.

Beside her, Lina was still talking. 'First they closed the Jewish schools and stopped them using public transport. Then the lawyers and doctors lost their professional licences.' She stopped walking and turned to Zofia, forcing her to come to a stop, too. 'You never met Rachel, did you?'

Zofia shook her head.

'She'd been at the Department for years, putting her heart and soul into her work. She was the first in the office every morning, the last to leave at night. People were desperate to have her as their case worker, because she put everyone else's needs ahead of her own. She was the kindest person I've ever met. And then…' She paused and tossed her cigarette to the ground, crushing it with her foot. 'She didn't come in one morning, which was wholly out of character, and later that day we were told she'd been sacked. Because she's Jewish.'

Zofia frowned. 'I didn't know that.'

'Wójcik was her replacement. Couldn't wait to move into her office and badmouth her achievements to anyone willing to listen.'

'What happened to her?'

Lina shrugged and her look grew sad, then bitter. 'I suppose she had to move into the ghetto, like the rest of them. I've tried looking, but there's no trace of her.'

'I'm sorry,' Zofia said softly. She didn't really know what else to say.

'And you know they force the Jews to work for a pittance in Polish factories?'

'Yes, I'd heard.' Zofia knew of this, because her father's competitors employed men and women from the ghetto. 'I will have nothing to do with slave labour,' he had said bitterly when someone suggested it was good for business.

'They round them up in the ghetto,' Lina was saying. 'Pulling them off the streets at random. Last year, as a joke, they rounded up Jewish women who were deemed "too elegant", because they wore nice clothes and lipstick. They had them picking potatoes for months.' She twisted her mouth angrily.

They continued walking in silence. On the corner of Leszno Street, a group of men – construction workers, judging by the plaster dust on their clothes – stood talking, passing around a bottle containing amber-coloured liquid. *Krupnik*, by the look of it; a cheap, homemade, honey-flavoured schnapps. The men clicked their tongues as Zofia and Lina passed by, but the two women ignored them.

'I was born here in Warsaw,' Lina said finally, breaking the silence. 'But it hasn't felt like home for a while now. It's as though… Oh, I don't know how to describe it. This street, for example.' She swept her arm in front of her. 'I used to come shopping here with my mother when I was a little girl. You see that fountain? I remember a really hot summer, when I was about six, and my mother let me take off my shoes and splash about in there. The cold water on my bare feet – it felt so good! And over there,' she pointed to a bakery on the opposite side of the road, 'is where I'd buy *paczki* filled with strawberry jam. Delicious!' She smiled at the memory. Then her face turned dark again. 'This street has always held happy memories. But now, knowing that this very street leads straight towards the ghetto … it makes me want to cry!'

She blinked away angry tears. Zofia knew Lina to be a high-spirited, passionate woman, ready to stand up against any perceived injustice, but this level of distress was new. It made Zofia slightly uncomfortable. She tried to shake the feeling off. There was nothing she could do about the situation, was there? The Germans had all the power, and if they chose to stop the Welfare Department from helping the Jews, there was very little Zofia could do about it. She recalled the first time she had come face-to-face with Nazi brutality. It was her second week at the Department, and a group of uniformed officers had stormed into the offices, unannounced, yelling '*Kontrolle! Kontrolle!*', knocking over furniture and throwing files to the floor. For three hours, Zofia and her colleagues were forced to stand in a line, facing the wall, like naughty school children. One of the secretaries had fainted, and a soldier had waited for her to regain consciousness and then slapped her hard across the face and made her stand in line again. The experience had left Zofia completely shaken.

Lina continued. 'The Nazis claim that sealing the Jews inside the ghetto is to stop the spread of typhus, but what they've done in reality is create the perfect conditions for the disease. And now they're preventing us from helping those who need us the most. It's plain *evil*!'

Zofia slowed her pace and pulled her collar tight. Her friend was right, it *was* evil. But at least Lina was trying to do something about it.

'You've been changing things, small details, in your case files,' she said quietly.

A spark of panic crossed Lina's face.

19

'I haven't told anyone!' Zofia assured her quickly. 'I would never do that. I understand why you do it. It's just…'

'What?'

'Isn't it terribly dangerous? I mean, what if someone found out? Wouldn't it be better to wait for the war to end?'

'And what then?' Her voice was angry again, though Zofia knew Lina's rage wasn't directed at her, but at the situation. 'The Soviets and the Germans have divided us up. Do you really think they're going to give us our country back when this damn war is finally over? Whenever that might be.'

Zofia reddened. 'I haven't … I haven't really thought about it.'

'Well I have,' Lina said. A few strands of blonde hair had come loose from her braids and the wind was whipping them around her face. 'And we've decided that the only way to change our future – the very fate of Poland – is to fight.'

'We?'

Lina stopped walking again. She looked around and lowered her voice. After a moment's hesitation she said, 'Me and Elżbieta.'

'Elżbieta?' Zofia almost laughed out loud. Straightlaced Elżbieta? The woman who never overran her lunch break by a minute, who tidied her desk before leaving every afternoon, whose stocking seams were always as straight as a ruler?

Lina nodded. 'And Dawid, from the Civil Status Division. Birth and death certificates and such. And … others. But this new announcement is a real blow. We'll have to find some other way to redirect funds to Jewish families.' She suddenly reached out and grabbed Zofia's hands. 'You must swear, on the life of your family, that you will never, *ever* repeat any of this to anyone.'

'I won't, I—' Zofia swallowed. 'Your secret's safe with me.'

A young man on a bicycle sped past, his coat flapping in the wind. Zofia watched him as he disappeared around the corner, in the direction of the ghetto entrance on Chłodna Street, and she wondered how many of the rumours about the ghetto were true. Initially, no one really knew how many Jews had been forced to move there; most people, including Zofia, had no real idea what was going on inside – as far as she knew, the Jewish community was a tight-knit one, and this way they were close to their own hospitals, schools, and synagogues. But after the ghetto had been walled off, terrible rumours began seeping out, of deplorable living conditions, arbitrary beatings and arrests by German soldiers, young Jewish men being snatched off the street into forced labour.

Zofia hadn't quite known how much of it to believe. She hated to think human beings were capable of such atrocities; besides, gossip and rumours were always to be expected in circumstances in which the reporting of real news was censored. And her work at the Social Welfare Department, she told herself, was her own small contribution. But if she were honest, she was fooling herself. Five years ago, she'd left school with excellent grades, ready to make a difference, ready to change the world! Five short years, and yet it seemed like a lifetime ago now. Back then, Hitler was still considered a nasty yet ultimately harmless little man whose bark was worse than his bite, Austria was still a sovereign nation, and the Germans and Soviets hadn't yet carved up Poland between them.

And then – everything had fallen apart. The bombing raids in the early days of the war, long nights spent in cold, damp shelters, measly food rations, chopping up furniture to keep the fire going in the winter. But all of that was nothing compared to what the Jews were living through, she thought now. Lina was right. If every righteous-minded person just sat back and let things happen, merely hoping and praying things wouldn't get too bad, who knows where it would end? And did Jesus not teach them to embrace the down-trodden, the excluded, the sick and the poor? He had stood up to all forms of injustice.

She turned back to Lina.

'I want to help,' she blurted out, surprising herself.

Lina's eyes widened. 'Zofia, I … I'm not expecting you to—'

'I mean it. I want to help. You're right, you're right about everything.' Saying it out loud made her feel breathless and oddly liberated. 'It's my duty as a Pole, as a Christian, to help if I can.'

Again, Lina took her hands. 'I know you mean well, Zofia, but what we do is extremely dangerous.'

'I'm willing to take that risk.'

Lina took a deep breath. 'I don't mean a fine, or even a prison sentence. Have you heard the name Ania Kowalska? Perhaps you read about her in the newspaper.'

Zofia nodded numbly. She not only recognised the name, she and Ania had been members of the same congregation at St. Kazimierz church.

'Oh yes, she was executed last week,' Zofia whispered. 'She'd been found guilty of sabotage, for blowing up a railway line outside Łódź. I couldn't believe it when I heard. She was always so … so kind and gentle.' Her voice wavered.

'I'm not surprised you couldn't believe it. It's because it wasn't true. The whole trial was a sham.' Lina swallowed. 'Ania was a member of our group. The Nazis found her smuggling ampules of the Weigl vaccine into the ghetto to give to a baby.'

Zofia let out a small moan and then made a hasty sign of the cross, murmuring a brief prayer.

'She was hanged because she tried to save a child's life,' Lina said, her voice thick. She sounded close to tears.

Zofia's felt her earlier boldness begin to fizzle out. Hanged, to save a life? Was she really that brave herself?

'What else does your group do?' she asked, digging her nails into the flesh of her palms in an attempt to stop her courage from deserting her.

'False identities, mainly. For Jews who managed to stay out of the ghetto. And bringing in supplies of food and medicines to those trapped inside. It's *good work*,' she said passionately. 'Important work.'

She paused as a horse-drawn cart passed by, the sound of unoiled wheels squealing and horses' hooves clopping loudly on the cobbled street.

'Listen.' She leaned forward conspiratorially. 'If you're serious about this, I can introduce you to some people. We need all the help we can get.'

'All right,' Zofia said with a tumbling feeling in the pit of her stomach, like she was riding on a fairground carousel. She took a sharp breath. 'I'm in. I want to help.'

Lina paused for a moment and looked away, rubbing her hands together for warmth. Zofia wondered if she was worried she'd revealed too much.

On the opposite side of the road, several school boys began kicking a tin can among themselves, whooping whenever they managed to hit one of the gas lampposts that lined the street.

'I would never betray you,' Zofia said finally, to dispel the awkward silence that had fallen between them. 'Please, you can trust me.'

Lina looked straight into her eyes. 'I do,' she said earnestly. Then her face opened into a smile. 'Yes, I do.'

Relieved, Zofia gestured for them to continue their walk home. When they got to Bankowy Square, they said their goodbyes and embraced briefly.

'You should sleep on it,' Lina said. 'What we do is very dangerous, and you should make the decision to join with a clear head. You can let me know on Monday, and if you've changed your mind, I won't think any worse of you.'

Zofia shook her head. 'I want to help. I'm absolutely sure.'

Lina gave her a smile, and as Zofia watched her turn into the road that led her home, she felt a stirring combination of excitement and dread in the pit of her stomach. What on earth had she just agreed to?

3

Seattle, Present Day

There was a sudden noise from outside – the mournful howl of some nocturnal animal – and Lizzie startled from her sleep. She looked up from her computer, noticing only now how stiff her shoulders were. She checked the time on her phone – five past midnight. Too late to call Alex, and besides, there was nothing to say to him. She'd sent him a message earlier but he hadn't responded. He obviously didn't have anything to say either. Pushing down the bruising feeling that they might have lost the ability to comfort each other, Lizzie rubbed her eyes.

Beyond the small attic window pane, the night sky was black with a scattering of stars. Lizzie reached up and stretched, hearing the soft pop of her stiff bones cracking. *I really should start doing yoga again*, she thought, and then, with a somewhat painful tug to her heart, she realised she hadn't thought about the miscarriage all day. That was something to be grateful for, surely? She got up to stretch her legs and crossed the small room to the window, catching her reflection in the glass. She looked a fright; her hair hung limp and greasy onto her shoulders, and only when her stomach let out an enormous rumble did she realise she hadn't eaten since lunchtime.

Her mother had called up to Lizzie a couple of times during the course of the evening, and Lizzie knew she was a little worried about her. She had been up here for hours, consumed with research into her great-grandmother's past. Her mother hadn't been able to shed any light on the mysterious photos; all she knew was that Zofia had been somehow involved in the Polish resistance during the war, but she said Zofia hadn't liked to talk about it.

'I think they were very difficult times,' Lizzie's mother had said earlier at lunch. 'Your great-grandmother might have been afraid of tearing open old wounds. And you know,' she reached out and put a hand on Lizzie's, 'perhaps she had good reason to want to leave the past in the past.'

Lizzie had made a noncommittal sound and let her mother change the subject. But as her mother told her all about the upcoming Fourth of July celebrations, where the entire neighbourhood would be a red-white-and-blue frenzy of barbeques and fireworks, Lizzie felt her curiosity catch and hold, like an itch that needed to be scratched. So, after lunch, she'd retreated to the attic and begun her research. The past was, if nothing else, a welcome distraction from all the sadness she was feeling in the present.

She had started with a straightforward online search about Poland during the Second World War, then about her great-grandmother's hometown of Warsaw. Inevitably, the first sites she came across were about the destruction of the city towards the end of the war, and, of course, the Jewish Ghetto. Lizzie scrolled through a number of disturbing images: destitute people of all ages in ragged clothes, emaciated children begging on sidewalks, people selling the last of their personal possessions at makeshift markets... She squeezed her eyes shut and closed the tab. Reading about the horrors the Nazis had inflicted on the Jews, and seeing pictures of actual victims, never failed to upset her.

She kept her eyes closed for a moment to dispel the images. Then she typed 'Polish resistance WW2' into the search engine and read several articles about the *Armia Krajowa*, the Polish Home Army, and the Polish Socialist Party, organisations that operated with cells providing food, medical care, money, and false identities to thousands of Polish Jews hiding outside the ghetto on the so-called 'Aryan' side of the German occupation zone. It was fascinating to read, but didn't shed any light on Lizzie's great-grandmother's involvement, so she typed in 'Zofia Szczesny', sighing disappointedly when her search brought up no results.

She had to narrow it down somehow. Thinking about the photograph of Zofia with the children, she typed in 'Polish resistance + children', and came across an organisation run by a woman called Irena Sendler. She had been a social worker during the war and was one of the best-known activists from that time. Lizzie clicked on another link and there she was again: Irena Sendler, recognised by Yad Vashem as one of the Righteous Among the Nations for saving countless Jewish children's lives. Sendler had smuggled the children out of the ghetto, placing them with foster families and convents, many of them in the Orphanage of the Franciscan Sisters of the Family of Mary in Warsaw.

Lizzie's eyes were itching with tiredness now. Maybe she should call it a night. But just as she went to switch off her laptop, she changed her mind and quickly googled 'Irena Sendler images'. There weren't many pictures of her – most of them showing an elderly lady with grey braided hair and a round, friendly face – but Lizzie continued to scroll down and her eye snagged immediately on an old black-and-white image. She peered at it more closely and gasped. Could it be?

Scrabbling through the piles of papers and notes beside her on the small desk, she found the second photograph, the one showing her great-grandmother and the group of women. She held it up against the screen and – yes, it was the same woman! So her great-grandmother had actually known the group's leader. Lizzie thought back to what her mother had said at lunch, that Zofia hadn't liked to talk about her time during the war. But why? Surely these resistance fighters were among the bravest people imaginable – Lizzie couldn't begin to conceive the fear and apprehension they must have lived with every single day. So why not be proud of it? Why keep it a secret from your own family?

Lizzie rubbed her eyes and then switched off the computer. Perhaps she should heed her mother's advice and leave the past in the past. But at the same time, she felt a rising sense of curiosity unfurling inside her, and it felt good not focusing on herself for a change. The decision was made as quickly as it had arrived: she would spend the summer finding out more about her great-grandmother.

4

Warsaw, September 1942

'You look terrible, *kochanie*. Another bad night's sleep?'

Zofia's mother ladled a spoonful of watery semolina into her bowl. Zofia looked down at it despondently.

'I'm not hungry, Mama.'

Her mother straightened up and clucked her tongue. 'Nonsense. You need to eat, even though I'd rather be serving you something more nutritious. But the butcher was out of pork again yesterday, and who knows when we'll ever see fresh eggs again!'

She sighed loudly and crossed herself.

Zofia's father Ludwik was sitting opposite her at the kitchen table reading the newspaper, her younger sister Zuzanna by his side. Zuzanna was very pale this morning, though she was tucking into her semolina porridge with an appetite that belied her small frame. She had just turned fifteen, but looked more like a twelve-year-old.

'Izabel,' Ludwik said without looking up from his paper. 'Stop worrying. We have enough to eat, and if we have to make do with more vegetables than meat for a while, then that shan't do us any harm.'

'Is there any coffee?' Zofia asked. She felt bone-tired. She had hardly slept the last two nights, replaying the conversation she'd had with Lina over and over in her mind. Why had she blurted out she wanted to help? The Nazis were known for the brutality with which they quashed any form of resistance, and if she *did* get involved and was found out, she'd be risking not only her own safety but also that of her family. At best, her father's business would be closed down and they wouldn't be able to afford Zuzanna's medical treatment. At worst… Zofia bit down on her lip. She didn't want to think about that.

'Chicory coffee only,' her father said, pulling a face. 'It's so bitter, you need to add five spoonfuls of sugar to make it drinkable, but your mother won't let me.'

'Well, you let me know when they've doubled our sugar rations,' Zofia's mother replied sharply, 'then you can have your five spoonfuls.'

Ludwik let out a small snort.

'Please don't argue,' Zuzanna said, looking from one parent to the other.

Izabel chuckled softly. 'We're not arguing, are we, my love?' She leaned forward and kissed her husband on the top of his head, whereupon he grabbed her waist and pulled her onto his lap.

'Argue? With this beautiful woman?' he said. 'Never!'

Izabel let out a squeal as he tickled her waist, making Zuzanna giggle.

'Now me, Papa!' she said, nudging her mother gently out of the way and sitting on her father's lap.

She'd been a surprise baby, born when Ludwik and Izabel were in their early forties and Zofia was eight. She was everyone's darling, nicknamed *Żabka* – froggie – because of

30

how she used to pump her little legs when she was a baby. Her weak heart had been diagnosed just before her first birthday, when she had failed to put on weight and was still wearing the baby clothes of an eight-month-old. The doctors had predicted she wouldn't survive past ten years of age, but she was a teenager now, and Zofia suspected her sister's fiery spirit and propensity for mischief had a lot to do with her not giving in to the illness. But she still needed to visit the doctor regularly, and her heart medicine was costly.

No, thought Zofia now, as she stirred her rapidly cooling porridge, becoming involved in the resistance was too risky. There was no way she could possibly jeopardise her little sister's safety. Besides, it was impossible to change the minds of those who so hated the Jews. It was much easier to turn a blind eye. She'd have to tell Lina she'd made a mistake. She was sure her friend would understand.

'If you're not eating that, Zofia, you'd better start getting ready,' her mother said as she wiped down the kitchen counter. 'You don't want to be late for work.' She held the washcloth under the tap and then wrung it out. 'Oh, and I spoke to Igor's mother after mass yesterday,' she said, the corners of her mouth tugging into a smile. 'A lovely young man. He's still working in the Civil Status Division, isn't he? And he's single, too.'

'Ooh, is Zofia in love?' Zuzanna laughed.

Zofia rolled her eyes. 'No, *Żabka*, I most definitely am not.' She yawned and got to her feet. She had a full day's work ahead of her, and an awkward conversation with Lina.

Later that afternoon, Zofia and Zuzanna stood in line outside the bakery on Stara Road to see if they could buy a cheap bag of breadcrumbs. Their mother had been foraging for mushrooms in Las Bielański forest on the outskirts of the city and had brought home a basketful of winter chanterelle mushrooms, which she would cut into slices, batter in breadcrumbs, and fry. It was an inexpensive, delicious meal but the downside was that they would all have to sit through Ludwik's bad jokes about how his wife was trying to poison him with dodgy fungi.

A car drove past them, expelling a stinking cloud of exhaust and making Zuzanna cough. She wore a headscarf tied below her chin, and her face, as small and delicate as a doll's, was pale. Zofia looked at her with concern, but Zuzanna shook her head to let her know she was all right. The sky was a cloudy grey and so low you might reach out and touch it. Zofia looked up at the clouds. They had a long and cold winter ahead of them. Her sister thrived during the summer, but after the damp, chilly autumn they'd had, she now looked as ill as ever. The doctor feared that the recent wet and cold weather had exacerbated not only her heart condition, but also adversely affected her lungs. Zofia took Zuzanna's hand and squeezed it gently. Although she had no memory of it, Zofia herself had been very ill as a young child. She had contracted typhus when she was two years old and according to her mother, it had been a miracle she'd survived. But unlike Zuzanna's illness, it hadn't left a trace. Their parents prayed daily their youngest daughter would experience a similar miracle.

There were six women in the queue ahead of them, and tensions were already running high. Most people baked their own bread to save money, but you had to buy flour and yeast somewhere and supplies were always hard-fought over.

'You were here this morning,' one of the customers said rudely to a woman stepping out of the shop and carrying a mesh bag containing a paper sack of flour. 'Where are you getting those extra rations from, hmm?'

'Mind your own business,' the woman snapped, equally rudely, and elbowed her way past.

'Someone should call the authorities on you,' the first woman said. She wore a scarf tied up around her grey hair, from which two curlers poked out.

The woman with the flour spun around. 'Oh really? So why don't you tell us all—' she gestured to the other women in the queue, who were observing the exchange with interest, 'what *you* were doing here this morning? Because that would mean this is your second trip to the bakery today as well.'

'I don't think—' the grey-haired woman began, but at that moment the baker popped his head out of the door.

'Ladies,' he said sternly, 'any fighting, and I will not hesitate to ban you from my shop.'

The woman who had already been served turned on her heel, made a small snorting sound and walked off quickly. The grey-haired woman fell into a grumpy silence and the queue shuffled slowly forwards.

Zofia gave her head a little shake. She understood the frustration of not knowing how to make ends meet, how to fill your children's bellies, how to survive from one day to the next. But surely it would be better if people came together to support one another. Fighting among themselves like this only played into the hands of their occupiers, who loved to stir up animosity among the city's residents. Sometimes, Zofia managed to block everything out and day-dream herself into a

33

future without war, without ration cards, without the gnawing guilt that she should be doing more about helping

She rolled her head on her neck, trying to ease some of the tension she'd stored up throughout the day. Everyone in the Department had been frantically busy all day, as a long-awaited delivery of typhus vaccines had come in and lists of potential vaccination candidates had to be drawn up. As ordered by the Germans last week, the names of Jewish families in need of welfare support had been deleted from the Department's records. Zofia was glad she hadn't been tasked with this particular job, as she was feeling guilty enough already about her change of heart. Thankfully, the commotion at the office meant she had managed to avoid Lina all day. Unfortunately, though, postponed was not abandoned. She would have to carve out a spare moment to talk to her tomorrow; if she had changed her mind about helping, being honest with Lina was the least she could do.

And there was something else troubling her now. There had been whispers at work about the sinister goings-on in Treblinka, a supposed labour camp that huge numbers of ghetto residents had recently been rounded up for transportation to. Mr Wójcik had shut down the conversation immediately, telling them that the Jews should stop complaining about conditions in the Jewish Quarter if they weren't willing to move to a labour camp and work for their upkeep. It was forbidden to use the word 'ghetto' in Warsaw, though everyone knew that was exactly what it was.

'Why are you so gloomy?' Zuzanna asked, tugging at Zofia's sleeve and tearing her from her thoughts.

'Oh, don't mind me,' Zofia said and tried to smile. 'I'm just tired from work.'

'I can't wait till I leave school and get a job,' Zuzanna said. 'If I have to learn one more Latin declension, I think I shall scream.' But then she began to cough again; this time it was a rough, sharp bark of a cough that sounded as though it were scraping at the insides of her lungs.

Zofia looked at her in alarm. 'Are you all right, *Żabka*? Do you want to head back home while I wait for—'

She was interrupted by a loud yell coming from the right, some twenty yards down the road. She and Zuzanna turned to see a couple of uniformed Germans pulling a woman out of the entrance to one of the tenement buildings that lined the street. She was crying and her dress had been ripped in several places. One of the soldiers had her arm twisted painfully behind her back and she screamed out as he pulled it even higher, trying to wrestle her into a truck that stood idling on the side of the road.

'That's Mrs Kamińska!' Zuzanna cried suddenly. 'What are they doing to her?'

Zofia knew Mr and Mrs Kamiński; they supplied tanning agents to her father's business.

'I don't know, *Żabka*,' she answered, stunned by what she was witnessing.

A moment later, two German soldiers dragged Mr Kamiński out onto the street. He'd obviously been beaten; he had a cut to his forehead and he could hardly stand up straight.

Zofia went to rush forwards, but another woman standing in the queue suddenly grabbed her arm and held her back. 'It's not worth getting involved,' she hissed. 'You'll only end up getting arrested yourself.'

'But—' Zofia began. 'Why are they arresting Mr and Mrs Kamiński? They're business partners of my father. I know them, they're law-abiding people.'

The woman let go of Zofia's arm and sighed. 'I thought it was a vicious rumour, but it turns out that Mrs Kamińska is Jewish. She converted to Catholicism when they got married.' She paused, her eyes darting around, then lowered her voice. 'But the Nazis don't care about that. They think mixed marriages will contaminate the race.'

On the pavement, Mr Kamiński was arguing with a soldier, trying to defend his wife. But the soldier just raised his rifle and struck him on the side of the head. It made a sickening cracking noise and the man reeled two steps backwards, obviously dazed. The soldiers grabbed him roughly by the arms and shoved him into the back of the truck.

'But what will happen to them now?' Zofia asked the woman beside her.

'He might be offered the option to divorce her. She will be taken to the ghetto.'

'But he is a devout Catholic!' Zofia said in disbelief, her eyes stinging with tears at the sight unfolding in front of her. 'He can't divorce her.'

The woman shook her head sadly. 'Then he will follow her to the ghetto.'

At that moment, the queue moved forward and the woman reclaimed her place.

Zofia stood and watched as the truck carrying Mr and Mrs Kamiński pulled away. Beside her, Zuzanna clenched her fists.

'Animals,' she whispered, a faint wheeze still audible in her lungs. Her eyes flashed furiously. 'If I were stronger, I'd … I'd fight them. I would throw petrol bombs into all the nice villas they've occupied, every night until they left. I wouldn't *care* if I were arrested.'

She was shaking with fury and her eyes were wet with tears. 'I feel so weak, so … so useless.'

'You are not useless, *Żabka*,' Zofia told her, her throat tightening while a fury of emotions swept through her. Anger, fear, disbelief – and strongest of all, shame. If her younger sister, suffering from a weak heart and damaged lungs, wouldn't hesitate to risk her own safety to help, how could Zofia in good conscience ignore the plight of these poor people?

She straightened up. 'Come on,' she said, her own voice now trembling with anger and determination. 'I'll walk you home. Then I need to pay Lina a quick visit.'

The Social Workers' Club was located on Dobra Road, a narrow, tree-lined street not far from the river. Zofia had been here once before, last Christmas, when her department had gathered for a party. A bomb had landed on the adjacent building, a haberdashery, some three years ago, destroying it almost completely. It was one of many buildings in the city that had been bombed out in the first few months of the war, now providing precarious playgrounds for children, who would play hide-and-seek in the cracks and crevices, and accommodating dozens of rats during the night. The bomb that had hit the haberdashery had also damaged the outside of the Social Workers' Club, leaving a pockmarked façade that was crumbling in places. No one thought it made sense to carry out any major repairs, not while the war was still raging. Besides, for Polish citizens, building materials were very hard to come by.

Lina pushed open the heavy wooden door and they entered the main area of the club, a large, L-shaped room with old blackish-brown wood panelling on the walls and milky windows that only let in some dull, grainy light. A dozen small round tables stood around the room, most of them occupied by people whom Zofia recognised from the Welfare Department. A blue cloud of cigarette smoke hung like a veil over the patrons' heads.

She and Lina nodded their heads in a greeting, and then Lina led Zofia across the large space towards a dark corridor at the back. There were several doors leading off the hallway, all of them closed.

'Where are we going?' Zofia asked, blinking to see through the gloom. It smelled of stale tobacco and mildew, and she let out a sudden gasp as she bumped her hip painfully against a large chest standing in the dark corridor. *What am I doing here?* she thought, suddenly anxious. After witnessing the arrest of Mr and Mrs Kamiński two days earlier, and shamed by her little sister's courage, she had gone straight to Lina's house to tell her she wanted to do something – *anything* – to help the resistance. She had felt so brave at the time, but here in this dark, unfamiliar place, she was close to losing her nerve again.

'The meeting is here, in one of the back rooms,' her friend said and walked ahead to the third door on the left, which had a sign attached announcing '*Mazurka Night!*'

Indeed, Zofia could hear lively music coming from inside the room.

'Dancing?' she asked, puzzled, and Lina shook her head with a laugh.

'Well, we can hardly advertise the resistance meetings, can we? They're usually at the headquarters on Żurawia Street, but there's a rat infestation there right now and the exterminators are in.' She wrinkled her nose in disgust. 'So, we're here tonight instead. Marek has brought his gramophone and some records, and if anyone happens to stumble across our meeting accidentally, we pretend we're having a night of traditional dance.'

She gave a little jolly swing of the hip. Then she knocked sharply on the door – *tap tappity tappity tap tap* – and pushed it open. A solemn-looking man greeted them, his eyes flicking from Lina to Zofia, holding her gaze for a few seconds, then back to Lina. He raised an eyebrow.

'She's with me,' Lina said and strode past him into the room. Zofia followed, rather shyly.

There were about two dozen men and women standing around in small clusters, most of them strangers to Zofia. All the same, she wondered how easily she had been let in, how – if she were a spy – could simply report them all to the German authorities. She said as much to Lina.

'You will have been screened,' her friend replied. 'Your family, too. To ensure there has been no contact with the Nazis.' She looked down at her feet. 'It isn't a nice thought, I know. But there are lives at stake here.'

Zofia swallowed. Lina was right, of course.

There was so much more she wanted to know – about how the group operated, and what exactly they did – but at that moment a young man approached them.

'Good evening.'

Lina went bright red and lifted a hand to rearrange a curl that had fallen out of place.

'Jakub,' she said. 'This is Zofia, a friend.'

The man – Jakub – greeted Zofia with a smile and a small bow of his head.

'Nice to meet you,' Zofia said, realising now why Lina had blushed so hard. He was tall and rather attractive, with short dark hair and a slightly chipped front tooth that gave him a rakish look when he smiled.

'A new recruit?' he asked, but before Zofia could reply, someone called his name from the other side of the room, and he shrugged.

'Sorry, I have places to be.' With a wink and another smile, he turned and left.

Lina watched as he walked away and let out a small sigh. Then she caught Zofia looking at her and cleared her throat.

'So, anyway, there's someone you have to meet.' She looked around. 'There she is,' she whispered, gesturing towards the far wall. 'Irena Sendler. She's a very important figure in the organisation.'

Zofia frowned when she heard the name, recognising it instantly. Miss Sendler was also a social worker, her office somewhere on the third floor of the labyrinthine department building they worked in. Zofia had never met her in person, but had often seen her name written on the outside of case files. Irena Sendler, a member of the resistance? She looked across the room towards where Lina was pointing and saw a slender woman, in her early thirties, standing at a table and leafing through some papers. She stood just over five feet tall and her dark hair was wrapped in a braid around her head, and even from a distance she had a sense of energy about her, something commanding, yet not dominant. Zofia could not quite put her finger on it. It was as though the woman were fully aware of her surroundings without losing focus of what she was doing.

'But … but … she's tiny!' she stammered quietly to Lina,

Lina grinned. 'You know what they say: small but mighty. Now don't be shy, come and let me introduce you.'

Zofia followed her friend across the room, nervously glancing around at the other people there. Most stood around in small groups of three or four, talking quietly among themselves. They stared at Zofia as she passed, some looking at her with suspicion, and she felt a little like an intruder. By the time they approached Irena, she had put down the papers and was deep in conversation with another woman.

'This is Zofia,' Lina said to Irena. 'The one I told you about.'

'From your office?' Irena asked, and without waiting for an answer, turned to Zofia and gave her a smile. 'Pleased to meet you, Zofia. I'm Irena – also known as Jolanta, for those who don't know me from work – and this here is Helena. She's been with us almost as long as I have.'

Helena nodded a greeting. She was older than Irena, in her late thirties perhaps, with dark, serious eyes and her hair scraped back into a no-nonsense bun. She was bent over the papers on the table and appeared preoccupied, fiddling with a small golden crucifix hung around her neck, and sure enough, she turned back to Irena a moment later, abruptly changing the topic.

'This new announcement means that we'll have to find some other way to get help to the Jewish families,' she said with an urgent tone to her voice.

'I've been thinking about that,' Irena said, 'and I have an idea. We can enter the names of Polish families as benefit recipients, and then redirect the funds to Jewish families.'

Helena tilted her head to the side. 'But what if the Germans investigate the Polish families?' she asked sceptically.

Irena shook her head. 'They won't, because the social workers will have them marked down as having cholera or typhus.' She smiled mischievously. 'You know how the Germans are terrified of illness and physical weakness. Well, let's use it against them. There's no way those cowards will enter a home if they think they might catch a disease.'

Zofia could tell that Helena wasn't entirely convinced, but Irena, for all her shortness of stature, didn't seem like the kind of person you would disagree with.

Irena turned to Zofia. 'So,' she said, 'you want to join us in our fight against the barbarians?'

There was something about her gaze, something energetic and intense that made Zofia blush.

'Yes,' she said, trying to sound more confident than she felt. 'I want to help.'

'Good,' Irena responded brightly. 'The more the merrier. Now, let me introduce you to the others.'

She took Zofia's hand and led her to join a group of three women and two men, who were deep in conversation.

'This is Zofia,' she announced, 'a new friend.'

The people looked Zofia up and down, making her feel rather like some exotic animal on display at the zoo, and she felt the heat rising to her face. Then one of the women smiled at her and introduced herself.

'I'm Nina,' she said, holding out her hand.

Zofia shook it, and this seemed to break the ice. Soon, she had been introduced to all the people in the room, far too many to remember their names. Or codenames, perhaps.

'Right,' Irena said eventually, leading Zofia back to the table. 'Enough of the pleasantries. We're here for business. Now let me let me ask you, has Lina told you much about us?'

Zofia hesitated for a moment. This was obviously a very secret organisation and she didn't want to get Lina into any trouble. 'False documents, smuggling food inside the ghetto. No details, I mean, she gave nothing away, really.'

'But the fact that she told you something means she trusts you deeply. And I trust Lina,' Irena said with a smile.

Helena, the only one who hadn't seemed to warm to Zofia so far, came and stood beside Irena. It was clear these two women formed a team.

'Well,' Irena continued, 'we have been active for several years, resisting the Nazi occupation wherever we can. As far as our section goes, we have passes for the ghetto, issued to qualified personnel by the head of the Health Department on Sokojnej Street.' She paused for a moment and frowned, a shadow crossing her face. 'Have you been inside the ghetto?'

Zofia shook her head. 'No, but I've heard stories.'

Irena's soft face briefly took on an expression of utter sadness. 'It is terrible,' she said quietly, and for a moment her brightness seemed to dim. 'It is far worse than any words can describe.'

Beside her, Helena bowed her head and mumbled a low prayer.

Then Irena seemed to shake her sadness off and her eyes sparkled again. Not with cheerfulness, but with resolve.

'I have a job for you, Zofia,' she said.

43

'Irena?' Helena said warily. 'Are you sure? This is—'

Irena interrupted her. 'Very sure,' she said.

'What have you got in mind?' Zofia asked, somewhat panicked. She hadn't expected to be given a task quite so soon.

Irena smiled. 'You will be given very detailed instructions. But you have to be able to think on your feet, always, because as carefully as these things are planned, it is always possible that something unexpected happens. A German soldier in the wrong place at the wrong time; someone getting unexpectedly sick; a delay in the tram schedule. So you have to be creative and flexible, and above all, courageous. Are you all of these things, Zofia?'

Zofia nodded and hoped her apprehension didn't show on the surface. Was she courageous? If truth be told, her heart began pounding at the mere thought of being here, among the other resistance members, but did she really have a choice? She thought of Zuzanna, of Mr and Mrs Kamiński. No, she didn't have a choice.

Irena seemed to read her thoughts and smiled again. 'It is good to be a little afraid. Fear prevents us from taking stupid risks. All of this—' she made a sweeping gesture around the room, 'is a huge risk. But it is a calculable one.'

And Zofia suddenly understood what it was about Irena's aura that she had noticed earlier, what it was that made her so special. It was the ability to make everyone around her feel powerful, to know that they too could make a difference.

'I will make all the arrangements and contact you with the specifics,' Irena said. 'Now,' she turned to the man standing beside the gramophone at the far wall, 'how about we turn the music a little louder, Marek? We're here to dance, aren't we?'

5

Seattle, Present Day

A sharp sunbeam sliced the heavy curtain in two and fell on Lizzie's face, waking her. From downstairs, she heard music coming from the radio in the kitchen, an 'oldie but goldie' station her mom always listened to.

She rolled to her side with a groan and checked the time. Eight thirty-five. It was two hours later than she normally got up when she was teaching, but she still felt bleary-eyed with exhaustion. For a moment, she wondered why she felt so tired, and then recalled that she had stayed up long past midnight in the attic room.

She sat up just as her mother knocked gently on the door and came in.

'I've made coffee,' she said, placing the cup on the nightstand beside Lizzie's bed and smiling at her daughter. 'You've got that "morning-after look" about you,' she said. 'Like when you were a teenager and had been out all night, partying.'

She went over to the window and pulled open the curtain.

Lizzie squeezed her eyes shut against the bright sunlight. 'Mom!'

Her mother chuckled and Lizzie lifted a hand to her hair; her curls were sticking out in all directions. 'I was up late,' she said wryly. 'Researching our family history.'

Her mother came to sit on the bed beside her and tilted her head to the side. 'You're really getting your teeth into this, aren't you?'

Lizzie took a sip of coffee. It was old-fashioned filter coffee, not the foamy lattes she and Alex made at home. The thought of her husband brought a momentary twinge of sadness, and guilt, but she brushed the feeling away. She'd come here for some breathing space.

'Yes,' she said in response to her mother's question. 'But I've found more questions than answers.' She pulled up her knees, making a small tent with the blanket. 'Is there really nothing more you can tell me about my *prababcia*?'

'Like what?'

'Does the name "Zielińska" mean anything to you?'

Her mother thought for a moment and then shook her head. 'I can't say it does. Why?'

'It was written on the back of one of those old photos I found in the trunk. I was wondering who the name belongs to.'

Her mom shrugged. 'Well, I wouldn't know anything about that.' She got up. 'I'm afraid I don't know much at all about my grandmother. Other than the fact she adopted my mom back in Warsaw and—'

Lizzie jolted upright, making a few drops of coffee splash onto the blanket. 'What do you mean, adopted?'

Her mom frowned. 'You didn't know? Oh look, you've spilled your coffee.'

'Forget the coffee, Mom. How did I not know *Babcia* was adopted?'

Her mother waved a hand in front of her face. 'I assumed you knew. It was different back then, I guess. These things were very secretive, not like today. Records were destroyed, new birth certificates were issued. Adopted children couldn't just go to some state agency and look up their birth parents in a register.'

Lizzie pushed the blanket off and swung her legs out of bed, keener than ever now to get back to her research. Hers wasn't a family that was big into stuff like family trees and ancestry, she knew that, but she'd assumed it was because there wasn't anything special about them. She was quickly beginning to change her mind about that, and it lent her a tingly feeling of excitement.

'Do you think *Babcia* is up for a visit?' she asked. *Babcia*, her grandmother, was living in a care home in Tacoma, just south of the city. She was old and in declining health, with her memory failing rapidly. Lizzie knew she had good days and bad, though recently, she was having more and more bad days.

Her mom pulled her eyebrows together in a frown. 'Now you don't want to go bothering her with all of this.'

'Why not?' Lizzie asked as she stepped out of her pyjama trousers and into her jeans. 'I won't be bothering her. She loves getting visits, and besides, she might enjoy talking about her past.'

'I don't know about that.' Her mother sighed. 'And she's getting more forgetful every day. What I'm saying is, she's vulnerable, so if you go talk to her, you must promise not to upset her.'

'Of course!' Lizzie replied, a little hurt her mom would think any different. But then again, she'd been guilty in the past of letting her enthusiasm get the better of her. Her unbridled optimism every time her period was late, for example. She swallowed hard to dispel the thought. 'I'll be kind.'

Her mom seemed to read her mood. She stretched out her hand and gently stroked Lizzie's cheek.

'Sure you will,' she said gently, then went to pull the blanket off the bed. 'I'd better put this in the wash before the stain sets. Oh, and before I forget – Hannah's coming tomorrow to stay for the weekend. She's having her dress made at Bella's Bridal Store and she's got a fitting in the afternoon. I thought we'd all go out for dinner together tomorrow night, what do you think?'

'That sounds great,' Lizzie said. She hadn't seen her sister for over a month, not since the last miscarriage. Hannah was one of the few people Lizzie couldn't keep any secrets from, and she had worried that her sister would see her for the wreck she was. Hannah was getting married in a few weeks' time and Lizzie hadn't wanted to burden her with her own troubles. But strangely, this whole business about her great-grandmother had begun to lift her mood. Only a tiny bit, but it was there, she could feel it. Perhaps this really could help her to heal.

After a quick breakfast of more coffee and half a slice of toast, Lizzie retreated to the attic. For the next couple of hours, she stared at the computer screen, going down one rabbit hole after the other. She furiously searched '1940's adoption', 'WW2 Poland', 'resistance' until her eyes itched and her back felt stiff for lack of movement. She had no luck with the name Zielińska either; all she discovered was that the male form 'Zieliński' was the name of a well-known Polish soccer player, a German immunologist, and that it was derived from the Polish word for the colour green. None of which helped her.

But she wasn't ready to give up. She clicked on an article about children in the Warsaw Ghetto and found it was written by Roksana Lewandowska, a Polish journalist who had published several articles and a recent book on wartime ghettos. Obviously someone who had researched the topic extensively. Lizzie bookmarked the article. Perhaps this Roksana might be able to shed some light on her great-grandmother.

She entered the woman's name in the search engine and got several hits, but she couldn't find an email address for her. With a groan of frustration, she let herself fall back in her chair, massaging her temples with her fingers, thinking. *Everyone is traceable these days*, she told herself, *surely it shouldn't be too difficult to contact a journalist. It's the age of the digital native, after all – everyone has social media*. She checked Twitter and – bingo – there it was: @roxiwriter.

Feeling oddly nervous, she typed in a brief DM.

Hi Roksana, my name is Lizzie Marshall, and I'm trying to find out more about my great-grandmother, Zofia Chesney (originally Szczesny), who was born in Warsaw in or around 1919 and was involved in the resistance in WW2. I read your articles on the subject and was wondering… Is there any chance I could pick your brains about this? Would be hugely grateful! Kind regards from Seattle, Lizzie Marshall

Then, before she could change her mind or worry obsessively about tone or typos, she added her email address to the end of the message and clicked 'send'.

Her mother's voice travelled up the stairs. 'Sweetie? You gonna be up there all day? You need to eat something.'

Lizzie called back, 'I'll be down in a minute', though eating was the furthest thing from her mind. But she couldn't sit here for hours refreshing her Twitter feed, so she got to her feet and headed downstairs.

'You hungry, sweetie?' her mom asked when she came into the kitchen. It smelled wonderfully of freshly baked bread and home-made chicken soup, and Lizzie felt her mouth watering unexpectedly. She was obviously hungrier than she'd thought. But before she'd even taken a step towards the pot simmering invitingly on the stovetop, a pair of hands cupped her eyes from behind.

'Hey, Bubbles!'

Lizzie turned around and saw her sister Hannah standing there, a huge grin on her face.

'Dimples!' she cried. 'Mom said you'd be here tomorrow!'

'Bubbles' and 'Dimples' were their long-standing nicknames for each other. Hannah had been born with the cutest dimples in her cheeks, a genetic quirk she'd inherited from their grandmother, and Lizzie had earned her nickname from when she used to blow spit bubbles as a baby; throughout her childhood, she had also been obsessed with soap bubbles and had spent hours silently transfixed by their perfect shape and shiny rainbow sheen.

Hannah took her older sister in a tight hug, then released her. She wrinkled her nose. 'Jeez, Lizzie. When's the last time you took a shower?' she said, laughing.

'Yeah, sorry. I've been busy.'

Their mother clattered a wooden spoon against a pan lid. 'Come on now, girls, set the table for me, would you? I have chicken soup waiting to be eaten.'

Lizzie and Hannah laid the table, jostling over the silverware and for a seat next to their mom. They laughed and teased each

50

other, and Lizzie realised how much she had missed this kind of sibling sparring. Best of all, she knew that Hannah wouldn't ask about the miscarriages or Alex or anything painful unless Lizzie initiated the conversation. With her sister, she always had their shared childhood to retreat to, a safe space where life was far less complicated, far less painful.

The soup was rich and salty. The flavours activated her tastebuds, and after only a few spoonfuls of the delicious broth she tore off a chunk of home-made bread and wolfed it down. Her appetite had returned with a vengeance. Looking up, she noticed that Hannah was staring at her from the side. She pulled a silly face at her and Lizzie chucked a small piece of bread in her direction.

'Stop that, girls,' their mother said, adding, 'I'm so glad to see you eating, Lizzie. You've become so thin and I've been worried about you.'

'I'm fine,' Lizzie mumbled quietly, even though her mother was right. She'd lost six pounds since the last miscarriage and none of her clothes fit properly.

'So,' Hannah said, 'what have you been up to since you arrived? You said you'd been busy.'

Lizzie swallowed her mouthful, and began to fill her sister in on what she'd found, from the mysterious photos in the attic trunk, to the message she'd sent to the Polish journalist, to the surprise revelation that their grandmother was adopted.

Hannah nodded casually. 'Yeah, I knew that.'

'What?' Lizzie was genuinely astonished. 'How come everyone knows but me?'

'I'm surprised you didn't know,' Hannah said, raising her eyebrows. 'It's not like it's a big secret. Mom told me years ago when I had to do a family tree project for school. And we were talking about it again just last year when—'

She stopped abruptly and put a hand over her mouth.

'Hannah!' their mother hissed.

Lizzie slowly lowered her spoon. 'When what?'

Both her mom and her sister had their heads down and were staring at their plates. It was as though a dark shadow had suddenly fallen over the room. Then her mom looked up with a pained smile and the penny dropped.

'You were discussing adoption,' Lizzie said quietly. 'After my miscarriage last November.'

'Oh, Bubs, I'm so sorry!' Hannah cried and got to her feet, her chair scraping noisily on the floor. She came over and put her arms around Lizzie. 'It just came up, you know? We were just so heartbroken when we heard, and … I dunno … Mom, or Dad, mentioned that it wouldn't be the first time someone in the family had chosen adoption.'

Lizzie put her spoon down. Her appetite had vanished as abruptly as it had arrived. She looked up to see her mom and her sister looking abject and she realised that they shared her pain. It wasn't their fault.

'It's okay,' she managed to say. 'I know you mean well.'

A hush fell over the table.

'Have to talked to her yet?' Hannah asked after a while.

'Who?'

'*Babcia*. About the pictures you found in the attic.'

'I was planning to go straight after lunch. Hey, you want to come? I'm sure she'd love to see us both.'

'I can't, sorry.' She furrowed her brows and tilted her head. 'I've got a fitting for my dress at three. But give Grandma my love, will you? I'll go and see her next time I'm up.'

6

Warsaw, October 1942

By now, the Nazi occupiers had given up any pretences that they were governing the city by rule-of-law – sham trials like that of supposed saboteur Ania Kowalska were a thing of the past – and there were announcements hanging on every street corner in the so-called 'Aryan' part of the city, warning residents that any attempts to help Jews would result in being shot on sight.

Zofia lowered her eyes whenever she came across one of these announcements, worried that she might have a change of heart. With every day that passed, though, she felt her resolve getting stronger and she couldn't wait to be given the task Irena had promised her. It felt oddly liberating to have taken the decision to join the resistance – as though she were shedding the constraints of powerlessness in the face of Nazi occupation like a snake sheds its skin. She had no idea what Irena had planned for her, but if she managed to help only one poor soul, it was a thousand times better than doing nothing.

Even though Lina, Elżbieta, and Zofia shared an office, they never spoke about their activities at work. It was a matter of principle; even when the others were out on their lunch break and with the office door closed, they could never be sure who might be listening. They were, Lina had told her, also strictly forbidden from discussing any resistance activities they themselves were not directly involved in.

'Better safe than sorry,' she had said, and they both knew that 'sorry' was a euphemism. Zofia tried not to think about it, but when she lay in bed at night, thoughts of being discovered by the Nazis – and what that would mean – revolved relentlessly in her mind.

Finally, almost a week after she'd been to the meeting at the Social Worker's Club, Lina took her to one side.

'Meet me outside in ten minutes,' she said quietly. 'At the back of the building, behind the fire door. We have to talk.'

They were never sure if and when the Germans would pay the Welfare Department a visit, and there were no office windows overlooking the small courtyard behind the building. But before Zofia could ask what she wanted to talk about, Lina had turned on her heel and left. Zofia finished typing the report she was working on, her fingers trembling with anticipation. Was this it? Was she about to be given her first mission? She took the paper out of the typewriter and left the office.

A rare slice of sunlight pierced the gap between the chimney stack that led up the side of the building and the space behind the fire door. Zofia crossed the small courtyard to where Lina stood in the shadows, the tip of her cigarette glowing orange in the dark. She smiled as Zofia approached.

'Sorry about all the cloak and dagger stuff,' she said, 'but I'm sure you can understand why we have to be so careful about everything we do.'

Zofia nodded, and her heart started suddenly pounding. Of course she understood why it had to be this way.

'I have a uniform for you here,' Lina said, holding out a small carpet bag. 'Irena got it for you.'

'A uniform?' Zofia stared at the bag as if it might contain a poisonous snake. What was Lina talking about?

Lina nodded. 'You'll be dressed as a nurse, so you can enter and leave the ghetto.' She shrugged. 'It might be a little big for you,' she said, 'but you can pin the waist and it should fit.'

'I'm going into the ghetto? But I'm not a nurse!' Zofia said, alarmed. 'What if they ask me something? Something medical that a nurse would know the answer to?'

Lina put her hand on Zofia's arm. 'You're nervous. And that's perfectly normal. I'm a bag of bloody nerves every time I go into the ghetto. But—' She tilted her head to the side. 'It's useful to be a little on edge. It enhances your perception.'

A little on edge?!? Zofia wanted to say. *You must be joking!* But she kept the words to herself and took a deep breath. She could do this.

As though reading her mind, Lina said, 'You can do this, Zofia, I have absolute confidence in you. But if you don't think you're up to it, it's better to tell me now.'

'No,' Zofia said, taking the bag from Lina and hoping her friend wouldn't see how much her hand was trembling. 'I can do it. I want to help. Just tell me what to do.'

'You'll meet Irena around the corner from the ghetto entrance on Muranowska Street. At three o'clock. She'll give you further instructions.'

'But that's … that's only an hour from now!'

Lina nodded. 'It's a general principle not to plan too far in advance. It helps to avoid information from leaking out.'

They both fell silent as somewhere behind them a door opened and closed. Zofia looked around, but there was no one to be seen.

Lina leaned in close. 'Irena will be waiting for you. Make sure to put the uniform on first.' She paused and gave Zofia an encouraging smile. 'You won't be inside the ghetto for long,' she said. 'You don't know your way around yet, and I'm sure Irena will be beside you every step of the way.'

'But what about Mr Wójcik? He'll notice if I leave early.'

'Don't worry about him. I'll tell him you're on a house visit. The Bartosz family have just had a baby, haven't they? It's standard practice to receive a welfare visit, especially as its their sixth child.'

Zofia bit down on her lip. It seemed a flimsy excuse, but she had to trust that Lina knew what she was doing. She nodded. 'Very well. I'll just file the report I've written.'

Unexpectedly, Lina took her in an embrace and hugged her tight. 'Welcome to the resistance,' she whispered.

It was just before three and Zofia stood at the corner of Nalewki Street, waiting for Irena. It was too early in the year for snow, but there was a bitter wind blowing in from the east, and a mass of thick grey clouds hung so low in the sky she felt she might reach up and touch them. Zofia glanced around, hoping Irena would be on time.

Just around the corner of the building she was standing at, a queue had formed at the ghetto checkpoint. Dozens of men from the forced labour brigade – among the only Jews allowed in and out of the ghetto – were returning from their backbreaking work at one of the German-run factories on the so-called 'Aryan' side of the city. Two guards were inspecting the bags of those entering, uttering curses every now and again.

Zofia plucked nervously at her uniform. As Lina had predicted, it was hopelessly baggy on her and the pin she'd used to pinch in the waist had fallen out. She fumbled with nervous fingers to tighten the band she was using as a makeshift belt and felt as conspicuous as a blood-red poppy in a snow-covered field.

When a hand tapped her shoulder, she almost jumped.

'Good, you're on time,' a woman's voice said, but when Zofia turned towards it, she was startled to see it was Helena, not Irena. She wore a brown coat and sturdy shoes, and like the last time, her hair was pulled into a tight bun. No sign of a nurse's uniform, though.

'Is Irena not … shouldn't she be…?' Zofia stammered.

Helena gave a short, sharp shake of her head. 'She couldn't make it. But no matter, I'm perfectly capable of giving you your instructions. Here is your pass.' She handed Zofia a slip of paper. 'This will get you inside the ghetto. The guards can be … well, let's say that most of them are there to do a job, and if you don't trouble them, they won't trouble you. A few others can be…' She frowned, looking suddenly older. 'A few others can be difficult. But I checked, and none of those ones are at the checkpoint today, so you shouldn't have any problems. If anyone asks, you are following up on reports of a new outbreak of typhus. Are you with me so far?'

Zofia's heart lurched. 'I'm going in on my own?'

Helena nodded. 'In and out. You're to go to the tram depot on Stawki Street. It's where the route of the number eight tram begins. Do you know where that is?'

'Yes.' Before the ghetto was sealed off, Zofia used to travel through the area all the time. The city of Warsaw had shrunk since its Jewish citizens had been locked away. 'But that sounds like an odd place for a nurse to be. What if one of the soldiers asks what I'm doing there?'

Helena shook her head dismissively. 'Don't worry about that,' she replied in a blunt tone. 'They won't look at you twice. Close to half a million people are crammed into that small place, squeezed into an area covering less than one-and-a-half square miles, drowning in filth and barely subsisting on meagre food rations of a few hundred calories. For the Nazis, everyone inside the ghetto walls is sub-human.'

She didn't make it sound particularly reassuring, but Zofia felt she had no choice but to comply. Despite Helena's brittle manner – or perhaps even because of it – Zofia thought it unlikely she would be anything but truthful.

'Good,' Helena said. 'You will go into the maintenance shed to the left of the depot. It's a wooden shed with a black door. You can't miss it. The door will be unlocked and inside, you will find a bag. A leather bag, similar to the ones doctors use. One of our friends will have placed it there. Do not open it. Just take it and board the tram that leaves at three fifty-two.' She checked her watch. 'You'll have plenty of time to get there. Does that all make sense?'

Zofia nodded, although there was an unpleasant rushing sound in her ears and she was finding it near impossible to concentrate. Helena didn't seem to notice; she continued in a calm and collected voice.

'Now, this next part is important: you must board the last carriage of the tram before any of the other passengers and take the seat closest to the back.'

A man carrying a briefcase walked past and tipped his hat at them. Helena gave him a polite smile and waited until he was out of earshot.

'Then place the bag beneath the seat,' she continued, quieter than before. 'Do not even acknowledge that it is there, you must not draw attention to it. Sit on the bench above it and your legs will hide it from view. Do you understand?'

Zofia nodded wordlessly, feeling slightly dizzy now. She realised she'd been holding her breath and exhaled slowly.

'The tram will stop when it comes to the checkpoint. A guard will board, likely even two, and you will show them your pass. If – God forbid – one of the guards notices the bag, you won't say anything. And if pressed, you will tell him you had no idea it was there. But that is a very unlikely scenario. We are excellent planners, if nothing else. When you are out of the ghetto, you must disembark at the stop on Olszowa Street. It's the second stop beyond the checkpoint, just across the river. Someone will be waiting to take the bag from you.'

She stopped speaking and her gaze softened. 'You look pale, dear. Are you all right?'

Zofia swallowed and her right leg began to twitch. It was only then she realised how tense her entire body was. With some effort she tried to relax her muscles, but it did nothing to calm her. This wasn't how she had imagined it at all. She assumed someone would accompany her, at the very least. She had imagined she might be smuggling in food and clothing, perhaps some medicine. But smuggling something *out of the* ghetto?

'What's in the bag?' she asked finally.

Helena didn't hesitate for a moment. 'A baby.'

Zofia's hand flew to her mouth and she let out a sharp gasp.

'Hush,' Helena scolded, and looked around nervously, but there was no one in earshot. She took a step closer. 'You want to be involved in the resistance?' she asked quietly. It was almost a hiss.

Zofia nodded numbly.

'Zofia, this is your task. It is too risky for us to send someone who is not committed so if you are not up to it, tell me now.'

Ahead of them in the queue, a small girl started coughing; it was a harsh, rattling cough that made the child double over while her mother stroked her back. Zofia thought of her sister Zuzanna and felt her courage return.

'I am up to it,' she said, lifting her chin and squaring her shoulders. Then something occurred to her. 'What happens if the baby cries?'

'Her mother will have given her a small dose of a sedative. Just enough to keep her asleep. But everything depends on timing. If you miss the tram, she will wake up and be at the mercy of the Nazis.'

Then she turned towards the checkpoint and Zofia followed her gaze. Above the gate hung a sign:

Typhus Infection Area
Entering and leaving is strictly prohibited unless authorised

The thought of it sent a shiver down Zofia's back. It was forbidden to call the place 'ghetto'; instead, the German authorities upheld the pretence that they were protecting the Aryan citizens from disease. It was a particularly cruel irony that the Nazis had forced Jewish labourers to build the ghetto walls with their bare hands, eradicating their very own freedom brick by brick.

'That's Wieland,' Helena said, tugging her away from her thoughts. She pointed at a young-looking guard in his olive-grey uniform. He had a rifle slung across his shoulder and was checking the passes of those wanting to enter the ghetto.

'He won't look twice at your pass,' Helena continued. 'But he will have a good gape at your legs. Just keep your eyes down and you'll be fine. Now — are you ready?'

Zofia let out a puff of air. 'Yes,' she said, and sensed her determination growing. 'I'm ready.'

It was a fifteen-minute walk from the checkpoint to the tram depot, and Zofia hummed a little tune to herself to keep her resolve up and her thoughts from wandering towards fearful territory. If she stopped for a moment to think about what exactly she was doing, about everything that could go wrong, she might freeze and become rooted to the spot. But mostly, she hummed the tune to distract her from her surroundings.

The ghetto was a living hell.

The first thing that had struck her when she crossed the checkpoint was the smell. A stench of faeces, unwashed bodies, and disease, so overpowering Zofia had to suppress the urge to vomit. But her visual senses were assaulted just as powerfully: filthy streets, dilapidated buildings, rubbish piling up at every corner, and people – *bodies* – just lying on the freezing pavements, looking more dead than alive. Two small children sat barefoot at a kerbside with a begging bowl, dark eyes huge in their emaciated faces. They looked up at Zofia pleadingly as she walked past, and she almost burst into tears there and then. It was all she could do not to gather them up on the spot and whisk them away. But that was completely unfeasible, and time wasn't on her side. She was on a mission and needed to prove to Irena that she was reliable and trustworthy. Picking up her pace, she swallowed down her tears and hurried on. *I'm just a nurse on her regular business*, she told herself.

The tram depot was a large semi-circular building off Stawki Street. Several trains stood waiting, and behind them, beneath a small shelter, were several drivers on their break, smoking and talking. Zofia scanned the area and yes, there it was, the maintenance shed with the black door. Head down, she slipped around behind a wall and made her way towards the shed, her heart pounding so hard she thought she might be sick. With a shaking hand, she turned the handle and pushed open the door, flinching at the squeal of the rusty hinges. She closed her eyes and waited a second, expecting a rough tap on her shoulder. Surely one of the drivers would have heard? But nothing happened.

Inside, the shed was a small and gloomy space, and just behind the door she found a black leather bag. She picked it up; it was lighter than she'd expected, but perhaps the adrenaline coursing through her body was making her feel stronger than she actually was. As casually as she could, trying not to think about what the bag contained, she left the shed and looked towards the passenger waiting area. No other passengers yet.

She checked the time. It was three fifty. Two minutes to go. The relief she felt that she had made it in and out of the maintenance shed without being caught was soon replaced with a nauseating thump of her heart that the worst lay still ahead of her. The number eight tram stood ready and waiting to start its journey through the ghetto, past the ghetto walls and across the Vistula River to the stop on Olszowa Street. Trying to look as inconspicuous as possible, Zofia crossed the road towards the tram, heading for the last carriage. A quick look left and right – the tram driver was still smoking a cigarette and chatting to a depot mechanic – and she stepped on board.

She let out a small gasp of relief – no other passengers had embarked and the seat at the back was free. She rushed over before anyone saw her and placed the bag under the seat, sat down and let out a long, shuddery breath. While she waited for the tram to start moving, several other people boarded, but no one paid her any attention. Finally, with a jolt and a judder, the doors closed and the tram started moving. About five minutes into the journey, the tram took a tight corner and a curse word escaped from her lips. The bag had slid forward with the movement of the tram. A woman on the opposite bench, wearing a tattered black coat that looked at least two sizes too big for her, tutted in her direction and she felt her cheeks burn. She'd forgotten how to breathe, feeling lightheaded as she bent down to scratch her ankle. Trying very hard to make it look casual, she pushed the bag right back into the recess. A man dressed in filthy overalls further along the carriage looked over and she stiffened, but a moment later he looked away.

The tram stopped three times inside the ghetto; at the last stop before the checkpoint, most of the passengers got off.

Only two other people remained on board, a bored-looking middle-aged woman with a basket full of kindling and the man in overalls. Zofia hoped he would get off before she did, as she would have to reach down to retrieve the bag. It would look tremendously suspicious if she suddenly 'discovered' a leather bag beneath her seat. And if she—

Her thoughts were interrupted by the sound of boots coming up the carriage. A German checkpoint guard. Not the young soldier she'd seen when she entered, but an older one, with a thin, ferret-like face and greased-down hair.

'*Passierschein*,' he barked at her.

She held out her pass and realised she was shaking violently. 'I–I … I'm from the Social Welfare Department,' she stammered. 'Infection control.'

The soldier took a step back, as though fearful she might be contagious. He took a cursory look at her pass and nodded curtly. 'Make sure to wash your hands properly,' he said with a sneer and went to disembark.

Zofia clenched her trembling muscles, forcing herself to regain control. She was through the checkpoint but not yet safe. If she lost her nerve now, she might still be at risk, as German soldiers patrolled the entire city of Warsaw, not just the ghetto, looking for suspicious activity. At the next stop, she sent up a frantic prayer that the man in the overalls would get off, and thankfully, her prayer was heard. As soon as he had disembarked and the tram door had closed behind him, she put her head in her hands and felt the weight of pressure evaporate from her body. *I've made it*, she thought. *I'm nearly safe.*

When the tram rumbled across the river onto Olszowa Street, she waited until it came to a complete stop, then leaned forward, slid the bag out and grabbed the handle. Without so much as a backward glance, she stepped off the tram and pretended to look for a handkerchief in her pocket while the tram trundled off. As soon as it was safely out of view, she looked around and spotted two women at the entrance to a narrow alleyway. Irena and Helena! Irena was beaming at her; Helena had a solemn kind of expression she couldn't read from a distance.

Holding back tears of relief, Zofia wanted to break into a run, but there were half a dozen other pedestrians on the pavement, and she didn't want to lose her nerve now. She strode towards the two women, as casually as she could, focusing on Irena's smiling face that seemed to draw her in like a beacon. When she'd reached them, the three of them stepped into the alley, out of sight of the main road. Zofia held out the bag.

'Well done, Zofia,' Irena said, taking it from her and placing it, almost carelessly, on the ground.

Zofia looked down at it, puzzled. 'The baby…' she began, but Helena was already crouching down and opening the bag. To Zofia's surprise – and horror – Helena pulled the baby out by the leg.

Except … it wasn't a baby. It was the right size, the right shape, but it was made of fabric, with button eyes and woollen hair.

'A doll!' Zofia exclaimed. She spun back around to Irena. 'Helena … Helena said it was a baby. She told me I'd be saving a *baby*, not a stupid rag doll!'

All her tension cascaded off her to be replaced by a rage and disappointment that made her heart flip wildly in her chest. A doll! She'd risked everything for a doll. How could they do that to her? How *dare* they? What kind of stupid game were they playing? She was so deeply upset she didn't notice at first that Irena had put her hands on her shoulders.

'Zofia,' she said softly. 'Zofia, calm down. Take a few deep breaths. Let me explain.'

Still shaking, Zofia let herself be led further down the alley, away from prying eyes and ears, to a small space between two buildings where the sun pooled on the ground in a golden light. A low brick wall, sprouting weeds from between the bricks, marked the end of the alley.

'Come and sit down,' Irena said, lowering herself onto the wall and patting the space beside her. 'You've had quite a fright.'

Zofia perched next to her on the wall. 'I don't understand,' she began. 'Why was I smuggling a doll out of the ghetto?'

'Baptism by fire, we call it,' Irena said quietly. She placed her hands in her lap and looked down at them, while Helena took a pack of cigarettes out of her bag and offered one to Zofia. Zofia shook her head.

'We are not just fighting the Germans, sadly,' Irena continued. 'There are some of us, some Poles, who hate the Jews just as much as the Nazis do, and would be happy to see every member of the resistance strung up for their troubles. And so…' She trailed off.

Zofia swallowed as the understanding dawned on her.

Then Helena spoke, and her voice was warm and gentle 'We're sorry for deceiving you,' she said. 'Truly we are. But there are some risks we just cannot afford to take. We have to make sure we don't invite any traitors into our ranks.'

At the word 'traitors', Zofia looked up at her sharply, but was met with a gaze so kind she dropped her eyes. Of course they had to be careful. This wasn't a game; this was a matter of life and death.

'Every new member is tested in some way,' Helena continued. 'It is unavoidable, I'm afraid. We had to make sure you wouldn't denounce us.'

As Zofia opened her mouth to protest, Irena said, 'And it wasn't just *us* testing *you*. Consider it a way of testing yourself, to see if you have the courage and resilience to stay calm under the worst kind of pressure.'

'But … but if I'd been caught?'

'All they would have discovered was a woman carrying a doll in a bag. Perfectly harmless, if a little … odd.'

She smiled, and Zofia found her anger had subsided completely. She smiled back.

Irena glanced towards Helena and back again. 'Helena and I have discussed it at length about you being a good fit.' She nudged Zofia gently with her shoulder. 'And if you can forgive us for this little ruse, then I'd like to extend a very warm welcome. You have great potential, and we need people like you. You've had a taste now, so to speak. Do you still think you'd like to join us?'

Zofia didn't hesitate for a moment. She still felt the fear and apprehension in her bones, yet strangely, she was more determined than ever. 'Yes,' she said, her resolve perceptible in her voice. 'I do.'

Both Irena and Helena smiled.

'Good,' Irena said. 'Welcome aboard.' She stood up and held out a hand to help Zofia up. 'But be under no illusion, this is no game. It will take over your life whether you like it or not.'

7

Seattle, Present Day

Spring Valley Residential Care Home was not in a valley, or anywhere near a valley. Rather, the care home was a low, bungalow-style building set well back from the road in a huge garden area, with a dozen apple trees and even a chicken run.

Inside, the décor was bright and cheerful, though on closer inspection Lizzie could see some paint peeling off the window frames and a few scuffs on the linoleum floor. But the floor-to-floor windows let in plenty of daylight, giving the place a pleasant, spacious feel. Lizzie plucked at her blouse to stop it sticking to her skin. *It's quite warm in here*, she thought; the air-conditioning was evidently set to a temperature more suited to the elderly. They must really be enjoying this unseasonably humid weather, Lizzie thought. She checked in at reception, writing her name in the visitors' register, and was told her grandmother would be in the community room, down the hall on the right.

Unlike other care homes Lizzie had heard and read about, Spring Valley didn't have that typical institutionalised smell of antiseptic and over-boiled vegetables. But as she entered the community room she became aware of another smell, something sharp and pungent that she recognised immediately. It was nail polish. She looked across the room and saw her grandmother sitting with a group of elderly women around a table, all giggling like school girls, and when she got closer, she saw a young nurse among them. Lizzie didn't recognise her; she must be new.

'No, Elsa,' the nurse was saying with a laugh, 'you gotta hold still, else I'll get the polish all over your fingers.'

'It's a new colour. It's called "Parkinson's Pink",' the old woman called Elsa said, setting off a wave of chuckles around the table. And indeed, her head was wobbling alarmingly on her neck.

'Hi,' the nurse said cheerfully as Lizzie approached. 'You visiting one of these lovely ladies? We've got a manicure going on here, as you can see. Go on, show her, girls.'

At this, the old women all laid their hands on the table, palms down, to show off their nails. Lizzie's grandmother had chosen a different colour for each nail.

'*Babcia*,' Lizzie said, bending over and giving her grandmother a soft kiss on the cheek. 'So nice to see you.'

Her grandmother looked up at her, a brief flash of confusion on her face. But then her lined face broke into a wide smile. 'Lizzie! How lovely to see you.'

Her dimples had deepened with age, marking two semi-circular wrinkles on her cheeks. On the left side of her face, she had a small star-shaped birthmark, something that had always fascinated Lizzie and Helena when they were young. Much to their delight, their grandmother had invented wild stories about the birthmark's origin – she had been kissed by a witch, breathed on by a dragon, touched by an angel… Lizzie bent over and gave her a soft kiss.

'Is this an okay time? Or am I interrupting you?'

The nurse stood up. 'Nah, we're pretty much done here. Magda, why don't you and – Lizzie, was it? – go and grab a coffee?'

Lizzie thanked the nurse and helped her grandmother to her feet. Magda had had both hips replaced a year earlier and still struggled with walking. Since the operation, her mental faculties had also been deteriorating steadily, and she had good days – when she would crack jokes and giggle like a teenager – and bad days, when she barely recognised her surroundings. Today, Lizzie was glad to see, was a good day.

'Let's not have coffee,' Magda grumbled as they crossed the room to a couple of armchairs near the window. 'It's awful stuff they have here. I'm pretty sure they reuse the grounds. Be a darling and get me a Coke, would you?'

'Sure,' Lizzie said, smiling. She went to a vending machine that stood in the corner and got two cans of Coke. Magda grinned up at her when she returned, her over-large dentures clicking out of place and back in again.

'So lovely to see you, dear. How are you? You still teaching?'

Lizzie nodded. She didn't know how much her grandmother knew about the miscarriages and she wasn't here to talk about herself, anyway. 'I'm fine, *Babcia*. It's summer vacation and I'm staying with Mom and Dad for a couple of weeks.'

'That's nice. So you can come and visit me more often?'

Lizzie put her hand on her grandmother's. Her skin was warm and paper-thin. 'Of course.'

'And how is that handsome husband of yours?' She looked around expectantly. 'Is he here?'

Lizzie straightened up. 'No, Alex … um, he's working. But he's fine, I'll tell him you asked after him.' She felt the heat rise to her face and distracted herself by opening the cans. 'Listen, *Babcia*, I wanted to ask you something. I, um … I was cleaning out the attic at home and found some stuff that belonged to *Prababcia*.'

'The encyclopaedias? Oh, my dear, those things have been gathering dust for years.' She chuckled. 'I've told your mom she can sell them. Or throw them out.'

'Actually …' Lizzie cleared her throat, unsure how to broach the subject. She'd rehearsed it on the drive out here, but the mention of Alex had thrown her. So she just launched right in and told her grandmother about the photographs, her research into the Polish resistance movement, her great-grandmother's involvement with Irena Sendler and helping people in the ghetto. 'Anyway, I was wondering what you can tell me?' she said finally. 'About Zofia.'

'Like what?'

'Like did she ever talk about it? I mean, when I first found the photos, there was one of *Prababcia* with a group of children, and at first I thought they were hers. They looked so intimate together, her and the kids, you know?'

She sighed, wondering for a moment whether to tell her grandmother how desperately unhappy she'd been. But her pain was still too raw – no, she was here because she needed a distraction from all of that. 'And today, Mom told me you'd been adopted. I mean, there's so much I don't know about my own family.' She let out a dry laugh. 'I genuinely thought we went back generations here in the States.'

Magda looked sombre for a moment, Then she waved a hand in front of her face, a gesture Lizzie recognised from her own mother when she didn't want to talk about something.

'Ah,' she said finally, her voice cracked with age. 'Old chestnuts.'

But Lizzie wasn't prepared to give up this easily. 'But she must have told you *something*, *Babcia*. Zofia was in the Polish resistance. That's … that's huge!'

'She didn't like to talk about it.' Magda's eyes flashed suddenly. 'You don't think I wanted to know, hmm? Who my birth parents were? But those were different times, things were often left unspoken. And perhaps that wasn't such a bad thing. Some wounds need to be left alone to heal properly.'

She leaned back in her chair and closed her eyes briefly. Lizzie wondered if she'd pushed her grandmother too far and was momentarily ashamed. Here was a frail old woman who had been through things Lizzie couldn't begin to imagine. But Magda soon opened her eyes and smiled.

'She was a good mother, Lizzie. She loved me unconditionally and I loved her right back. Now, if you don't mind.' She heaved herself out of her chair, her legs wobbling as she grabbed her cane for stability. Once up on steady legs, she announced, 'The girls and I are playing Mah-jongg in ten minutes.'

Lizzie gave her a kiss goodbye and left. And as she walked back out into the sticky, oppressive air, she felt a sense of deep frustration. She'd hoped her grandmother would know the answers to all her questions, but instead, all Lizzie had managed to do was to upset her. If she had known about the adoption earlier, she would have prepared better, addressed the issue more sensitively. As it was, she'd shown all the sensitivity of a bull in a china shop. She should have known better; she knew what it felt like when other people casually pushed her to talk about her failed pregnancies.

And was it so surprising that Magda didn't like talking about her adoption? It was a tricky topic at the best of times, one that Lizzie herself had avoided like the plague. She and Alex hadn't really discussed it. No – that wasn't true. Alex had mentioned it once and Lizzie had flown into a rage, shouting at him that he didn't understand, that he hadn't a clue how she felt. It had been a bruising argument. She pushed the painful memory aside. Part of her knew she would have to face him at some point, make a decision about whether they still had a future together. But now was not the time.

As she walked past the chicken run to her car, her phone buzzed and she pulled it out of her pocket. It was a text from Alex. She stared at her phone for a long moment, her grandmother's words echoing in her head. '*Some wounds need to be left alone to heal properly.*'

She deleted the message. She didn't want to deal with her own life right now – all she wanted was to lose herself in her great-grandmother's.

8

Warsaw, November 1942

It was now two months since she had officially joined the resistance. Zofia wasn't sure how, but Irena had managed to put her name on the list of nurses that had permanent passes to enter the ghetto for infection control. In a very brief induction session, Zofia had been shown the best way to smuggle items into the ghetto, which guards to avoid if at all possible, how to rotate checkpoints and which schedules the guard patrols used. She had expected some training on how to withstand interrogation if the worst happened and she was caught by the Germans, but Helena explained, almost casually, that that was something no one could prepare you for. 'Just pray it doesn't happen,' she had said in that blunt tone of hers.

Helena, it seemed to Zofia, had become hardened to all the agony and human suffering. She wondered if the other woman had always been this way, or whether it was an inevitable consequence of witnessing such wretchedness on a regular basis. As much as she prayed she would never get caught by the Nazis, Zofia also prayed she would never become quite as hard as Helena.

She had been in and out of the ghetto dozens of times now, smuggling in medicines sewed into the lining of her coat, or loaves of bread hidden in a secret compartment of her medical bag, and fear remained her constant companion. At every checkpoint crossing she expected to be pulled out of the line, searched, beaten, and worse. It took Herculean strength to stay calm when she presented her pass and had her bag rifled through. But every time she wavered, she told herself that every dose of vaccine she managed to smuggle in, every loaf of bread she gave to a hungry family, might save a life.

Besides, as Irena maintained, the Germans had no idea what was going on under their very noses. For them, Jews were subhuman, and even Poles were backward people. Too stupid, too primitive to organise in such a sophisticated way. They knew, of course, that there was some black-market activity going on, deals made with valuables – jewellery, keepsakes, watches and such – that all Jews should have surrendered to the German authorities when they had been forced into the ghetto. Early on, there had been regular raids of people's homes and anyone involved, or even suspected of involvement, ended up in the notorious Pawiak Prison. By now, however, the Germans thought they'd broken the resistance. They were arrogant fools, Irena had said, but that didn't mean they could afford to let their guard down. German spies and collaborators were everywhere.

Zofia was sitting at her desk one morning when Mr Wójcik entered the office.

'Miss Szczęsny?' he barked. 'My office, now.'

He turned and walked out, evidently expecting Zofia to follow him into the corridor. She put down her file and shot Lina a glance, who frowned and then shook her head nervously.

So much had happened since Zofia had joined the resistance, it was hard sometimes to recall how mundane her day-to-day life had been two months earlier. Her concerns over having to darn already threadbare stockings, feeling disappointed at the idea of cabbage and potatoes for dinner yet again, pretending to be overjoyed when all she got for her birthday was a leather belt made from offcuts from her father's workshop – all these things seemed unbelievably trivial now. It had only taken a single visit to the ghetto to realise how blessed her life had really been. She couldn't clear the images of destitution from her mind, particularly of the children, their large, mournful eyes and emaciated bodies.

Her life was drastically different now and the past two months had taken their toll, physically and emotionally. Every plate of food her mother put in front of her made her think of the starving children, and most nights she was assailed by nightmares that left her groggy and bleary-eyed in the mornings. Her skin was red-raw from perpetual scrubbing with cold water and carbolic soap, as she was terrified of bringing germs into the house. She herself was likely to be immune to typhus after her childhood infection, but Zuzanna's health was fragile and Zofia lived in constant fear of infecting her sister. But she clung on to the idea that she was making a difference, however small that might be.

She got up and left the office, taking her time as she crossed the corridor to Wójcik's office. When she got to the door, she smoothed down her skirt, trying to guess what he might want to speak to her about. It was, of course, entirely possible that she'd made some mistake in her office work, a stupid filing error or something.

She knew the importance of keeping her guard up in the ghetto, but it was exhausting and could lead to lapses of concentration. Thankfully, it had only happened once, when she'd gone to cross a checkpoint after delivering some vaccines, and couldn't find her pass to get out. For a panic-stricken moment, she'd imagined she would have to stay there, in hiding, until someone realised she hadn't returned and went to look for her. After a frantic, heart-stopping search of her bag she had finally found her pass and crossed the checkpoint without incident. There had been no harm done, really, but for days afterwards she'd found it impossible to still the little voice of doubt in her head that whispered, *Why are you doing this? You're not cut out to be a heroine. And what if you're discovered and arrested, what will happen to your family?* It didn't help that Lina had mentioned noticing increased soldier patrols on her recent visits to the ghetto and warned everyone to be aware of people snooping about. The spies and Nazi collaborators were everywhere.

These were Zofia's thoughts as she stood outside Wójcik's office. Although his door stood ajar, she knocked against the doorframe before entering. Wójcik was sitting behind his desk, a thick fug of cigarette smoke hanging just above his head. There were several open files in front of him. Zofia took a few steps forward, unsure whether to take a seat on the chair opposite his desk.

'No need to sit down, Miss Szczęsny,' Wójcik said, looking down at his desk and giving her the eerie feeling he was reading her thoughts. 'I won't keep you long.'

'What can I—' she began, but he cut her off.

'I'm wondering,' Wójcik said, his eyes still on the papers in front of him. 'I have five case files here for which the reports are outstanding.' He looked up. 'They were due last Tuesday and yet you have submitted nothing. Would you care to explain?'

Zofia's mouth was suddenly dry. She swallowed.

'I've also noticed you've been taking extended lunch breaks lately, leaving early, arriving late … in fact, you seem to come and go as you wish. Is there anything other than office work occupying your time?'

Zofia's heart fluttered in her chest like a trapped bird. *This is it*, she thought. *He's found out that I've been visiting the ghetto.* Her eyes darted to the door and back, as though there might be some hope of escape. She had been as careful as possible, only shaving off fifteen minutes here, half an hour there, hoping her boss wouldn't notice. But obviously, she hadn't been careful enough.

'Well?' he barked into the silence. 'What has been keeping you from your work? And I don't want to hear any excuses.'

'It's my sister,' Zofia said hurriedly, trying to keep the nervousness out of her voice. 'She is unwell and I have to accompany her to doctor's appointments sometimes, when my mother is otherwise engaged…' She trailed off, suppressing a twinge of guilt for using Zuzanna's illness as a pretext.

Wójcik sniffed. 'You are paid a full-time salary, and I expect you to work accordingly. I am sorry that your sister isn't well, but I expect you to be present during office hours. Do I make myself clear?'

Zofia nodded as graciously as she could. Wójcik gave her a cold stare and then dismissed her with a wave of his hand.

As she left his office and closed the door behind her, she wondered – not for the first time – how long it would be until she was exposed.

Both entrance and exit queues at the ghetto checkpoint were long. Zofia got in line, shivering despite her warm coat. It had snowed overnight, a thick white blanket covering the roads and rooftops. She smoothed the front of her coat down as best she could, praying the guards wouldn't make her remove it. She had stuffed a loaf of bread into the waistband of her skirt. It was uncomfortable, and a huge risk should she be searched. But she had donned plenty of layers beneath her coat – two woollen jumpers as well as a cardigan – and hoped this would conceal the bread and make her merely appear slightly chubby.

She was here to see the Bocheńskis, a family of six. Mr Bocheński had caught pneumonia and couldn't work, thus drying up the family's only source of income. The only effective treatment of pneumonia was antibiotics, but that type of medication was worth its weight in gold and impossible to source. With Irena's help, Zofia had managed to get her hands on some aspirin, which might at least help with Mr Bocheński's fever.

It was her turn at the checkpoint. She handed her pass to the guard and waited as he scrutinised it closely, keeping her head down and pulling up her scarf to cover as much of her lower face as possible. Although she had been trained to rotate checkpoints – entering and leaving by different routes, in order to spend more time inside the ghetto without arousing suspicion – it was prudent to stay as anonymous, as unrecognisable as possible. The guard handed her pass back and ordered her to open her bag. Hoping she appeared calmer on the outside than she felt, she opened it and let him root around inside. His nose and cheeks were red with cold and he looked decidedly uncomfortable in his thin uniform. He was a soldier, not an officer, and as such wasn't afforded the luxury of a thick, lined winter coat. Zofia studied his face as he continued to rifle through her bag. She watched his lips move as he mumbled silently to himself, saw his pale eyelashes blink, saw a small crease form on his forehead, just between his eyes. What she was looking for, she realised, was some indication, some feature, that marked him out as evil. But no – he looked just like a normal human being. It was unfathomable to her how a seemingly ordinary man could participate in this wicked regime. It would be less frightening, somehow, if the evil were visible on the outside – like a beast or a monster. But to believe that ugliness and hate on the inside permeated to the outside would deny that perfectly normal humans were capable of evil.

'What are you staring at?' he asked angrily, startling her out of her thoughts.

'Nothing, I-I was… Nothing.'

The soldier waved her through, spitting on the ground as she passed. As soon as she was out of sight of the checkpoint, she removed the loaf of bread from her waistband and put it in her bag. It wasn't a huge loaf, but it was better than nothing.

The fresh white snow, which made an otherwise grey and dreary Warsaw look rather beautiful, did little to hide the wretchedness in the ghetto. Here, the feathery, glittering flakes didn't soften the outlines of buildings or muffle the sounds of motor vehicles. Instead, it seemed to draw attention to the blackened façades, the ugly piles of rubble, the whole human misery.

There was a sound from the other side of the street; Zofia turned and saw an old man, who was no more than skin and bones, rattling a begging cup with an outstretched arm. He stood leaning heavily on a short tree branch he was using as a walking stick. Zofia paused for a moment, wondering if there was something she might give him. Eventually though, she moved on and tried to focus her mind on the Bocheński family. She couldn't help everyone, she reminded herself, but she could help some. She walked on.

There was the sudden rush of boots from behind her; turning, she saw two uniformed German soldiers running across the road to the old man. Without any warning, one of them kicked away the man's stick, sending him sprawling onto the icy pavement. His begging cup rolled away into the gutter, as the other soldier began kicking the man, shouting filthy slurs at him. Zofia let out a stifled cry, torn between wanting to go and help him, and knowing that if she did so, she would most likely face arrest herself. She looked away, trying to close her ears to the sound of him crying out. As ever, witnessing such monstrous cruelty left her trembling and afraid, and sick to her stomach. As she continued down the street, a feeling of agonising guilt rose up inside her as the old man's moans of pain rang in her ears. Not for the first time, she found herself wishing she were less sensitive to the suffering of others. It would make this so much easier. But if that was the case then, perhaps, she wouldn't be doing it at all.

Fifteen minutes later, she arrived at the tenement building where the Bocheńskis lived. Like so many other buildings in the ghetto, it hadn't seen any maintenance work for years, and the façade was pockmarked and crumbling. The main door hung precariously from a single hinge and Zofia entered the building with a sense of trepidation. Inside, paint was peeling off the walls, with Yiddish words scrawled there in a large, angry script. The whole place smelled of mould and human waste.

Zofia climbed the stairs to the second floor and knocked on the door, her breath a cloud of white. She waited a moment, then knocked again, but no one came to answer. She shivered slightly. Behind her, on the opposite side of the stairwell, a door opened and a woman appeared. She was quite tall, with chestnut-brown hair and a striking kind of beauty. She carried an air of sophistication that even her tattered clothing couldn't hide. In a previous life, she might have been a ballerina, or a film actress, Zofia thought. She wondered briefly if this woman had ever been forced to dig for potatoes because she was 'too elegant'.

'Can I help you?' the woman asked warily.

'I'm an inspection control nurse,' Zofia replied. 'I'm looking for Mr and Mrs Bocheński.'

The woman's face twisted into a mask of fear and distress and she let out a sudden sob. 'They're gone. Yesterday, they were taken to the *umschlagplatz* and they didn't return. The little ones were out playing and when they came back in, we had to tell them…'

She broke down in tears and couldn't continue. Zofia offered her a handkerchief and murmured some words of comfort. Empty words of comfort, for they both knew what it meant to be taken to the *umschlagplatz*. It was where people were forcibly gathered before being deported to Treblinka.

When the woman had calmed a little, Zofia asked, 'Where are the children now?'

The woman sniffed. 'They are with us. But—' She gave Zofia a stricken look. 'But we have three of our own already and I don't know how we are going to feed four more.'

Without thinking twice, Zofia reached into her bag.

'Here,' she said, holding out the loaf of bread. 'Take it. For you, and the children.'

The woman hesitated briefly, then quick as a flash took the bread from Zofia, turning it in her hands and inspecting it closely.

'No mould,' she said quietly. She gave Zofia a sad smile. 'That'll make a change.'

Back at the office, Zofia scribbled a note and placed it in a manila folder, then labelled it: *Miss Sendler, Dept. IV.*, to give to the in-house messenger. An hour later she received a reply, suggesting they meet at a *bar mleczny*, a milk bar, on Mostowa Street after work.

It was a long afternoon, but finally, five o'clock came around and Zofia hurried to the café. Irena was already there, sitting at a table close to the window. She smiled as Zofia came in.

'Nice to see you,' she said. 'I've ordered *kompot* and two slices of freshly-baked *makowiec*. I hope that's all right.'

Zofia sat down. 'Sounds lovely.'

A minute later, the waitress brought their hot drinks and two slices of poppyseed roll.

Irena speared a piece of cake onto her fork. 'My father always used to bake this every Christmas,' she said, smiling wistfully.

Zofia sighed. Christmas was just over five weeks away, but it had never been further from her mind. Usually at this time of year, she and Zuzanna would be busy with preparations, making straw stars for the tree, helping their mother bake honey-layered cake, attending Roraty Mass, whispering their most outlandish wishes for Christmas presents to each other – a proper fur coat for Zofia, a real camera for Zuzanna. But this year, all that seemed beyond frivolous. Zofia's lack of enthusiasm hadn't gone unnoticed by her family, but she had claimed, as usual, that she was just too busy at work.

Irena took a bite of cake, nodded appreciatively, and set her fork back down. 'Now, Zofia, what is this meeting in aid of?'

'It's the children,' Zofia blurted out, and proceeded to tell Irena about her visit to the Bocheński family that morning. 'Without their parents, the children stand no chance. There must be something we can do for them.'

Irena listened attentively. When Zofia had finished speaking, she looked out of the window and then back at Zofia.

'There is something we can do,' she said quietly.

'What?'

'You've heard about the infighting at the Committee?'

Zofia nodded. The Provisional Committee had been set up to provide assistance to Jews living in Poland, and was the umbrella organisation for the underground resistance groups. It was a relatively recent set-up, but there had been tensions among its more senior members from the beginning, and it was expected to fall apart any time soon. A number of donors had already backed out, leaving the organisation in a critical financial position.

'There is a newly formed branch of the resistance,' Irena continued. 'It's now called the Council to Aid Jews.' She sighed and waved a hand in front of her face. 'Council, committee, the name shouldn't matter, I think. Anyway, this new organisation will continue the work of the Committee with a slightly different structure.'

'What has any of this to do with the Bocheński children?' Zofia asked impatiently. She wasn't interested in the ins and outs of the resistance structure. What did it matter whether they were run by a council, or a committee, or any other type of board, so long as they did something meaningful to help people?

Irena raised her eyebrows slightly. 'You are very passionate about children, aren't you! And very impatient, too.' She smiled.

'I suppose I am, yes.'

'Well, this new organisation – codenamed Żegota – has a number of different sections. Medical care, housing etcetera. And I am heading up the children's section. It will—'

She stopped as two men in long overcoats passed by their table. She took another bite of cake and waited until the men were out of earshot.

She continued in a low voice. 'Over ten thousand children were deported in August alone. We have to try and save as many as we can before all the remaining children are murdered.'

'But how?'

Irena opened her mouth to speak, but there was the sudden, foreboding sound of boots on the pavement outside. Zofia cast

85

a nervous glance through the window and saw a group of German soldiers, marching rhythmically past the milk bar.

Irena caught Zofia's eye and tapped her lips with a finger, waiting until the footsteps had receded completely before continuing, even more quietly than before. 'You remember your initiation? The baby on the tram?'

'I certainly do.'

'We have been saving children from the ghetto. Children who would otherwise die from disease, or starvation. Many mothers cannot produce enough milk for their babies because they are starving themselves. So we smuggle them out. Not necessarily by tram, but there are other ways – underground passages, ambulances, hearses.' She leaned further forward, so that Zofia caught the faint smell of lavender soap. 'And we will need all the help we can get. Do you recall the time I said you had potential?'

Zofia nodded. It had been after her first 'mission', when she had smuggled out the doll.

'Well, Zofia, you have realised that potential, in fact you have exceeded my expectations. And I would very much like you to be a part of Żegota.'

Zofia's eyes widened as she felt a shiver of something that was closer to excitement than fear. She was ready.

9

Seattle, Present Day

Lizzie was relieved to return to an empty house. There were so many thoughts swirling around in her head after her visit to her grandmother, she wouldn't have known how to hold a meaningful conversation with anyone. She went to the kitchen to fetch a glass of iced water – the afternoon heat was seeping into the house – and headed up to the attic.

Upstairs, she tugged the thin curtain shut against the sunlight, and fired up her laptop. To her delight, there was a new email in her inbox. Roksana Lewandowska, the Polish journalist, had written back to her. Despite telling herself not to get her hopes up prematurely, Lizzie opened the email with an expectant click.

Dear Lizzie, thanks for reaching out! I'm glad you enjoyed reading my articles. Fascinated to hear that your great-grandmother was in the resistance! Hers is not a name I recognise, but I will definitely check to see what I can find. Please do not hesitate to ask any questions you may have! I'm happy to help if I can. Kind regards, Roksana

Lizzie couldn't help but smile and immediately began typing a reply, thanking Roksana for the quick response and her offer of help. Then she spent a good half hour summarising where her research had led her so far (which was a string of dead ends, basically), and told Roksana she would be hugely grateful for any help. As a last thought, she photographed the three pictures she had of Zofia and attached them to the email.

When she finally pressed 'send', she checked the time. It was almost six o'clock. She got up and stretched, then went to pull back the curtain and open the window. Outside, the air was still and warm, but the heat of the day was slowly waning. There was a nine-hour time difference, which meant it was three in the morning in Poland; any reply from Roksana would come tomorrow at the earliest.

Lizzie drained her glass of water and put the glass down, noticing how loose her wedding ring was on her finger. She really should eat something, keep up her strength. She'd not only lost weight since her last miscarriage, but her energy levels were also depleting.

A movement on her computer screen shook her out of her thoughts. It was an email from Roksana.

Dear Lizzie, thanks for your email. You certainly have many questions! I hope I'm not being presumptuous, but have you considered coming to visit? Warsaw is a beautiful and fascinating city, particularly at this time of year (I'm not at all biased LOL) and there is plenty of history to see with your own eyes. Please let me know if you plan to visit; I'd be delighted to show you around! But I will certainly get back to you if I find any more information about your great-grandmother. Kind regards from Warszawa, Roksana

The attic door creaked open and startled Lizzie.

'Hey, you still up here?' Her sister's head poked around the corner.

'How was the fitting?'

'Really good.' Hannah blushed a little. 'I'm getting so excited now, it's like I've got a thousand butterflies trapped inside me.'

Lizzie smiled. 'I'm really happy for you, Dimples. You're gonna be the most beautiful bride ever.'

Hannah blushed and clucked her tongue. 'Anyway, Mom says can you come down and help peel some potatoes for French fries? Dad's doing a barbeque tonight.'

After dinner, they all sat at the round wooden table on the terrace. The air was warm but no longer muggy and the embers of the barbeque glowed red in the dark. Lizzie sat staring at a dozen fireflies dancing about at the foot of the garden, half-listening to her mother and Hannah talking about Hannah's wedding dress.

'Oh honey,' her mother said. 'I really don't think that's suitable.'

Hannah scowled. 'Well, it's my wedding, not yours.'

'Let me see,' Lizzie said, and Hannah picked up her phone and showed her a picture of the fitting.

Lizzie let out an appreciative whistle. Her sister was wearing a red gown that complemented her dark hair beautifully and brought out the sparkle in her eyes.

'Looks good to me,' she said, smiling at her sister.

'But red? For a wedding?' their mother said.

'Oh Mom, this is the twenty-first century,' Hannah replied with an eye-roll. 'There's no law that says brides have to wear white.'

Lizzie's mother clucked her tongue and got to her feet. 'There's baked apples and home-made vanilla ice-cream for dessert. Any takers?'

Everyone gave her an eager 'Yes' and she went into the house.

Lizzie looked up at the night sky.

'Why so pensive, sweetheart?' her dad said. 'What's up?'

She shrugged a shoulder. Roksana's suggestion that she come to Warsaw had lodged itself into her brain and refused to move.

'She's been up in the attic for hours,' her mother said, as she came back to the terrace, expertly balancing four plates on her arms. 'Going through my grandmother's things.'

'You finally going to throw out that encyclopaedia?' her dad said with a laugh. 'Been sat up there for years, catching dust. Hey, maybe it's even worth something! We should put it on Craigslist.'

Lizzie paused a moment as the others tucked in to their baked apple and ice-cream. 'The journalist wrote back,' she said. 'The one in Warsaw.' She laughed to herself. 'She said I should come and see the city for myself.'

Her mother raised her eyebrows. 'Go to Warsaw? You, on your own?'

'I know,' Lizzie said. 'It's a dumb idea.'

But Hannah threw up her hands. 'Are you kidding? Of course you should go!'

'Mom? Dad?' Lizzie turned to her parents. 'What do you think?'

'Why not?' her dad said. 'School's out for the summer, though Eastern Europe wouldn't be my vacation destination of choice.' He looked at his wife. 'You know I would much rather go bird-watching in Toledo, but—'

She interrupted him. 'If you think I'm spending our next vacation hidden in a bush looking through some binoculars for a purple-spotted tit-babbler, think again.'

'Now you're being ridiculous, Agnes. It's a fluffy-backed tit babbler, and you won't find them in Toledo, anyhow.'

Hannah gave Lizzie a look and they both grinned. Then Hannah's face turned serious.

'Seriously though, Bubs, it's a great idea,' she said. 'It'll distract you, and who knows what you'll discover about our family history. I'm a little jealous, to be honest.'

Lizzie sat back and took a sip of wine. Visiting Poland on a whim – what a ridiculous idea! But maybe her sister was right, maybe it was the distraction she needed.

Her phone buzzed. Without even looking, she knew it was a text from Alex. The familiar mix of guilt and anger, and the underlying ache of grief, gave way to a sudden urge to escape. She got to her feet.

'Off to bed already?' her dad asked.

'Um, yeah. It's been a long day,' she replied. Then she went inside, headed up the stairs, past her room and up to the attic.

Ten minutes later, she had booked a flight from Seattle to Warsaw, leaving tomorrow. All it had taken was a few simple clicks. How, she wondered as she climbed into bed, did people like those her great-grandmother had helped, escape from their awful realities back then with the Nazis watching their every move?

10

Warsaw, November 1942

Today, Zofia was facing a far larger, more terrifying challenge than bringing in vaccines and food. She and Helena were smuggling out the four Bocheński orphans, along with two others from a different family Irena knew. They were taking the children out through an underground passage beneath the courthouse, and Zofia's nerves were more tightly strung than she could have imagined possible. So far, entering the ghetto had been relatively uneventful, but now, as they approached the checkpoint, her fear was as fresh as that very first time, when she smuggled out a doll. Fear was a good thing, she told herself. It kept her senses alert.

Irena wouldn't be joining them for this part of the operation; there was a bout of acute typhus sweeping along the eastern part of the ghetto, and Irena's skills as a trained nurse were increasingly in demand. For the past few weeks, she had been busy sourcing and smuggling in the Weigl vaccine, which didn't provide full immunity against the disease, but did reduce the symptoms. It didn't help Zofia's nerves that Irena wouldn't be there; she had come to rely on her almost like a good luck charm.

She and Helena got off the tram at Złota Street. The ghetto checkpoint was only thirty metres ahead of them, but Zofia's legs felt as heavy as if she were wading through treacle. Helena appeared to notice her trepidation.

'You must have faith,' she said quietly. 'The first time is always the worst, but we have done this several times before and no one has been caught.' She swiftly made the sign of the cross.

The soldiers at the checkpoint seemed bored and waved Zofia and Helena through after a quick inspection of their passes. Once they were on the other side, they carried on straight ahead down Śliksa Street. They were due at the home of Mr and Mrs Dawidovicz at five o'clock to pick up their two children, and would meet another Żegota member there, who would be bringing the four Bocheński children.

Żegota members worked within separate cells, and Zofia would have been hard pushed to explain the structure of the organisation. This was intentional, Irena had explained; if a single member was discovered by the authorities, they would only be able to give up the handful of members they were in contact with. Zofia had insisted passionately she would *never* betray anyone to the Nazis, but Irena just shook her head unhappily and said, 'Bless you, Zofia, for not even contemplating the absolute evil these people are capable of.'

Zofia cheeks had burned when she realised Irena was talking about torture.

The cell she worked in included Helena, Lina, Elżbieta, and the young man she'd met at the Social Workers' Club – Jakub – who smuggled food, medicines and clothing into the camp. As the head of the children's section, Irena was familiar with each and every cell, and Zofia could only guess how much of a burden it was, the responsibility of knowing so much. If Irena were ever exposed, then they would all be at risk. Zofia often wondered how she hadn't collapsed under the pressure.

Keeping her own activities hidden from her family was one of the most difficult things she'd ever had to do. She rarely kept secrets from them normally; she was used to coming home from work and telling them all about her day, sharing anecdotes about Mr Wójcik's temper tantrums and gossip about who might be courting whom. Now, she barely mumbled a word at the dinner table, forever fearful she might inadvertently blurt something out. Not that her parents would report her, she was certain of that, but they would be terrified on her behalf and probably pressure her into stopping. But having seen the misery and wretchedness of the lives on the other side of the ghetto walls, she had no choice but to continue. So she remained largely silent at home as she was having to hold so many thoughts in her head at once that it was safer not to talk at all. Her parents, she knew, held the quiet hope that Zofia would come home one day and disclose that she'd met someone, a kind and loving man who would marry their daughter and settle down with her. But thoughts of romance couldn't be further from Zofia's mind. How could she think of love and marriage when the world was burning around her?

By contrast, Lina's romantic streak hadn't been dampened at all by her resistance activities. She had recently confided in Zofia that she found Jakub 'easy on the eye', and though Lina had fleeting crushes on any number of young men that crossed her path, Zofia had also caught herself glancing at Jakub a few seconds longer than strictly necessary, taking in his strong jaw, his dark hair and very white teeth. He worked as a joiner when he wasn't smuggling things in and out of the ghetto, and had the muscular physique of someone accustomed to physical labour. Unlike the Żegota women who posed as inspection control nurses, Jakub didn't have a pass to enter and exit the ghetto, yet he somehow managed to get in and out without detection. Lina reckoned he had used his good looks to charm a guardian angel. But regardless of how he did it, he was a valuable asset to the group, often bringing back useful intelligence, like the patrol routes and schedules of the German soldiers, or advice on how to rotate the checkpoints they used to avoid the more sociopathic guards who took pleasure in humiliating the nurses, tradesmen, and labourers who were allowed to enter and exit the ghetto. Only last week, Zofia had witnessed a man being forced to get on his hands and knees and crawl through the gate while two soldiers kicked him until he had a black eye and a bloody nose.

Helena stopped in front of a dreary-looking tenement building. Paint was flaking from the doors, the frames were rotting, and several of the windows were missing the glass and had been hastily boarded up. From a distance, they heard the sound of church bells from nearby St. Alexandra's chiming the call to evening mass. It was incredible to think how close the outside world was – from where they were standing, the church was a mere five-hundred metres as the crow flies – and yet the distance between the ghetto and the 'Aryan' side of the city couldn't be greater.

Helena looked up at the building. 'Third floor, Mr and Mrs Dawidovicz, with their children, Aneta and Aaron.' She turned to Zofia. 'Come on, they'll be waiting for us.'

They entered the house and made their way up to the third floor. There were all manner of sounds coming from the flats in the building – hammering, someone crying quietly, a couple arguing. Zofia and Helena didn't exchange a word as they climbed the stairs; they were both acutely aware of the solemnness of the task ahead. They would be taking children away from their parents, tearing the family apart. Zofia hated every minute of it, but what other options were there? Almost daily they heard new stories about more and more men, women and children ordered to go to the *umschlagplatz*, the transhipment point at the northern tip of the ghetto, where large trucks waited to take them to the labour camp at Treblinka. Hundreds of thousands had disappeared to the camp over the past few months, and no one had heard anything of them since.

When they got to the third floor, Helena took a deep breath and knocked softly on a door that looked to be rotting in its frame. A moment later, Mr Dawidovicz opened it. He was a tall, dark-haired man with sunken cheeks, and was wearing a suit that had seen better days. The knees were worn and shiny, and he exuded an air of complete resignation. Zofia looked away so he wouldn't catch her staring. Mr Dawidovicz had once been a lawyer, Helena had told her, but was now forced to sweep the streets or shovel snow to earn money to feed his family.

'Come in,' he said, greeting them with a smile that didn't quite reach his eyes. 'Your friend Jakub is already here. He arrived ten minutes ago, with the Bocheński children. They are in the kitchen.'

Helena and Zofia stepped inside the flat and followed Mr Dawidovicz along a dark and narrow hallway. Just before they got to the kitchen door, the man turned and spoke in a low whisper.

'My wife is a little … upset, but she is trying hard not to frighten the children. We've told them they're going on a trip, a winter excursion, but I'm not sure Aaron quite believes us. He's a very intelligent boy, you know.'

Zofia could see how much effort it was costing him not to break down and had to stop her own tears from falling.

Helena laid a hand on his arm. 'You have made the right decision. And we will keep them safe, I promise you.'

He swallowed and for a moment, it seemed as though he was going to say something. But then he just nodded and opened the kitchen door.

'They're here,' he announced with a false cheerfulness in his voice.

Jakub was standing by the small window, looking out, and turned when Zofia and Helena came in. He looked tense and only nodded a curt greeting. Zofia didn't take it personally – her own nerves were so tightly wound they felt close to snapping. Four young children stood beside him, aged between three and seven, all dressed in dark clothing several sizes too big for them. The Bocheńskis. Zofia crouched down and smiled at them, but they just gave her earnest stares in return. *Poor things*, she thought. *They must be terrified.*

The air in the room was warm and stuffy, with a lingering smell of boiled cabbage. Mrs Dawidovicz was sitting at the small kitchen table, a fearful look of pain and dread on her face. Her daughter Aneta, probably no older than five, sat on her lap with her head her mother's shoulder. She had a slightly stunned expression on her face, as though she wasn't quite sure what was happening. Aaron, the son, looked about eight or nine, and stood pale-faced beside his mother.

'Is it time?' Mrs Dawidovicz said. Her eyes were red-rimmed, and Zofia doubted she would have slept at all last night.

At the window, Jakub took a last look out and straightened up. 'A few minutes more,' he said, 'to say your goodbyes.'

At this, Mrs Dawidovicz let out a small, sad mewing sound and hugged her daughter tightly. Then she kissed her face over and over again, until the girl began squirming on her lap.

'Come now, my love,' her husband said, his voice trembling, and gently took his daughter from his wife's embrace. 'It is for the best.'

Mrs Dawidovicz gripped Zofia's wrist and pulled her forward. Her face was a mask of utter despair. 'Look after them,' she whispered.

'We will,' Zofia replied. 'And God willing, you will be reunited soon.'

The little group – Zofia, Helena, Jakub and the six children – made their way down the stairs. Outside on the street, Jakub turned left while the others carried on straight ahead down a narrow side street. His task was to scout their route to the courthouse, making sure there were no German soldiers or other nasty surprises along the way.

Zofia and Helena continued eastwards with the children, careful to stay close to buildings, ready to duck and hide in any number of entrances that opened onto the street. Zofia didn't know what the children's parents had told them, but they were exceptionally well-behaved, keeping very quiet and obeying every instruction she or Helena gave them. Perhaps, Zofia thought, the children believed it to be a game. Only Aaron seemed to realise the seriousness of the occasion and walked beside her with his face set in an expression of solemnity too old for such a young child.

When they got to the corner of Nowolipki Road, the streetlamps suddenly went off. Helena checked her watch.

'Curfew,' she mouthed.

Zofia looked around and indeed, they were the only people left on the street. This was the riskiest part of the operation. If they were spotted, they had no excuse for being out and about after curfew.

'We'll wait five minutes and then head for the courthouse,' Helena continued, her voice so low Zofia had to lean in to hear her. 'Jakub will be waiting for us.'

They snuck deeper into the shadows of the building behind them, and then Aneta tugged on Zofia's hand.

'Excuse me, miss,' she whispered. 'I need the toilet.'

Zofia gave Helena a nervous glance, and then leaned over to Aneta. 'Can you wait a moment longer?' she asked quietly. 'We're nearly there.'

The little girl shrugged. 'I don't think so. I really need to go. Please.'

Helena murmured something under her breath. 'All right,' she said eventually. 'Zofia, you stay here with the others. I'll take Aneta behind one of the buildings. We won't be long.'

Zofia nodded, though she was terrified at the thought of being left here on her own. But she put a brave smile on her face so as not to make the other children anxious. Helena disappeared down the lane with Aneta, leaving Zofia to wait for what seemed like an eternity. And then she spotted something and her stomach dropped to her knees. A movement at the other end of the lane. She pressed her body up against the brick wall behind her and gestured for the children to do the same. Hardly daring to move, she turned her head and saw the silhouettes of two men standing at the entrance to the lane, the moon casting two long shadows onto the ground. One of them pulled out a packet of cigarettes, offered one to his friend and lit his own. For a few moments, they stood there smoking, just behind the corner. *Please let them be ghetto residents late for curfew*, Zofia thought. Then one of them said something, and her stomach heaved again when she realised they were speaking German. They must be soldiers out on patrol. The children glanced up at her with fearful, glazed eyes, and Aaron looked as though he were about to speak, so she clamped a hand over his mouth.

'No,' she mouthed silently as she shook her head. She removed her hand and Aaron nodded, pressing his lips together.

Zofia looked around wildly, her breath coming in snatches, and spotted the shell of a bombed out building a little further down the lane. She gestured towards it with her head and took the two younger children by the hand. They crept as quietly as they could towards the ruin, a dark silence draped around them like a thick blanket, disturbed only by the occasional moan and sigh of the wind. Zofia trod softly across some rubble, expecting one of the soldiers to call out at any minute. When they reached the building, which was little more than a pile of bricks and debris, Zofia and the children crouched down behind the remnants of a brick wall and waited.

For a long while, there was no movement, and all Zofia could hear was the rush of her own heartbeat in her ears. Then the terrifying realisation dawned on her: Helena and Aneta would be back any minute and she had no way of warning them. She straightened up, praying she wouldn't be seen, as pure panic surged through her body. There, tiptoeing down the lane towards her, were Helena and Aneta. Zofia took a silent step forward.

'Get back!' she hissed quietly, and thankfully, Helena obeyed instantly, ducking into the building behind and dragging poor Aneta with her.

Zofia crouched down again and instinctively put her arms around the children, knowing at the same time there was no way she could protect them if they were discovered. The footsteps came closer – the soldiers were only ten metres away now and were arguing about something, but they were speaking so quickly Zofia couldn't understand them. And then they came to an abrupt halt. Zofia squeezed her eyes shut in panic, holding her body completely rigid, and felt her heart hammering wildly in her chest. Had they been spotted? She tried to close her mind against the horrifying thoughts that began spiralling inside her head – discovery, arrest, torture … death. The tension was unbearable and she had to suppress the urge to let out a scream. One of the little girl's hands was in hers, clutching so tightly Zofia could feel her nails almost pierce the skin.

And then she heard the sound of footsteps shuffling again, but this time they were receding. By the time they were almost out of earshot, Zofia's mouth was so dry she could hardly move her tongue. Had she waited long enough? Her terror of getting caught had completely distorted her sense of time. She counted to fifty in her head. She didn't want to open her eyes, but she knew she had to: Aaron was staring at her, his expression one of utter terror.

'It's all right,' she said and instinctively took him into a warm embrace. 'They're gone. They're gone.'

A moment later, Helena appeared, pale-faced and trembling. Little Aneta was at her side, clinging onto her hand.

'They turned right,' Helena said. 'Looks like they're heading for the checkpoint on Żytnia Street, so we should be in the clear.'

The small group stepped out of the lane and continued to make their way towards the courthouse. When they got to Leszno Street, they paused, looked left and right, and then continued across the road. During the day, this was a busy, bustling road, but now, just after curfew, it was ghostly quiet. In the absence of street lighting, the shadows seemed alive. Zofia took some deep breaths to steady herself. Everything depended on Jakub now.

The courthouse was a wide, sandstone building that spanned some three hundred yards, and the large inscription above the entrance read: *Justice is the mainstay of power and the durability of the public.* Zofia had read somewhere that it was the largest court building in Europe, and it was a veritable rabbit warren of corridors and offices and larger court rooms. The courthouse was not only a place where cases were heard and ruled on, it was also used for socialising, business meetings, and to buy or sell things. But the reason they had come to the courthouse tonight was that it formed the border between the ghetto and the rest of the city. The entrance to the building was here on Leszno Street, and the back faced out onto Ogrodowa Street on the so-called 'Aryan' side. If they could get inside the building undetected, they would be able to take the children through to the other side.

Helena took some pebbles out of her coat pocket and tossed them across the street.

'What are you doing?' Zofia asked, worried the sound might carry. She was still shaken from their near-discovery by the soldiers.

'It's the signal,' Helena replied softly. 'Don't worry, the soldiers are out of earshot.'

A moment later they heard a low whistle coming from the other side of the road.

'The coast is clear,' Helena said. 'Come on, children. Time to go.'

She took Aaron and Aneta by the hand, while Zofia reached out for the youngest of the Bocheński children. They emerged from the shadows and dashed towards the courthouse as silently as they could.

Jakub took a step forward as they approached. 'I was worried you'd been caught,' he whispered, and Zofia could hear the strain in his voice.

'We nearly were,' Helena replied. 'We came as quickly as we could.'

'I'm glad you made it,' Jakub said, his eyes darting left and right as he spoke, constantly on the lookout. 'But we have to hurry now. The janitor won't wait much longer.'

He instructed them to stay under cover of the trees for a moment and crept around the corner of the courthouse past the main entrance, towards a small black wooden door that was almost hidden from the street. There he gave a series of knocks, stepped back and waited. Almost immediately, the small door opened. He turned back to the two women.

'Come, now!' he whispered urgently and waved them towards him.

Zofia held out her hands for Aneta while Helena ushered the others along. All six children were looking more dazed than ever and Zofia prayed they would be out of danger before one of them started crying or panicking.

Once inside the building, Zofia nodded a greeting to the janitor, a tall elderly man with a shock of grey hair. The man, who knew Irena from before the war, had contacted Żegota through the whispered underground network of the resistance and offered his assistance. With his help, they could access the courthouse with its escape route to the other side of the ghetto walls.

He tipped his head to the women in greeting and then gave the children an encouraging smile, before reaching into his pocket and pulling out a handful of boiled sweets. The children looked up at Zofia, waiting for her approval.

She nodded. 'You can have one each.' And to the janitor she whispered, 'Thank you.'

Grinning with delight, the children took the sweets and popped them into their mouths. It was a small but valuable comfort. They followed the janitor through another set of doors – Jakub leading the children, Zofia and Helena bringing up the rear – and down a long, dark corridor. Although this wing of the building was empty at this hour, they heard sounds everywhere: the hiss and clank of heating pipes, the ghostly squeaking of an unoiled door hinge, an odd pattering noise that might have been pigeons nesting in the eaves, or rats in the wall spaces. It was as though the courthouse was settling in for the night and needed to first rid itself of the life it had held during the day. There was an echoey bang from somewhere up on one of the higher floors and they all startled. Aneta, who was walking in front of Zofia, stopped and began to weep softly.

'It's all right, sweetheart,' Zofia whispered. 'There's nothing to be frightened of.'

Then she picked her up, startled at the child's bones jutting into her as she held her onto her hip. The girl weighed next to nothing.

Up ahead, the janitor came to a halt at yet another door. 'There's a set of stairs through here,' he said quietly. 'Twelve steps in all. There's no lighting, so make sure to count them as you go down. We don't want any accidents.'

They managed to climb safely down the steep stairwell and turned some sharp, twisting corners, and then made their way through a long, dark tunnel that sloped downwards. The air was stale and damp; they must be quite far underground now. Zofia could feel her heartbeat pounding in her chest, and the light thrumming of Aneta's heart as she clung to her. Then, just as Zofia thought her shredded nerves would finally break and snap completely, they climbed a final long set of stairs. There, the janitor unlocked a door and ushered them out onto the dark pavement.

'This is it,' he said, nodding towards the street. 'Stay safe.'

And with that, he stepped back into the building, closed the door behind him, and locked it.

11

Warsaw, Present Day

The taxi pulled up outside a six-storey building, and the driver jumped out to fetch Lizzie's suitcase out of the boot. Lizzie thanked him in broken Polish and paid him, then picked up her suitcase and entered the building using the keycode she'd been provided.

She was feeling strangely wired after the fourteen-hour flight from Seattle; a bone-aching tiredness coupled with a fizzing sense of excitement that she'd finally made it here to Warsaw. It was just after midday, but her internal clock was set to the early hours of the morning. It would take several days to get back into synch, but she was meeting up with Roksana later this afternoon and decided that several cups of strong coffee would have to do to kill off the worst of the jetlag.

The hotel room she'd booked was on the fifth floor; it was a small but clean and modern space that looked out onto a grand avenue – Aleje Jerozolimskie – to the west, and the Vistula river to the east. A white sun hung in the very blue sky above, covering the city with a sheen of summer sunlight, making the glass façade of a tall building opposite glint. Lizzie stood at the window looking out, trying to imagine the city eighty years earlier, thinking past the skyscrapers and grandiose Stalinist architecture and picturing pre-war tenements and cobbled streets. She had only been here for an hour, but this view alone told her that the city had undergone radical change over the past decades. Instinctively, she grabbed her phone to take a picture to send to Alex, but then remembered how cold he had been to her at their last parting. 'If this is what you want, Elizabeth, then I can't stop you,' he'd said as she told him she needed some time away from him. He had helped her load her bags into the car, and even now she wasn't sure if he was being considerate in doing so or whether he wanted her to leave as quickly as possible. It wasn't the first time their separation had caught her out like that, and it left her feeling dull and miserable.

Then her legs became so heavy she found herself swaying with tiredness and had to sit down on the bed. Just for a moment, she told herself, then she would unpack.

She was dragged up from a deep sleep by the shrill sound of her phone, feeling groggy and disoriented. It took her a few seconds to remember where she was, then she sat up heavily and scrambled around in her bag for her phone and answered it.

'Lizzie?' the voice said. 'It's Roksana. I think we were scheduled to meet at three?'

'Um, yes,' Lizzie croaked. Her voice was thick with sleep and she cleared her throat. 'Yes, sorry. What time is it?'

'Twenty past,' Roksana said. 'I'm downstairs.'

'Oh my gosh, I'm so sorry. I fell asleep and forgot to set my alarm.'

Roksana laughed, a light, cheerful sound. 'Don't worry!' she said. 'I was a little worried you'd changed your mind about coming.'

Lizzie rubbed some sleep from her eyes. 'No, I'm here. Give me a couple of minutes and I'll be right down.'

When she stepped out onto the pavement five minutes later, she was met by a young woman in sunglasses with cropped, bright red hair and a wide smile. She was holding a cup in one hand and an ice-cream cone in the other.

'Lizzie?' she said. 'I'm Roksana. Now, first things first. Coffee, or ice-cream?'

She held out the cup and the ice-cream, which had begun to melt down the cone in thick creamy drips.

'It'll have to be coffee,' Lizzie said. 'I'm still half asleep.'

Roksana grinned. 'Correct choice. I've had about five coffees today already and this ice-cream looks delicious.'

They began walking down the street. It was a busy main road, with cars, buses and trams roaring down it at speed. On the cycle path on Lizzie's left, a man on an electric scooter suddenly whizzed past, so fast and so close she almost dropped her coffee. Roksana shouted something after him.

'They're such a bloody nuisance, those things,' she said irritably. Then she smiled and added, 'When I'm not using one myself.' She looked at Lizzie. 'Seriously though, they're quite handy for getting around the city, if you're too tired to walk.'

Lizzie gave her a mock-horrified look. 'If I'm too tired to walk, then I'm definitely too tired to operate any kind of machinery in unfamiliar traffic.'

Roksana laughed and they continued walking in silence.

'So, your family is from Poland?' Roksana asked after a while.

Lizzie nodded and drained her cup, looking around for and then finding a litter bin to throw it in.

'*Czy mówisz po polsku?*' Roksana asked.

Lizzie pulled a face. 'If you just asked me if I speak Polish, then I'm afraid the answer's no. Just a few words, unfortunately. Like I wrote in my email, my great-grandmother was born here, but she emigrated to the States sometime after the war. She spoke Polish with my grandmother, as far as I know, but the language got lost after that. That's one of the reasons I came here, I suppose. It's a part of my history I've never really had access to.'

Roksana smiled. 'Well, I'm happy to help as much as I can. I can't promise that we'll find anything about your great-grandmother herself, but I can certainly show you where she might have grown up.'

They crossed a large, busy junction, and walked up a long road with broad pavements full of street cafés, and quirky little shops full of tourists and locals, mostly young people. Zofia had visited several European cities before – London, Amsterdam, Prague, Berlin – and Warsaw seemed to have the same kind of feel about it. *It's probably because these cities are so old*, she thought, *and built to last.* They'd grown organically over time, allowing for them to be shaped over generations by the people who lived here, rather than by bureaucratic city planners. Roksana, who had presumably grown up here, seemed less interested in her surroundings and set a quick pace.

They walked for a good fifteen minutes until finally, they turned a corner into a quiet, narrow street and came to a stop in front of a five-storey tenement building with crumbling reddish brickwork. The windows were all bricked or boarded up, and a five-foot-high metal fence that separated the building from the pavement was covered in graffiti. The house had obviously been standing empty for many years.

'This is one of the few remaining ghetto buildings,' Roksana explained. 'The Nazis destroyed most of the ghetto after the uprising, and went on to raze the rest of the city to the ground once they knew the Russians had made it to the eastern side of the river.' She looked around. 'They left an ocean of rubble. And a world of sadness and grief.'

The two women stood in silence for a while before Roksana turned to look across the street. 'And that,' she said, indicating the building opposite, 'is a remnant of the ghetto wall.'

They crossed the road and Lizzie looked up. It was a red-brick wall, also crumbling in places, about twenty feet high. Someone had laid flowers and candles at its base.

'They made Jewish labourers build the wall, incarcerating themselves in the ghetto.' Roksana spoke in a heavy voice. 'Just imagine, it's like building your own tomb, with you trapped inside.'

Lizzie reached out to touch the brick and felt her throat close up with tears.

'You know,' Roksana continued, 'Warsaw used to be the Jewish capital of Europe. Now we have only around ten thousand Jews living here. For most of the survivors, Warsaw was no longer their home. The Communists didn't exactly make them feel welcome, either.'

They walked on. All the while, Lizzie looked around, trying to transport herself back in time, imagining how these streets had looked eighty years ago. Had her great-grandmother ever walked beneath this oak tree, waited at that tram stop, bought a magazine or newspaper at that newsagent, whose sign purported it was established in 1924? It was an oddly magical feeling, to be this close to one of her ancestors, as if at any moment, she might walk through some kind of time/space curtain and be right back there, in 1940s Warsaw, alongside Zofia.

The sun-baked pavements were hot beneath her feet and she felt a prickle of sweat beneath her arms, but she was fully absorbed in all the sights and sounds and barely noticed. Roksana showed her the Nożyk Synagogue on Twarda Road, the sole surviving synagogue in Warsaw, and a monument to the *umschlagplatz*, the place Jews were gathered for deportation to concentration camps. Lizzie made a mental note to read up on all these places when she got back to the hotel.

They were walking down a main road with a long, seemingly unpronounceable name, when Roksana came to a sudden halt.

'Oof, it's hot,' she said. 'Do you mind if we sit down in the shade for a bit?'

Lizzie, whose legs had felt like jelly for the past half hour, gladly agreed. They left the main road and entered a small, shaded park. At it its centre, a fountain sprayed jets of water several feet into the air, much to the delight of a group of kindergartners, who ducked in and out of the falling water.

Lizzie and Roksana found a bench beneath a large beech tree and sat down. They each got a water bottle out and drank thirstily. Roksana took out a pouch of tobacco and rolled a cigarette.

'You don't mind?' she asked, squinting into the sun.

Lizzie shook her head and looked back at the children, splashing barefooted in the water. One little girl slipped and fell, and began wailing. Immediately, a young couple rushed over and the father scooped her up in his arms, kissing away her tears. The sight of them provoked the familiar combination of longing and sadness in Lizzie, and she looked away.

'What's that?' she asked, pointing to a large bronze statue of a man standing with his arms wrapped protectively around a group of children. He was looking down at them with great tenderness, reminding Lizzie momentarily of the photograph of her great-grandmother sitting with the children.

'Funny you should ask,' Roksana said. 'I'd actually forgotten about this. It's a monument to a man called Janusz Korczak. He was the head of the Jewish orphanage, in the ghetto. When the Nazis came to round up the children to take them to Treblinka, he was offered the chance to escape, but he refused and insisted he go with the children. *His* children, he called them.'

She sank into silence for a moment. *How incredible it must be*, Lizzie thought, *to have grown up in a place bursting with living history, full of sorrow and struggle, but also beauty and hope.* Here was a statue to a man who had sacrificed himself and been murdered for his principles, not ten metres away from a new generation of Polish children playing in the sunshine. Lizzie hoped they would be taught about the courage of their ancestors. For a brief moment, she felt ashamed of her self-piteous thoughts a moment earlier. In the face of so much tragic history, shouldn't she appreciate how much in her own life was good? True, she had also suffered loss, but didn't she have every kind of support imaginable – her family, her friends and, most importantly, a loving husband? The thought of Alex made her heart suddenly heavy as she realised how much she missed him. She hoped she hadn't damaged her marriage beyond repair.

'You okay?' Roksana said beside her.

Lizzie nodded. She wasn't here to think about all that. She was here to find out about her great-grandmother, to try and discover something more about her roots, to anchor herself. Her and Alex … there was plenty of time for that in the future.

'Irena Sendler,' she said. 'She was the head of the children's section of the resistance organisation, wasn't she?'

'She was. No one quite knows how many children she saved – some sources say it was hundreds, others say thousands – but even if it was only a single life, it would have been worth it to her.'

'I sent you the photos, of my great-grandmother Zofia, one of them with Irena Sendler. Were you able to find out anything more, perhaps where the pictures were taken?'

'No,' Roksana said. Then she smiled. 'But I managed to get in contact with someone very special.'

'Who?'

'Aliza Blumsztajn.'

Lizzie frowned and a look of puzzlement appeared. 'I'm sorry, I don't think I've ever heard that name before.'

'She is the daughter of one of them. One of the children Irena saved.'

Lizzie sat up excitedly. 'And she's here, in Warsaw?'

Roksana nodded. 'She is. And I've arranged for us to meet her tomorrow morning. If you have time, that is? She might be able to shed some light on your family history.'

Lizzie's pulse was racing. 'Oh, yes, I have time.'

12

Warsaw, November 1942

'*Ojcze nasz, któryś jest w niebie, święć się Imię Twoje.*'

Zofia pointed at a young boy with sandy hair and a missing front milk tooth. 'Artur, you go first. Repeat after me: *Ojcze nasz…*'

Artur recited the words of the Lord's Prayer perfectly, making Zofia smile. It never ceased to amaze her how quickly children learned, even in such dire circumstances, and she had become very attached to them. Irena had asked her to come here to the youth centre, to teach the children Christian prayers, so that they would be less likely to be identified as Jewish once they'd been smuggled out successfully. Getting the children out was one thing; housing them safely on the other side was another. The options were fairly limited: orphanages, Catholic convents, or foster parents who were willing to take the risk of hiding a Jewish child. The children had to be coached meticulously, which was easier said than done, and though learning Christian prayers was straightforward, there were other complications to hiding the children. For one, most of the boys were circumcised, making them easily identifiable as Jewish, though in some cases, if the boys were young enough, they could be disguised as girls.

Each child they managed to smuggle out was given a new name, but Irena wrote their real names, their aliases and their whereabouts on pieces of paper and kept them safe, as she never lost hope that one day, the children would be reunited with their parents. It was what Zofia most admired about Irena: her unwavering hope for the future, the conviction that goodness would – *must!* – ultimately triumph over evil. And indeed, the more time Zofia spent around strong, fearless women like Irena and Helena, the greater her own confidence was becoming. Following the rescue of the children through the underground passages of the courthouse, she and Helena had handed them over safely to a contact from the Żegota network to be taken to convents or foster families. Zofia had felt a rush of invincibility, and although Helena had warned her to be wary of feeling over-confident, as this inevitably led to mistakes, she couldn't help thinking that perhaps, in the not-too-distant future, she might be leading her own missions. The thought made her feel excited and apprehensive in equal measure.

She continued the Lord's Prayer with the other children, before showing them the sign of the cross. Some of the younger children found this a little tricky, not sure whether to touch the top of their head, or their belly button, or whether the cross went left to right or right to left. Soon, there were arms flailing all over the place, causing even the most earnest children to giggle. Zofia let them. These were rare moments, carefree moments in which the hunger and fear and deprivation could be forgotten. If everything went well, most of these children would be saying goodbye to their parents soon, with no guarantee whether they would ever see them again. The youth centre was much more than a place where the youngsters came to gather. Before the outbreak of the war, children and young people had gathered here for homework tuition, music lessons and Talmud classes, but over the past two years, it had evolved into a meeting place for the community, with a makeshift library, small classes for the young children, and a few rooms used as basic accommodation for people whose homes were so overrun by rats they had become uninhabitable. The centre was situated within the ghetto, only a few streets from one of the checkpoints, and also had a soup kitchen, which was run from a window facing onto the street. Here, watery soup was distributed to long lines of desperate people who waited patiently in all weather. They had no choice – it was either this, or starve. The ghetto inhabitants were allowed daily rations of only a few hundred calories, which inevitably led to a slow, painful death of starvation.

Zofia knew that there were small gaps in the ghetto walls, through which children slipped in and out and smuggled in food. Children as young as seven or eight were tasked with this as the gaps were too narrow for adults, even emaciated ones, to get through. It was highly risky, as Nazi soldiers thought nothing of shooting even the youngest children on sight.

The centre also provided basic medical assistance – though medicines were as rare as gold – and delousing programmes. Many of the children had head lice; even now, Zofia could see two of the younger children scratching furiously at their hair. In a predictable sub-conscious reaction, her own scalp began to tingle, but she was distracted by a scuffle near the entrance. She jumped to her feet, ready to run and hide in a neighbouring room that had a hidden trapdoor, but it was only two elderly men arguing over a woollen scarf one claimed the other had stolen. It wasn't, as Zofia had feared, a group of German soldiers. Now and again, the youth centre was visited by the soldiers, who tipped over tables and tore books off shelves in an attempt to harass and bully the people there, but they were so afraid of lice and disease their visits were thankfully a rare occasion.

Zofia yawned and sat back down. She was exhausted, physically and emotionally, and tears were never far from the surface. She couldn't remember the last time she hadn't cried herself to sleep. Weeks ago, probably. She was fairly sure Zuzanna had heard her, but hadn't said anything, for which Zofia was grateful.

There was a tap on her shoulder and she turned to see Jakub standing behind her, a steaming cup in his hands. She shouldn't be surprised to see him here, as his work for the resistance took him all over the ghetto, but it was unexpected nonetheless. *An unexpected pleasure*, she caught herself thinking.

'I thought you might like a cup of coffee,' he said with a smile. 'Chicory is all they had, but it's better than nothing, I suppose?'

Zofia got up and smoothed down her skirt.

'Thank you,' she said, her finger grazing his as she took the cup. The touch made her heart give a light skip. She drank a sip and grimaced, hoping he wouldn't notice her blushing. 'Bitter.'

Jakub nodded in the direction of the children, who had retreated to a corner of the room to play marbles. 'How are they doing?' he asked.

'Their prayers are coming on nicely. But they know their time here is running out and…' She trailed off.

Jakub frowned. 'That's a good thing, surely?'

'Of course,' Zofia said. 'But what of their parents? Stuck here, in the ghetto. Or worse, taken to a labour camp. I just wish we could help them, too.'

Jakub shook his head. 'Too risky. It's difficult enough finding new homes for the children. We can pass them off as orphans, or refugees, but if entire families started turning up on the Aryan side, it would—'

Zofia interrupted him. 'I wish you wouldn't call it that.'

'What?'

'The "Aryan" side,' she said. 'This whole talk of races, it makes it sound like some people are superior to others. I mean, look around.' She gestured towards the others in the room, the children playing in the corner, a woman sitting at a table reading a book, two men playing chess. 'Why does there have to be sides?' she said, her voice rising in anger. 'We're all just human beings, aren't we?'

'Yes,' Jakub agreed quietly. 'You're right.' He was still for a moment and took a sip of his own coffee. Then he pulled a face. 'This tastes awful,' he said, changing the subject and leaning in closer. 'But I have something to make it better.' He smiled and pulled two sugar cubes from his pocket.

'Where did you get those from?' Zofia asked, but Jakub just tapped the side of his nose and dropped a cube in each of their cups.

'*Na zdrowie*,' he said, tapping his cup against hers.

They sipped their coffees in silence – it tasted so much better with sugar, Zofia had to admit – and then Jakub nodded towards the children.

'How many more prayer lessons do you have planned?'

118

'A few more,' Zofia answered. 'The children have to be as well prepared as we can get them.'

They were planning their most ambitious smuggling operation to date, this time through the sewage system that ran below the ghetto. It would be dark and cramped and filthy, and Zofia was hoping that none of the children would be overcome by claustrophobia. Since the escape through the courthouse, she and Helena had managed to extract an eight-year-old girl in an ambulance, claiming the girl had died of typhoid and they needed to incinerate the corpse as soon as possible. The brave child, her skin whitened with face powder, had lain completely still beneath a sheet while the guard took a quick look inside the ambulance before letting them pass. Like most of the soldiers, he had presumably been terrified of infectious disease.

And last week, a Żegota member had heard of a newly appeared gap in the ghetto wall well away from any of the checkpoints, and Zofia and Helena had swooped in and carried out a three-year-old boy who was so malnourished he could no longer walk. The gap had been discovered and bricked up hours later. For Zofia, these had been heart-stopping operations, and every success was exhilarating, doing wonders for her ever-growing confidence. But this upcoming mission would be a far bigger challenge, not just because of the precariousness of the sewers, but because they were going to try to get more children out than ever before.

'How many children are you taking out in total?' Jakub asked, as though he'd read her mind.

'We've selected twenty children for the next move. Many of them from the ghetto orphanage on Sienna Road.'

It was a huge number for a single operation, and it made Zofia slightly nauseous to think about it, but there were urgent and terrifying rumours that the next wave of deportations to Treblinka was due to take place any day now. Reports were never completely reliable, but they had heard that the Nazis would be targeting the orphanage, and Irena had decided – in that gentle but uncompromising way of hers – that they were going to try and rescue as many orphans as they could. The sheer number increased the risk, of course, but time wasn't on their side. Yet what to do with the children when – if – they got them safely to the other side? There were only so many foster families willing to risk taking in a Jewish child and trying to pass them off as Christian. The Catholic orphanages in Warsaw and its surroundings were full to the brim, housing refugee children who had become separated from their parents, or whose parents had died along the way. But like Irena said, what other choice did they have?

'Have you decided on a date yet?' Jakub continued.

Zofia shook her head. 'It'll be determined at the very last minute. You know how it is – the information isn't shared until just beforehand to keep us all safe.'

Jakub opened his mouth to speak, but at that moment, one of the youth centre managers came up to Zofia. He apologised for interrupting and held up a small camera.

'Would you mind?' he asked. 'It would be nice to have a memento. There are so few memories worth capturing in this place.' His smile disappeared from his face for a moment. 'But perhaps one of you with the children?'

Zofia glanced towards Jakub, who smiled encouragingly.

She shrugged. 'All right then. Why not?'

'Just one thing.' The man grimaced apologetically. 'We'd have to go outside. I have no flash tube and it's too dark in here.'

Zofia called over to the children and asked if they'd like their picture taken, and they went outside, where a round, white sun had broken through the clouds, taking the sting out of the cold air. The man with the camera asked Zofia to take a seat on a wooden bench and instructed the children to sit beside her. Two of the younger children seemed reluctant, hanging back at the door to the youth centre, but Jakub bounded over to them making silly noises, and scooped one up under each arm. The children squealed with delight as he spun them around, finally plonking them down next to Zofia. Then he took a position behind the photographer, making funny faces to get the children to smile into the camera. Zofia couldn't help but smile with them. *He evidently has a way with children*, she caught herself thinking.

The man took a couple of snaps and promised Zofia to get her a copy of the pictures when he could. They all went back inside then, where Zofia handed the children slips of paper with some more Christian prayers written on them.

'Let's see how many of these you can learn off by heart,' she said, trying to sound chirpy. She knew that some of the more devout parents struggled with their children being introduced to this religion. But Zofia had told them to think of the prayers as nursery rhymes, and besides, most of the parents realised they had no other option.

She checked her watch. It was quarter to two.

'I have to be off,' she said, turning back to Jakub. 'My boss, Mr Wójcik, has added a dozen new cases to my workload. I'm starting to think he suspects something and wants to keep me busy at the office.'

121

As she went to leave, Jakub took her hand and said, 'You're very brave, Zofia.'

She felt herself blush. 'No, I'm not,' she said. 'I mean, no more than others.'

'You're so dedicated,' he continued. 'Coming here, day after day. I only manage two or three times a week, but you're here every time I come. You're inspiring, do you know that?'

He looked straight at her and his slate-grey eyes seemed to see right inside her, momentarily making her feel like the only person in the room. It was the first time he had spoken to her in this way and she became uncomfortably aware of the rapid beating of her heart. But then she thought of Lina, dropped her gaze and looked down at her hand, still resting in his. His skin was warm and dry.

'Well … I do what I can,' she said, hoping he wouldn't notice how flustered she was feeling. 'We all do as much as we—'

There was a sudden commotion in the corner of the room as the children began fighting over the marbles. Zofia slid her hand out of Jakub's, feeling the warmth linger on her skin.

'I really have to go now,' she said and turned away without another glance. Flustered, she crossed the large room and headed quickly for the door, trying to shake off the self-conscious feeling that Jakub might be watching her leave.

But when she got to the door, she spotted a woman sitting on a chair beside the window. The woman had a worn blue shawl wrapped around her shoulders, and she was crying softly. In her hands she held a greying handkerchief, which she now lifted to wipe her eyes. Zofia took a step closer and crouched down.

'Are you all right?' she asked. 'Is there anything I can do to help?'

The woman raised her head and Zofia could tell she was younger than she'd first appeared. Her face was gaunt and pale, her eyes red-rimmed with crying, but her skin was smooth and youthful. She was probably not much older than Zofia herself. She shook her head and swallowed, then her chin trembled and she began to cry again. Zofia took a seat beside her. She really needed to get back to the office, but the woman's obvious distress tugged at her. She felt suddenly foolish, almost ashamed, for her thoughts about Jakub.

'I'm Zofia,' she said. 'What's your name?'

'Julia,' the woman whispered. 'Julia Zielińska.'

'Are you hungry, Julia?' Zofia asked. 'The kitchen is closed for another hour, but I can go and see if they have some bread, if you like.'

Julia shook her head and began twisting her handkerchief between her fingers. Zofia could make out an embroidered monogram – *P. Z.* – on the corner of the fabric. Julia saw her looking.

'It's my husband's,' she said quietly, evidently holding back tears. 'Pavel. This is all I have left of him.' She paused and sniffed. 'He had to report to the *umschlagplatz* two weeks ago. I haven't heard from him since.'

'Oh,' Zofia said, 'I'm so sorry.'

Julia wiped her eyes. 'My daughter, Ola, keeps asking when her papa will come home.' She glanced across the room towards a young girl with dark curly hair, who had taken a picture book off a shelf and was leafing through it. 'I don't know what to tell her. She's only five years old.' With this, she began weeping openly.

Zofia didn't hesitate. She put her arm around Julia's shoulders and hugged her, wishing she could take the woman's grief away. When Julia eventually fell silent, Zofia took a slip of paper and a pencil out of her bag.

'Here,' she said, 'write down your address. Perhaps I can come and visit you.'

It was an impulsive thing to do, and went far beyond her remit. Thus far, she had been doing what she was instructed, sticking to what she knew. Helena would presumably warn her against forming emotional attachments in this place. But there was something about this woman, and her daughter, that made Zofia want to show some genuine human kindness that went beyond vaccines, extra rations, and pre-planned logistical operations. Perhaps she also needed to prove to herself that her work in the ghetto hadn't hardened her heart.

Julia took the paper and pencil and jotted down her address. 'Thank you,' she said, her voice still thick with tears. 'Thank you for your kindness.'

'It's nothing,' Zofia mumbled as she stood up and buttoned her jacket. Just as with Jakub's compliments, she felt ambivalent at hearing the woman's expression of gratitude. In light of all the suffering she had witnessed over the past few weeks, her own actions seemed like a drop in a very large ocean. At least she was going home to a warm meal and a soft bed. Julia, by contrast, was probably living in a cold, cramped flat somewhere inside this hellhole. She said her goodbyes and tried to shake off her negative thoughts.

Outside the youth centre, a queue had begun to form at the window; dozens of wretchedly hungry people hoping to fill their bellies with a crust of stale bread and a soup made from potato peelings. Zofia turned right and headed towards the checkpoint, barely noticing that the sun had retreated and had been replaced by an icy drizzle.

13

Warsaw, Present Day

'Sorry about the weather,' Roksana said as she held the café door open for Lizzie. 'We usually have nice summers here, but the rain gods obviously have other plans today.'

Lizzie laughed. 'Don't worry. I grew up in Seattle, so I'm familiar with rain gods,' she said as she stepped inside the café and looked around. It was a small space, with seating nooks fitted along the far wall, the benches upholstered in soft, though worn-looking, fabrics. Sounds were muted by the thick carpeting and velvet curtains that hung at the windows, and the whole place smelt wonderfully of freshly ground coffee and cinnamon. It felt like a cosy little cave.

After their walk through the city yesterday, she had returned to the hotel with her mind whirring and buzzing, overwhelmed by all the impressions. Twice she had picked up her phone to call Alex, needing, almost instinctively, to share everything with him. But both times she had changed her mind. Her head was too full to deal with the complications of her relationship. Instead, she had gone to bed early and slept unexpectedly deeply.

Behind her, Roksana shook out her umbrella and stuck it in a tall brass stand near the door, then gestured towards one of the seating nooks. 'Shall we sit there?' she asked. 'Then I can keep my eye on the door.'

'Perfect,' Lizzie answered.

When they'd taken their seats, the waitress, a small round woman with fluffy grey hair, came and took their orders. Roksana persuaded Lizzie to order a slice of *szarlotka*, telling her it was the café's speciality, home-baked in the back of the small shop.

Lizzie hadn't thought she had much of an appetite, but when the waitress placed the slice of apple cake on the table in front of her, her stomach let out a loud growl.

'I'm so sorry,' she said. 'I guess I'm hungrier than I thought.'

Roksana waved her apology away with a smile and started to say, 'You don't—', but then stopped as the café door opened with a pleasant chime. 'There she is!' she exclaimed and jumped to her feet to welcome the woman who had just entered.

The woman was in her late fifties, Lizzie guessed, and wore a green raincoat, which she slipped off and shook out. She wore scuffed jeans and a rose-coloured blouse, with dangling silver earrings that swung from side to side as she moved her head. Roksana was already greeting her and saying something in rapid-fire Polish that Lizzie had no hope of following. The woman laughed and said, '*Tak, tak bardzo,*' and then came over to Lizzie.

'*Dobry dzień,*' she said, holding her hand out to shake.

Lizzie took the woman's hand and repeated the greeting, feeling somewhat foolish she'd assumed Roksana's contact would speak English.

Roksana took her seat and gestured for the woman to sit down beside her. 'This is Lizzie Marshall,' she said. 'And Lizzie, please meet Aliza Blumsztajn.'

While Lizzie scrabbled around furiously in her brain for the Polish for 'Nice to meet you', Aliza leaned across the table and said, 'It is such a pleasure to meet you. Roksana tells me you are from Seattle? A beautiful city. I have visited many times. Now tell me, how may I be of assistance?'

Lizzie almost laughed out loud in surprise. But she managed to rearrange her face and said, 'It's lovely to meet you, too. And may I say, your English is fantastic! Where did you learn it?'

'Aliza is a professor of archaeology,' Roksana said.

'Yes, I was a lecturer at the University of Manchester for many years,' Aliza added, smiling. She had dark, expressive eyes that made her seem younger than she was. 'And you have Polish ancestry, I hear?'

Lizzie nodded. 'My great-grandmother was from Warsaw. But sadly, her native language got lost through the generations,' she said. 'My grandmother speaks a few sentences, but as for me…' She trailed off with a shrug.

'And now you are researching your family history?' Aliza asked.

'Yes, but I'm afraid I know very little.' She went on to tell Aliza how she'd found the three photographs at her parents' house. 'It all started from there.'

The waitress came over and Aliza ordered a *pączek*, a type of filled doughnut, while Roksana ordered more coffees for herself and Lizzie.

'My mother was two years old when they smuggled her out of the ghetto. You know about the Żegota?' Aliza asked.

'A little. I did some research before I came, but there's only so much you can find out on the internet.'

'I understand,' Aliza said. 'But you will have heard of the leader of the children's section, Irena Sendler?'

Lizzie nodded. 'She's in one of the photographs with my great-grandmother. She smuggled Jewish children out of the ghetto.'

'My mother was one of those children,' Aliza said. 'They took her across the checkpoint in a hearse. Hidden inside a coffin. She was only two, did I mention that? She was given a sedative to keep her quiet, and also, I assume, to stop her from panicking.'

She fell silent for a long moment.

'My mother's very old now,' she said finally, 'and getting frustratingly forgetful. She called me last week complaining that the remote control was gone and she was missing her daily soap opera. I went round to find she'd put it in the fridge.' She smiled gently. 'But her memories of that time are as keen and fresh as ever. You'd think that a two-year-old can't form memories, but to this day, she cannot bear to be in a room with the doors closed. And she has always slept with a night-light. The darkness frightens her beyond belief.'

The waitress arrived with the order and Aliza took a sip of coffee before continuing.

'You know, some of them – the children who survived thanks to Irena and her helpers – meet up regularly. Sadly, most of them were never reunited with their families.'

Her dark eyes clouded over with a deep sadness and she raised her hand and began twirling one of her earrings, as though trapped in thought. After a long silence, she continued.

'But I tell myself that for every evil act committed against humanity, there is at least one act motivated by genuine goodness. It ensures a kind of cosmic equilibrium, I suppose.' She let out a bright laugh. 'Cosmic equilibrium? Goodness, I sound like a bit of a wacko, don't I?'

Lizzie shook her head. 'No, not at all.'

'To believe otherwise,' Roksana added, 'would be terrifying.'

A brief silence descended on the three women.

'Coffins weren't the only methods used for smuggling, of course,' Aliza said after a while. 'They were a very creative bunch. They hid children in potato sacks, in ambulances, walked them through the sewers.' She wrinkled her nose. 'Roksana, did you show her the courthouse?'

'No, not yet. Warsaw is a big city. There's only so much you can cover in one day.'

'The courthouse had underground passages,' Aliza said, turning back to Lizzie. 'If you knew where they were, it was fairly simple to use them to get out of the ghetto. I know that Irena – and perhaps your great-grandmother – used the courthouse in their smuggling operations.'

'But why didn't more people escape that way?' Lizzie asked, remembering the terrible images she'd seen online – men, women, and children starving to death, sitting on pavements begging.

Aliza nodded. 'Early on, when the ghetto was first established, it was a functioning community, with Jewish hospitals and schools and synagogues. For many, it seemed the best and safest place for Jewish people and their families. So many stayed, not believing – not *wanting* to believe – that things might get a lot worse. And when they did—' She paused for a moment and stirred her coffee pensively.

'Escaping the ghetto was one thing,' Roksana continued in Aliza's stead. 'But where were they to go once they'd got out? Many Warsaw Jews didn't speak Polish, only Yiddish. And even if they did, the streets on the so-called "Aryan" side were teeming with German patrols. If you didn't have the correct papers, you would be shot on sight.'

'But I read that the resistance movement forged documents for Polish Jews,' Lizzie said.

Aliza nodded. 'They did. But the Nazi soldiers wouldn't think twice of forcing a man to drop his trousers if they had any suspicions. And if he was circumcised … well, they wouldn't bother asking further questions. But children were another matter. They could be hidden in foster homes or orphanages with new names and identities, and they would grow up to become perfectly assimilated in terms of language and religion.'

'Which reminds me,' Roksana cut in. 'I must show you the church that was used as a safehouse. The Church of St. Joseph of the Visitationists. Perhaps they have records of your great-grandmother.'

A flicker of excitement grew inside Lizzie. Back in Seattle, all of her questions had led to dead-ends. Now she was here, she was sure to find answers.

'Does the name "Zielińska" mean anything to you?' she asked.

Aliza pulled her eyebrows together, thinking. She shook her head. 'It's not uncommon in these parts,' she said. 'But I don't know anyone by that name. Why?'

'It's someone my great-grandmother might have known. The name was written on the back of one of the old photographs. I hoped it might be a way of finding out more.'

The door opened and a group of young Spanish tourists entered, chatting excitedly. Aliza took out her phone.

'I'm afraid I haven't much more time,' she said, 'but I'll give you my number. Please call me if you have any more questions. It's great to meet someone who cares about their history.' She smiled, her eyes flashing. 'But then again, I'm an archaeologist, so I tend to find the past infinitely more interesting than the present.'

14

Warsaw, December 1942

'You are heading out again?' Zofia's father asked one Saturday afternoon as she slipped on her shoes at the front door. 'You've only been back from work less than an hour. I thought we'd spend some time together as a family. Perhaps go to the forest for a little foraging.'

'Lina's going to the Saxon Garden with some others from the social club,' Zofia replied, turning away and pretending to fasten her jacket so he wouldn't see her face. 'For a walk. She asked if I'd like to join them.'

It wasn't a lie, strictly speaking. Lina *had* asked if she wanted to come along to the Saxon Garden, to try, as Lina put it, 'to forget everything for a couple of hours'. But Zofia had turned her down. Instead, she was planning to visit Julia and her daughter Ola in the ghetto. She wasn't sure why, but the woman's plight had touched her deeply that day in the youth club. There was something in her eyes that had captured Zofia's heart. Perhaps it was because Julia reminded her of herself, so she had wanted to make good on the promise of visiting. Tearing children from their parents' arms – even if it was to save their lives – was a dreadful and distressing thing to have to do, and despite anything Helena might think, Zofia was desperate to make a more lasting human connection with someone inside the ghetto.

'Isn't it a bit cold for that?' her mother asked.

'Well, we'll all be wrapped up warm, and someone will probably bring some hot *grzaniec* to drink.'

'Not laced with vodka, I hope,' her father said.

'Of course not, Papa.'

'Can I come?' Zuzanna said excitedly. 'I haven't been to the Saxon Garden for ages.'

'Um, it's only a bunch of grown-ups,' Zofia said. 'You'll get bored.'

'No I won't!' Zuzanna cried. 'Mama, can I not go with Zofia? Please?'

'Oh, let her go out and enjoy herself with her friends,' their mother replied. 'We'll go for a nice walk, *Żabka*, just the three of us. The forest air will do you good.'

'But Zofia hardly spends any time at home, these days,' her father complained. 'All those long hours she has to work at the office.'

Zofia picked up her bag. 'I've told you, Papa, there are more and more people relying on soup kitchens and only so many helping hands to go around.'

Her father raised his hands above his head and sighed. 'I know, I know. These are difficult times. But I wish Wójcik would see to it that you are paid for all the overtime.'

Zofia felt the heat rise to her face and before she could stop it, her eyes had filled with tears. She hated lying to her parents, but if she told them even a fraction of the truth – that she had been risking not only her life, but their lives, and Zuzanna's – her father was likely to prevent her from ever leaving the house again.

'I … I won't be long,' she said, almost choking on the words. She quickly fished a handkerchief from her pocket and pretended to blow her nose, then wiped the tears from her eyes.

Her mother, always sensitive to her daughters' emotions, however carefully hidden, cupped Zofia's face and then gave her a kiss on the cheek. 'You go and have some fun, *kochanie*. We should all make the most of the little pleasures in life.'

Unable to look her mother in the eye, Zofia squeezed her eyes shut and turned away.

Julia lived on Ostrowska Street, only a ten-minute cycle from the checkpoint, but Zofia soon had to get off her bike and push. As always, the streets were teeming with people, even in this weather. Hardly surprising, given that hundreds of thousands of inhabitants were forced to share an area of three square kilometres. Beyond the ghetto walls, people were indulging in Advent cheer in the run-up to Christmas, but it was like a separate universe in here: the desperate conditions, the sense of claustrophobia, and the unbelievable human misery. And if the streets seemed crowded, this was nothing compared to the conditions inside the buildings. Every open doorway let out a smell of unwashed human bodies, over-boiled food, and decay. No wonder people preferred the outdoors, even with the sharp winds and freezing temperatures. *At least the sun is out*, Zofia thought. It was the small mercies one had to be grateful for.

She walked up the stairs to the third floor, pulling out a handkerchief and pressing it over her mouth to stifle the stench of mildew and something unpleasantly sharp and sweetish. On the door to the left she found Julia's family name – Zieliński – attached to a makeshift cardboard nameplate. There were three other names written there, indicating that Julia shared the flat with at least three other families. From behind the door, she could hear a couple arguing in ugly, bitter voices. A baby cried out and the argument stopped abruptly. But a moment later, it flared up again. Zofia let out a sad sigh. The cramped living conditions were a strain on even the happiest of marriages. At home, Zofia shared a bedroom with Zuzanna, but even so, there was always a space to retreat to when she wanted or needed to be alone. For most of the ghetto residents, there was absolutely no privacy to be had; every corner of every space was used as a place for sleeping or cooking or just living.

She raised a hand and knocked on the door, and immediately the arguing voices fell silent. There was a shuffle of footsteps and then a brusque voice asked, 'Yes? What do you want?'

The man who opened the door looked as though he hadn't slept in weeks. His cheeks were sunken and his eyes appeared unnaturally large in his face. His clothes hung off his thin frame and his cheeks bore the scratches of a blunt razor. Zofia could barely suppress a grimace at the stench wafting from him.

'Good day. I, um … my name is Zofia. I'm here to see Julia Zielińska.'

The man looked her up and down and frowned. 'You're not from the ghetto,' he said. It was a statement, not a question.

They could tell, always. In the beginning, when the Jews had first been imprisoned behind the ghetto walls, many of them had been wealthy, well-nourished, well-dressed. But now, a few years later, clothes had turned to dirty rags and forced starvation had turned previously healthy bodies into walking skeletons. By contrast, Zofia's relative comfort was unmistakable. Embarrassed, she shook her head.

Instantly, the man's gruff demeanour changed into something akin to desperation.

'Do you have any bread? Or … or perhaps potatoes?' His voice became almost tearful. 'Anything to eat? My wife, she hasn't eaten in two days. She gives her rations to her sister Agata, so she can produce milk for the baby. My wife is so thin, I tell her she must eat her rations, but she…' He trailed off, seemingly deflated.

Zofia's heart sank at his words. She had a small bar of chocolate hidden in an inside pocket of her jacket, but she'd brought that for Julia to share with her daughter. Julia was just as underweight as this man, and Zofia could imagine Ola was undernourished, too.

'I'm sorry,' she whispered, unable to meet the man's eye.

He shook his head, dejectedly, and took a step back. 'Come in,' he said.

Zofia followed him inside the flat. The small hallway was windowless and dark; the air was thick and stale, and smelled slightly sour.

The man pointed to a door to the left of the shabby hallway. 'Julia is in there.'

'Thank you,' Zofia whispered, and knocked on the door and entered. Julia was sitting on a chair, listlessly staring out of the window, while her daughter Ola was sitting on the floor in the corner, leafing through a tattered picture book. Julia jumped up as Zofia entered.

'You came!' she said.

'I'm sorry I couldn't come sooner. I've been so busy.' Zofia's gaze swept the cramped, dark room. There was a narrow bedframe at the far wall covered in a greying knitted blanket, a sideboard with drawers so warped they didn't shut properly, and some poorly washed laundry hanging on a piece of string that stretched from corner to corner. A small broken window pane had been half-covered with some cardboard, blocking out most of the light.

'Please, sit down,' Julia said, clearing some books from a chair. 'We don't have much space, I'm afraid.' She blushed slightly.

'It's fine,' Zofia said, 'I'm not—'

She was interrupted by Ola, who had come over to stand beside her mother. The child had messy brown hair and eyes as dark as chocolate. She put her hands on her hips and gave Zofia an earnest look. 'Who are you?' she asked.

'I'm a friend of your mama's,' Zofia responded.

'Very nice to meet you,' Ola said. 'But I'm afraid I'm busy reading.' Then she turned and went back to her book in the corner.

Zofia let out a soft laugh, instantly charmed by the girl's confidence.

'She can't even read yet,' Julia said quietly, 'but I like to let her pretend.'

'Has she started school yet?'

Julia shook her head. 'She was meant to start in September, but there are too many children and too few teachers. The Jewish Council does what it can, but…' She trailed off.

Zofia took the chocolate bar from the inside pocket she'd sewn into her coat and handed it to Julia. 'It's only a small bar,' she said, 'but I thought you and Ola might like something sweet for a change.'

Julia reached out tentatively, as though afraid the chocolate might disappear into thin air at any moment. 'Thank you,' she said quietly. 'That's very kind.'

Then she unwrapped the bar, broke off a square to give to Ola and wrapped the chocolate again.

'I'll save some to give to Agata,' she said. 'She lives in one of the other rooms and she had a baby six weeks ago. She can't make enough milk and has to feed her son sugar water to make up for it.'

It wasn't the first time Zofia had been profoundly moved by the selflessness and sense of community among the ghetto residents. 'And how are you?' she asked.

Julia kneaded her chapped hands in her lap. 'I'm all right. I haven't been sleeping well, to be honest, worrying about Pavel. But I'm sure he will write soon. He won't have much time, he'll be busy working. They don't call it a labour camp for nothing.' She attempted a smile but Zofia could see that tears pricked her eyes.

They fell silent for a moment, avoiding each other's eyes, both knowing this wasn't true. It was only the most naïve of people who believed the rumours that Jews were being deported to Treblinka to work.

Zofia changed the subject. 'Does Ola have any toys?' she asked, thinking of the box containing her and Zuzanna's old toys gathering dust in a corner of the flat. 'I could bring some the next time I come.'

Julia smiled. 'That would be lovely. We had to leave everything behind when we moved here from Konstancin-Jeziorna. Do you know it?'

Zofia nodded. Konstancin-Jeziorna was a small wealthy town just outside Warsaw that had once had a large Jewish population, with tree-lined streets and beautiful houses with manicured gardens. Two years ago, the Jews had all been rounded up and transported to the ghetto, leaving the Nazis to take over the grand villas.

'Pavel, my husband, was an engineer,' Julia continued. 'We bought a lovely house there when we got married. Nothing grand, but it was our very own.'

She looked around the small, dark room and bit down on her lip.

'We had such lovely things,' she continued quietly, her voice cracking. Her pained expression softened for the briefest moment, as though the reminiscing were bitter-sweet. 'Persian rugs, mahogany furniture, a piano. There was a little stream at the bottom of the garden where I would take the little ones to splash about in.'

'The little ones?'

Julia frowned and brushed a strand of hair out of her face. 'Ola, I mean. And … and a little puppy we'd bought. I don't know what became of him. It was such a lovely life, and now … this.' A shadow of anguish crossed her face. 'Please don't misunderstand me, Zofia. I don't mean to say we have it any worse than people who came here with nothing, it's just that I realise how little I appreciated everything I *did* have.' She dropped her hands into her lap. 'I don't even think Ola can remember any of it. Her memories will always be of this terrible place.'

On hearing her name, Ola came over and pulled at her mother's sleeve. 'Can I have some more?' she asked, and when Julia shook her head, she looked at Zofia. 'Do you have any more chocolate?'

'I'm afraid not,' Zofia said. 'But I'll bring some more the next time I come.'

Ola frowned, then put her hands on her hips. 'When are you coming again? Tomorrow? Perhaps you should go now. If you go now then you can come back sooner, can't you?'

Both Zofia and Julia laughed.

'Don't be rude, Ola,' Julia said gently. 'Zofia is our guest. You shouldn't ask guests to leave or they might not want to return.'

Ola's eyes widened in alarm. 'But you do want to return, don't you?'

'Of course. Now,' Zofia said, standing up, 'do you know a game called *ciupy*?'

They played for a good twenty minutes, until Ola's attention started to wander and she asked Zofia to read to her. Zofia had just lifted the girl onto her lap when Julia started coughing, barely managing to draw a wheezing breath between coughs. It was a deep, rasping sound, reminding Zofia of her sister Zuzanna's cough.

Zofia looked at her, alarmed. 'We should go outside,' she said, once Julia had her breath back. 'It's cold, but the sun is shining, and the clean air might do you some good.'

Ola didn't need much coaxing, so a few minutes later, they stepped out onto the crowded pavement. It seemed as though everyone would rather be outdoors on a day like today.

'There's a small square down here,' Julia said, still somewhat breathless from her coughing fit, and pointed down the street. 'It used to be a little public park, but all the trees have long since been chopped down.' She wrapped her arms around herself. 'The winters are so cold…'

Ola ran ahead and Julia and Zofia had to hurry to catch up with her. From Julia's concerned expression, Zofia could tell she was worried she might lose sight of her daughter in the crowd. When they reached the square, Ola went to play on the grassy area, doing cartwheels. Zofia nudged Julia's arm.

'Look, there's some ground ivy,' she said, pointing at a creeping plant with little purple flowers. 'We can use it to make tea. It's good for coughs and has lots of vitamin C. My mother is an expert forager,' she added by way of explanation.

While Ola whooped and danced on the grass, singing a made-up song and charming everyone around them, the two women picked ground ivy, dandelion roots and even stinging nettles. Nettles, Zofia knew from her mother, could be dried well and used during the winter, when their immune-system boosting qualities were most needed. Zofia put the nettles in a paper bag and paused for a moment. Spring would invariably follow winter, but the warm weather was still months away and she didn't like to think how many people would not survive that long.

She shook the thoughts away and glanced across the small square to see a man taking photographs. He was tall, with long arms and legs that made him look somewhat lanky. He wasn't wearing an armband, so he wasn't a ghetto resident, but he wasn't in uniform, either. When he noticed her looking, he smiled and made a beeline for her and Julia.

'Is that your daughter?' he asked Julia, nodding towards Ola, who was whirling around with her arms stretched out, face turned towards the sky.

'Yes,' she replied.

'May I take a picture of her?'

Julia gave him an uncertain look. 'What for?'

'She is naturally photogenic, I think,' he said with a smile. He wasn't a handsome man, and his smile was a little crooked, but it was warm and genuine. 'Every photographer is looking for the sort of vibrancy your daughter has.'

Julia seemed flattered.

'Yes, why not?' she said and called Ola over, but Zofia placed a hand on her friend's arm.

'I don't know if that's wise,' she whispered in her ear. 'We don't know who he is.'

The man must have caught her words, because he turned back. 'I don't mean any harm,' he said to Julia. 'And if you'd rather I didn't…'

By now, Ola had joined them. Her curly hair was a little wild and her cheeks were flushed.

'Who are you?' she asked the man, her breaths coming out in puffs of white.

'My name is Filip,' he said.

'And what's that thing?' Ola continued, pointing at his camera.

The man crouched down and showed her the camera. 'This is a very special camera. A Leica III. It takes the most wonderful pictures. Would you like to be my model?'

'Your what?'

'Would you like me to take a picture of you?'

Ola stuck her bottom lip out and considered the question. Then she shrugged with a cheeky grin. 'Err … okay!'

The man laughed and asked Ola to go and sit on a low wall that was covered in small white blooms of winter honeysuckle. Then he slipped a roll of film into his camera, aimed it at Ola and pressed the shutter a few times.

'Now one with your mother, if you don't mind?' He gestured towards Julia, who gave Zofia a look as if to say, *See, he's harmless*, and went to sat beside Ola.

The man took a few pictures, telling jokes to get Ola to laugh. Zofia went to stand beside him and watched as Ola posed for the camera, then climbed onto her mother's lap. Julia gave her a soft kiss on the cheek and then began smoothing down her daughter's unruly hair before carefully braiding it. It was an exquisite image of the intimacy of a loving mother and her daughter, Zofia thought. The photographer must have seen it too, and he snapped another several pictures until a small *click* indicated the film was empty.

While he wound the film, she said, 'Why are you taking pictures? Here, in the ghetto?'

'My name is Filip Kamiński. I work for the Governor General's office. Officially, I'm tasked with taking nice photographs of life inside the Jewish Quarter. For propaganda purposes.' He pulled the corners of his mouth down. 'I fell into the job, if you want to know. The wife of the Governor General saw a picture I'd taken for someone's wedding and I was offered the position. It wasn't the kind of offer I was permitted to turn down.'

'So why do you want a picture of Ola?' Zofia asked. She wasn't entirely sure she trusted this man. She didn't really trust anyone these days.

Filip sighed. 'I take the pictures the Nazis want. I don't have much choice. But I always have a second roll of film with me, which I use to capture life in here. *Real* life.' He spoke emphatically. 'It isn't much of a contribution, but it's important to keep a record of what is happening to these people. The squalid conditions, the begging children, the sheer *inhumanity* of it all.' His voice cracked and he cleared his throat. 'But when I see someone as vibrant – as full of life! – as that little girl, I want to capture that too, because it shows that as much as these monsters want to break these poor people, the human spirit will prevail.' He stopped and gave her a sheepish smile. 'I'm sorry, I got carried away. There are very few people I can talk to about this.'

'Will you give those pictures to the Nazis?' Zofia asked. 'The ones of Ola?'

Filip shook his head. 'No! Of course not. I mean, it's the kind of image they love – a Jewish child playing happily in the ghetto – but she's too…' He seemed to struggle to find the right word. 'She's too *pure* to feed their propaganda machine. I would be loath to share her spirit with them.'

Zofia felt herself relaxing. This man was friend, not foe. 'I know the feeling. I'm Zofia, by the way.'

'Nice to meet you.' He held out his hand to shake. 'But you don't belong in here, either.'

'How do you know?'

'I'm a friend of Jolanta's,' he said quietly, without looking at her.

Zofia's eyes widened. Had she just heard him correctly? 'Jolanta' was Irena's code name.

He seemed to read her thoughts. 'I went to school with Jakub; we've known each other for years. And he told me about a young social worker who spends every spare hour helping people in the ghetto. I can tell from your clothes that you don't live in here. So I put two and two together.'

'Excuse me? Filip?' Julia called over. 'Would you take a photograph of all three of us?'

Filip smiled and looked at Zofia.

'Yes, that's a lovely idea.' She brushed off what Filip had said and went to join Julia and Ola on the wall. It took several attempts to take a picture, as Ola had obviously had enough of being a 'model' and squirmed on her mother's lap.

When they were done, Zofia asked Filip if they could have a copy of the photograph after he'd developed the film.

'Of course,' he said, clicking the lid back onto the lens. 'You can ask Jakub where to find me. If I don't run into you sooner.' He looked around. 'Well, I'd better be off. The light is fading fast and I'm still in need of a suitable image for the Nazi propaganda machine.' He grimaced. Then he said his goodbyes and headed off down the street.

Zofia, Julia and Ola slowly made their way back to Julia's flat. It was still a few hours until curfew, but Julia was evidently weakened by their short outing. When they got upstairs, Zofia instructed her to sit down, and made her a pot of tea from the wild herbs they'd collected.

'I'm afraid I'll have to leave soon,' Zofia said.

'Will you come back?' Ola piped up.

'Of course. As soon as I can.'

'Will you bring chocolate?'

Zofia nodded. Ola beamed, her dimples spreading across her cheeks. Zofia smiled back. *She's stolen my heart*, she thought fondly.

'It was so kind of you to visit,' Julia began, but then started coughing again. She leaned forward in her chair and Zofia spotted a dark mottled rash on her chest.

'How long have you had this rash?' she asked, but Julia pulled her blouse tighter around her neck and shook her head.

'It's nothing. Bed bugs, probably.'

'I'll ask one of the nurses to take a look,' Zofia said. 'If you make an appointment at the youth centre, someone can examine you properly.'

'It's nothing,' Julia repeated.

'Even so,' Zofia insisted. 'You must see a nurse. Promise me?'

Julia nodded, and looked away.

On her way home, Julia was all Zofia could think about. A purple mottled rash was a telltale sign of typhus. Thousands of ghetto inhabitants had perished from the disease, and if Zofia was right, then there was little hope for Julia, even if she did see a doctor. She said a silent prayer that she was mistaken and then tried to think of solutions. Antibiotics were the only medication that might give her a fighting chance. But they were hard to come by even outside the ghetto. And what would become of little Ola then?

She picked up her pace, keen to get home now. On the other side of the street, she saw a group of people, carrying suitcases and other possessions wrapped in makeshift bundles, heading north down Zamenhofer Street. Zofia stopped and watched them; she counted at least fifty people, among them a number of children. They were all walking slowly, shuffling forwards as though unsure whether they wanted to reach their destination. An old man in a dusty black suit walked past Zofia, then stopped a few feet away and watched the strange procession.

'Where do you think are they going?' Zofia asked him.

The man sniffed and at first, Zofia thought he was somehow annoyed by her question, but when she turned to him, she saw him wiping away a tear.

'They're heading for the *umschlagplatz*. The Germans are clearing out the streets of the ghetto, one by one. I live in the northern part, so my name won't be on the list for a while, but I'd be happy to swap places with one of those poor souls if I could.'

Zofia looked at him questioningly, and he returned her stare with rheumy eyes.

'You think it's bad in here? From what I've heard, it's paradise compared to where they're going. I'm an old man, my life is almost over. But these young, young people – they don't stand a chance.'

Then he lumbered on, mumbling a chanted prayer under his breath.

The *umschlagplatz* could only mean one thing. Treblinka. That's where those poor people were going. Zofia thought of the upcoming operation and felt a sudden sense of urgency that made her heart race. She turned and hurried towards the checkpoint. It might be risky, but, she began to think, she would take a thousand children out of here if she could.

15

Warsaw, Present Day

That evening, Lizzie sought out a small restaurant a twenty-minute walk from the hotel. It was off the main road in a rather ugly residential area with buildings looking like something out of a Cold War spy movie. The architecture was functional and dreary, and the buildings looked like they hadn't been renovated since the 1960s. But Lizzie wasn't here for the sightseeing, she wanted to avoid the crowded avenues and tourist sites and find a quiet place to sit and eat and think.

She had plenty to think about after the meeting with Aliza. She recalled the look of profound sadness in the woman's eyes when she spoke about her mother. Lizzie had once come across the term 'intergenerational trauma', the trauma that is passed on from one generation to the next. It was what she had seen in Aliza's eyes.

She entered the restaurant and was greeted by the patron, an elderly man with a bushy moustache and round cheeks that bunched up when he smiled. He spoke to her in rapid Polish and seemed not at all perturbed when she answered in English, and continued to talk as he led her to a small table near a tall counter. The restaurant had only six tables, all with wax tablecloths in a red-and-white chequered pattern and a candle in the centre.

The man, smiling broadly, thrust a menu at her and said, '*Moja żona!*', which Lizzie knew meant 'my wife'. At that moment, a small, stout woman in a chef's jacket appeared from behind a door.

'He say, I am cook,' she said, adding, 'All homemade. All good food.'

Lizzie smiled and nodded, and ordered a braised cucumber soup for a starter, and stuffed cabbage with tomato sauce as her main. When the soup arrived ten minutes later, she smiled to herself at a memory of Sunday lunches at her grandmother's house, when Magda was still sprightly enough to cook for the whole family. They would say grace before eating and then tuck into a meal of *borscht* and *pierogi*. She finished her soup and put her spoon down, just as the patron arrived with her main course. He placed it down in front of her and then disappeared again, only to return quickly with a bottle of ice-cold vodka and two small glasses.

'*To na koszt firmy,*' he said as he poured two measures. The small glasses frosted up immediately.

Lizzie looked at him questioningly. She hadn't ordered a drink, but she didn't want to be rude by refusing.

Then his wife called from behind the counter, 'On the house.' She beamed at Lizzie. 'First time you are here, you drink vodka.'

The man picked up his glass. '*Na zdrowie.*'

'*Na zdrowie,*' Lizzie repeated, clinking her glass against his. Cheers.

The vodka spread through her veins like icy lava. Her appetite was suddenly huge and she tucked into her stuffed cabbage rolls with enthusiasm. They were delicious – hearty and salty, just like the meals her grandmother used to cook. She finished off everything on the plate, sitting back and feeling pleasantly full. When the patron approached with the vodka bottle, she happily let him refill her glass. She would come back here tomorrow evening, she decided, and suddenly realised that ever since she had started retracing her great-grandmother's history, her appetite had returned. It had been months since she had enjoyed eating so much. Later, she would call her mom and tell her she was on her way to becoming a plump Polish woman. The thought made her smile.

On the walk back to the hotel, she remembered what Aliza had said about the courthouse. Pulling out her phone, she checked her navigation app and discovered it was only a twelve-minute walk from where she stood. It was a warm evening, and she didn't fancy going to bed quite yet, so she set off towards the courthouse with quick, confident strides and a quiet sense of excitement.

She reached the main entrance in under ten minutes. It was on Aleja Solidarności, a wide, six-lane thoroughfare that Lizzie presumed dated back to Soviet times. The courthouse was older though, a large, elegant sandstone building that spanned almost the entire block, with a low, wide set of steps that led up into the building. Two security officers stood to the left of the entrance, smoking. Lizzie went up to the doors but, predictably at this hour, they were locked. There was only a dull yellow light coming through the glass, and the security officers threw her a scowling look, so she descended the stairs again. Taking out her phone, she did a quick search on the history of the building. This entrance had been on the so-called 'Aryan' side, and the building stretched back to Ogrodowa Street, which had been in the ghetto. *So*, she thought, taking a few steps back, *this is where the lucky escapees emerged*. Again, that poignant feeling of retracing her great-grandmother's footsteps overcame her. Perhaps she had stood at this very spot, a child on her arm, or a baby in a sling. How had she felt? Nervous? Terrified? Or had she been so immeasurably brave she'd had nerves of steel? Lizzie lifted her phone and took a couple of photos of the courthouse, but then one of the security guards called out something gruffly in Polish. Maybe it was illegal to take photos of government buildings, Lizzie thought, and she certainly didn't want to risk trouble with the local police. She turned and started to make her way back to the hotel, reflecting on everything she'd experienced since she arrived in Warsaw.

But as she walked, a sadness came over her. She had been harbouring hopes of finding the 'Zielińska' child in the photograph; it was the main reason she had come all the way here to Warsaw. But now, after talking to Aliza this afternoon, she realised the child might not even have made it out of the ghetto. Even if she did, she would have been given a new identity – and surname – once she was safely smuggled out, wouldn't she? A cold feeling of defeat crept up on Lizzie, and a familiar sense of loss. It was almost as though she had lost a child all over again. *How did the mothers feel back then*, she thought, *sending their children away, probably never to see them again?* And how did they bear it not knowing what would become of them? She touched her face, realising it was wet from a single tear.

It was nine-thirty when she arrived back at her hotel room. She hadn't managed to shake off the jetlag completely, and she was still feeling slightly tipsy from the vodka. She got ready for bed and slipped between the sheets. She felt herself drifting off into sleep almost as soon as her head hit the pillow. But then her phone buzzed. *It'll be Alex*, she thought, and at first decided to ignore it. But then again, it might be her mother, wanting to know how her day had been. She fumbled for her phone in the dark and recognised Roksana's number.

'Hello?'

'Hi, Lizzie. It's Roksana. I'm sorry for calling so late.'

'That's okay.'

'It's just that I got a lead on the Zieliński family.'

In an instant, Lizzie was fully awake. She sat up. 'What have you found out? And are you sure it's the family I'm looking for? Aliza said it was a common surname.'

'It is. But I'm pretty sure this is who you want.'

Lizzie could almost hear Roksana smiling on the other end of the line.

'I'll pick you up at eleven tomorrow, if that's okay,' she said.

'Yes.' Lizzie's heart did a light little dance. 'Yes, that's more than okay. See you in the morning!'

16

Warsaw, December 1942

Two weeks after her visit to Julia, Zofia stood on the corner of Żelazna Street at the entrance to an alleyway, waiting for the signal, rubbing her shoulders for warmth. Night had fallen hours ago; she couldn't see the horizon from where she stood, but the winter sky above her was a deep inky blue, and a few purple-grey clouds had blossomed there like ink on wet fabric. It should be beautiful, but amid all the anguish and suffering, she feared she'd lost the ability to see beauty. Irena would chide her for these thoughts. Irena, so full of hope, so full of strength, said that once you begin to lose faith, you lose everything. Zofia envied her that conviction.

There was a man on the opposite side of the street, leaning against the wall of a dilapidated tenement building. He wasn't looking directly at her; he appeared to be staring into the middle distance, lost in thought. Or not lost – trapped. Inside this hell, everything was trapped; your body, your thoughts, your soul. Perhaps the man was reminiscing about his former life; perhaps he had led a safe, comfortable existence outside these walls, before he and his family had been herded into this hellhole, where a crust of mouldy bread constituted a full meal and a lungful of fresh air was a long-lost memory.

Zofia's toes were freezing and she stamped her feet. It was ten minutes to curfew and if they didn't show soon, she would have to leave. *What's keeping them?* she thought, her nerves cranked so tightly that even the smallest sounds caused her heart to race painfully in her chest.

Tonight, Jakub's role was that of lookout. Right now, he was waiting on a roof somewhere above her, ready to give the signal that the operation was about to take place. Zofia raised her head and let her glance sweep the rooftops, but he was, of course, out of sight. Despite herself, Zofia found herself looking forward to seeing him again.

Lina had switched her affections from Jakub to Igor – the young man from the Civil Status Division Zofia's mother had had hopes for. When Lina had confided this, Zofia felt strangely relieved as it meant her own fondness of Jakub no longer needed to be tinged with feelings of guilt. Perhaps notions of love and romance weren't as far from her mind as she liked to think, even though her and Jakub's paths didn't cross very often, and Zofia knew very little about him, other than that he worked somewhere in the west of the city as a joiner. The last time she'd seen him was a week ago, when she and Helena had smuggled some children out through the tram depot. Jakub had been waiting for them on the other side to help transport the children to a safe place. Before they parted, he had pressed a small envelope into her palm. 'A couple of aspirin tablets, for your sister,' he had murmured, and then rushed off. It had been such a thoughtful act, Zofia thought; she had only mentioned Zuzanna's poor health in passing and yet here he was, sourcing such valuable medication for a girl he'd never met. If only circumstances allowed, she might have occasion to really get to know him—

A sudden sound to her left ripped her painfully from her thoughts. She spun around, constantly and painfully vigilant, but it was only an elderly woman, rushing indoors and slamming the door behind her. Zofia let out a shuddery breath.

She was waiting on a corner where Żelazna Street was dissected by one of the main roads, Leszno Street, and with each passing minute she felt increasingly nervous that she was so far from the checkpoint. She was wearing her sensible shoes, flat lace-ups that made her ankles look thick, but in which she could run if she needed to. Another five minutes and she'd have to put them to the test. She had rehearsed half a dozen cover stories, and tonight's story – if she were approached by a soldier – was that she'd been visiting a family to check on a suspected typhoid patient and had got lost on her way out of the ghetto. The family had been briefed and would confirm her story if necessary. Tomorrow, it would be a different story, a different family, a different alibi. Every single step had to be planned meticulously. Nothing could be left to chance. There was no margin of error.

Zofia checked her watch again and stamped her feet again against the cold. The electricity would go off in less than ten minutes, and already she could smell the oddly garlic-like odour coming from the carbide lamps that people were switching on in the buildings around her. The man opposite was still there, but now his gaze had sunk to the ground in front of him. He was tall, and as emaciated as most people here; his clothes were well-worn and stiff with dirt. Soap was a most precious commodity – apart from food of course – for the unhygienic conditions meant that disease was rampant, and very few people wasted their soap on laundry. The man looked no different from all the other poor souls in the ghetto – malnourished, filthy, desperate – but Zofia knew it would be foolhardy to make assumptions. After all, a spy wouldn't be much of a spy if he couldn't blend in. She looked away so he wouldn't catch her staring. Maybe Jakub had spotted him from the roof and was waiting for him to leave before giving the signal.

Zofia's mouth was uncomfortably dry and her thick woollen stockings itched uncomfortably. She tried to calm her wildly beating heart by telling herself that the smuggling operations had all been successful so far. Last week, they had taken four children through the tram depot, using trained dogs to distract the guards while the children had squeezed through a narrow gap in the wall behind the depot. Those children had been Catholic Jews, which meant they knew their prayers and the boys weren't circumcised. It was one less thing to worry about in case they were stopped by a German soldier on the Aryan side. It was always far riskier for the Yiddish-speaking children, who never quite understood the dangers they faced if they slipped up. Zofia knew Irena had been working desperately behind the scenes to find new homes for the children they were taking tonight. They would first be taken to the Rodzina Marii Orphanage on the other side of the river, where they would be given clean clothes and a warm meal. Then, depending on how many foster families Irena had managed to find, they would be driven there, or else remain in a convent or other religious institution run by nuns in nearby Chotomów and

Lublin. It would be the beginning of a very unsettled time for the children, but at least they had a future to look forward to.

Finally, the man opposite pushed himself from his leaning position and began to make his way down Żelazna Street, head down, walking carefully so he wouldn't slip on the icy pavement. And sure enough, a moment later Zofia heard it: the softest whistle, a low warbling sound, coming from one of the rooftops above.

Jakub.

It was Zofia's cue. She ducked into the alleyway and hurried to the manhole. Irena had told her to wear thick gloves, not just to keep her hands warm, and as she slipped her fingers into the holes of the manhole cover, she understood why. Not only was the metal cover heavy enough to snap her fingers like twigs should she get them trapped, but when she pulled a gloved hand away, it was covered in something dark and slimy.

'You'll need help with that,' a low voice behind her said.

Zofia's heart flip-flopped. She turned to see Jakub, and an icy rush of relief slunk up and down her spine. She straightened up.

'They're on their way,' he said quietly, then reached out his hand and pulled something from her hair. A small twig; it must have become lodged there while she was cycling through the small copse of birch trees in Kazimierzowski Park.

Jakub smiled and pressed the twig into her hand. 'In case you want to keep it,' he said and folded her fingers around it. 'For luck.'

His touch, warm and soft, caused something inside Zofia's stomach to tighten. She turned away slightly, embarrassed at the inappropriateness of her feelings. She was about to embark on an illicit and highly dangerous mission, and yet right now she was behaving like a love-struck teenager. She cast a glance towards him and their eyes locked for a second, but then he pointed at the manhole cover and the spell broke.

'It's heavy,' he said, crouching down. Together, they managed to lift it and push it to the side.

Zofia bent over to look inside and took an involuntary step back. The ghetto smelled bad, of refuse and rotting food and unwashed bodies, but this was something else. It was indescribably foul, assaulting her senses and making her eyes water.

'They're here,' Jakub said, and before she could say her goodbyes, wish him well, or tell him she hoped they'd meet again soon, he had disappeared.

Irena and Helena were making their way down the alleyway, pressed into the shadows of the buildings, leading a group of children. Zofia counted eighteen of them – a huge number, more than they'd ever moved before. But there were two missing. Zofia had seen Irena write down all their names. Where could they be? She watched as they made their way towards her, counting them again.

The children moved slowly, their limbs uncoordinated and floppy. Irena would have given them a mouthful of vodka each, to keep them drowsy and subdue the natural exuberance of seven- and eight-year-olds. Medicinal sedatives were hard to come by and had to be rationed carefully, administered in tiny doses only to the babies they smuggled out to stop them crying. These children would have been told they were going on an outing, and Zofia was absurdly grateful she wouldn't be there when they discovered the truth.

'Quickly, in you go,' Irena said, without so much as a greeting. But this was not a time for such niceties.

'There are two children missing,' Zofia whispered, but Irena just shook her head as if to say, '*Not now*', so Zofia lowered herself into the sewer, using her foot to feel for a slippery rung. She climbed down and reached the bottom, then waited as the children made their way down, one by one. Irena was last, pulling the manhole cover shut again with a strength that belied her small frame.

In the muffled dark, their breaths sounded impossibly loud, but the stench was so overpowering they couldn't possibly breathe through their noses. Several times, Zofia gagged, and after a few minutes she couldn't help herself: she bent over and vomited. Ashamed, she wiped her mouth with the back of her hand and went to apologise, but Irena gave her a sympathetic look.

'It's a physical response,' she said softly. 'And that's what makes you human.'

They walked painfully slowly through the dark in single file, Helena at the back, Zofia in the middle and Irena leading the group. It was warmer down here than up in the wintry air, and the ground was slick. Zofia was constantly afraid one of the children might slip and fall into the reeking wastewater that flowed through the duct beside them. They might be able to fish them out, but if a child ingested any of the germs and bacteria in the water, they were likely to become severely ill. The scuttle and scurry of rats also sent shivers of disgust through Zofia, but she kept her thoughts tightly focused on their destination. She knew the sewer ran in a straight line underneath the ghetto and that they didn't have far to go.

And indeed, it wasn't long before Irena stopped and gestured upwards. Thin fingers of orange light from a nearby lamppost shone through a manhole cover.

'Shall I go first?' Zofia whispered.

Perhaps Irena opened her mouth to answer, Zofia wasn't sure. All she knew was that in the next moment, they heard something so terrifying she felt her knees give way and barely stopped herself from sinking to the filthy ground.

Male voices. German. Zofia spoke a little of the occupiers' language, but even so she couldn't quite make out what they were saying, until she heard the words, '*Da unten.*' Down there.

'What do we do now?' She could hear the panic in her own voice and several of the children let out frightened whimpers.

A flash of fear crossed Irena's face and she closed her eyes. For the longest time, she was silent. Then she opened her eyes again, her expression now almost unnaturally serene, and whispered, 'Now we pray.'

And there, in the stinking darkness, she dropped to her knees and made the sign of the cross.

For a panic-stricken moment, Zofia thought the woman must have lost her mind. But as Irena began to recite the Lord's Prayer in a gentle, monotone voice, the children became calm. Zofia bowed her head and joined in with the prayer, when there was a sudden jolt to her elbow.

'Go!' Helena whispered fiercely. 'You must go back now.'

She pushed past Zofia and dragged Irena to her feet. 'You have to go back,' she hissed. 'Or we will all be shot.'

She fell silent at the sound of the men's voices. '*Hörst du was?*' Can you hear something? Then in response: '*Sind bestimmt nur Ratten*', and, '*Nein, das hier ist die Stelle. Wir sollten nachschauen.*'

There were at least three of them, saying that they'd found the place and deciding whether to check the sewer. They were very close; they must be standing just above them on the street. Irena took a deep breath and crossed herself to complete her prayer.

'You're right,' she said to Helena in a low voice. 'You must all go back. As quickly as you can. I'll stay here and distract the—'

Helena shook her head. 'No. You and Zofia take the children back. I'll wait a minute or two until you're out of sight and then show myself.' She let out a shaky breath and tried to smile. 'I have plenty of cover stories to choose from.'

Zofia could just about make out the whites of Helena's eyes, but even in the gloom she could tell the woman was terrified. She wasn't going to sacrifice herself, was she? Irena, it seemed, was contemplating the same question. She stood there, very still, her hands clenching and unclenching.

When Helena next spoke, her voice was trembling. 'I won't take no for an answer, Irena. The organisation needs you. The *children* need you. Let's be honest – I am dispensable.'

Zofia's throat tightened. For a long moment, a moment that seemed to stretch beyond time, Irena stared at Helena. Then she put her hands on Helena's shoulders and leaned forward to kiss her forehead.

'God bless you, Helena,' she whispered, then turned to Zofia. 'Come now, we have to hurry.'

Zofia had no choice. She mouthed 'Good luck' to Helena, then whispered to the children that their outing had come to an end and they were going to hurry back.

They had no option but to take the children – hungry, exhausted and foul-smelling – back home: the orphans to the orphanage on Sienna Road, and the others to their bewildered parents. Thankfully, there were no patrols of the empty ghetto streets, and they managed to return the children without incident. The parents were, without exception, overjoyed to take their children back into their arms, yet at the same time distraught that they hadn't managed to escape. Irena promised each and every one of them they would try again soon, but Zofia wasn't sure they would all agree to a second attempt.

All the while, she felt numb, her thoughts wrapped around the look of terror in Helena's eyes. When she and Irena finally passed through the checkpoint – a tired-looking guard gruffly asking why they were coming out so late, but evidently satisfied with Irena's excuse that they'd lost their way in the labyrinthine ghetto – they came to a stop beneath a hissing lamppost.

'What will happen to Helena now?' Zofia asked.

For a while, Irena was silent, staring out into the black night. 'Her fate is in God's hands now.' She gave her head a tiny shake and turned to Zofia. 'Say a prayer for her tonight, won't you?'

17

Warsaw, December 1942

The next morning, after a restless night haunted by nightmares of the night before, Zofia told her parents she had a migraine and wouldn't be going to work. She knew her father would be at his workshop, and her mother had planned another day foraging for wild mushrooms, berries and herbs after she had walked Zuzanna to school.

As soon as they had left the house, Zofia got dressed in a hurry and rushed out, cycling as fast as she could to Irena's flat. The sun was out and the winter air was crisp and fresh, a perfect day for a walk on the riverbank. But Zofia's mood was dark. She still had the stench of the sewer in her nostrils and the sound of scurrying rats in her ears. And worst of all, she couldn't shake the image of the whites of Helena's eyes. It was haunting her, reminding her of the failed mission. She thought back to how invincible she had felt after the first few operations. How arrogant, how foolish she had been to feel that way! All the doubts she had had right at the beginning, when Lina had first told her about the resistance, rushed back into her mind, but this time, those doubts had increased a thousandfold. She pedalled harder, trying to focus on the burning sensation in her thighs to clear her mind, but the lingering doubts refused to be dismissed so easily.

When she arrived at Irena's building, she leaned her bicycle against the brick wall and rang the doorbell to the flat. A few seconds later, the lock buzzed and she pushed against the heavy door to let herself in. Irena, who lived on the second floor of the tenement building, was standing in the dark stairwell, waiting.

'Why are you not at work?' she asked.

Zofia, her legs heavy after the fast cycle, took the stairs as quickly as she could.

'I told my parents I have a headache,' she said breathlessly, and added, 'Have you heard anything?'

Irena looked around as though fearful someone might overhear, and beckoned Zofia inside the flat. She led her into a small kitchen and gestured for Zofia to sit down. It smelled comfortingly of tea and biscuits, and for a moment, Zofia longed to leave all the terror and hopelessness behind. What she wouldn't give to just sit and chat with her friend!

'You should have gone to work today,' Irena said. 'Everything must appear normal. Especially after last night.'

'I couldn't … I can't think of anything else. My mind is spinning around and around in circles.' She briefly shut her eyes, but was immediately beset by the haunting image of the terror in Helena's eyes. 'I keep thinking of poor Helena. Do you know what's happened to her?'

'She was arrested as soon as she emerged from the sewer,' Irena said in a tight voice. 'My sources tell me she's in Pawiak Prison.'

'The one inside the ghetto? The Gestapo prison?'

Irena nodded. She busied herself filling the kettle. 'We mustn't dwell on it,' she said, placing the kettle on the hob and clicking on the gas. 'Helena is a strong woman. And we have work to do.'

Is that all you can say? Zofia wanted to shout. *Don't you have any feelings at all?*

But when Irena turned back around, Zofia could see a look of pure anguish in her face. 'She is strong,' Irena repeated in a wavering voice. 'She will be back with us soon and she'll be stronger than ever before.'

She took two cups from the cupboard, added some dried camomile leaves, and poured over the boiling water. Then she took a cloth and began to wipe the spotless counter. Zofia realised she was trying to keep busy to distract herself.

'Irena?' Zofia said quietly.

'Yes?'

She took a deep breath. The time had come. She would tell Irena it was over, that she couldn't possibly face the fear and danger any longer. She had done what she could for Żegota, and now she had nothing more to give. But as she looked at Irena, she faltered. As ever, Irena's proud, straight posture made her appear taller than she was. Despite everything that had happened, she still exuded extraordinary strength.

'Are you all right, dear?' Irena asked, turning to face her.

Zofia swallowed, the words she had just been thinking dissolving on her tongue. She couldn't tell Irena now, it would have to wait. So instead, she said, 'There were only eighteen children with us last night. Who were the missing two?'

'Seven-year-old twins, Rachela and Adam Joselewicz. Their parents – particularly their father – were hesitant about letting us take them, but I thought I'd made a convincing case.' She sighed. 'That's what makes it so much easier with the orphans. There is no one we have to persuade.'

She brought the cups over to the table and sat down. 'I understand the parents, I do. What a terrible decision to have to make – saying goodbye to your own children, not knowing if you'll ever see them again. I know Mr and Mrs Joselewicz want the best for their children, but…'

'What happened?'

'When Helena and I went to fetch them, Mr Joselewicz wouldn't open the door. He is orthodox, and was profoundly troubled that his children might be raised in a different faith. We urged him to reconsider, that this might be the only way his children will survive, but he said that God would protect them.'

Zofia let out an involuntary huff. 'God won't though, will he? It takes only a single visit to the ghetto to tell you that He doesn't care much.'

Irena's head snapped up, eyes blazing. 'You mustn't speak like that, Zofia. I understand how you feel, believe me. All this evil … it burrows its way inside your head, your memory, your thoughts, be they waking or sleeping. But you must resist, and at the same time you must beware of becoming accustomed to it. One may get used to certain sights, certain sounds, but we must never accept them, or tolerate them. We must never stop being entirely committed to eliminating this evil from God's earth. You mustn't lose your faith, promise me.'

Zofia gave a small nod, although it was an impossible promise to give. The things she had seen and heard since she joined the resistance had called everything into doubt. Her faith in a just and loving God, the thread that had run through her life for as long as she could remember, was threatening to unravel. The feeling was painful and liberating in equal measure. If there was no God, then they only had each other. But would that be enough? And yet, Irena's words – or more precisely, the *passion* with which she spoke them – had reignited the dying fire of her determination. Despite her doubts, despite the fear that had accompanied every waking hour since she had joined the resistance, the thought of returning to a life of ignorance was impossible. The Nazis would still be transporting Jews to the death camps, the remaining ghetto inhabitants would still be starving. Julia's daughter Ola would be facing certain death. Zofia took a sharp intake of breath, and realised Irena was still talking.

'We must be extra vigilant,' she was saying. 'Though we will have to speed up operations. The deportations are continuing unabated – those monsters won't stop until they've killed each and every Jewish man, woman and child.' She sighed in despair and her round youthful face looked as though it had aged several years overnight.

Zofia sipped her tea slowly. How much more vigilant could they be? The smuggling operations were so precisely planned, because any wrong step could result in capture, but you always had to factor in human error – a misunderstanding, a breakdown in communication, or something more sinister…

A terrible thought began forming in her mind. 'You … you don't think the twins' father might have betrayed us?'

'Why would you say something like that?' Irena said, horrified.

Zofia swallowed. 'I don't know. It's just...'

'What?'

'The German soldiers. They knew exactly where to wait. Almost as though they were expecting us. And given that Mr Joselewicz was so against you taking his children, well ... I thought that perhaps...'

Irena frowned and clicked her tongue. 'No. I refuse to believe that.'

Zofia felt foolish. Irena was right; what father would sacrifice the lives of others' children? There would be nothing for him to gain, anyway.

The two women both fell silent for a long moment. Then Irena said, 'But you might not be entirely wrong. There might well be a spy among us.'

They exchanged a look of fear, both comprehending the terrible implications if that were true.

That afternoon, Zofia entered the ghetto with dozens of sugar sachets sewn into the lining of her coat. Someone had sourced the sugar – Zofia had no idea who, or how – and she'd been tasked with distributing it among breastfeeding mothers and small children.

By now, she was familiar with many of the guards, knew which ones would wave her through, which ones would closely and lengthily inspect her ghetto pass, which ones would make her remove her coat, hat and shoes and rifle through her bag looking for items to confiscate. Today's senior guard was a man called Buchholz, a middle-aged man with round, horn-rimmed glasses who looked like he'd never smiled a day in his life. He was one of the supercilious ones who looked at any non-German as though he had found something objectionable on the sole of his shoe. He would, Zofia knew, make a great fuss of her pass, ask her name and date of birth, how long she intended to stay in the ghetto, and inform her she was at risk of catching one of any number of diseases.

She kept her face as expressionless as possible as she approached him.

'*Den Passierschein, Fräulein,*' he said.

Zofia handed over her pass. As expected, he began to question her about her details, which authority had issued her pass, who she was here to visit. She answered all his questions patiently, and finally, he handed her pass back and dismissed her with a curt nod of his head.

'Filthy place,' he said, as she stepped past him into the ghetto.

Around the next corner, she patted down her coat to ensure the sugar sachets were still in place. Sugar was not the most nutritious food, but it was light and therefore easy to smuggle, and the simplest way to provide additional calories to people's diet. What they really needed, she thought as she passed by an emaciated young man sitting on the pavement with a begging bowl in front of him, was meat, and eggs, and fresh fruit. She slowed as she passed the man; his skin was stretched tight over his face, his eyes sunk deep into his skull and his hair was missing in patches. It took all Zofia's willpower not to rip open the lining of her coat there and then and give him some of the sugar.

But she didn't. There were thousands of people here who were just as needy, and she had come to appreciate the need to prioritise, as painful as it was. Today, there were five families on her list whom she had selected because the women were either pregnant or breastfeeding, or where one of the family was on the absolute verge of starvation. The vast majority of people here were starving – with the exception of some particularly skilled and unscrupulous black marketeers – but two of the mothers she was going to visit might not last another few weeks without the additional calories. And if they died, their newborns would die soon afterwards.

She gave the man a tight smile and picked up her pace, suddenly needing to escape his pain and desperation, to feel less helpless.

When she had finished her last visit, it was five o'clock. Her parents would be expecting her home soon, but she needed to make one final stop.

At the flat on Ostrowska Street, the same man as last time opened the door, but his greeting was kinder today.

'Julia's in her room,' he said. 'My wife is looking after Ola to give Julia some rest. She was up for most of the night.' He drew his eyebrows together in a troubled frown. 'We are hoping it is just a stomach upset.'

'Has she seen a doctor, or a nurse?' Zofia asked. 'I told her to go to the youth centre.'

But the man just shrugged and walked down the hall, back to his room. Zofia heard Ola's bright laugh from behind the door and felt a sharp tug to her heart. The girl was the living embodiment of joy and optimism, and Zofia would have given anything to feel that way again herself. She knocked gently on Julia's door and opened it. Inside, the air was fetid and close, and the curtains were drawn, making the room feel oppressive. Julia lay beneath a sheet on her narrow bed in the corner, her laboured breathing audible from where Zofia stood at the door.

On the floor beside the bed was a bowl, and when Zofia came closer, she realised it was the source of the smell. It was full of watery, greenish vomit.

'Julia,' she whispered. 'It's me, Zofia.'

Julia opened her eyes and tried to sit up. She groaned with the effort.

'Please, don't try to get up.' Zofia's voice was firm. 'You're not well.'

She put a hand on Julia's forehead. It was burning hot.

'That feels nice,' Julia said with a weak smile. 'Your hands are so cool.'

'How long have you felt like this?' Zofia asked, trying to keep the alarm out of her voice. Julia was very, very sick. She had deteriorated significantly since the last visit, and any hope Zofia had had that Julia might miraculously recover now seemed pathetically naïve. It made her feel completely hopeless. 'Did you go to the youth centre, like I said? Have you seen a doctor?'

'No, I…' She swallowed painfully. 'I've been very tired. My legs, they are so weak.'

Zofia looked around for a water glass, but there was just an empty chipped mug on the windowsill. 'I'll go and fetch you some water,' she said softly.

In the kitchen, she found a kettle on the gas stove; thankfully, the water was lukewarm, so someone must have boiled it earlier. She took a cup from one of the cabinets and went to rinse it under the tap, but the water that came out was brownish and smelled rusty, so she wiped out the cup with a tea towel instead.

'It's the bad water that makes so many people sick,' a woman's voice behind her said.

She turned to see a thin young woman in a black dress and a brown scarf covering her head.

'That and the lice,' the woman continued. She took a step towards Zofia and held her hand out. 'I'm Sara Friedman,' she said. 'I think you've already met my husband, Eliasz.'

Her collarbone jutted out sharply, and the dress looked like it belonged to a woman three sizes larger.

'Zofia. Nice to meet you. I'm a friend of Julia's.'

'Do you have any food with you?' Sara said, blushing slightly and then raising her chin, almost defiantly, as if to show she wasn't begging, she was – quite simply – starving. How much self-esteem it must cost her to demean herself like that, Zofia thought. And a second later, she remembered she had promised Ola some chocolate, which she had forgotten about. She shook her head.

'I'm sorry, I have nothing with me. I'll try and bring something the next time I visit.'

Sara let out a long breath and seemed to deflate. But she gathered herself again quickly. 'Julia is very sick,' she said. 'She has been for some time, but last night … I'm not sure even a doctor can help her now.'

Zofia gave her head a small, almost imperceptible shake, as though she could unhear Sara's words, and the truth they contained. She hurried out of the kitchen.

'I want to ask you something,' she said as she returned to Julia's room.

Julia frowned and licked her dry lips. 'Of course. Anything.'

Zofia handed her the glass and waited until she had taken a sip. What she intended to suggest might cause Julia incredible pain, but this was the harsh reality of war, not a fairytale. There wasn't a happy ending for everyone.

'I … I'm not sure how to say it. It's just … I'm part of an organisation that helps children. We smuggle them out of the ghetto and place them with families who can keep them safe. Until—' She paused and looked away for a moment. 'Until this is all over and we can reunite them with their parents.'

She turned back to find Julia staring at her with unbearably sad eyes. 'You want to take Ola,' she whispered.

Zofia had to fight the urge to look away again. Julia blinked once and a tear escaped her eye. Again, she tried to sit up, barely managing to prop herself on her elbows. Zofia's heart gave a lurch at the sight of her friend's frailty.

'It's all right,' Julia said softly. 'We shouldn't pretend I have a common cold that will be over in a few days.' As if to underline the point, she let out a sudden, dry rasping cough and fell back onto the mattress. For a long moment, she lay there, her eyes closed, her chest rising and falling heavily as she breathed. The room was so quiet it was almost as if Zofia could hear Julia's heartbeat slowing.

'It will shatter my heart to pieces,' she said then, so quietly Zofia had to lean in close to hear her. 'But you must take Ola. You must save my daughter.'

Zofia's throat tightened painfully as she fought a sudden urge to weep. She had thought her capacity for tears was long since drained, but now she felt more vulnerable and heartbroken than ever before. With a huge effort, she swallowed her tears down. Now was not the time to weep. She had to be strong. For Julia. For Ola.

18

Warsaw, Present Day

Lizzie woke just after nine o'clock, after the deepest sleep she'd had in months. Roksana had sent a message asking if they could meet a bit earlier than planned, at ten-thirty instead of eleven, and by quarter past, Lizzie was waiting outside the hotel, pacing the pavement impatiently.

Roksana arrived five minutes later, carrying two cups of steaming coffee.

'You ready for the next stage of your adventure?' she asked with a grin.

'I certainly am. And Roksana … I can't thank you enough for all of this. None of this would have been possible without your help.'

Roksana blushed, making her look like a bashful teenager. She handed Lizzie a coffee and ran a hand through her short hair, making it stand up on end. 'You're welcome. And I'm a journalist, so I have a natural curiosity. Come on then, it's a half-hour trip to get there.'

The woman who went by the name Zielińska lived in Żoliborz, a small suburb to the north of the city centre. Lizzie and Roksana took the metro there and emerged from the station onto a busy street.

Roksana took out her phone. 'She lives on Stefana Pogonowskiego Road,' she said, reading from her phone. 'I spoke to her grandson, Tomasz, and he said as long as we're there before the old lady's lunchtime nap, she'll be happy to talk to us.'

They made their way up the street, Lizzie turning her head this way and that to take in as much of the city as she could. Unlike the district she was staying in, this was very much a residential area she doubted many tourists got to see, a pretty neighbourhood with tree-lined streets and children's playgrounds, and plenty of people out and about on their bicycles. It was the first time since Lizzie had been married that she had travelled alone, and the urge to share all these impressions with Alex was almost overwhelming. She wasn't sure if she should feel irritated by this urge, or whether it was an indication that no matter what, Alex had a fixed place in her heart. What she was sure of, though, was that coming here had been the right decision: uncovering her family history was a way to cut through the emotional turmoil she'd been feeling and give her some sense of clarity.

'This is it,' Roksana said as they came to a small, two-storey house with a red sloping roof. It had small arched windows and white shutters, and with its stump of a chimney poking out of the roof, the house looked like something from a child's drawing.

Roksana rang the doorbell and stepped back, giving Lizzie an encouraging smile. Not for the first time, Lizzie felt profoundly grateful to have found a friend in her.

The man who came to the door was huge – well over six feet tall and as broad as a bear and seemed altogether too massive for such a dainty house.

'I'm Tomasz Broński,' he said in fluent but heavily accented English. 'You must be Roksana – and Lizzie. From America,' he added with a grin, showing off a missing incisor. It made him look almost jaunty, Lizzie thought, and returned his infectious smile.

'Come in, come in,' he said, gesturing widely with his large hands.

The women followed him inside, down a narrow hallway and into the living room. Even at first glance, Lizzie could tell this was a multi-generational household – the wicker basket in the corner containing wool and knitting needles, the PlayStation controller on the coffee table, a few gardening magazines and a crime novel Lizzie recognised; one she'd been meaning to read herself but had never got round to. Everything was mismatched and put together in a rather random fashion, but despite this – or perhaps because of this – the place was warm and cosy. The smell of over-brewed tea and potpourri hung in the air. It was a homely atmosphere that made her want to stay a while.

Tomasz gestured towards a large sofa that was worn in places, but looked very comfortable.

'Please, sit down. My wife will bring some tea and cake.' He called out a name Lizzie knew to be a pet name, and the response came immediately that tea and cake were on their way.

A moment later, the door opened and a young boy poked his head around the door.

'*Witam*,' Roksana greeted him, but he retreated as quick as a flash. There was some giggling on the other side of the door, and then a girl ventured into the room. She was about nine years old and was wearing jeans and a home-knitted jumper.

For a moment, Lizzie thought the girl looked a bit like Hannah when she was that age, with her frizzy hair and heart-shaped face. The girl took one look at Lizzie and Roksana, gave them a cheeky smile, and dashed out again.

'My daughter, Maja,' Tomasz explained. 'And the first one was my son, Aleksander. It seems they need some work on their manners.'

He smiled apologetically, but Lizzie could see the paternal pride in his eyes. She had only been here five minutes, yet it was evident that this was a loving, close-knit family. They all turned as the door creaked open, and a very old woman entered. Her back was alarmingly hunched, and when she raised her head to peer over towards Roksana and Lizzie, she looked like a tortoise poking its head out of the shell.

'*Babcia*,' Tomasz said, 'you have some visitors.'

He turned to Lizzie. 'I'm afraid she doesn't speak English,' he said, 'but I am happy to translate.'

'And me,' Roksana added.

The woman ambled forward, leaning heavily on her stick, and sat down in an armchair opposite the sofa. She had small round eyes that were almost black.

At Lizzie's request, Roksana made a brief introduction, telling the old woman that Lizzie had come from America to find out more about her family's history. Mrs Zielińska listened thoughtfully, nodded and spoke some words.

'She is happy to help if she can,' Roksana said.

Lizzie took a deep breath to still her fluttering nerves.

'Do you know Zofia Szczęsny?' she asked. Roksana translated.

The old woman's face brightened.

'*Tak*,' she responded, and launched into an excited string of Polish.

'What? What's she saying?' Lizzie asked, looking from Tomasz to Roksana.

Tomasz asked his grandmother something, and she nodded. He turned to Lizzie.

'She says she was saved by Zofia. Smuggled out of the ghetto. She was hidden at a convent for a few months, but then she was adopted by a Polish family – this family.' He patted his chest and smiled. 'They were very good to her, she says. Loved her like a child of their own.'

He reached out and stroked his grandmother's hand.

Something occurred to Lizzie. 'Tomasz, when you greeted us at the door, you said your name was Broński. So I'm wondering – perhaps it's a cultural thing I'm not familiar with – why your grandmother's surname is Zielińska. Was she not given the same name as her adoptive parents?'

At the mention of the name Zielińska, the old woman's eyes snapped towards Lizzie. She began talking again, and not for the first time, Lizzie cursed the fact she had never put much effort into learning the language of her great-grandmother. She waited as the old lady spoke, her eyes flicking from Tomasz to Roksana to see their reactions, but they just listened, nodding occasionally.

'She says,' Roksana began when the old woman had finished talking, 'that she was moved from the convent to the Broński family. Then, several months later, a nun came to visit.'

'And she can remember all of this? She was only a young child.'

'I remember *everything* about Zofia,' the old woman suddenly croaked in English, surprising both Lizzie and Roksana. She grinned at them, her small button-like eyes full of mischief.

'*Babcia*,' Tomasz said, equally astonished. 'You said you don't speak English!'

She grinned again, showing off her dimples. 'Only a little. But that is enough now. Too tiring for my tongue.'

Then she lapsed back into Polish.

'A few months later,' Tomasz went on to translate, 'a nun came to visit to check on her. The nun told her she'd been sent by Zofia Szczęsny, that it was too risky for Zofia to visit herself.'

The old woman nodded. 'She was … a true friend to my mother,' she whispered.

'You want to tell the story yourself, *Babcia*?' Tomasz said archly, but she drew a pretend zip across her mouth and leaned back, a mischievous smile twitching on her lips.

'So,' Tomasz continued. 'The nun, sent by Zofia, informed her adoptive parents that my grandmother was a very special girl. She asked that when the girl was old enough, when the war had ended, that they tell her that her real name is Zielińska. It was the name her father gave her, and one that she should be proud of.'

His grandmother smiled and said something else. Tomasz nodded.

'When she was a teenager, her adoptive parents – my great-grandparents – told her of her real name. When she heard this, she decided to revert back to the use of Zielińska – even kept it after she got married – which is very unusual in these parts.' He glanced at his grandmother, knowingly. 'She's a headstrong woman.'

Mrs Zielińska straightened up. '*Silna kobieta.*'

This, Lizzie understood. 'A strong woman.' She beamed at her and said, 'I'm so glad you are, because otherwise, I would never have found you.'

For a long moment, she was overcome with emotion, and a strange, unfamiliar sense of serenity. Finally, a piece of the puzzle had fallen into place.

'Is there anything else you can tell me about my great-grandmother? Exactly what she did during the war? I want to know as much as possible about my family history.'

With Tomasz and Roksana translating, Mrs Zielińska went on to say she wished she could help Lizzie, but she only had vague moments of recollection from her time during the war.

'I thought you said you remembered everything,' Lizzie said, trying to keep the frustration out of her voice.

Mrs Zielińska spoke. Tomasz translated.

'She only remembers Zofia well. She was, um, *była aniołem*—' He searched for the words.

Roksana interjected. 'An angel. Zofia was an angel.'

Lizzie couldn't help but smile. She felt an odd sense of pride that her great-grandmother elicited such pleasant memories. Then a familiar feeling of grief and sadness assailed her – she herself would never have descendants, no children to tell her stories to, no grandchildren wanting to know what life was like 'in the olden days'. Without warning, the blackness closed in on her briefly. When she looked up, she noticed Mrs Zielińska staring at her. Then the old woman spoke to Tomasz. He paused and looked at her quizzically, but she gestured for him to translate.

'She asks if you have a deep sadness inside?' He shook his head slightly. 'That is a very personal question. I apologise for my grandmother.'

Lizzie felt the heat rising to her face. 'No, please, don't apologise.' She looked down at her hands. 'You can tell her she's right. But … but it's not something I feel comfortable talking about.'

Mrs Zielińska tilted her head to one side. 'You are a kind woman,' she said in English. 'But sad.' Then she leaned back and let out a soft breath. A moment later, she had closed her eyes.

'I'm sorry, but I think it's time for her nap, now,' Tomasz said quietly. 'It was very nice to talk to you, though.'

'Thank you so much for inviting us in,' Lizzie said. 'What a lovely lady your grandmother is.'

Tomasz chuckled quietly. 'That's one way to describe her, I guess.'

'One more thing,' Lizzie said. 'I don't want to be impolite, but would you mind telling me her first name?'

'Of course,' Tomasz replied. 'Her name is Ola. Ola Zielińska.'

Lizzie and Roksana rose from their seats and said their goodbyes. On the way to the front door, the young girl, Maja, peeked out from behind a door. She smiled at them, two dimples forming in her cheeks. Then she said something and disappeared again, giggling.

19

Warsaw, December 1942

Zofia stood at the back of the smoke-filled room at Żegota headquarters, which were located in a flat on Żurawia Street. She'd wanted to go to the ghetto to visit Julia after work, but Lina had insisted she come here. The group had been in disarray after the terrible incident in the sewer and Helena's arrest, and Irena had called them together to discuss their next actions. The mood in the room was a palpable mix of anger and fear. People were talking over each other, some shouting, some crying.

'We'll have to lay low for a while,' a man was saying. 'It's too risky.'

'Shut the operation down?' another shouted. 'We can't do that. People are being deported as we speak. Lives are lost with every day that passes.'

'What's the alternative? That we sacrifice ourselves?'

Zofia listened to them numbly; she was still feeling the ache of shock after Helena's arrest. Somewhere in their midst, Irena stood talking to a man with greying hair and a noticeable scar on his right cheek. They looked to be arguing, the man's arms gesturing wildly and Irena's face flushed with anger.

'Enough!' Irena shouted, loudly enough to make everyone fall silent. 'Helena's trial is next week,' she said, her voice as assured as ever. *This*, Zofia thought, *is what a true leader looks like, composed in the face of crisis.* And indeed, a sense of calm appeared to fall across the room.

Then Irena looked at each one of them in turn. 'Some of you have known Helena for years, others know her only by name. For those of you who aren't aware, she lost her husband and two-year-old son to a German bomb at the beginning of the war.' There was a small gasp from the back of the room. Irena continued. 'Helena has suffered more than any young woman should suffer, and now she has made the ultimate sacrifice. She has likely given her life to save ours.' She paused for a moment. 'I would like us all to take a moment to pray for her safety.'

She folded her hands and bowed her head, and while the others in the room did the same, Zofia just stood there, stunned. How had she not known Helena's terrible story? Losing a husband, and a small child – what could be worse than that? Zofia had never felt particularly close to her, but at that moment, she felt acutely ashamed of all the times she'd thought of Helena as cold and aloof, when in fact the woman was carrying the heaviest of burdens. But for what? *It's hopeless*, she thought suddenly. For all their compassion and selflessness and noble intentions, Żegota would never win the fight against the sheer brutality and inhumanity of the enemy.

She clasped her hands together to stop them shaking. Her hope and optimism were all but gone, and her faith in the cause and strength to see it through were being pushed to the limit. She forced herself to close her eyes, but just saw an image of the terror in Helena's eyes. When she managed to shake that image, her mind immediately turned to Julia, lying sick and dying in her cramped, dirty room.

She couldn't take it anymore. The danger had always been present, and with it the heart-stopping fear, but it had always seemed abstract. Now, with Julia dying and Helena almost certainly facing a death sentence, her worst nightmare had seemingly come true. She managed to get out of the room and into the small dark corridor before she broke down in huge, heaving sobs. But every gulp of air made her more breathless and her heart was pounding so heavily she was afraid she might be sick. Finally, her trembling legs couldn't hold her anymore and she sank to the floor, dizzy and struggling to breathe.

'Oh, Zofia,' a soft voice whispered.

With great effort, Zofia raised her head. It was Irena.

'It's … it's too much,' Zofia gasped. 'I can't do this anymore, I can't … I can't breathe.'

Irena crouched down. 'You're hyperventilating, that's all. It's frightening, I know; it feels like you're suffocating.' She put her hand on Zofia's back and instructed her to take some deep breaths. Finally, the oxygen streamed back into her lungs and the dizziness subsided.

'You are stronger than you think,' Irena said finally, handing her a handkerchief. 'But you would be less than human if it didn't affect you.' She stroked Zofia's back. 'When this is over – and my faith tells me it will be, one day – then we will all be very different people. Scarred certainly, but not broken.'

Zofia wiped her eyes and took a deep, shaky breath.

'We cannot afford to lose you, Zofia. Our resistance is more than the sum of its parts, but each and every small part is crucial. With Helena gone…' She paused for a moment and cleared her throat. 'With Helena in prison, we need you to take over in her stead. There are many, many more children whose only hope of survival lies in your hands.'

'I … I don't know if I can,' Zofia whispered.

'You have no choice.'

Her voice was kind, yet firm. Zofia looked up at her and realised she was right. They had reached the point of no return; everything Zofia had witnessed, every person she'd met, every child she'd helped – it would all amount to nothing if she gave up now. And Helena's sacrifice would be meaningless. She held out a hand and Irena helped her to her feet.

'Now,' Irena said, 'go and wash your face, if you like, then come and join us again. We have to decide how to move forward.'

When Zofia returned from the bathroom ten minutes later, the room had all but emptied. Lina was stacking some chairs, and Irena was clearing up the papers from the table. Zofia approached her.

'Everybody has left?' she asked.

Irena nodded tiredly. 'Too much emotion in the air. Decisions made that way tend to be poor ones.'

'How can we carry on, Irena?' Zofia said. 'Without knowing if there's a spy among us.'

Irena sighed heavily. 'I've been thinking of nothing else. But there's only one way to find out.'

'How?' Lina asked.

Irena's face took on an expression Zofia couldn't read. 'I will think of something.'

Without another word, she briskly crossed the room to fetch her coat and hat from the coat stand. She was trying not to show it, but Zofia could tell she was emotionally exhausted, and by the way her lips were moving soundlessly, it was clear that she was deep in thought.

Lina finished stacking the chairs and came up to Zofia, putting a hand on her shoulder.

'Everything all right?' she asked.

'Yes.' Zofia nodded. 'Just … all of this … it's so upsetting. I daren't imagine what Helena must be going through.'

Lina opened her mouth to speak, but Irena came back towards them, a look of determination on her face.

'We were going to move the children out on Tuesday, weren't we?'

Lina nodded.

'We will move them tomorrow night.'

'But we can't!' Zofia cried. 'That's far too risky. It's a full moon and the forecast is for clear skies. We'll stand out like sore thumbs.'

'We'll be careful,' Irena replied. 'We've done it before. It'll be no different this time.'

'But—'

'We're all tired and on edge,' Irena said, interrupting her. 'I would suggest we leave it for tonight and reconvene tomorrow when we've had some sleep.'

20

Warsaw, December 1942

The following evening, Zofia stood outside what used to be a wigmaker's shop, but was now boarded up and shuttered, home only to colonies of rats. She looked up and down the eerily silent street. Curfew had just begun and the ghetto lay in complete darkness. At one time, this had been a vibrant quarter, with music halls and cafés, places you might bump into an artist or a musician. But now … now all of that had gone. It was more like a graveyard for the living.

Zofia shivered and blew into her hands. It was another crisp winter's night and she was glad she'd put a layer of newspaper inside the bottom of her boots to keep out the worst of the cold. But still, if she had to wait here much longer, the cold would come creeping up through the soles. She held her wristwatch close to her face to check the time, squinting to make out the time in the gloom. Eight minutes past seven. In about two minutes, she would hear Jakub's signal, and then she would make a move to the meeting point, where Lina would have brought the children.

The moon hung plump and bright in the inky sky. Not for the first time, Zofia wondered why Irena had decided to move the smuggling operation forward. The conditions were all wrong, and Irena was usually so rigorous, so careful. Early on, she had told Zofia that the risks they took were calculable. These conditions – the sudden rush to move the children, a potential Nazi collaborator among them, the bright moonlight – made the risk anything but calculable. Was Irena becoming careless in her desperation to save as many children as possible, Zofia questioned? Why had she decided to push through, regardless of the risk?

There was a gunshot somewhere in the far distance, and Zofia hoped the shooter was only using rats as target practice. She pushed herself further into the shadow of the building and tried to focus her mind. She had been so deep in thought it occurred to her she might have missed Jakub's signal. *You need to concentrate*, she chided herself. *Lives depend on it.*

Then, the sound of feet scuffing the ground and a hand on her shoulder. She spun around with her fists clenched, every muscle in her body tensing, ready to fight. But it wasn't a soldier, it was a young man in dark clothes, and he looked familiar, though it took her a moment to place him as the photographer who had taken pictures of Ola in the park. What was his name again? Filip.

'What—?' she began, but he put his fingers to his lips to indicate she should be quiet. He leaned in closer.

'Jolanta sent me,' he said, so softly she could hardly hear him. His dark hair was ruffled and he was out of breath. 'You need to come with me.'

'Where's Jakub?' she said. 'What's going on?'

'It's not safe.' He turned his head and scanned the street. 'Come on, we have to leave.'

He cupped her elbow and began to lead her down the road, but she shook him off.

'Where's Lina? What about the children?'

'I'll answer all of your questions soon enough.'

There was a sudden banging sound from nearby and Zofia startled.

Filip nodded towards the end of the street. 'It's dangerous out here in the open,' he hissed. 'We have to go. *Now!*'

Zofia had no choice but to follow him. He was setting a quick pace and she struggled to keep up. Despite the damp, cold mist that had settled between the buildings, she began to sweat, and her footsteps seemed alarmingly loud in the ghost-like silence of the ghetto. Her head was spinning, torn between fear and her mistrust of this man. What was going on? Why would Irena send the photographer to get her? She stumbled on a protruding cobblestone and almost fell. *Oh God*, she thought then, *something must have happened to Lina and the children*. Why had she let Irena talk them into moving the children tonight? It was madness, she'd known it all along. And now several innocent children were at the mercy of the Nazis. And Lina… Zofia stifled a sob as her legs threatened to give way beneath her.

Filip must have noticed, because he slowed down and turned towards her. His face took on a gentle expression and he held out his hand. 'Everything is fine,' he said quietly. 'We just have to get indoors, out of sight, then I'll explain everything.'

Zofia looked at him, puzzled, but then they heard loud footsteps from around the corner, the echo of boots on stone, and they ducked into a narrow passage between a tenement building and a ruin. The beam of light from a flashlight swept the blackened wall above them, but then disappeared again.

'Keep your head down,' Filip whispered. 'I know a place we can hide.'

Zofia's heart was hammering against her ribs, but she crouched down and followed Filip through the passageway. It stank of human waste and rotting vegetables, and the telltale rustling of rats came from the shadows. They made their way along a labyrinthine route of dark side streets and alleyways, pausing every so often for Filip to peer around corners to make sure they weren't spotted, until they finally reached a small, derelict one-storey building.

'In here,' Filip said and led the way inside. Zofia followed hesitantly. The building must have been hit by a bomb in the early days of the war and looked as if it might collapse on itself at any moment, with crumbling brickwork and window panes hanging from their hinges. Inside, Zofia could smell the sharp, musty smell of rat droppings. She fumbled her way through the dark space, keeping a hand to the wall for orientation, before it hit something cold and slimy. She pulled it away in disgust.

'We'd best head upstairs,' Filip whispered and began climbing a wooden staircase.

The stairs felt spongey beneath Zofia's feet, and creaked and groaned disturbingly, but she made it upstairs safely and followed Filip from the dark hallway into a room on the left. It was unexpectedly bright in here, but looking up, Zofia saw that a section of the roof was missing, letting in the silver moonlight. Her gaze swept the room. A small pile of books stood in a corner, and several filthy cups stood on an upturned wooden crate. At the far wall, there were four filthy mattresses with crumpled blankets, beside them a newspaper, some empty bottles and several candle stubs. A thin sheet hung as a makeshift curtain at the window. It looked as though someone had been living here not too long ago.

They both stood there for a moment, their breaths forming clouds in the air. Zofia's damp skin was uncomfortably clammy.

Filip looked at the mattresses. 'We'll have to spend the night here.'

'You must be joking!'

'Come here, take a look.' He crossed over to the window and crouched down before pulling the curtain back a little. 'See?'

Zofia joined him and looked out. There, on the corner, were a couple of soldiers, talking and smoking. Further along the street, a group of them marched purposefully down Karmelicka Road, towards the entrance to the sewer Zofia and Lina had planned to take the children through.

'They're out in force tonight,' Filip said quietly. 'And not just on the streets. They're patrolling the sewers, and the courthouse, and the tram depot.'

'But those—' Zofia's mouth was suddenly as dry as sandpaper. 'But those are the routes we use to smuggle the children. How do they know?'

Even before she stopped speaking, she knew the answer to her question. Someone had betrayed them and her eyes widened in disbelief. Filip pointed at her, then at himself.

'You knew of tonight's operation. So did I. Irena, too, of course.'

'And … Lina?' Zofia whispered. 'But surely, she can't…' Her words trailed off.

191

'I was delivering some photographs to the Commandant General's office this morning and overheard the adjutant discussing the patrols. They were planning to step them up tonight. I informed Jolanta immediately.'

'But why didn't she tell me? She almost let me walk right into their trap!'

Filip sniffed and lowered his head. 'She knew it was either you or Lina.'

Zofia swallowed, caught between feelings of anger and disappointment and disbelief. How could Irena possibly have thought that of her?

'But if they'd caught me, I might have been shot on sight. Does Irena really think I am that expendable?'

Filip leaned closer, so she could feel his breath on her face. 'You know Irena better than that,' he said. 'This was not a decision she took lightly. But she had to be sure. And I was watching out for you. As soon as I saw you in the ghetto, I knew you couldn't be the traitor.'

'I can't believe Lina betrayed us,' Zofia said quietly. Her head was spinning and time felt as though it was standing still. Lina was her friend, her comrade. The thought made her nauseous.

Then, unexpectedly, Filip put his arms around her and drew her into a tight embrace. His entire body was trembling and she realised that she wasn't the only one whose emotions were so close to the surface. Everyone in the resistance lived in constant terror of being found out, and their nerves were frayed beyond belief. She leaned into the embrace, glad for the warmth and strength of Filip's body, and sobbed openly.

After a long while, when her tears had subsided, Filip straightened up and went to the mattresses at the other side of the room. He picked up a blanket and shook it; thousands of dust motes flew up into the air, dancing on a beam of moonlight that streamed in through the window.

He's serious, Zofia thought. They were going to sleep here. She turned and cast another glance out of the window. More soldiers had turned up; they were swarming the place now. Zofia shivered involuntarily. Getting safely out of the ghetto would be impossible tonight, pass or no pass. And if Filip hadn't come for her, she would have been caught.

'Are we safe here?' she asked.

'Safer in here than outside, at any rate,' Filip replied, shaking out a second blanket. 'We've got enough blankets, so at least we won't have to worry about freezing to death.' He gave her a shy smile. 'Can't promise you any breakfast in the morning, though.'

It was still dark when Zofia woke. The air was freezing; dawn was still hours away and it was completely silent outside, just the lone hoot of an owl disturbing the perfect quiet. Zofia looked up towards the gap in the roof to see the sky pinpricked with stars. For a long moment, she gazed at them, wondering if it was possible to read her fate there, then chided herself for her naivety and turned towards Filip. He was lying on his side, eyes closed and his long, dark eyelashes resting on his cheeks. His breathing was regular, though every now and again, his body twitched. He wasn't a beautiful man, Zofia thought, not in the way Jakub was, with his muscular build and hazel eyes. Filip's nose was rather large, and he didn't have Jakub's plump lips and winning smile. Zofia chided herself for her shallow thoughts. Filip was a good man. He had saved her life.

Where is Jakub tonight? she thought then. He was supposed to have given her the signal. If he had, she would have turned down Wiezienna Road, then onto Pawia Street, where she would have been right in the open for several minutes, making her ripe pickings for any German patrol. Suddenly, the fear she'd felt earlier rose up inside her violently and it took her some effort to dispel it. She took a few deep breaths. Irena would have warned Jakub, that was why he didn't come.

Beside her, Filip twitched again. A bad dream, presumably. Zofia had had plenty of those. She watched him for a while until she felt her own eyes grow heavy. Then she reached out and slipped her hand into his, and fell back into a shallow, fitful sleep.

21

Warsaw, December 1942

At home, Zofia took off her shoes at the door and slipped into the kitchen. Although she felt frozen through, she washed her hands, arms and face with icy water, wincing at the sting of the carbolic soap on her chafed skin. Then she crept silently up the stairs, avoiding the squeaky treads she knew might give her away. It was still pitch dark; it would be several hours before the early morning light would seep into the house through the small, latticed window on the landing.

Filip had woken her by gently shaking her shoulder. He'd said he had to leave because his pass, in contrast to hers, was issued daily and it was too risky to try one of the checkpoints.

'How are you going to get out?' she'd asked, her voice still thick with sleep.

'There's a gap in the north side of the wall on Mławska Road. It'll be a squeeze to get through, but it's my best bet.'

Zofia hadn't wanted to be left there alone, so she had insisted she would go with him. Together, they had made their way through the ghostly quiet streets, their footsteps unnaturally loud on the frozen ground. But Filip evidently knew the ghetto like the back of his hand, and after a short ten-minute walk they had come to a hidden gap in the ghetto wall and slid through easily. They had parted wordlessly.

On the landing, she gently pressed down the doorhandle to her and Zuzanna's room and entered. Her sister lay on her bed, turned towards the wall. Zofia waited a few seconds to make sure her breathing was slow and regular, and then went to slip beneath the covers of her own bed. Her limbs ached after the restless night on the cold, hard mattress, and the anxiety of sleeping in unfamiliar and dangerous surroundings. But just as she closed her eyes, hoping to get at least another hour's sleep before getting up for work, she heard the squeak of springs from Zuzanna's bed.

'I'm not stupid,' Zuzanna said, turning to face her. 'I know you've been out all night.'

'Shhh, *Żabka*,' Zofia said quietly. 'You'll wake Mama and Papa.'

'Don't call me that. I'm not a little frog, and I'm certainly not a baby.' Her tone was laced with indignance.

'Sorry.'

Zuzanna waited a moment, then said, 'So, where have you been?'

Zofia just shook her head. Of all the things to share with her sister, this was the most impossible. It wasn't that she didn't trust her; she needed to keep it a secret in order to protect her.

Zuzanna sat up. 'Tell me or I'll tell them you've been out all night.'

'I can't,' Zofia insisted. 'I'm sorry, and I hate keeping things from you, believe me. But you mustn't tell them, please.'

Zuzanna gave her a long stare. 'You've been helping people in the ghetto.'

'Zuzanna, no … I—'

'I saw you. A few weeks ago, on Grzybowska Street. You were coming through the checkpoint and you were wearing a nurse's uniform. But you're not a nurse, are you?'

Zofia opened her mouth to deny it, but then shook her head. 'No, I'm not.'

Zuzanna got out of bed and came over, sliding under the blanket beside her. Her eyes were alive with excitement. 'Do you bring them food? Medicines? You can confide in me, you know. I won't tell a soul, I swear.'

A thousand thoughts tumbled around in Zofia's mind. So her sister knew part of her secret; Zofia couldn't deny she'd been in and out of the ghetto in a uniform. But she couldn't tell her the truth, it would put her at risk.

'I can't talk about it, *Żabka*,' she said. 'All I can say is that you must never, ever tell anyone you saw me. Promise me.'

To Zofia's surprise, Zuzanna beamed and took her in a tight hug. 'I'm so proud of you, Zofia!' Then she dropped her arms and her face turned serious. 'I only wish I could do something, too.'

Zofia took her hand and squeezed gently. 'I know how brave you are, Zuzanna. And I understand how badly you want to help. But the best way you can help is to keep silent about what you know.'

Zuzanna looked down glumly.

'Promise me, Zuzanna,' Zofia said. 'Promise me you won't breathe a word of this to anyone.'

Her sister nodded, just as the door opened. It was their mother.

'Good morning, girls. You're both up early!' She crossed the room and pulled open the curtains. 'It looks like another chilly day. But the forecast is for sunshine, so it's not all bad.'

Zofia and Zuzanna exchanged a silent look, then got out of bed and headed downstairs for breakfast.

At the office, Zofia couldn't concentrate on a single thing. She had managed to file three reports in the wrong cabinet, while Lina kept up an uninterrupted stream of chatter, telling her and Elżbieta about a hosiery she'd discovered that sold cheap silk stockings, her and her family's plans for Christmas Eve, and the entire plot of a novel she had recently read. Zofia found it excruciating. How could Lina behave as though nothing had happened? Was she really that good an actress? Or was she talking so much to cover her nerves?

During the course of the morning, however, Zofia began having doubts. Perhaps Lina was as innocent as she was. The Nazis had other spies, she was certain of it; or perhaps it was only a coincidence that they had stepped up their patrols last night. They might even have been trying to prevent a different operation altogether – there were a whole host of black market activities going on in the ghetto, many of them highly sophisticated.

When lunchtime came around and it was time for their break, Elżbieta wordlessly slipped her a message. Zofia frowned and opened her mouth to ask who it was from, but Elżbieta gave her head a tiny shake and put a finger to her lips, her meaning clear: *don't speak*. Zofia unfolded the piece of paper.

Dear Zofia, I hope this finds you well. It is such a wonderful sunny day, I thought you might like to join me for a walk in the Saxon Garden. Please make sure to bring your blonde friend! Kindest regards, Jolanta

Zofia read Irena's message twice and her hands began to shake. Irena was asking her to bring Lina to the park. She walked over to Lina's desk, where she was taking a paper-wrapped sandwich out of her bag and setting it on the table.

'I fancy a little walk,' Zofia said, trying to keep her tone casual. 'How about we take our sandwiches to the Saxon Garden? The sun's out, and it's too lovely outside to stay cooped up in here.'

Lina looked up at her. 'Um, I'm not sure. Will we have enough time to get there and back?'

'It's only a ten-minute bicycle ride. We'll have plenty of time.'

'I thought you fancied a walk?'

Zofia cleared her throat. 'Oh, yes, what I meant was, we could bike if you are worried about the time. And anyway, do you really want to spend your lunch break in here?'

They cycled for ten minutes, Zofia setting a fast pace, pushing down hard on the pedals. The icy air was painful in her lungs, but she wanted to avoid talking to Lina.

Once they had reached the Saxon Garden, they got off their bikes and pushed them, white billows of frosty breath escaping their mouths. The pine trees stood rigidly, sharp with frost. As they walked along the small gravel path, Zofia glanced around. Where was Irena?

At a small clearing that featured a marble sundial, Lina stopped. 'This is a nice spot,' she said. 'And we don't have too much more time.'

'Yes, I suppose so.' Zofia's heart was beating uncomfortably in her chest. She hated lying to her friend like this. *But Lina may well be a traitor,* she reminded herself.

They sat down on a bench facing the water feature. Nearby, a group of school children stood in a circle, while their teacher explained something about the naked trees and the cycle of life.

'You're very quiet today,' Lina said, startling her out of her thoughts.

'Um, yes, I—' She stopped as a figure suddenly appeared in front of them. It was a man Zofia recognised from the social club, but she couldn't recall his name. He leaned in towards Lina.

'Irena wants to speak to you,' he said gruffly. 'Now.'

Lina lowered her hand to her lap, a flicker of panic in her eyes. Her sandwich had a perfect semi-circle of teeth marks on it.

'Does she?' she asked. 'Whatever for?'

Her voice sounded strangled, as though she were squeezing the words out, and all of a sudden, her hands started trembling violently.

'Come on,' the man said, cupping her arm and pulling her to her feet. Her face was as white as a ghost.

'Zofia?' she said, staring at her with a puzzled and frightened look. 'Is this why you brought me here?'

I'm sorry, Zofia almost replied, but she stopped herself. Lina was a traitor. She had risked Zofia's life – and that of innocent children. She lifted her chin defiantly. Anything that happened now was the result of Lina's own actions.

'Where are you taking me?' Lina asked the man, but he didn't respond. He tugged her forward, making her almost lose her footing on the tufty grass.

One of the school children turned his head towards them, but the man smiled and waved at him. The child waved back. If Lina decided to start screaming now, there were plenty of people to come to her rescue. But she didn't.

Zofia followed them, wordlessly. She didn't know where they were going, and what was going to happen now. She wasn't sure she wanted to know. The man marched Lina towards a small, wooden structure behind a copse of trees. They had left the main area of the public park and there was no one else around. The man turned to Zofia.

'Open the door,' he said, and she did as he asked, turning the metal knob and pushing it open. The wood was warped and groaned as the door moved. It took a few seconds for Zofia's eyes to adjust to the gloom and at first, she could only make out a figure.

'Thank you, Zofia,' a voice said. 'This can't have been easy for you.'

It was Irena. She stepped forward into the light that shone in through the door, just as the man and Lina entered.

'Come in,' Irena said. 'Lina, please sit.' She pointed to a wooden crate in the centre of the shed. It was a small, dark space with gardening tools hanging from nails on the walls, and a rusty-looking lawnmower in the corner. The shed had the sweetish, mushroomy smell of composted leaves and grass.

'Irena,' Lina said, her voice threatening to break with tears. 'It's not what you think … I didn't … you have to understand, I—'

'She told you to sit down,' the man said brusquely and pushed Lina forward. She let out a frightened sob but lowered herself onto the crate.

'Marek,' Irena said softly, 'there is no need for that.'

In an instant, Zofia realised he was the man who had brought the music the night she went to her first resistance meeting. She had discovered since then that Marek was Helena's cousin and had been a member of the resistance almost as long as Irena. He was an expert forger and had created hundreds of false identity documents for Jews who had managed to flee the ghetto. Zofia saw him clench and unclench his fists. *He must be terrified for Helena's safety*, she thought, *and angry beyond belief at the betrayal by one of our own.*

'Lina,' Irena said, and her tone was soft but firm. 'Did you betray us?'

Lina gave a barely perceptible nod and let out a small, mewling sound, like a frightened kitten. Then she broke down completely, falling forwards onto her knees on the cold ground, her body racked with huge, heaving sobs. Her distress was so genuine, Zofia could barely watch.

Irena also seemed greatly affected by this display of raw emotion. She took an unsteady breath and began to wring her hands. She seemed torn between wanting to comfort Lina and wanting to hurt her for what she had done.

Zofia looked away. Lina's wretched sobs continued unabated inside the small shed, and suddenly, it struck Zofia that she might just be crying for herself. Not for Helena, not

202

for putting Zofia and Filip and Jakub and a dozen innocent children in harm's way. An enormous wave of rage rose up inside her and she couldn't keep it inside.

'But why did you do it?' she shouted at her.

Irena flashed her look to say, *Keep your voice down*.

Zofia took a deep breath and tried to calm herself. 'Why, Lina? Why would you possibly work for those monsters?'

Lina looked up, her mascara running in streaks down her face. 'They … they threatened my family,' she said between sobs. 'My brother was caught chopping wood in Las Bielański forest several weeks ago. Firewood, for heating. He knows it's illegal, but one of my sisters almost died from pneumonia last year, and he was desperate to help. He went during the night, thought he'd be safe in the dark. But two German soldiers discovered him and took him into custody. When they found out I worked at the Welfare Department, they summoned me.'

Marek took a step forward. 'How much do they know?' he barked.

Lina shook her head. 'I don't know. They haven't got any names, they just suspect that the Jews are getting help from our department. They don't know who is involved.' She looked up at Irena, then at Zofia. Her eyes were huge and wild with fear. 'I didn't give them any details,' she said. 'I just … I just told them I'd heard about escapes. That Jewish children were being smuggled out.'

'How could you, Lina?' Zofia said, struggling to keep her voice down. 'I was there last night, waiting for you to arrive with the children. There were hundreds of German soldiers on the streets. I could have been caught!'

'I didn't have any choice! They would have arrested my whole family, and then…' She didn't finish the sentence.

'Come on, Lina, let's get you up off the cold floor.' Irena held out her hand and helped Lina back onto the crate. For several minutes, Lina just sat there, drawing long shuddering breaths.

'Who do you report to?' Irena asked when she had calmed down a little.

Lina pressed her lips together and shook her head a fraction. Irena crouched down beside her. 'You are frightened, I know. But we need to know everything. Are there any other spies among us?'

Marek took a step forward. His rage was simmering just beneath the surface, but Zofia could also see a deep sadness in his eyes. She understood how he felt. There was something profoundly upsetting about knowing a trusted friend had betrayed you.

'I'll get the truth out of her,' he said, his voice barely a growl.

But Irena stood up to face him, forming a barrier between him and Lina. 'There's no need for that,' she hissed angrily. 'Absolutely no need at all. That is not who we are!'

Zofia had never seen Irena so angry, and Marek seemed equally surprised by her ferocity. He backed away and went to stand by the door, his jaw clenched.

Irena crouched down again. 'Lina, I promise you will come to no harm if you tell the truth. But there is no going back for you now. You must tell us everything, starting with your contacts. Who do you supply the information to?'

Lina shivered and squeezed her eyes shut for a moment. Then she swallowed and said, very quietly, 'Jakub.'

22

Warsaw, Present Day

'What a delightful old lady,' Roksana said as they emerged from the metro station and made their way down Marszalkowska Avenue.

'Yes,' Zofia agreed. 'I'm so glad that we found her. Well, that *you* found her. Thanks, Roksana.'

Roksana shrugged. 'You're welcome.'

'And even if she couldn't tell me more about my great-grandmother, just talking to her was worth my trip over here.'

'I'm glad. Hey, you fancy an ice-cream? There's a stall up here. The best in town.' Roksana smiled broadly.

'Sure,' Lizzie said, and they walked further up the street to a tree-lined square. Right in the centre was a stall with a colourful marquee. There was a long queue, but Roksana swore it was worth the wait. They joined the line and Lizzie looked around. A group of teenage boys were showing off their skateboarding skills, while several girls were filming them and making jokes. Lizzie smiled as she watched them. *They're the same all over the world*, she thought.

Further along, twenty or so younger children sat cross-legged on a patch of grass, listening to a young woman speaking. It looked to be a teacher with her primary school class. The young woman was pointing at various things – a tree, a building, a statue – and asking questions. When a boy raised his hand and gave what appeared to be the right answer, the teacher nodded and clapped, making the boy smile proudly from ear to ear.

Lizzie felt a tender ache in her heart. How could she ever have considered leaving her teaching job? Working with children was the most fulfilling job she could ever have imagined, and for the first time in ages, she thought fondly of going back to work after the summer vacation. She only hoped she would return from this trip feeling a little stronger. However untethered she had felt in recent months, she had the unmistakable feeling that she was gradually beginning to heal.

On a low wall nearby sat a family of four, with the Palace of Culture and Science stretching up into the satin-blue sky behind them. The daughter held a selfie stick out in front of her and instructed everyone to smile.

Lizzie let out a gasp, making Roksana turn. 'The photo!'

'What photo?'

'I forgot to show Mrs Zielińska the photograph, the one I found in the attic back home.' Lizzie looked back down the street towards the metro station. 'Do you think we can go back quickly?'

Roksana pulled the corners of her mouth down. 'She's probably taking a nap, and if she's anything like my grandmother, she won't want to be disturbed. But listen—' She pulled her phone out. 'Why don't I give you Tomasz's number and you can call him later? Maybe we can go back tomorrow.'

Feeling a little disappointed and annoyed at herself for forgetting the photo, Lizzie typed Tomasz's number into her own phone.

'Thanks, Roksana,' she said. 'I owe you.'

Roksana smiled as they nudged a little further along the queue. 'You're very welcome. I don't come across such interesting family histories every day, you know. It's a shame my family tree doesn't stretch back across the ocean, because then I'd have a reason to fly over and visit you in Seattle.'

Lizzie laughed. 'Are you kidding? You're welcome to visit me any time! With or without a family tree.'

'You know what?' Roksana said. 'I might just do that.'

They had reached the front of the queue.

'Now, what'll you have? They have a peanut butter ice-cream that's to die for.'

Lizzie's phone rang just as she opened the door to her hotel room.

'Good morning, sweetheart. It's your mom.'

'Hi, Mom. And it's afternoon here.'

'Oh, of course. I forgot. Anyway, just checking in to see how you're doing.'

'I'm fine. We just went to visit this old lady, and—'

'We?'

'Yeah, this journalist I told you about, the one I'd emailed from Seattle. Roksana. She's lovely.'

'That's nice.'

'Anyway, we've just been to see this old lady, Mrs Zielińska. Mom, you'll never believe this, but she actually knew *Prababcia*!'

'You're kidding me.'

'No, and get this – Zofia saved her life by smuggling her out of the ghetto! Mrs Zielińska called her an "angel". She remembers her to this day. I mean, she's over eighty now.'

'Oh, Lizzie, that's amazing! I was talking to your grandmother about this yesterday when I visited.'

'Really?'

'Yes. In fact, I think you might have stirred something up.'

'Oh, I'm sorry, I didn't mean to upset her.'

'No! I meant that in a good way. In fact, she seems really excited about your whole Warsaw trip. You know, she's never liked to talk about her past, but I think she's coming to realise that it isn't just *her* past. It belongs to the whole family. Her being adopted doesn't mean our family tree is somehow broken, or wrong. The roots are just as strong, only different.' She paused. 'Does that make sense?'

Lizzie smiled to herself. She felt a stillness inside her, as though she had been rescued from a stormy sea and tethered in a calm port. 'Perfect sense.'

'By the way, Alex called yesterday.'

The feeling of stillness dissolved instantly and was replaced by an odd sensation of guilt and longing. Unbidden, a memory of their last argument came to her, in which he'd accused her of closing herself off from him, saying that he could only help her if she let him in. She'd tried to explain that it wasn't a choice. If she let him in, she would be letting in all of the pain, too. But he couldn't – wouldn't – understand her, and when she had suggested taking some time apart, he had let her leave without a word of protest. For a while she had tried to come to terms with the thought that this could mean the end of her marriage. But over the past few days, she'd realised how much she missed him, how much she still needed him in her life. The time to talk to him would come, she was sure about that, but it wasn't now, not while she was here in Warsaw. For a long moment, she didn't speak.

'Lizzie? You still there?'

'Yeah.'

'I wasn't sure whether to tell you. He was asking after you, said you're not answering his messages.'

Lizzie cleared her throat. 'Listen, Mom—'

'I know, I know, it's none of my business. And I didn't tell him you're out of town. All I said was I'd pass it on that he called. And I've done that now.'

'Okay.'

'But, sweetheart, don't you think it's time you and Alex talked? I know how much you love each other.' She paused. 'You do still love him, don't you?'

Lizzie didn't hesitate a moment. 'Yeah, Mom. I do. Very much so.'

'Okay, well, I won't keep you. Just wanted to hear you're well.'

'I am, Mom. Bye now.'

23

Warsaw, December 1942

Like every other winter for the past few years, the icy cold affected Zuzanna badly. Her body was racked with coughs every few minutes and at night, her temperature rose to worrying heights. Their mother fretted terribly, cooking broth and oatmeal porridge to keep Zuzanna's strength up, and administering cool compresses around her calves to bring the fever down. Zofia helped where she could, cycling to the pharmacy to buy cough syrup, reading to her sister in the evenings, and keeping watch over her as she slept.

Yet all the while, her thoughts circled around the betrayal. Despite herself, she had some understanding for Lina's motives – what might she do if her own family were threatened? Lina had felt she had little choice, and had acted accordingly. The day after she had been exposed, she had handed in her notice to the Welfare Department and had gone to stay with an aunt and uncle who lived just outside Łódź. Irena was convinced she was no longer a threat, that she was genuinely contrite for what she had done. There had been some argument in the group, but Irena had remained insistent, saying that Lina would face a reckoning with God.

Jakub's betrayal, by contrast, cut Zofia more deeply than she would have liked to admit, and the romantic notions she had held about him now made her feel oddly shameful. How childishly pleased she had felt on the days she knew she would be seeing him! How his rakish smile had warmed her from the inside! But all along, he had only been trying to get close to her for information, the same way he had with Lina. He had probably known that Lina had a thing for him, making it easier to get her to do what he needed. And Zofia had almost fallen into the same trap. Now, she was left replaying conversations she'd had with him in her head; how he'd quizzed her for the dates and times of planned operations, asking how many children they were taking, whether they were planning to use the courthouse, underground passages, ambulances. It also now made sense that he had always known so much about the Germans' movements, and it was clear now that some of the intelligence he had been feeding them had been flawed.

The ripples of Lina and Jakub's treacherous actions continued to make large waves. Sources had told Irena that the Germans had been furious when they had discovered children were being smuggled out under their very noses, and now it appeared they were determined to put a stop to any resistance activities. They had begun patrolling the ghetto more heavily than ever, and not just during the day. Zofia had been in twice this week to visit Julia, and her neighbours had informed her that there were groups of Nazi soldiers out every night, roaming the streets, 'like the rats they are'. There were also alarming reports of random arrests and people being shot on the street.

Zofia didn't know what had become of Jakub, other than that Żegota would never have allowed him to walk away, if only for reasons of self-preservation. He knew things about the resistance – its members, codenames, modes of operation – that would amount to a death sentence for many of them if the Germans found out. Part of Zofia hoped he was facing the same terrible fate he had inflicted on Helena, that he would be locked up in a dark, damp hole somewhere, not knowing if this day would be his last. It was hard to suppress these thoughts, even though Zofia understood that holding on to them caused her bitterness. She knew she would feel that sting of betrayal for the rest of her life.

On a cold Tuesday evening, Zofia was at Irena's flat and the two women were discussing the way forward. The parents of the children they had tried to take out last time were desperate; most of them were waiting in anguish for the order to report to the *umschlagplatz* from where they would be deported to Treblinka, and they were anxious to get their children to safety beforehand.

For hours, Zofia and Irena had been poring over a map of the ghetto, coming up with ever more elaborate ways to sneak through the area without being seen. The 'safe' nighttime routes – the sewers, the courthouse, the tram depot – were all compromised now, thanks to Lina and Jakub. Zofia once again felt the dull throb of anger inside her.

'It's hopeless,' Irena said finally with a loud sigh and threw her hands up. 'It can't be done.'

Zofia thought of Ola and Julia, who were never far from her mind, now. It was touch and go whether Julia would survive the week. Her neighbours had been lovingly caring for her, day and night, but there was very little they could do, other than placing a cold, damp towel on her forehead to try to reduce the fever, or keeping Ola occupied. *The poor child*, Zofia thought. She would soon be an orphan. It was now six weeks since she had met Julia and Ola in the youth centre, but it seemed much longer – or rather, the relationship she'd formed with them reflected something far deeper than a mere acquaintance. She drummed her fingertips on the map in front of her. She couldn't help Julia, but she could try to ensure her daughter had a future.

'But we can't leave the children in there to die! They are relying on us. We have to do something.' She leaned forward in her chair. 'There's only one option. I will have to move them during the day.'

'What?' Irena looked stunned. 'That's madness! How can you possibly take twenty-five children out single-handedly in broad daylight?'

'I won't be on my own,' Zofia said. 'I will ask Filip, I'm sure he will help me.'

'Filip?'

'I know he's been more of a – how shall I put it? – a quiet supporter of the movement so far. Documenting the suffering in the ghetto with his camera. That's where I first met him.'

She recalled the afternoon with Julia and Ola when Filip took their picture. Then she remembered the warmth of his hand in hers that night they were trapped in the ghetto, and felt the pounding of anger inside her dampen down. She was still capable of positive feelings.

'When I was in the ghetto that night, after Lina's betrayal,' she continued, 'he saved me. He didn't have to, he was risking his own life. But I realised how much the situation is affecting him, too.'

'I didn't know,' Irena said.

'He is as brave as any of us. I know he will want to help.' She cleared her throat. 'And if I can't smuggle the children out at night, then I have no choice. I'll have to take them during the day.'

Zofia and Elżbieta spent three nights sewing school uniforms. They were planning to smuggle the children out through the courthouse, and then dress them as pupils from a Catholic school, enabling them to blend in on the Aryan side. Zofia couldn't take the children through the checkpoint, for obvious reasons. Even if Żegota managed to make enough forged documents, there was no plausible explanation for leading a group of children through a ghetto gate. Some Jewish workers were granted passes for forced labour in factories that lay beyond the ghetto walls, but they were mostly adult men.

'You're completely mad, you know that,' Elżbieta said, pumping the treadle of the Singer machine with her foot.

They were sitting in Elżbieta's kitchen, in the flat she shared with her elderly aunt, each with a steaming cup of tea in front of them. They had been working for three hours now, a comfortable warmth coming from the tiled oven close by. The rhythmic *tack-tack* sound of the sewing machine was hypnotic, causing Zofia to feel heavy.

She sighed. 'I know.'

'But for what it's worth, I think you are terribly brave.'

Zofia reddened. If Elżbieta only knew how many times she had come close to giving up, how many nights she'd lain awake planning to tell Irena she wasn't up to it.

She cleared her throat. 'We have to get as many children as possible out of that hell,' she said. 'It just breaks my heart for the ones we have to separate from their parents.'

She lifted the needle and snipped a thread. Another pair of trousers finished. Tomorrow at three o'clock she would be collecting eighteen children from the orphanage on Sienna Road; Filip would fetch the Joselewicz twins and three other children from their parents. That made twenty-four children.

Ola was number twenty-five.

Elżbieta lifted her arms above her head and stretched. 'There, I think that's it.' She stood up and began folding the skirt she had been sewing. 'Let's hope the uniforms fit.'

'That's the least of my worries,' Zofia said quietly and plucked a stray thread from the fabric in front of her.

The cover story was that she and Filip were teachers taking the children out on an excursion. That way, they could move around the ghetto in a group and make their way to the courthouse, where the children would change into the uniforms and then emerge as 'Polish' children on the other side. It was a huge risk moving such a large group during the daytime, but with the Germans now patrolling the ghetto in force, any nighttime operations were impossible. It was the only way, but it troubled Zofia deeply that there were so many unknowns – would they even be allowed inside the courthouse? What if they were caught changing into the uniforms? Filip had never been involved in any smuggling operations – what if he wasn't up to the task? And, most troubling of all, was he really

215

trustworthy? In her heart, Zofia felt sure of it, but then she had trusted Lina and Jakub, hadn't she? And they had turned out to be traitors.

'Would you like to stay for supper?' Elżbieta asked, breaking into her thoughts. 'I have some bread – though it's rather stale, I'm afraid – and some plum jam my aunt made. It's really quite good.'

Zofia turned to look out of the window. It had snowed and the temperature was below freezing now, turning the pavements into ice rinks. It would be a slow and slippery walk home.

'Thanks for the offer,' she said with a sigh. 'But I'd better be on my way. My parents will be waiting.'

Elżbieta tilted her head to one side. 'What have you told them?'

'That you and I are making clothes for children the Department supports.' She pulled a face. 'It's as close to the truth as I can make it, but I'd feel guilty stretching the truth any further. I'm fairly sure they know that something is going on.'

Elżbieta nodded and began to tidy up the remaining buttons on the table. 'It is awful, all of this deception. I've stopped counting the number of lies I've told my aunt. It certainly keeps me busy in the confessional every Sunday.' She attempted a smile that faded again quickly. 'But never forget who is responsible for this. One day, this will be over, and then every one of them will be held accountable.'

One day. But who knew how far that day lay in the future? And what might happen before then? Zofia began to get to her feet, realising how tired she was.

'Here, before you leave, let's get you warmed up inside,' Elżbieta said, fetching a bottle of rum from a kitchen cabinet and pouring a glug into Zofia's teacup. 'It's freezing out there.'

Zofia smiled and sat back down. She took a sip of tea and rum, feeling the warmth from the alcohol making its way down her throat and into her bloodstream. It felt good. Elżbieta was right, it was just what she needed before heading out into the freezing cold. Then she noticed Elżbieta staring at her.

'What?' she asked, smiling.

'This man, Filip.'

Zofia's smile dropped from her face and heart did a fearful little jolt. 'What about him? Is he not to be trusted? Elżbieta, you must tell me if you know something.'

Elżbieta raised her hands. 'No! I don't know him at all. And I've certainly never heard anything untoward about him.' She let out a soft laugh. 'It's just…'

'What?'

'The way you've spoken about him over the last few days is quite … tender, if I may say so.'

Zofia felt herself blushing and looked down. It was the rum, she told herself.

'Oh, no, well … he saved my life. You see … that night in the ghetto, he really did save me.' She stopped when she noticed she was rambling. That must be the rum, too.

'I'm sorry,' Elżbieta said kindly. 'I didn't mean to pry.' She reached out and placed a hand on Zofia's. 'But if I might just say one thing? If you like him, let him know. If all of this has taught me anything, it is that we shouldn't waste the precious time we have on this planet.'

24

Warsaw, December 1942

It had stopped snowing and the temperature had risen to a few degrees above freezing, turning the old snow into grey slush. Zofia entered the ghetto with her pass, feeling strangely calm. She wore her winter coat and thick woollen stockings that scratched her skin, but they kept her legs warm. The uniforms she and Elżbieta had spent so many hours making had been smuggled in yesterday in a hearse, hidden inside a coffin. It was one of many ways of smuggling goods into the ghetto, and the Nazis were by now well aware of it, but it seemed they were still concentrating on nighttime activities, and Zofia had received word from the orphanage that the uniforms had arrived safely.

The first child Zofia went to collect was Ola. The neighbours, Mr and Mrs Friedman, had dressed her in as many layers of clothes as they could find.

'So you stay nice and warm on your day out with Miss Szczesny,' Sara Friedman said, fastening the buttons on Ola's coat.

Ola looked up at Zofia and gave her a dimpled smile. Zofia wondered how much the girl had been told. She glanced at Mr Friedman.

'Julia is sleeping,' he said quietly. 'We thought about waking her, so she could say a final goodbye, but...' He couldn't finish the sentence and looked down at the floor, his lip quivering.

Zofia put a hand on his arm and squeezed gently. 'I think that's best. I will ... I will return when the girl is in safe hands.'

Ola let Sara wind a woollen scarf around her neck and came up to Zofia.

'Do you have chocolate with you? Are we going on a trip? Have you ever been to the zoo? I never have but I'd like to go because there's elephants in my favourite picture book and I'd very much like to see a real one.'

Zofia smiled. 'I have been to the zoo before, and I saw some real elephants. Perhaps we might go to the zoo together one day.'

'Today?'

'No, sweetheart. The zoo closed a few years ago. But when it reopens, I promise I will take you.'

Ola pulled her eyebrows together in contemplation. Then she gave a sharp nod of her head. 'All right,' she said earnestly. 'We shall go when the zoo opens again.'

Zofia held out her hand. 'Come on then, sweetheart. We must go or we'll be late.'

Ola reached up and took her hand. On the way out, she turned back to Sara Friedman.

'Please give Mama a kiss from me when she wakes up. I will try and bring her something back from my outing if I can.'

219

Sara let out a strangled sob and ran inside, her husband following a moment later.

They arrived at the orphanage with several minutes to spare. Zofia had told Ola they were collecting some more children for the outing, which seemed to please Ola greatly.

'I'll make lots of new friends,' she said excitedly. 'Then we might *all* go to the zoo when it opens again.'

The poor child has no idea what is happening, Zofia thought, and had to resist an urge to hold the girl, tight, and never let her go. Zofia did her best to put Julia to the back of her mind. She had to – if she didn't, she would go mad with guilt.

A few minutes later, she saw Filip approaching from a distance, that look of gentle concern on his face. He had his camera bag slung around his shoulder, and he was holding hands with the Joselewicz twins. The three older children were right behind him. Zofia's thoughts turned to Elżbieta's words the previous night. *If you like him, let him know.* But did she like him? In that way?

'Everything all right?' he asked.

'Everything is going to plan, so far.'

He gave her a relieved smile, and she knew then that, yes, she had come to like him. She cleared her throat. There was no time for such things now.

'We mustn't linger,' she said. 'Accompanying such a large group of children can be demanding at the best of times.'

'And this isn't the best of times.'

Zofia shook her head. 'No.'

Together, they headed into the orphanage. The staff had been saying tearful goodbyes to their charges. They had been caring for some of the children since they were babies; others had come to the orphanage after their parents had been deported to Treblinka. When one of the smaller boys became inconsolable, refusing to leave the arms of an elderly nurse, Zofia opened her bag. She had spent the morning making chocolate treats by melting a large bar and dripping it in small circles onto greaseproof paper. She hoped the chocolate buttons might sweeten the children's farewell from all they knew; even if the conditions in which they had been living were awful, they were looked after by people who cared for them.

'Here, darling,' she said, holding out the bag of treats.

The boy looked at the chocolate suspiciously at first, but when the other children crowded around and began taking one each, the boy reluctantly let go of the nurse and came towards Zofia.

The twenty-five children she and Filip led along the street were aged between four and twelve. Zofia had paired them up so that an older child each held the hand of a younger child, and they all carried small knapsacks containing their uniforms. Zofia held Ola's hand and Filip walked alone at the back of the group. Zofia would have liked him to walk beside her, not least because the closer they came to the courthouse, the more her nerves began to tingle. She could feel the adrenaline coursing through her and would have welcomed Filip's conversation as a distraction. They marched in this manner along the streets, Zofia thankful that the temperature was a little milder today, and that the sharp, icy winds of the last few days had fallen away. On the other side of the ghetto walls, the Polish children would be taking part in similar processions, but they would be carrying torches and lanterns in honour of St. Nicholas, and would be looking forward to returning to a warm home and loving parents. *They certainly are not facing the uncertain future of these children here*, Zofia thought. If they were facing any future at all.

The group stopped on the corner to Krochmalna Street and Filip made his way to Zofia at the front.

'We're coming up to the bridge,' he said. Then he turned to the children, most of whom had long stopped holding hands with their assigned partner and now formed a higgledy-piggledy group.

'Um, perhaps you might want to get back into pairs,' Filip told them. 'Because … when we cross the bridge, we don't … we can't…'

Zofia had noticed that he was a little awkward around the children, as though he didn't quite know how to talk to them. For a brief moment, she recalled how naturally Jakub had played with the children at the youth centre, and with a dark sense of shame she remembered she had found that attractive about him. And yet he had happily risked those very same children being captured and murdered by the Nazis. She shook the thought off.

'Everyone get into line, now,' she told the chattering children, sparing Filip's blushes. The children obeyed and they made their way along Chłodna Street to a wooden bridge that formed a link between the 'small ghetto', as it was known, with the larger section of the ghetto in the north. Dozens of people were crossing the bridge, which had been built at a two-storey height to allow for trams and buses to pass below. The bridge appeared to creak and wobble as people crossed and Zofia looked up with concern, hoping none of the children were afraid of heights.

Filip noticed her hesitation.

'It will be fine,' he said encouragingly. 'I've crossed the bridge many times before and it's sturdier than it looks.' He smiled at her. 'I'll go first.'

He began to climb the steps and Zofia told the children to follow him. It was a squeeze, as the large number of steps – Zofia counted fifty-two – were effortful for people already suffering from malnutrition, and the pedestrians moved slowly. Four guards stood below them on the street, rifles slung around their shoulders. One of them glanced up to the bridge and shouted something to the people crossing above. Everyone looked down at their feet as they shuffled across the wooden bridge, trying to stay as inconspicuous as possible, desperate not to attract any attention and be dragged down to face a beating, or much worse. Zofia, Filip and the children crossed the bridge without incident and climbed down safely to the other side. Zofia kept her eyes left and right, constantly vigilant, but they didn't see a single Nazi soldier on this road. This was what every operation was like. A sequence of small trials to overcome, each presenting its own challenge and risk of being caught. One false step, one word said too loudly, one look in the wrong direction – that was all it took for an operation to fail. And the only way to see it through was to focus on each and every small challenge and be thankful if it succeeded.

As they turned a corner onto Ogrodowa Street, Zofia stopped short and let out a gasp. Ahead of her were two men pushing a handcart with the bodies of children inside. Those who had perished during the night were gathered up the next morning and taken to the cemetery at the north-western tip of the ghetto. Zofia had seen adult corpses being transported away, but never children. Their small, pale limbs flopped lifelessly about as the men tried to negotiate the uneven ground. It was a hideous, heart-breaking sight.

'Keep your eyes ahead, children,' Zofia called, tears choking her voice, but these children were so familiar with such sights – and worse – that they merely nodded wordlessly and continued walking.

Finally, they reached the courthouse on Leszno Street. Unlike the time she and Helena had taken the children during the night, the place was a hive of activity now. The steps leading up to the main entrance were crowded; a group of young people was standing there, chatting, and the large doors swung open and shut as people entered and left. Some ten metres from the entrance stood an old man churning thin, mournful sounds from a dilapidated barrel organ, a tin cup in front of him on the pavement.

They were about to cross the road when Zofia spotted two German soldiers heading for the building. She froze and gestured for the children to be quiet. There were constant patrols inside the ghetto, so it was inevitable that they would run across some guards, but as they had come this far without incident, she had hoped they would make it all the way without being stopped and questioned. The guards were walking towards the courthouse with long, purposeful strides and Zofia felt a sudden flash of fear. Had they been betrayed again? She looked around anxiously, wary of panicking the children. There was a crumbling brick wall several metres from where they stood, tall enough to hide the children if they crouched down. Filip seemed to have had the same thought. Quickly, they herded up the children and led them to the wall.

'Everyone get down, quickly,' Zofia told the children, adding, 'We're playing hide-and-seek.'

The children did as she asked, some of them giggling, others – older ones – looking at her with concern. She took a clumsy step to the side and slipped on an icy patch, falling onto the muddy ground.

Filip rushed to help her up. 'Are you all right?'

She nodded wordlessly, embarrassed more than anything. Other than a large smudge of mud on her coat, she hadn't hurt herself.

'Stay here,' Filip murmured, and crossed the street to head off the soldiers.

From her hiding place, Zofia watched as he approached them, gesturing towards his camera and saying something in a casual, friendly voice. The soldiers looked at each other and nodded. Then they took a few steps back and struck a pose in front of the courthouse. Filip took several snaps and thanked them profusely. Then he pointed towards the organ grinder and led them towards him. They were still very much in sight, but their backs were now turned to the wall behind which Zofia and the children were hiding. Filip took some more pictures and then one of the soldiers took out a pack of cigarettes and offered one to Filip. He accepted, and as he leaned forward to light it off the German's lighter, stole a glimpse at Zofia and nodded.

She understood the message. As she motioned for the children to start moving ahead, Filip kept the soldiers' attention distracted by taking his camera from his neck and showing them how to remove the lens. Zofia and the children crossed the street and reached the steps of the courthouse, just as the doors to the building swung open and a crowd of people surged out.

'Quickly,' Zofia said to the children, 'follow me.'

She pushed her way through the crowd, looking back over her shoulder every few seconds, terrified she would lose one of the children in the crush. When they entered the building, she did a quick headcount. Twenty-five children. Good. She felt a small weight lift from her shoulders. Now she had to keep her eyes open for the janitor, who would take them through the underground passage to the other side. It would be a different man than last time, Irena had told her. They had two janitors aiding the resistance, one on night shift, the other here during the day. Tonight, they were looking for a youngish man, Irena had said, mid-thirties with dusty-blond hair and a pronounced gap between his front teeth. Zofia craned her neck to look across the packed courthouse lobby. There was a stairwell curving up the left side of the space, beyond which, she knew from her last time here, a narrow set of steps led to the cellar.

It was busy in here, with dozens of people milling around, some standing in small groups, and others passing in and out through the doors. Across the hall, two men began to have an argument, their voices raised. People turned towards the commotion and Zofia prayed the noise wouldn't draw the attention of the Nazi soldiers they had seen outside. Then an old man dressed in black, with a long white beard and curls hanging from his temples, went over and began talking to the men. A rabbi. Zofia couldn't hear his exact words, but he spoke calmly, in a low and gentle monotone. Soon, the men

226

had calmed down and shook each other's hand. Zofia let out a long sigh. Crisis over.

Finally, Filip appeared beside her, just as the children were becoming restless.

'We shouldn't dawdle,' he said quietly. 'I didn't manage to get any details, but one of the soldiers mentioned that they'd been sent to the courthouse to keep their eyes open. He wouldn't say much more, but it might have been suspicious if I'd pressed him.'

'Thank you,' Zofia said. She reached out and touched his hand. 'It isn't the first time you've saved me.'

Filip looked down at her hand and then back up into her face. It was only a fleeting moment, but Zofia had the feeling that he saw deep inside her, and it was a warm, exhilarating feeling. Beside her, one of the children coughed, and their eye contact broke.

'There,' Filip said, looking over Zofia's shoulder. 'That looks like our man.'

She turned and saw the janitor; a youngish man with short, light hair and a blue janitor's overcoat. He glanced across at her and gave his head a little nod. Zofia turned to the children.

'This way, boys and girls,' she called, trying to keep her voice steady.

They passed quickly through the large hall, pushing their way through the groups of people. Thankfully, none of them gave Zofia, Filip and the children a second glance. When they reached the janitor, Zofia gave him the code words she'd received from Irena – *the mercury has risen* – and without another word, the janitor turned and led them around a corner into a smaller hallway. There, he unlocked a narrow door that led to the underground passage. Zofia told the children they would have to be very quiet down here and followed the janitor. Filip brought up the rear, closing the door behind him when he'd ensured they were all inside. They were enveloped in sudden darkness and one or two of the children let out a startled cry.

'Hush, children,' Zofia said softly. 'We're all very safe here, but we need to stay as quiet as mice. We haven't got far to go. Just stay together and hold your partner's hand.'

There were a few scuffles and giggles as the children bumped into one another in the dark, but soon their eyes became accustomed to the gloom. After a minute or so, a child suddenly grabbed Zofia's hand, evidently frightened. Zofia looked down and saw Ola, staring up at her with huge eyes. Her chin was trembling as she was trying not to cry.

'It's all right, sweetheart,' Zofia said gently. 'We'll be out on the other side very soon.'

When they had climbed safely up and down the stairs and reached the end of the passage, she instructed the children to change their clothes. Filip went back to the rear to make sure they hadn't been followed, while Zofia helped the younger children slip on their uniforms and button up their jackets.

'It's time,' the janitor said and opened the door.

Zofia stepped out onto Biała Street, her heart thrumming so hard she thought she might be sick. *Don't panic now*, she told herself as she blinked in the sudden brightness. *We've very nearly made it.*

The pavements were busy; busy enough for her group of children not to be all too conspicuous. She turned back, just about to beckon the children through the door and out onto the street, when she noticed something. Several of the children were wearing their armbands, marking them out as Jews. They were so accustomed to wearing them, they must have thought they needed to wear them over their uniforms. If they were caught like this on this side of the ghetto wall, it would be a disaster. This street was full of *smalcownicy*, Polish blackmailers who made a living from reporting any escape attempts to the Nazis.

Zofia ducked back inside and instructed the children to remove their armbands, then took them and stuffed them into her bag. She would burn them as soon as she had the chance.

'Now,' she whispered to the children, 'hold hands with your partner and keep very quiet. No talking until I say so.'

By the time they reached the Visitation Church, the children were quickly becoming irritable and tired. Up until now, they had been so well-behaved, Zofia marvelled as she and Filip led them through a wooden gate into the churchyard. It was as though even the youngest among them had understood the seriousness of the situation, that this operation was a matter of life or death. *Children should not have to consider such things*, she thought. It was too heavy a burden for them, and not for the first time, she wondered what this might do to their little souls, whether they would carry the scars of it for the rest of their lives. And yet, she told herself, at least they now had a chance to live.

Beside her, Filip was silent. Zofia turned to look at him. He had a serious expression on his face and he appeared preoccupied. Was he having the same thoughts about the children? Or perhaps, she caught herself thinking, about what a good team the two of them made?

Abruptly, Filip stopped walking. 'I have to leave,' he said.

Zofia nodded. It had been agreed that they should be in each other's company for the shortest time possible. Filip glanced down at her bag and frowned.

'What will you do with the armbands?'

'Take them home and burn them,' she replied.

He waited a moment, then said, 'It's probably best if I take them. I live alone, just on the outskirts, and I can dispose of them in the forest without drawing attention to myself.'

'Yes, that's probably best,' Zofia agreed. She took the armbands out of her bag and handed them to him.

'Well, goodbye,' Filip said, stuffing the thin fabric bands into his pockets.

'Goodbye. And thank you.'

Zofia held her hand out for him to shake and he took it, held it for a long moment, then turned and walked back down the path, the frosty blades of grass crunching beneath his feet. Zofia watched him leave, wondering with an unexpectedly heavy heart when she would see him again. Behind her, one of the children sneezed.

'Come on, children, let's find a place to wait.' She tried to sound cheerful, although cheer was the furthest thing from her mind. 'We can do some jumping jacks to keep warm.'

She ushered the group around the back of the church where there was a small copse of beech trees. The winter sun had come out and a delicate web of light fell through the leaves onto the ground, giving the place a magical feel. It was as nice a place as any to wait for the contact to arrive, and Zofia had the children jump up and down to ward off the creeping cold, even though she was wary about making too much noise.

'I'm thirsty,' one of the younger children said, and instantly, the other children fell in saying they were thirsty too, or hungry, or tired, or cold.

'You will all get something to eat and drink soon,' Zofia said. She checked the time. It was five to three. Her contact was due to meet her here at three o'clock. It was someone she had not met before, and she felt uneasy. Ever since Lina and Jakub had betrayed the group, her mistrust of friends, let alone strangers, was as acute as ever. How could Irena ever possibly know which resistance members were trustworthy, and which ones were traitors? She recalled her own initiation, when she'd thought she was smuggling a baby that turned out to be a doll. Hadn't Lina and Jakub been put to the test? Lina certainly; she had acted despite herself, to protect her family. But Jakub…

'I need the toilet,' a little boy named Rubin said, snapping her out of her thoughts, 'very badly.'

'All right,' she replied. She looked around and saw some bushes about ten metres away, close to the back of the church. 'Come with me, and I'll—'

'What a nice day for an outdoor lesson,' a female voice said from behind her.

Zofia spun around to find a nun in a black habit standing there.

'So long as it doesn't snow,' she answered, hoping this was her contact. Like with the janitor, she had been given a code for this encounter. If the woman replied with, 'But we might have a white Christmas yet', then this was the person who would help her take the children to the convent.

'Ah, we might have a white Christmas yet,' the nun said with a knowing smile.

Zofia breathed a sigh of relief. She was safe. The children were safe. And suddenly, the tension left her, flowing off her body like water.

'We made it,' she said in a trembling voice, and gestured towards the children standing near the tree. 'All of us. Twenty-five children.'

'You are very brave,' the nun said. Then she took Zofia in a tight embrace. 'Come now, Father Franciszek and three sisters are inside, waiting. They will feed the children and take them to their new homes.'

Zofia called over to the children, telling them they would now have something to eat and drink. 'And yes, Rubin, you may use the lavatory.'

Rubin nodded eagerly, and at that moment, Zofia realised she had almost forgotten Irena's final instruction. She quickly took two folded sheets of paper from her bag and proceeded to tear them into small squares.

'What are you doing?' the nun asked.

'I'm writing down the children's names,' she explained. 'Their new Christian names, and their real names with their birthdates. If there is no record of who they really are, how will they ever be reunited with their parents?'

Keeping a record of the children's identities had been Irena's idea. It was a risk, of course; they tried to avoid any kind of paper trail that might lead the Nazis – or their spies – to the activities of the resistance. But it was testament to Irena's profoundly held belief that someday, the war would be over, the ghetto liberated, and the Jews free once more. And when that day came, these children would want to trace their families. Zofia wrote down the names, surprised at how steady her hand was. As she wrote, it slowly dawned on her what she had achieved: she had successfully led twenty-five children to safety, twenty-five children who would now have the chance of a new life, who might grow up and start families of their own, become doctors, musicians, teachers. And who one day would be old enough to tell their grandchildren about their fight for survival. A warm feeling of pride overcame her and she smiled to herself at the thought of the anxious, timid young woman she'd been when she had first joined Żegota.

She finished writing down the children's names and then gave each child a hug goodbye. When she came to Ola, whose 'new' name was Maria Nowak, she crouched down to the girl's eye level.

'It's time to say goodbye,' she said, her throat tight.

Ola looked at her solemnly. 'Will you come back tomorrow?'

'I don't … I don't think I'll see you for a while. But I will come and visit you as soon as I can. I promise.'

'But where am I going? Will my mummy be there?'

Zofia swallowed hard. 'No,' she whispered. 'Your mummy won't be there. You're going to go and stay with some lovely people. They will look after you and make sure you have plenty to eat and clean clothes to wear. And maybe they'll have some chocolate for you. You like chocolate, don't you?'

She forced a smile and then, without warning, Ola threw her arms around her and hugged her tight.

'Don't go, please,' she said, pressing her small face into Zofia's shoulder, and from the shudders going through her small body, Zofia could tell she was sobbing.

'I'm sorry,' Zofia whispered, barely able to hold back her own tears. She bit down hard on her lower lip. 'Ola, *kochanie*, please don't cry. I will come and find you; I promise. I will come, and then we might be together for good.'

She held Ola for a long time, until the girl's sobbing had subsided and the nun suggested kindly that they needed to move on. Reluctantly, Zofia released Ola from her arms and pressed a handkerchief into her hand.

'Wipe away your tears, *kochanie.* You don't need to cry.'

'Come now, little one,' the nun said and took Ola's hand. Then she led the girl away, throwing Zofia a reassuring glance over her shoulder as if to say, *The girl will be fine, we will look after her.*

Zofia watched the group of children disappear into the church, one by one, then turned and left the churchyard. With tears stinging her eyes, and thoughts of her achievement marred by the painful parting from Ola, she hurried along the road, further and further away from the child she had come to care for so deeply.

25

Warsaw, December 1942

The sun was warm on her face, but Zofia felt frozen to the core. The relief that the operation had been successful only lasted for a moment as she made her way down Królewska Road towards home, before a bone-aching exhaustion made its way over her body, making her long for a bath and twelve hours of deep sleep. But worse than the tiredness was the image of Ola's bright eyes and the echo of her words, *Don't go, please.* Zofia stifled a sob.

She turned onto Dąbrówki Road, hoping there would be enough hot water at home so she didn't have to make do with a lick and a promise at the sink. She was so lost in thought that she didn't see the German soldier approaching, and ran right into him. She apologised quickly and went to walk on, but he called her back. '*Halt!*'

Zofia froze. For a moment, she was back in the ghetto, trying to lead a group of children down the street without drawing attention to herself. Her frayed nerves, always just below the surface, were instantly fizzing and her heart began flip-flopping in her chest.

I'm safe, she reminded herself. *I'm just out for a walk in the sunshine, I'm not breaking any laws.*

But the soldier, it seemed, had other ideas.

'*Machen Sie Ihre Tasche auf!*' he barked. 'Open your bag.'

Zofia took a deep breath and did as he'd ordered. Residents were regularly searched on the street for no apparent reason – it was a type of harassment designed to remind the Polish who was in charge in their country – and the best response was just to do as they were ordered. Zofia always told herself not to let the Germans get to her, that her pride and dignity were unassailable.

Thank goodness she had given the armbands to Filip! If she had kept them, she would most likely be facing death from a Nazi bullet here on the street. The soldier, who stood uncomfortably close to her and smelled of cheap tobacco smoke and tooth decay, rifled through her bag, taking out her handkerchief, her comb, her keys, and dropping them to the ground. She waited patiently, biting her tongue, and when he was done, she bent down to retrieve the discarded items.

She was about to leave when the soldier grabbed her sleeve.

'This,' he said, pointing to the mud on her coat. 'What is this?' He took another step closer, so that his face was only inches from hers. His stinking breath turned her stomach. 'And here, on your cheek. You have been rolling around in the mud? Like a pig?'

Zofia's hand shot up to the side of her face, desperately trying to think of a credible reason why she might be covered in mud.

'It's— I, um …' Her voice trembled. 'I slipped on the ice … I fell!'

The soldier wiped her words away with his hand.

'You go,' he said with a sneer.

She nodded and turned. As she walked away, he called after her, 'And wash yourself, you filthy Polack!'

It took all Zofia's strength not to turn around and spit in the man's face. Instead, she gripped her hands into fists, so hard her nails dug into her palms, and continued on her walk home.

The following afternoon, Zofia arrived home from work at four o'clock. Mr Wójcik hadn't been in the office all day, so she had used the opportunity to leave work an hour early. In fact, she wanted to nip home for a change of clothes before she went to see Julia in the ghetto. She hadn't been able to face her yesterday, after the heartbreak of saying goodbye to Ola, but she also knew it wasn't fair to let Julia wait much longer. Besides, the woman's health was deteriorating so quickly, it was possible she might die before hearing the news of her daughter's escape to safety.

But as Zofia stepped into the hall, she heard unfamiliar voices coming from the living room. Her heart started thrumming as she took off her coat and went to stand behind the door, which stood ajar. She heard an unknown man's voice, low and droning, and her insides turned to ice. But on closer hearing, she could tell he was speaking Polish. And then a second voice, a woman's, and this one she recognised. It was Mrs Galińska, a neighbour from across the road. Zofia had known her for a number of years, and disliked her, but not as much as she disliked the woman's husband. Mr Galiński was a pushy, arrogant man. He owned several clothing workshops in Warsaw, where a large proportion of the workforce was made up of Jewish labourers. Zofia suspected, although her father had never said, that Mr

Galiński was one of those Polish businessmen who had happily participated in the 'Aryanisation' of the economy, buying up Jewish businesses at ridiculously cheap prices. To her mind, this was nothing short of looting.

Zofia avoided the Galiński's company where she could, but for her father, it was a different matter. Like it or not, he was forced to trade with people like Mr Galiński if he wanted to provide for his family – and afford medical treatment for Zuzanna. Zofia closed her eyes for a moment, took a deep breath, and entered the living room.

Mr and Mrs Galiński were sitting side-by-side on the sofa opposite Zofia's parents, a pot of tea and a seed cake on the table in front of them. Zuzanna was sitting on an armchair with a blanket around her shoulders. Zofia's mother gave her a pained smile as she came in.

'Zofia! There you are. How was your day at work?'

'Fine, Mama.' She greeted Mr and Mrs Galiński politely and received a curt nod in response. It was probably the mention of work, Zofia assumed. To people like the Galińskis, Zofia should long be married and producing babies. That she was a working woman in her twenties without so much as a fiancé on the horizon was perhaps not quite scandalous, but certainly shameful. She took a seat beside Zuzanna, who rolled her eyes in the direction of Mr Galiński, who was speaking to their father.

'…And as I was saying, Ludwik, the Jews have a way with business, am I right?' He chuckled horribly. 'You have to watch them at every turn, believe me. You get the occasional malingerer, but all in all, it's a good deal. Cheap employment. Or two for the price of one, as I like to say.'

He leaned back and spread his legs, so wide that his wife had to shift position to accommodate him.

Zofia's father cleared his throat. 'I understand what you are saying, Sławomir. But I am perfectly content with my employees. They do good work and for that, I am happy to pay them a proper wage. I have no need for "cheap employment", as you so eloquently put it.'

They were talking about forced labour. It was the worst possible topic Zofia could have walked in on. She clenched her teeth, so tight it almost hurt, and hoped they would change the subject. But Mr Galiński wasn't finished.

'But Ludwik, we're businessmen, aren't we? And it's the bottom line that matters in the end.'

Izabel leaned forward and poured the guests more tea. 'Some of them don't look well enough to work,' she said softly as she sat back down. Her voice wavered with concern. 'I've seen men so thin they can barely stand, let alone work.'

Zofia turned to look at her. She had never heard her mother mention this, the fact that she cared. Perhaps it would be best, after all, to let her parents in on her secret activities.

Mrs Galińska took a sip of tea. 'Malingerers, like my husband said.'

Izabel turned the corners of her mouth down. Zofia could tell she wanted to say more, but daren't. She, by contrast, had heard enough.

'As my mother rightly explains,' she said, as calmly as she could, 'it is not right to exploit other people's suffering, business or no business.'

Mr Galiński let out a surprised huff, but she continued. 'You call yourselves Christians, but surely, if the Bible teaches us anything, then—'

Mr Galiński cut her off. 'Religion has absolutely nothing to do with this, my dear. These *people* have weaker constitutions than we do. They are more susceptible to disease, let's not pretend otherwise. Besides, I am reliably informed that they are provided with sufficient rations – better rations than us, some of them! And they have nurses and doctors to take care of any little aches and pains they might have. Yet at the same time, my wife must wait *weeks* for a doctor's appointment.'

Beside him, his wife nodded sourly.

Zofia couldn't stop herself and blurted out, 'Better rations? Doctors and nurses? Is that really what you think?'

Mr Galiński drew himself up in his seat. 'You have no idea what conditions they are living in, young lady,' he said condescendingly, adding, 'unless you choose to believe the communist propaganda?'

Zofia jumped to her feet, her fists clenched. 'It is no communist propaganda, believe me.' She was almost growling. 'If you knew how these people were living, then even you would—' She stopped as she felt Zuzanna clutching her sleeve and turned to see her sister sitting forward, warning her with her eyes.

'Zofia,' she said with a false smile. 'These are Mama and Papa's guests. Let's not argue, please.'

Her breathing was laboured and she was pale and sweating. Zofia sat back down, trembling. *My sick little sister just saved me*, she thought and her heart thumped uncomfortably against her ribs. She had almost exposed herself, almost told that horrible man that she had seen with her own eyes how the Jews were being treated, that their diseases were due to filthy sanitary conditions and starvation rations. That three-year-old children were forced to sit in the snow, begging, because their parents had been forcibly deported and they had no one to look after them.

An awkward, stony silence filled the room, until Izabel said, 'Shall we have some more tea?'

But Mr Galiński got to his feet. 'It is time my wife and I left. We are much obliged for your hospitality.'

He took his wife's elbow and guided her towards the door. Turning, he said, 'And Ludwik, perhaps you might want to teach your daughter some manners.'

He and his wife left the room, leaving them in stunned silence.

Zofia cycled hard towards the ghetto checkpoint, trying to shake off her anger at the Galińskis – and also at the thought that she had almost betrayed herself so stupidly. She should be stronger, less susceptible to such vicious, hateful talk. But it was like salt in an already inflamed wound. By the time she got to the checkpoint, her hands were red-raw with cold and her nose was running, and she snapped at the guard who asked to look inside her bag.

'There's nothing in there,' she said. 'What are you looking for, anyway?'

She was lucky on two counts: first, that she didn't have so much as a boiled sweet on her, let alone potatoes or even vaccines, and second, that the guard inspecting her bag was a very young man – no more than nineteen years old – who blushed and shrank back timidly when she admonished him, then waved her through without another word.

She turned a corner, out of sight of the checkpoint, and stood with her back pressed flat against a brick wall, steadying her breath, eyes closed. *That could have gone very wrong*, she thought. But how much more of this could she take? The constant fear of discovery and arrest, the human suffering she witnessed almost daily, Julia's pain at having to give up her daughter, Zofia's own heartbreak at bidding the child farewell, not knowing when she might see her again, or what kind of future Ola had.

She kept her eyes forward as she made her way along the pavement, yet she still couldn't fail to see the beggars that lined the streets, some of them calling out, some singing mournful Jewish songs, and others too limp and weak to draw any attention to themselves at all. She turned a corner and nearly stumbled over something lying at a courtyard entrance. Taking a closer look, she let out an involuntary cry when she saw it was a body; a naked corpse covered haphazardly with newspaper. She looked away quickly, to see two boys on the other side of the road taking the clothes and shoes from another body. It seemed such a barbaric thing to do, to steal from the dead, but the clothes the boys themselves were wearing were little more than rags. The children were, she realised, merely trying to survive. And yet, even taking the clothes from a corpse was a dangerous endeavour, as all and any raw materials – fabric, wood, scrap iron – had to be handed over to the Nazi authorities for reuse. There was no escape from Nazi tyranny, even inside this hellscape. It put her own wretched feelings into perspective instantly.

She arrived at Ostrowska Street feeling contrite, though a lot calmer, and knocked at the door. Eliasz Friedman opened almost immediately.

'Is she safe?' he asked with concern. 'The little one, is she safe?'

Zofia nodded. 'Yes, I got all the children out. How is Julia?'

The man gestured towards the door to her room. 'Not well at all. She is deteriorating fast.'

Zofia followed him inside the flat, noticing how the bones jutted out through his shirt at the back. How could anyone, least of all a fully grown man, survive on four hundred calories a day? She wished she could force the Galińskis to experience something like this, the purposeful, systematic starvation of human beings, people who were facing a slow, demeaning, prolonged death.

'She might be sleeping,' Eliasz said as they came to Julia's door. 'She does little else. Her strength is almost gone entirely, and now with her daughter no longer here…'

Zofia thanked him and went inside. Julia lay on her bed, seemingly asleep. Her skin was parchment dry and the colour of an old candle. She stirred as Zofia came closer and opened her eyes. A flash of panic crossed her face.

'Is she safe?' she whispered.

Zofia sat down on the bed next to her. 'Yes, Julia. We made it across and Ola is safe.'

'Thank you,' Julia said weakly and let out a ragged sigh. 'I can't tell you—' She broke off, her poor body racked with a coughing fit.

Zofia put a hand on her forehead. She was burning up.

'I should go and find a doctor,' she said. 'There might be some medicine, or something, to help your fever.'

Julia shook her head. 'It would be wasted on me.'

'No, it wouldn't be wasted! If you saw a doctor, if you got some medicine, you—'

Julia held up a trembling hand to interrupt her.

'You must promise me something,' she said. Her voice was nothing more than a thin rasp, and Zofia had to lean in closer to hear her properly. 'You must protect Ola as though you were her second mother.'

'Of course.' Zofia thought of Ola's sweetness, her boundless curiosity and her infectious laugh. It made her sad beyond belief, and she couldn't begin to imagine Julia's pain at having had to let her go. 'I promise. I told one of the nuns to keep a close eye on her. In a few days' time, I'll go back to the convent, and they should be able to give me the address she's been taken to.'

'It makes it easier for me, you know?'

'What?'

'I know that I am dying. Very soon, I think.' Julia blinked, and a tear escaped her eye and ran down her cheek. 'But to know there are people like you, with your kindness and love – despite everything. This is the worst time in humanity, and yet there is still some light in the darkness.'

She let herself fall back limply onto her pillow, drawing breaths that made her chest rattle. Zofia squeezed her hand and pushed back a strand of hair from her clammy forehead, trying to stop her own tears from falling. Her throat was painfully tight and she knew that if she started sobbing now, she might never stop. This was a level of sorrow she would never get used to.

Then she noticed Julia's lips moving; she was trying to speak. Zofia bowed her head towards her, her ear close to Julia's mouth, and listened, wide-eyed, as Julia began to whisper something.

26

Warsaw, Present Day

The following afternoon, Lizzie and Roksana took the metro back to Ola's house.

Tomasz opened the door. 'Oh, hello,' he said. 'You said on the phone you'd forgotten something?'

Lizzie gave a small shrug. 'Actually, I forgot to show your grandmother something.' She opened her bag and took out the photo. 'It's a picture of her, with my great-grandmother Zofia. I really don't want to bother her, but I meant to show her this yesterday and I was so absorbed in her story that I completely forgot. Do you think—?'

Tomasz opened the door wider and smiled. 'Of course! She talked of nothing else yesterday afternoon, and yesterday evening, and this morning at breakfast. I think she will be delighted to see you again.'

He led them inside and into the kitchen. Ola was sitting at a large oak table, its surface bearing the marks and scratches of time, showing her great-granddaughter how to form small round *jagodzianki*, buns made with leavened dough and filled with blueberries. Lizzie had seen her own grandmother make them many times.

They both looked up, and Lizzie was once again puzzled by the resemblance the young girl had to her own sister Hannah. *Must be the Polish genes*, she told herself.

'*Dzień dobry!*' Ola said, smiling. She patted the empty chair on her left. '*Usiądź.*'

'She wants you to sit down,' Roksana said.

Lizzie did as requested. 'I forgot to show you something yesterday,' she said, and began to explain how she had found a photograph in her great-grandmother's attic; a picture that had set this whole investigation in motion. 'I thought, maybe the picture can jog your memory.'

She held out the photograph. Ola wiped the flour from her hands and took it. She stared at the picture for a long time, first impassively, but then the corners of her mouth turned up in a smile, making her dimples appear. There must be almost eighty years between then and now, Lizzie calculated, but Ola was still recognisable as the bright young child in the photo.

She waited for the old woman to speak, trying not to let her impatience show. Finally, Ola handed the picture back and spoke to Roksana.

'What did she say?' Lizzie asked eagerly, when the old woman had finished talking.

Roksana shook her head. 'She is very sorry, but she cannot help you. She does remember this photograph being taken, she recalls the photographer, a friendly young man, but it has done nothing to – how do you say? – shake loose any other memories.'

Lizzie almost groaned out loud. She felt suddenly defeated and realised how many hopes she had pinned on this one picture. That was it then, she had come to a dead end.

Then, suddenly, the old woman's eyes flashed and she said something in rapid-fire Polish to Maja. The girl jumped up and left the room.

'What is it?' Lizzie said, turning to Roksana.

Roksana shrugged. 'She told Maja to go and fetch the wooden box from underneath her bed.'

They sat in silence for a few minutes, waiting for the girl to return, while Lizzie tried not to get her hopes up again.

'Ah,' Ola exclaimed as Maja returned, carrying a small wooden box with resin inlay in the lid. It looked very old, yet well taken care of and polished to a high shine. Her fingers trembling with age, Ola fumbled open the locket she wore around her neck and took out a small key, with which she unlocked the box. There was a tense, anticipatory silence as she slowly opened the lid. Then she let out a sudden shriek.

Lizzie, Roksana and Maja jumped.

'*Prababcia!*' the girl cried.

'Ola, is everything all right?' Lizzie asked with genuine concern.

But then Ola started laughing; a long, infectious chuckle.

Maja rolled her eyes. 'She think she is funny,' she said. 'My *prababcia* is a—' She frowned. '*Żartowniś.*'

'A joker,' Roksana translated, a smile tugging at her lips.

Ola wiped her eyes. 'Sorry, sorry,' she said when she'd finished laughing, and proceeded to open the box. Serious once again, she removed some letters and laid them to one side with great care, then took out a handkerchief.

'From Zofia,' she said, stroking the yellowing fabric. She sighed, then laid it on top of the letters and went back to the box, from which she retrieved a photograph. Like the one

Lizzie had shown her, this one was in black-and-white, with crinkled edges and faded with age. The old woman looked at it briefly and passed it to Lizzie. She spoke to Roksana, her voice breaking with sadness every now and again.

'It was sewn into her coat,' Roksana translated. 'When she left her mother behind. She says she can't remember it being taken, she was only two or three at the time. It was before – before they were sent to that godawful place.'

'The ghetto.' Lizzie looked at the picture. It showed a toddler on the lap of a young woman, and, to Lizzie's surprise, another child sitting beside them. She had the same dark curly hair as Ola, and was perhaps a year or two older.

'Who is this?' she asked.

With Roksana's help, Ola explained that the other child was her sister. She was eighteen months older, but Ola had very few memories of her, as her parents never really liked to talk about her. She had kept this photograph safe all her life. It was the only reminder she had of her.

'She assumes her sister died in the ghetto, like so many others,' Roksana said. 'Perhaps that's why her parents didn't speak of her – it was too painful.'

But Lizzie wasn't really listening; she was staring at the photo, her heart pounding.

'Ola,' she said slowly. She wanted the old woman to understand exactly what she was about to say. She didn't want anything getting lost in translation. 'Ola, what is that mark on your sister's face?'

Ola frowned. 'Mark of birth,' she said in English and looked up to Roksana for confirmation. '*Znamię.*'

Roksana nodded. 'Birthmark. Her sister had a birthmark.'

As though in a dream, Lizzie took her phone out of her bag and scrolled through her picture gallery. Her hands were shaking like a leaf.

'Here,' she said, when she had found what she was looking for. She held up the phone to Ola. 'This is my grandmother, Magda. She has the very same mark.'

27

Warsaw, December 1942

Zofia sat back, astonished.

'Why didn't you tell me? Whatever became of her?'

Julia tried to sit up, but she was too weak. 'I don't know,' she said, her breath shallow and rattling. 'She managed to get out of the ghetto a year ago, through a gap in the wall, and found her way to our old neighbour's house. Their daughter was her friend and she wanted to see her again.' She sniffed. 'Just to play with her. They were best friends.'

'So she never came back?'

'No. We were worried out of our minds, Pavel and I, but then we received word of where she was, and we managed to get a letter to our neighbours, begging them not to hand Magda over to the Nazis. The last thing we heard was that she'd been taken in by a family in Poznań.' Julia closed her eyes briefly and a tear rolled down her cheek. 'So far away.'

'Oh, Julia, I'm so sorry.'

Julia swallowed. 'I need you to find her.'

'I … I'm not sure I could, I—'

Julia suddenly gripped Zofia's arm with surprising strength. 'You must find her. Magda and Ola are sisters, they need each other. Especially because…' Her words faded for a moment and she took a rattling breath. 'Because they have no parents. They only have each other.' She stared at Zofia, pleading with her eyes. 'This war will come to an end, sooner or later. And you need to make sure my daughters have a good life, free from the atrocities of their past. They are young, with their whole futures ahead of them, and they should grow up knowing only love and compassion.'

She paused to cough again and then continued in a whisper. 'I'm sorry to burden you with this, Zofia, but there is no one else to ask. And to know my daughters will be well looked after, loved … well, it's all a mother can hope for, isn't it?'

Zofia sat silently for a while, contemplating the impossibility of the task. Find Magda? Where would she start? And yet she understood Julia's profound need to know her daughters would be reunited.

'I'll do my best to find her and reunite them,' she said finally, praying she hadn't just made a promise she had no hope of keeping.

'Where have you been?' her mother asked as Zofia stepped through the front door.

'I was busy and—' Zofia began, but one look at her mother's worried face made her pause.

'Mama, what's wrong?'

Izabel wrung her hands. 'It's Zuzanna. She hasn't been able to get up all day, just coughing and coughing, barely able to

251

breathe. Papa has made up a bed for her downstairs, so she can be close to the fire, but she is as weak as ever.'

'Has the doctor been?'

Her mother nodded.'He gave her the usual cough syrup, but it's her heart that's the problem. Her condition is exacerbated by an infection of the lungs. All he could suggest was bed rest and cold compresses to fight the fever.' Her shoulders slumped. 'Oh, Zofia, I don't know if I could bear it if … if…'

She started weeping, very softly. Zofia rushed towards her and took her in her arms while a surge of guilt washed through her. She had been so caught up in the lives of others that she had been neglecting her own family.

'Zuzanna is strong,' she whispered into her mother's ear. 'She will rest, and then she will fight this damn infection.'

Her mother released herself from the embrace.'We will pray for her. She is an innocent soul, God will look over her.' She made the sign of the cross.'Now, I have managed to get my hands on some scraps of beef and bone. I am making a nice savoury broth. Perhaps it will help Zuzanna get back onto her feet.'

Zofia waited until she had retreated to the kitchen and then went into the living room. As her mother had said, their father had made up a bed for Zuzanna on the sofa. A few orange coals glowed in the fireplace, lending the room a strange, alien light. But at least it was warm in here.

Zuzanna lay on the sofa, her skin pale and clammy. She opened her eyes as Zofia approached and tried to sit up, but couldn't.

'*Żabka*,' Zofia said tenderly, taking her sister's hand.'Are you causing trouble again?'

Zuzanna gave her a weak smile.'If only.'

Again, she tried to sit up, but was overcome with a coughing fit. Immediately, Zofia was reminded of Julia and struggled to keep her tears back.

'It's all right, *Żabka*,' she said, stroking her sister's back. Zuzanna smelled of cold sweat and camphor from the cough syrup. 'And I'm so sorry I haven't been here for you. Will you forgive me?'

Zuzanna's cough subsided and she lay back down again slowly.

'Zofia?' she said, when she had found a comfortable position. 'Today, were you – were you out again helping those poor people in the ghetto?'

Zofia nodded.

'Then you were doing the right thing,' Zuzanna said, and in a hoarse whisper continued, '"Carry each other's burdens, and in this way you will fulfil the law of Christ."' She turned her head and gestured towards the Bible lying on the table.

'Ephesians, four thirty-two.' Zofia gently pushed back a strand of hair from her sister's forehead. 'You really must be poorly if you're reading the New Testament.'

'Bored, more like.'

The two sisters smiled at each other. They heard the kitchen door opening and the rich, aromatic smell of bone broth wafted into the room.

'Will you eat something?' Zofia asked.

Zuzanna nodded. 'If I get well, then perhaps I can join you in helping those people.'

Zofia took her sister in a hug. 'If everyone had as kind and strong a spirit as you, *Żabka*,' she whispered, 'then this world would be a very different place.'

When Zofia arrived at Ostrowska Street early the next morning, she knew even before she knocked on the door that Julia had gone. Death had visited this house before; an elderly couple on the first floor had succumbed to pneumonia and starvation-induced exhaustion three weeks earlier. But this was different. A dull silence emanated from inside the flat, so physical Zofia could almost grasp it. She tapped her knuckles gently against the door.

As always, Eliasz Friedman answered.

'I'm sorry,' he said quietly, shaking his head. He had dark purple shadows beneath his eyes. 'She passed during the night.'

He rubbed his face and sighed heavily. Zofia could see he had been crying.

'It was peaceful,' he said after a moment. 'My wife and I sat with her and she just … she just closed her eyes. I think,' he continued, 'she was at peace knowing her daughter was safe.'

'Thank you,' Zofia murmured, for what else was there to say? Then she turned and hurried back down the stairs so he wouldn't see her tears. She had witnessed so much suffering in the ghetto, but this was the first time she'd been confronted with the death of someone she had felt so close to. She wiped her eyes before stepping onto the cold street. She knew that the grief she felt now was the consequence of becoming emotionally attached to Julia, and yet she had no regrets. If anything, it made her even more determined to do the right thing by as many more children as she could.

28

Warsaw, Present Day

Ola held Lizzie's phone with trembling fingers. She had turned white as a sheet, and for a moment, Lizzie was worried she might faint. But then the old woman looked up at her, eyes full of tears.

'I cannot believe it,' she whispered, stroking Magda's image on the phone. '*Moja siostra. Moja starsza siostra.*'

Lizzie glanced up at Roksana, who had also turned pale.

'My big sister,' Roksana translated, her tone reverent and incredulous in equal measure.

Ola placed the phone on the table and opened her arms wide. '*Chodź tu*, Lizzie,' she said.

Lizzie didn't wait for a translation and rushed into her great-aunt's embrace. For a long time, they hugged each other, both women crying, then the kitchen door flew open and Tomasz came in.

'What is going on?' he called, anxiously. '*Babcia*, are you all right?'

Maja stood up, smiling. 'It's okay, Papa. She is happy, that's all.'

Half an hour later, sitting at the table with coffee and cake in front of them, Lizzie did her best to answer Ola's many questions.

'Magda is living in a care home close to my parents' house,' she said. 'Her health is declining, sadly, but she is still very sharp-minded on her good days.'

Ola smiled and then sighed, as if to say, *Age catches up with all of us in the end.* Lizzie reached out and stroked her hand. She felt a sudden urge for physical closeness, now she knew she was related to the old woman.

Ola sighed again and spoke.

'She wishes she could meet with her,' Roksana translated, adding loudly, 'Oh, I wish *I* could meet with her!'

Tomasz had opened a bottle of vodka to celebrate, and Roksana had already had three shots. Lizzie had declined; it was a little early in the day and she wanted to keep her wits about her until she and Ola had finished talking. Besides, she might have Polish ancestors, but she wasn't exactly practiced in the art of drinking hard spirits. But tonight, she had promised Roksana that they would go out together and drink champagne.

She glanced over at Maja, only now realising it was hardly a surprise the girl had more than a passing resemblance to Hannah. They shared the same genes, after all. She picked up her phone.

'May I take a picture of you?' she asked the girl. 'It's just, you look very much like my sister Hannah when she was your age. I'd love to send her a picture.'

Maja agreed, and Lizzie snapped a photo. A moment later, Tomasz – who had also drunk his fair share of vodka – insisted on taking some group selfies, and they spent the next fifteen minutes posing in different formations, jostling for position and giggling like children. It was a feeling of total abandon, Lizzie suddenly realised. She was among her family, and it felt perfect.

'If Magda and Ola are sisters,' Tomasz said, frowning, 'then what are we to each other?'

'Cousins?' Lizzie ventured.

'No.' Roksana shook her head. Her cheeks were flushed rosy red. 'Second cousins, I'd say.'

'Ah, you're wrong,' Tomasz continued. 'We are first cousins twice removed.'

Lizzie grinned. 'Or perhaps, second degree cousins once removed, depending on whether you are part of my parents' generation or how many aunts and uncles are in between. Is your mother's father my aunt's brother-in-law, or is your father's mother my sister's great-aunt?' She was babbling nonsense and she laughed as Tomasz actually frowned to consider her question.

Maja pointed to the vodka bottle. '*Usunięto*,' she said, drawing a circle at her temple to suggest they were behaving crazily.

'She thinks we are *all* a bit removed,' Tomasz chortled. 'Perhaps she isn't wrong.'

They fell about again, laughing like children, while Ola demanded, and received, an explanation. She chuckled at length, then asked Tomasz to pour her a glass of vodka, too.

When they had all settled down, Roksana suddenly blurted out, 'Video call! You should organise a video call!'

'What a wonderful idea, Roksana,' Lizzie said.

Ola asked something in Polish, and Tomasz translated. Instantly, the old woman's eyes lit up.

'*Tak!*' she said. 'Yes, yes, yes!'

Lizzie turned to Ola. 'I'll try to get a flight home as soon as possible, and go and see Magda. Oh my goodness, she will be so pleased to hear about you, I just know it!'

After a very emotional goodbye, Lizzie and Roksana left the Broński house and stood silently on the pavement for a while. Lizzie closed her eyes and held her face up to the warm sun, smelling the sweet, fruity scent of the freesias that grew in the front garden, and listening to the high-pitched, melodious song of a couple of nearby thrushes. All of her senses were alive.

'It's incredible,' Roksana said finally. 'I mean … just incredible!'

'It is,' Lizzie replied and rubbed her jaw. Her face was aching from smiling so much.

Roksana went to speak, but then closed her mouth again.

'What is it?' Lizzie asked

'Would it be okay with you if I wrote this up as an article? I know this is a very personal story, and perhaps it isn't something you want to share with the world, but I think such a story of resilience and joy would appeal to lots of readers. And happy endings are in short supply these days.'

Lizzie beamed and then threw her arms around her in a tight hug. 'Of course you must write about this!' she said. 'I would never have found Ola if it hadn't been for you.'

29

Warsaw, December 1942

Zofia and Irena stared up at the gnarled branches of the tree. The bark was dark, almost black, and the boughs were naked, but a light layer of snow had settled there, making the tree look like something out of a fairytale.

'It doesn't look like much now, during the winter,' Irena said, 'but in autumn it holds the reddest, plumpest apples you can imagine.'

They were standing in the garden of a house in the eastern suburbs of the city, intending to bury two jars containing the names of the children they had smuggled out; their true names as well as their Christian codenames and locations. The house belonged to a friend of Irena's, a woman she had known for many years and who had offered her garden for this exact purpose. It was only a small garden, but it had a few nooks and crannies and was hidden from the road by a tall hedge. In its midst grew an apple tree, and beneath it, Irena had already hidden several jars.

Zofia gazed up at the tree for a long moment, imagining the coming seasons – spring, summer, autumn – when the air would be warm, bees would be pollinating the flowers, and the trees would be full of verdant leaves. *Will next year be the year this damned war ends?* she thought despondently. There had been promising news on the forbidden wireless channel, BBC, that the Sixth Army of the German Wehrmacht had been surrounded in Stalingrad, leading to huge losses for the German army. But still, from everything Zofia had heard about Hitler, it seemed unlikely he would just capitulate. *No*, she thought, *he won't rest until he has dragged the whole world into hell.*

Irena pulled Zofia out of her thoughts with a nudge to her elbow.

'Now, let's get to work,' she said and took two small trowels from the bag she was carrying.

The two women kneeled on the frosty grass and began to dig. It was hard work; the soil was frozen and hard, and Zofia's fingers were soon numb with cold, despite the gloves she wore. Eventually however, they had managed to dig a hole some forty centimetres deep.

Irena placed the jars of names into it and then sat back on her heels, made the sign of the cross, and began to pray. Then, as though a floodgate had opened, Zofia was filled with a sudden rush of faith, so strong it almost took her breath away. There *would* be an end to this war, humanity would prevail and – God willing – these children would be reunited with their parents. Zofia put her hands together and closed her eyes, the long-forgotten prayers bubbling up inside.

It was a moment later that Irena put a hand on Zofia's arm.

'Shh, there's someone there.'

They fell silent and heard a rustling sound somewhere to the left. They scrambled quickly to their feet, Zofia snagging her tights on some brambles in the process. Irena placed her large bag over the hole in a vain attempt to hide what they had been doing.

Another *crack* as someone stepped on a frozen twig.

'Who's there?' Irena called out.

A man stepped forward from behind the hedge and Zofia let out a sigh of relief. It was Filip.

'I'm sorry,' he said awkwardly, 'I hope I didn't startle you.'

'Well, you did,' Irena said, not unkindly, 'but it's a good thing it's you, and not a Nazi soldier.'

She retrieved her bag from the ground where it was covering the hole and started to shovel dirt in over the jars.

Filip took a step towards Zofia. 'I saw you both getting off the tram and I wasn't sure when I would next see you, Zofia.'

'Oh.'

'So I followed you.' He gave a small laugh. 'Took me a while to find you, but you both left footprints in the snow, small ones, so I thought…' He trailed off, blushing.

He is such a sweet man, Zofia thought suddenly, surprising herself. *He is brave and selfless and modest. If there were more men like him, this world would be a better place.*

Filip put his hand into his coat pocket and pulled something out. 'I've been meaning to give you this.'

Zofia's heart did an excited little skip, but then she saw what he was holding out. It was the picture he'd taken in the ghetto, of her with Ola and Julia.

'The photograph,' she said, taking it from him. She felt momentarily foolish. What had she been expecting? A gift? Some chocolates?

'That's lovely,' Irena said, coming to stand beside her. 'And who is this little girl?'

Zofia didn't answer straight away. She was staring down at Julia, who had tried so bravely to smile for the photograph, despite her illness. Beside her, Ola's head was thrown back in a laugh, her dark curls bouncing around her face. Zofia's throat tightened. This little girl would grow up without a mother. She recalled the tearful farewell outside the church and her promise to find Ola. *No*, she thought, a fresh determination growing inside her, *the girl will not grow up without a mother. She will just grow up with a different mother.*

'She's a girl we helped smuggle out,' she said, hearing her voice catch. 'And I need to find her.'

Irena gave her concerned look. 'The children's whereabouts are kept confidential for their own protection, as you know. This girl may have been placed in foster care, or an orphanage, or even found a family willing to adopt her.' She looked down to where they had buried the jars, and then back at Zofia. 'I can see you have become attached to the child, but I fear it will be very difficult to trace her until all this is over.'

'Difficult perhaps,' Zofia replied. 'But not impossible.'

'No.' Irena smiled gently, perhaps noting the defiance in Zofia's tone. 'Nothing is impossible.'

After they had finished burying the jars, Zofia and Irena returned to the Żegota headquarters on Żurawia Street. Several of the group's members had already gathered there and for a moment, Zofia believed they might have come together for a social gathering, perhaps to celebrate today's Fourth of Advent. It would be Christmas in less than a week. But there was a strange, heavy silence in the room, and as soon as they entered, a man hurried towards Irena. It was Marek, Helena's cousin, and it was obvious he had been crying.

'They've sentenced her to death,' he said in a thick voice. 'She will be executed by firing squad on New Year's Eve.'

Then the bear of a man broke down in huge, gulping sobs. Irena rushed towards him and hugged him, whispering words of comfort into his ear as he slid onto his knees. The rest of the group stood there in a dull silence. Zofia looked away, unable to bear the sight of his distress. At the back of the room, a middle-aged woman stood wringing her hands nervously. Her name was Anna, and although Zofia didn't know which cell she was a member of, or what her role in Żegota was, she knew Anna had been with the resistance since the outbreak of the war.

Someone placed a glass of vodka in Marek's hand and he sat on a chair, slumped forward. He had stopped crying, but looked utterly broken. There was a small murmuring as Anna stepped forward. For a long moment, she just stood there, looking from Marek to Irena, then casting an anxious look over her shoulder to the others.

'I'm sorry, Irena,' she said finally, 'but I can't do this anymore. I have a family to think about. This has become too risky.'

She squeezed her eyes shut for a moment. 'I'm sorry,' she said again, then turned and left the room hastily.

Irena waited until they had heard the front door close. Then she turned to the rest of the group.

'There is no shame in leaving,' she said gently. 'Anna has been incredibly brave. She has three young children and I think we must all honour her courage to have been a part of the resistance for this long. Now…' She crossed to the window and Zofia's gaze followed. Outside, thick snowflakes fell from the sky, illuminated by the light as they floated past the window. Irena turned back around. 'If anyone else feels they have to leave, please don't hesitate to say so. Everything you have done this far, small or large, is highly appreciated, and no one – absolutely *no one* – should feel obliged to continue with this work if you are frightened. For yourself or others.'

When she had finished speaking, Zofia looked around the room, wondering if anyone would take this opportunity to leave. No one moved. After a long silence, Irena cleared her throat.

'Let us pray for our comrade Helena.'

Everyone present got down onto their knees, including Marek, whom Zofia knew was not devout in any way. She also got onto her knees, closed her eyes and bowed her head. As Irena softly began reciting a prayer, Zofia found herself recalling the last time she had seen Helena, down in the sewer, just before she had given herself up to save the lives of the others. She had been an unapproachable, often stern woman, who hadn't always been easy to like, yet her bravery had been unsurpassed. Zofia listened as Irena prayed, reflecting on whether she herself could ever do what Helena had done, and waiting, almost instinctively, for the familiar nagging voice of doubt to appear. But amazingly, it was silent. She was still frightened, exhausted and at times despairing, but then she recalled something Irena had told her a while ago: that the most difficult struggle of all was the one within ourselves, and that if we became accustomed to the conditions we found ourselves in, we might lose the ability to discriminate between good and evil. This painful state of being – the fear, the anguish, the uncertainty – was the price we had to pay for knowing what was good.

When Irena closed the prayer with an 'Amen', it was clear to Zofia that the best way to honour Helena would be to continue her work. With her knees pressed against the hard wooden floor, she felt her resolve growing. There was no way back; she had seen too much sorrow for that. Not just sorrow, she had seen pure evil.

Yet although she was more determined than ever to save as many children as possible, it was one particular child who had won her heart, and she knew she would never rest until she'd found her.

30

Warsaw, January 1943

When Zofia got home, she put her key in the front door and pushed with her shoulder. The wooden doorframe always warped in the cold temperatures, and the Advent wreath Izabel and Zuzanna had made in early December released a shower of pine needles as she bumped the door open. It was the first week in January, and the decorations would be taken down on the sixth. Zofia doubted the wreath would last another few days.

Christmas had been a muted affair. Zuzanna's health had deteriorated badly the day before Christmas Eve, so instead of enjoying the *Wigilia* supper their mother had lovingly prepared, their father had set out in the freezing, snowy cold to try and coax the doctor away from his own family celebrations. The doctor had come, but had charged twice his usual fee. Thankfully, Zuzanna's fever had broken two days after Christmas, and although her coughing was as bad as ever, she had slowly begun to regain a little strength.

But even if there had been no worries over Zuzanna's health, Zofia would not have been in a mood to celebrate. On

New Year's Eve, the date of Helena's execution, all she could do was sit in her dark bedroom, completely drained of emotion, not even able to cry.

The Welfare Department had remained closed over Christmas and New Year, and Zofia had used the time to search for Ola. The last time she'd seen her was at the churchyard at St. Joseph's. All they were able to tell her was that she had been moved to the Rodzina Marii Orphanage here in Warsaw, but when Zofia went to speak to the nuns who ran the orphanage, they weren't sure where exactly Maria Nowak had been sent. Instead, they had referred her to a convent in nearby Chotomów. It felt increasingly like a wild goose chase, but giving up was out of the question. Tomorrow was Saturday, and Zofia planned to visit the convent. She had yet to think of an excuse to tell her parents – though perhaps, she thought now, it was time to tell them everything. When she found Ola, she intended to bring her home to live with her, and then, at least the truth would be out.

She was about to step inside the house when she had the odd, unmistakable feeling she was being watched. Turning quickly, she scanned the street and saw a figure in a long coat beneath a lamppost, looking in her direction. It was a man, smoking. For a brief moment, she thought he was going to cross the road and approach her, but he tossed his cigarette down and crushed it out with his shoe, then turned and walked away.

A cold shiver slunk down her spine. It wasn't the first time she'd thought she was being followed. Earlier that week, she had been sitting on the tram, reading, and had noticed a young man staring at her. When she looked up, he had looked away, but a moment later, she felt him staring in her direction again. Then, when she'd got off at her stop, he had also disembarked, and followed her a few hundred metres down the street until she'd taken a sudden sharp turning into a lane, then doubled up and walked the long way home. If he really had been following her, she must have managed to shake him off, because she hadn't spotted him again.

She slipped off her coat and hung it on the rack. She may well have been imagining things, but all the same, it had left her feeling troubled. *Perhaps I should mention it to Irena,* she thought as she tossed her keys into her bag. She hadn't seen her since the night they'd found out about Helena's death sentence. The heavy familiar cloak of sadness descended on her at the thought of her brave friend, but then she became aware of the sound of quiet sobbing. She followed the sound into the kitchen, and found her mother sitting at the kitchen table, holding a handkerchief to her face. When she looked up, Zofia knew as soon as she saw her mother's expression that something was terribly wrong.

'What is it?' she asked, letting her bag drop to the floor. Her heart began thumping painfully. 'Is it Zuzanna?'

Her mother shook her head. Her eyes were red-rimmed. 'No, it's Papa.'

'What? What's happened? Has he had an accident?'

At that moment, her father entered the kitchen and Zofia scanned him for visible signs of injury. But there was nothing – no blood, no bandages, not even a scratch.

'Papa, what's wrong?' she asked.

Ludwik sat down heavily on a chair beside his wife. 'I received a visit today,' he said in a low, trembling voice. 'From the SS.'

Zofia clapped a hand around her mouth and felt the blood draining from her face.

'They wanted to know if I had any dealings with Jews,' Ludwik continued. 'If I use any labourers from the ghetto in my workshop. Or if I do … deals with them.'

'What did you tell them?' Zofia said. Her words were barely a whisper.

Her father spread out his hands in front of him and shrugged. 'What could I tell them other than the truth? I know nothing of these things they were suggesting.'

'They must have the wrong person,' Izabel said. 'I can think of quite a number of people who exploit those poor Jews, paying them pennies for hard physical labour. They must have mistaken you for someone else.'

Zofia looked her father up and down again. 'Did they … hurt you? Or threaten you in any way?'

He just shook his head.

'Their visit alone is a threat,' her mother said darkly. 'Once you know they are watching you, you will never feel safe.'

The following morning, Zofia made her way to the Rodzina Marii Orphanage. She knew it would be foolish to try and visit the convent in Chotomów if she was under surveillance by the SS, so instead, she packed some leftover cake from the holidays in a basket and took the tram across the river. If anyone stopped her, she would say she was bringing the children some treats. On the way, she thought of little else than the Nazis visiting her father. What had they wanted from him? Did they really suspect him of helping the Jews? Or did they know about her Żegota activities and were using a threat to her family to frighten her? She looked around at her fellow passengers on the tram. Were any of them watching her? There, that old woman with the scraped-back hair, she was looking in Zofia's direction. Zofia looked away, then glanced back quickly, trying to catch her out. But the old woman was just staring out of the window now, swaying slightly as the tram turned a corner. Zofia sighed. She would have to be more vigilant from now on, but she would also have to ensure she wasn't becoming paranoid.

The nun who opened the gate to the orphanage was Sister Bernadyna, the one who had given Zofia the address in Chotomów on her last visit. She smiled when she saw Zofia.

'Miss Szczęsny, so nice to see you again. Do come in.'

'Good day,' Zofia replied, following Sister Bernadyna inside. 'I'm so sorry to trouble you again, but I was wondering if you could help me.'

Sister Bernadyna led her into a spacious room, where children were sitting at a large, round table, drawing.

'Oh, and I brought some cake,' Zofia said.

At the word 'cake', the children jumped up and gathered around her, trying to peer inside the basket.

Sister Bernadyna called them to order. 'Now, children, settle down. I'm sure there's enough for everyone.'

'Actually, I'm not sure there is,' Zofia said apologetically.

'Then it'll be just a small piece each.' The nun lowered her voice. 'They get such few treats, even a mouthful is something to be grateful for.'

Feeling a little guilty for not bringing more, Zofia let Sister Bernadyna cut up the cake into very tiny pieces and hand them out to the children. When each child had their portion, she turned to Zofia.

'Now then, my dear, you said you needed some help. Does this have anything to do with the child you've been looking for?'

Zofia nodded. 'You told me she'd been sent to Chotomów. I … I haven't been able to go there myself. You see … it isn't safe for me to go and I—'

Sister Bernadyna laid a hand on her arm. 'I understand,' she said gently. 'But as it happens, Sister Magdalena, one of the nuns here, will be travelling to Chotomów early next week. I will ask her to enquire about Maria Nowak.'

'She also goes by the name of Ola Zielińska,' Zofia said, knowing, but not caring, that she was breaking every rule by mentioning her true name.

The nun tilted her head to one side. 'She means a lot to you, this child, doesn't she?'

'She does,' Zofia said. 'More than I can say.'

31

Warsaw, February 1943

While Zofia waited on news about Ola, she continued her work in the ghetto, visiting almost every day, usually smuggling in food and sometimes medicines. And even if she had nothing to bring, she went anyway, if only to provide emotional comfort to those she visited. There were noticeably fewer people living there; the streets were no longer as crowded, but most of those who remained were unlikely to survive much longer. The ones who weren't sick were starving, and there were increasing numbers of those who had decided to take their own lives rather than suffer the slow death that was surely inevitable.

Her guard was up and she hadn't noticed anyone following her for a while, but nevertheless, every knock on the door, every ring of the telephone, sent her stomach plunging. Ever since the SS had paid her father a visit, she had been expecting the Gestapo to come and arrest her. How long could this war possibly go on? It was a question never far from her mind. The Americans had begun bombing Germany relentlessly, and news was that the Red Army were making their way through Ukraine, having successfully retaken Kharkov. But that was over a thousand kilometres away from Warsaw, and every day that passed meant another dozen deaths in the ghetto – and another day of danger for Zofia.

During her last visit to the ghetto, she had spoken to two families who had heard about the possibility of getting their children out. The mass deportations to Treblinka had begun again, with the Nazis working their way through the ghetto in an efficient, organised, calculated manner. Street by street, from south to north, east to west, the residents were instructed to report to the *umschlagplatz* to await transportation to a 'labour camp'. The families Zofia had spoken to were waiting to receive such orders any day now, and even if a miracle occurred and they were somehow spared, there were other dangers on the horizon. A Jewish resistance within the ghetto had been forming, unbelievably brave men and women arming themselves with weapons and explosives, planning to revolt against the deportations. No one believed they would ultimately defeat the huge Nazi military machine, but they considered it a battle for the honour of the Jewish people, determined not to allow the Germans alone to pick the time and place of their deaths. It was both admirable and courageous, Zofia reflected, as the resistance fighters were very likely to die, but at the same time, she knew the SS would hunt down everyone who survived, and would exact terrible revenge on the rest of the ghetto inhabitants. And that included children.

The biggest problem was that the escape routes Żegota had been using to smuggle out the children were now largely defunct. With routine patrols of the courthouse and the entrances to the sewer system, and ambulances and hearses subjected to random searches, the Germans were doing their best to plug any gaps. Yet despite these setbacks, Zofia had found herself promising the families she would help their children escape, and she knew she would now have to find a way to honour that promise.

Leaving work on a cold, wet February afternoon, she spotted Filip waiting on the corner and her heart did a little skip. She hadn't seen him December – she didn't even know where he lived, or worked – and it was only now she realised how much she had missed him.

'Zofia!' he called when he spotted her, approaching her with long strides. 'Is this a good time? I know you work here, so I thought I'd… I hope you don't mind, but if you're busy, or if you have to get home, then I…' He trailed off and gave her a shy, lopsided smile.

'No, not at all. It's lovely to see you. Let me get my bike, though.'

She went to unlock her bicycle and they began walking down Towarowa Street.

'There are some more children I want to get out,' she said quietly. 'I've discussed it with Irena, but we are running out of options. And I'm trying not to become paranoid, but I've come to suspect I might be being followed.'

Filip nodded. 'That's why I came to see you. Well, that's not the only reason.' He smiled shyly again, then his face turned serious. 'I think I have discovered a new escape route,' he said. 'But it's risky.'

'Isn't it always?'

'This is more exposed than usual.' He stopped and pointed to a milk bar across the road. 'May I treat you to a coffee?'

They crossed the street and found a table in the milk bar close to the back, where they were less likely to be overheard.

'So,' Zofia said once they had two cups of coffee in front of them, 'what is this route you've found?'

Filip went on to explain that on his photographic trips around the ghetto, he had found a gap in the wall behind the Jewish cemetery on Młynarska Street, where the Jewish cemetery bordered the Evangelical-Augsburg cemetery. The Germans had found the gap and closed the section off with a wire fence.

'But we would only need a pair of bolt cutters to get through. I've been observing the guards for a few weeks now. They stop patrolling at around four o'clock – they've stepped up patrols all over the ghetto and presumably don't have enough men to guard the spot day and night – and they only resume after dark, so that would give us half an hour or so to get the children out.'

'Half an hour should be enough.'

'But we won't have time to scout the place first,' he continued. 'And we would have to get the children through as quickly as possible without being seen. That part of the cemetery is out of bounds. It's awfully risky.' He paused and looked up at her. 'Perhaps we should wait. They can't guard the sewers and the courthouse forever.'

'We can't wait,' she said desperately. 'I promised the families I would help. The deportations are continuing relentlessly, and every day we wait, the risk to them increases. This might be our last chance to save any of them.'

'How old are the children?'

'The Kostek children are eleven, eight, and three. Then there's Benjamin Lieberman. He's six months old.'

Filip let out a long sigh. He looked down at his coffee and a deep crease of concern appeared on his forehead. Zofia had noticed her own face showing premature wrinkles of worry. What was it Irena said? When this was all over, then they would be very different people. Scarred, but not broken. Yes, she thought now, her wrinkles were the visible marks. But the marks no one could see cut much deeper.

Finally, Filip looked up. 'You're right, we have to do everything we can to save as many children as we can. But we will have to plan this right up to the smallest detail.'

Zofia put her hand on his. 'Like always.'

'Yes, like always.' He looked down at their hands and blushed slightly.

Zofia felt her own face reddening. Perhaps, when the war was over, their friendship might have a chance to blossom into something closer, something more tender. But now was not the time. And then a familiar, gnawing voice of doubt crept into her mind. Since the betrayal by Jakub and Lina, there was no one she trusted fully, not even Filip. There was a time she would have trusted Lina with her life, and look what had happened! How could she be so sure Filip wasn't working for the Nazis? He took photographs for them in the ghetto, after all. She slipped her hand away.

'Is anything wrong?' he asked.

Zofia drew her hand onto her lap and avoided looking at him. For a moment, neither of them spoke. Then Filip leaned forward.

'Do you not trust me, is that it? I thought I'd proved … that night … you know, the night we spent together in the ghetto.'

Zofia looked up and saw him blushing furiously now.

His eyes widened in alarm. 'I don't mean … it's … we didn't spend the *night* together. Not like that. Oh God,' he groaned, putting his head in his hands. 'I can't believe I'm getting this so wrong.'

Zofia had to smile, despite herself. 'Don't worry, we both know what you meant.'

He smiled back awkwardly, then his expression became serious. 'It's what they do, you know.'

'Who?'

'The Nazis. They don't just use brutality and violence to keep us down. They try to hurt us here,' he pointed at his head, 'and here.' He laid a palm against his chest, just over his heart. 'They sow suspicion and mistrust in order to divide us. It's psychological manipulation. And it works, perhaps even more effectively than violence.' He paused as a waitress passed with a tray full of coffee cups. 'I trust you wholeheartedly, Zofia,' he continued in a low voice, 'but I understand if you can't reciprocate.'

Zofia glanced to the side, saw a young couple feeding their toddler a jam-filled bun and laughing as the child smeared icing sugar all over his face. She thought of the children in the ghetto, of the families she'd promised to help. She owed it to them to take this leap of faith.

She took Filip's hand again and gave it a squeeze.

'You saved my life that night,' she said, 'and I do trust you.'

Filip gave her a smile so heartfelt it made her ashamed she'd doubted him even for a second. She checked her watch and let out a small gasp.

'I'm sorry,' she said, 'but I have to get home now. My sister is not very well and my mother needs my help to care for her.'

They rose from their seats and Filip accompanied her to the door.

'Your parents are lucky to have such a dutiful daughter,' he said, but Zofia shook her head. She had been lying to her family for months now, and that felt anything but dutiful.

She returned home feeling strangely energised, despite the worry of what lay ahead. Filip was right, it would only play into their enemies' hands if they allowed themselves to become paranoid. She and Filip made a good team, and with his help, she would be able to make good on the promise she'd made to the two Jewish families.

Her mother came into the hall as she hung up her coat.

'How is Zuzanna?' Zofia asked. Her sister had spent half the night coughing and had still been asleep when Zofia left this morning.

'A little better this afternoon. But she is not eating enough.' She tilted her head to one side and gave Zofia a long, hard look. 'And neither are you, child. But I have managed to get my hands on some fresh tripe, so I'm making *flaki* for dinner.'

'Good luck trying to get Zuzanna to eat tripe,' Zofia said with a smile.

Her mother sighed. 'I know. There is hardly anything to buy in the shops, and yet your sister still manages to be such a picky eater.'

She turned to go into the kitchen.

'Mama?' Zofia said.

'What?'

'Has Papa had ... has he had any more visits? From ... you know.'

Izabel shook her head. 'No. Like I said, they probably mistook him for someone else.' She crossed herself quickly, as if to ward off evil spirits. 'Oh, a letter came for you,' she said and picked up an envelope from the sideboard. She handed it to Zofia with a puzzled and somewhat anxious expression.

Zofia took the letter from her and shoved it in her pocket. She could guess who it was from. It was now three weeks since she had been to the orphanage to enquire about Ola, and she hoped the reply was what she'd been waiting for.

'I'll, um … I'll go and wash my hands for dinner,' she said, then turned and rushed up the stairs to read the letter in the privacy of her bedroom. She felt bad doing so. Her double life had created a distance between herself and her parents over the past few months and it was deepening with every additional secret she held. Only Zuzanna knew part of the truth, but Zofia knew she couldn't confide fully in her sister.

She closed her bedroom door and took the letter from her pocket. Perhaps this was finally good news, and by God, she could do with some. She tore open the envelope with shaking fingers.

Dear Miss Szczęsny,

I am delighted to inform you that we have managed to locate Ola Zieliński. She has been placed with the Broński family, who have a daughter of a similar age. I enclose their address and wish you the best of luck.

God bless,

Sister Bernadyna

Zofia let out a joyful gasp. Finally! Tears pricked her eyes at the thought of seeing Ola again. She knew the street, it was in the Wawer district of Warsaw, east of the river. She folded the letter and stuffed it into the back of a drawer in her bedside table. She would go to Wawer on Saturday and fetch Ola. She could hardly wait.

On Saturday morning, Zofia took the tram to Wawer. It was a grey and windy day, and she had butterflies in her stomach, almost as though she were about to go on stage and sing in front of a crowd of thousands. She hoped Ola would be as excited to see her as she was, and would be happy to come with her. Zofia knew there was a chance that the Broński family had taken Ola into their hearts and wouldn't want to give her up, but she would explain about Julia's dying wish, that she had asked Zofia to care for Ola and to reunite her with her sister, Magda.

The search for Magda was proving even more frustrating, however. How did one possibly go about finding a child that had disappeared from the ghetto over a year ago? All Zofia knew was the girl's name, and that she had been taken in by a family in Poznań. For want of other ideas, Zofia had contacted a branch of the Welfare Department there and asked if they might help locate a missing orphan named Magda Zielińska. Thankfully, it wasn't an obviously Jewish name, so that was one fewer risk. The Welfare Departments all over the country were hopelessly overworked, and Zofia was still waiting for a response, but she was sure she would find Magda, and then she would adopt both girls and provide a family for them. It was the thought of Ola and Magda that made her want to survive the war.

For days now, ever since she'd received the letter from the orphanage with Ola's address, she had been mentally rehearsing how to explain everything to her parents, once she turned up at home with a five-year-old girl in tow. Of course, she daren't tell them about her involvement with Żegota, not least to keep them safe. Instead, she had decided on a white lie: that Ola was an orphan the Social Welfare Department had had problems placing with a family. Zofia was sure that given time, when this blasted war was over, she would be able to confess that Ola was, in fact, a Jewish orphan from the ghetto.

The address she had been given by the nuns was a five-minute walk from the tram stop. It was even windier on this side of the river, a cold, relentless eastern squall, and Zofia had to hold down her felt hat to stop it being blown off by the wind. When she finally reached the address, she stopped outside the house on the pavement to calm her heartbeat. Now she had found Ola, she could hardly wait to see her. The Brońskis lived in a tiny brick house, with a flat roof and blue shutters outside the windows. It was winter, so the garden was rather dreary, but from where she stood, Zofia could see a few rhododendron bushes and forsythia and lilac shrubs. In springtime, the garden would be lush with colour, and looking further, Zofia spotted a wooden swing attached to an old beech tree. It was just the kind of house she would like to think of Ola living in. Perhaps, one day, she might be able to buy a house like this for her and Ola to live in. And once she had found Magda … well, then they would be a perfect family. She walked up to the front door, smiling at the thought. From a distance, she heard church bells calling the congregation to ten o'clock mass.

Oddly, the curtains were drawn in every window – perhaps everyone was still sleeping? It was Saturday morning, after all, though with two young children – Ola and the Broński's daughter – it was strange that no one was up and about at ten o'clock. Zofia rang the bell and heard the sound echoing inside the house. Apart from that, she heard nothing. She rang again, then knocked. Waited. No one came to the door. She was about to step around the side of the house to see if she could look inside a window, when a voice called out.

'Miss? Hello? What are you doing?'

Zofia turned and saw a plump, elderly woman with a colourful headscarf tied beneath her chin. She was standing on the threshold of the house next door, arms crossed over her ample chest. She took a few steps towards Zofia, giving her a quizzical, though not unfriendly, look.

'Can I help you?' she asked as she came up the path.

'Good day,' Zofia said. 'I'm looking for the Broński family. They live here, don't they? With two little girls?'

A shadow crossed the woman's face. 'They left,' she said sombrely. 'Several weeks ago. There were—' She paused and looked around before continuing in a quiet voice. 'There were rumours, about that little girl they were fostering. That she was – that she was a Jewess. I mean, I don't like such gossip at all, and the child looked perfectly normal to me. In fact, she was a very friendly little girl, always wishing me a good day, or a pleasant afternoon.' She smiled fondly at the recollection.

'But where have they gone?' Zofia asked, a sense of dread rising up from the pit of her stomach.

The woman shook her head. 'I have no idea. They were here one day, and gone the next. They must have moved out during the night. Perhaps there was some truth to the rumours, who knows?' She shrugged.

The blood rushed from Zofia's head to her feet and she thought she might faint. She put out a hand to steady herself against the wall of the house.

The woman took a step forward. 'Goodness, are you all right, my dear? You look awfully pale. Would you like to come to my house for a cup of tea?'

Zofia swallowed and blinked back her tears. 'No, I'm fine,' she mumbled, feeling her heart crumble inside. 'I-I have to go.'

32

Warsaw, February 1943

On the day of the operation, time seemed to lose all shape. The morning at the office dragged by, each minute as long as an hour, but then after lunch, Zofia checked the time and it was finally two o'clock. She quickly packed her things together and went into Mr Wójcik's office to tell him she had a migraine, adding that it was to do with 'women's troubles' when he seemed to be about to question her further. It did the trick, and he reluctantly agreed to let her off work early.

She hurried home to prepare. She had told the families she would come to collect the children at exactly quarter to four that afternoon, and instructed them to have the children ready and waiting. They would also have to have already said their farewells, as time was of the essence for a safe escape. In Zofia's experience, it was always better to be upfront about these things; the shock of a hurried goodbye was painful for both parents and children.

'It's me,' she called as she opened the front door, but there was no response. Her father would be at work, but her mother and Zuzanna should be here. Zuzanna had been off school for many weeks now and was bored to tears. She took off her coat and went into the living room. Zuzanna was lying down, reading.

'Hello, *Żabka*,' Zofia said. 'Where's Mama?'

'You've just missed her. She heard there was pork loin to be had in Ursus.' Zuzanna rolled her eyes. 'You know what she's like when it comes to meat.'

Ursus was on the other side of Warsaw; it would take their mother over an hour to get there and back – not counting the time spent in the inevitable queue. It was convenient that she was out, Zofia thought guiltily, as she wouldn't have to face her mother's scrutiny when she had to leave in just under an hour's time.

'Are you all right to be on your own?' Zofia asked. 'How are you feeling?'

Zuzanna scowled. 'You sound just like Mama. I'm not an invalid, I'm perfectly capable of—' She stopped to cough. When she finally caught her breath back, she was pale and wheezing. 'I'm fine,' she repeated.

Zofia came to sit on the bed beside her. 'I know you're not an invalid. But you have to rest. How about I make some tea?'

Zuzanna nodded. She was worryingly pale. Zofia understood full well her sister's frustration at her illness, but ignoring it wouldn't help. If only the winter would finally give way to spring! Then Zuzanna's lungs at least might have a chance to recover. But the air was as cold and heavy as ever, and it would be weeks, if not months, before Zuzanna would enjoy any respite.

'Would you put the radio on for me? I'm sick of reading.'

Zofia smiled and went to switch on the radio that stood on a sideboard at the far wall. She fiddled with the knob until she found some swing music.

'Thanks,' Zuzanna said and leaned back, tapping her hand to the beat.

Zofia went into the kitchen and filled the kettle, her thoughts soon focused away from Zuzanna's illness and towards the upcoming operation. She hoped the parents had managed to find sturdy shoes for the children – not an easy task in the ghetto, where more and more children were forced to go barefoot, even in winter. But they would have to walk across rubble and ice-covered pavements on their way to the cemetery, and there would be no time to stop. The baby, Binjamin, shouldn't be a problem, though. Zofia had fashioned a fabric sling with which to carry him; it was waiting upstairs at the back of her wardrobe.

She and Filip had met twice to discuss the operation. Each time, they had studied the ghetto map, hoping they might discover an escape route that was less risky than the cemetery. But it had been in vain. The Germans had become wary; an increasing number of weapons and explosives were being smuggled into the ghetto, and just a few weeks ago, a group of armed Jewish men and women had successfully resisted efforts to deport several thousand ghetto inhabitants. The Germans had cracked down hard, executing anyone who even appeared to have had anything to do with the resistance.

Finally, they had agreed that Filip would be waiting at the cemetery at four o'clock, with the wire fence already cut open. Zofia would collect the children and meet him there, and together they would slip through the hole. They would then wait on the other side of the ghetto boundary for the sun to set properly, giving them the opportunity to lead the children to safety under the cover of darkness. Zofia had already contacted the nun at the Visitation Church, who said she would be waiting with hot tea and blankets.

'I know it's not a very brave thing to admit, but I don't like cemeteries,' Filip had said with a shudder. 'They bring bad luck.'

'We both know that luck has nothing to do with anything,' Zofia had replied. 'And don't for a moment think you aren't brave. You are the bravest man I know.'

Then he had looked straight at her, and she knew that he was also thinking about a time beyond this one, when they might meet and talk about books or travel or music. Zofia felt the same sweet, painful longing, but as ever, that longing had to be stifled. Yet she was sure the time would come when they would be able to speak openly and honestly about their feelings.

The doorbell rang just as the kettle came to the boil, bringing Zofia out of her thoughts.

'I'll get it,' Zuzanna called, and was up and out of bed before Zofia could stop her.

She heard the front door open, a short conversation, and then the door close again. A minute later, Zuzanna came into the kitchen with an envelope.

'It's for you,' she said, handing it to Zofia.

Zofia looked at it, noticing immediately that there was no stamp or return address.

'Who delivered this?' she asked.

287

Zuzanna shrugged and sat down heavily. The sudden rush to the door had left her weak and breathless. 'A boy. About my age, I'd say. Red hair. Never seen him before.'

Zofia turned her back to her sister and tore open the envelope. It was a brief note, written in hurried, untidy handwriting.

Dear Zofia, BEWARE! Patrol at Cmentarz Żydowski scheduled for 4 p.m. God bless, Jolanta

Zofia lowered the note to her table with trembling fingers. A patrol of the cemetery! She swallowed, though her mouth was suddenly and painfully dry. They must have been exposed – or at least, their plan had been discovered. And if Irena's message hadn't reached her, she and the children would have walked right into the trap. Her next thought set her heart thumping. Filip! He would be waiting for her and the children in the cemetery, close to the wire fence. He had no reason to be there and would most certainly be arrested if the Germans found him there. And if he was caught with bolt cutters…

'Zofia, is everything all right? Who was the letter from?'

She looked up at Zuzanna. 'Um, a friend. It's … it's not important.' She checked her watch, but had to wait a few seconds before the hands stopped dancing in front of her eyes. Quarter to three. *There is enough time*, she thought. She hurried into the hall, stuffing the note into her pocket, and Zuzanna followed her.

'I have to go out for a while,' Zofia said, opening the front door and letting in an icy draught. 'I won't be long. You'll be all right on your own?'

Zuzanna stood leaning against the kitchen door. 'Is it … is it about them?' she asked. 'The people you're helping in the ghetto?'

'No, nothing like that, *Żabka*.' She flushed – lying still didn't come easily, even after all this time – and she quickly grabbed her coat. 'You go and lie down again, please. I'll be back very soon.'

Zuzanna gave an irritable grunt, but turned and went into the living room.

Zofia's thoughts were tumbling around inside her head as she headed towards the door. Of course there was no way she could fetch the children; she would have to return another time and explain everything to the parents. Her main priority now was to warn Filip. She knew he would be entering the ghetto through the checkpoint on Wolność Street; she had just enough time to head him off there. If she took a shortcut through the main railway station, rather than go around it, she would risk passing by the German guards there who liked to select people at random and detain them for a whole host of arbitrary reasons. But the shortcut would shave ten minutes off her journey and then she would reach Filip in time, before—

There was a sudden scraping sound from the living room, followed by a thump. Then a terrifying silence. Zofia rushed in to find Zuzanna collapsed on the floor. She froze. It was as though she had just been plunged underwater. All her senses were dulled; the sound of the radio became muffled; the overhead light seemed to dim; time slowed, then stopped.

A long second later she was on her knees beside her sister.

'Zuzanna! Can you hear me? Zuzanna!'

She patted her sister's ashen face, first gently, then harder, but her sister didn't wake. Panicked now, she put two fingers on her wrist and held them there. A pulse. Weak, but perceptible. There was only one thing she could do. She would go to the closest public telephone booth, call an ambulance, and wait until it arrived. Then she would rush to the cemetery to warn Filip. It was a fifteen-minute cycle to the closest ghetto checkpoint if she hurried. She wouldn't get to him before he entered the ghetto, but there should be – *there had to be!* – enough time before the patrol arrived. She rushed outside and unlocked her bicycle with trembling fingers. Filip wasn't stupid, he would be on his guard and looking out for any signs of the Germans, she told herself, even though the thought of leaving him exposed twisted inside her like a knife. But what choice did she have? If anything happened to her little sister, she would never be able to forgive herself.

The public telephone booth was on the corner at the end the street. Close to tears, Zofia cycled down the road as fast as she could, letting her bicycle clatter to the ground when she reached the booth. It was unoccupied, and she threw a small prayer of thanks up to the sky as she entered and dialled the emergency number.

'Hello? I need an ambulance. You must hurry.'

It was twenty-four minutes past three when the ambulance arrived and took Zuzanna to the Children's Hospital on Świetokryska Street. Zofia left a scribbled message for her mother, her insides churning with guilt that she hadn't accompanied her sister. But Zuzanna was in safe hands, and Zofia had another life to save.

She slipped on a patch of ice as she went to mount her bicycle and fell to the ground, tearing her stocking and grazing her knee. But she barely felt any pain. Rather, there was a ringing in her ears, a raging pressure building up inside her head that threatened to make her skull explode. She cycled faster than she had ever dared, sounding her bell to warn pedestrians and other cyclists, shouting when they didn't move fast enough, and pulled up just ahead of the checkpoint eight minutes later. There were only two people waiting to enter. Zofia went to stand behind a young man in overalls, and her vision was suddenly beset by a thousand dots swirling in front of her eyes. She forced herself to take some deep breaths to dispel the dizziness. If she passed out now, it might mean a death sentence for Filip.

The guard called out something; it was her turn. With legs like jelly, she approached him and handed him her pass.

'Name,' he growled.

'Zofia Szczęsny.'

'Leave your bicycle here.'

'Why?'

The man drew himself to his full height. 'Are you questioning my order?'

Zofia shook her head hurriedly. 'No, of course not. I'm sorry.'

She quickly pushed her bicycle to the nearest wall and propped it there, not bothering to lock it. It would take her twice as long to get to the cemetery without the bicycle, but what could she do? It was three thirty-two. If she ran, she should have enough time.

The guard studied her pass for what seemed like an eternity and she had to clamp her hands behind her back to prevent herself from snatching it back off him.

'Date of birth?'

'It says on my pass,' she blurted out, and immediately regretted it when he raised his head slowly to look her in the face.

'I asked you to tell me your date of birth,' he said sharply.

'Twenty-fifth of May, 1919.' She raised the corners of her mouth in an attempted smile, but the tension made her cheeks twitch.

'What's your business in the Restricted Area?' the guard continued. He had a thin duelling scar on his left cheek that puckered as he spoke.

'Um, there's…' Zofia's voice caught. She cleared her throat. 'There's a suspected case of typhus north of Mylna Road. I'm here to impose a quarantine order for the people living on that block.'

The man sniffed, then wiped his nose on his sleeve. He leered at her.

'You're a nurse, then?'

She nodded.

'Where's your uniform?'

'I … I didn't have time, I…' She threw him a pleading look. It was all she had.

The soldier grabbed her upper arm and drew her in close. It took all her effort not to show her utter repulsion for him.

'This—' he said, pointing at the tear in her stocking on her left knee, 'is quite unbecoming for an otherwise attractive girl.' He grinned at her, displaying a row of crowded, greyish teeth.

Then he thrust her pass back to her. 'Next time, you wear your uniform. I like a girl in uniform.'

He barked a laugh and let her go.

Zofia hurried down the street and turned the next corner out of sight of the checkpoint. Then she ran. She ran as fast as she could, past a woman with open sores on her legs begging and moaning, past a group of young men collecting glass bottles, past two filthy, half-naked children with matted hair and distended stomachs. She was driven by fear, but also by a sudden, fuelling rage against Jakub and Lina that she might ever have questioned Filip's loyalty. Her lungs were soon screaming for air, but she didn't stop running. Her long hair had come loose from its braid and strands of it whipped across her face. Tears were streaming down her cheeks, icy hot as the sharp wind buffeted her from the front. An elderly man in a torn black coat held out an arm as she ran, trying to stop her, calling, 'Careful, slow down! You will draw attention to yourself!', but she ignored him, down Nowolipie Street, taking a sharp turn onto Smocza Road, not daring to look at her watch, yet hearing the seconds ticking loudly in her head, *tick tick tick*.

Finally, she reached the entrance to the cemetery and stopped short. There he was! Filip, some fifty metres away, making his way through ivy-covered trees towards the far end of the cemetery. He was dressed in a dark brown jacket and black cap, a leather bag slung over his shoulder. Zofia almost howled with relief. Thank God, she had caught him in time.

And then – a sight she would replay in her head for years to come, a sight she would later wish she could delete from her memory forever: four green-clad figures emerged from behind a huge oak tree on the left, surrounding Filip before he had time to run. He raised his hands immediately, but one of the soldiers hit him on the side of the head – the crack of it loud enough for Zofia to hear – and he fell heavily to his knees. The bag was ripped from his shoulder and opened. The bolt cutters were removed. A guttural laugh, followed by a sharp string of words.

Almost mechanically, Zofia lifted her wrist and looked at her watch. It was three fifty-two.

No! she wanted to scream. *It isn't time, you're too early! The patrol was due at four o'clock!*

But she didn't scream. Instead, she doubled over and vomited. When she looked up again, the soldiers had pulled Filip to his feet and were dragging him out of the cemetery. A thin stream of blood was dripping down the side of his face. Zofia stepped behind a tree and put a hand to her mouth to prevent a moan of despair escaping. She closed her eyes, the taste of bile sour in her mouth.

Then she heard the voices coming closer. If she stayed where she was, they would discover her. Trembling violently from head to foot, she turned and fled up the street, the shattered pieces of her heart stabbing at her chest like broken glass. She didn't know how they would ever possibly heal.

33

Warsaw, Present Day

It took Lizzie a couple of attempts to get the keycard into the hotel room lock. She chuckled to herself when the green light finally lit up and the door opened.

She'd had a great night out with Roksana – first they'd gone for dinner at a restaurant that served the best pot roast and napkin dumplings Lizzie had ever eaten. Then Roksana had taken her to a bar on Masowieka Street, where she had sampled some delicious local vodka. Finally, they'd crossed the river Vistula and ended up in the district of Praga, where they enjoyed the warm summer night, listening to a live band while relaxing on deckchairs and sipping cocktails. Now, Lizzie was pleasantly tipsy, and very, very happy.

All night, she and Roksana had talked about everything they had found out since Lizzie had arrived in Warsaw – the meeting with Aliza Blumsztajn, the tour of the ghetto, the afternoon with Ola, and most of all, the heroic actions of a courageous woman named Zofia Szczęsny – an entire lifetime squeezed into four days. When Lizzie and Roksana had eventually run out of words, they had hugged, tearfully, and promised to stay in touch.

Lizzie slipped off her shoes now and went to get a glass of water, then fired up her laptop and checked flights from Warsaw to Seattle. There was a flight leaving tomorrow at eleven thirty, with a layover in Frankfurt. It was slightly more expensive than her flight out here, and she wasn't sure she'd be free of a hangover in the morning, but she bought a ticket anyway. She just couldn't wait to get home and tell her family – most of all her grandmother – what she had found out.

When she had packed her few belongings into the suitcase, she went to the bathroom to brush her teeth. Looking into the bathroom mirror, she found herself staring intently at her reflection, seeing her own face as though for the first time. Whose genes was she carrying? From whom had she inherited the oval-shaped face, the dark shiny hair, the left eyebrow that was ever so slightly higher than the right? She might never know what had become of Julia, her biological great-grandmother. It made her momentarily sad, that some questions would forever stay unanswered, but then she thought back to the very beginning of this journey, when she had discovered three photographs of her great-grandmother. It had turned out that Zofia Szczęsny was not her biological great-grandmother after all. And yet … without Zofia, and her selfless actions, Lizzie would not be here. Surely *that* was the meaning of family – and unconditional love.

Lizzie's journey had resulted in her finding her family, her Polish family, and discovering so much about herself. She thought of Ola, and Tomasz, and Maja. She was incredibly grateful to have found them, and it made her a little wistful to think it might be months before she saw them again. But it wasn't just the Broński family; Lizzie had fallen in love with the city of Warsaw itself, and she knew she would be back here to visit before long.

She was overcome by a sudden desire to share everything she had discovered, and decided she couldn't wait until she got back home. She quickly rinsed her mouth, dropped the toothbrush in the sink and hurried into the bedroom. There was only one person she wanted to talk to now, one person who knew her better than anyone, one person who would understand what she had come to realise: with adoption part of her story already, why couldn't it be again?

Her hands shaking slightly, she dialled Alex's number. It was mid-afternoon back on the west coast, and he might be busy at work. The call rang out four times, five, and then—

'Hello?'

34

Warsaw, June 1945

The sky was a clear blue with just a handful of feathery clouds floating up high. It had been four weeks since the Germans had surrendered, but Zofia still had to remind herself that Europe was at peace, and no longer at war. Two years and four months since she had last seen Filip, and she still thought of him regularly. Though it was undoubtedly painful whenever such memories surfaced, she clung on to each and every one of them. It was all she had left of him.

She and Irena were digging beneath the apple tree, and the early summer sun shone down on their backs as they worked. They had already uncovered four of the jars they had buried last time they were here, but there were still one more left somewhere under the earth.

Irena's friend Karolina, the woman to whom the house belonged, came out into the garden.

'Here, I thought you might like some lemonade,' she said, holding out two glasses.

Zofia and Irena thanked her and took a lemonade each. The digging was thirsty work and they both emptied their glasses quickly.

'How is it coming along?' Karolina asked.

Irena gestured towards the jars they had placed near the back wall, each containing slips of papers with the names of the children they had saved. 'Nearly done. Sorry about your lawn. I should have made a map, like a pirate.'

'X marks the spot.' Karolina laughed. 'And please don't worry about the lawn. It will grow back.'

Irena handed her glass back to Karolina, thanking her again, and then put her hands on her lower back and stretched. She turned to Zofia.

'Back to work, then. It must be here somewhere.'

As they continued digging for the final jar, Zofia threw an occasional glance towards Irena. It was unusual seeing her in trousers, though as always, she wore her long brown hair piled up on her head in a complicated braid. It was incredible, what she had been through over the past two years. Irena's story was terrifying, and yet she was here to tell the tale. She had been exposed and arrested in October 1943, eight months after the failed smuggling attempt that had seen Filip being arrested. She was sent to Pawiak Prison and tortured, though she didn't give up a single name, and had quickly been sentenced to death. But, it seemed, God had had other plans for her. Żegota members had identified German officials who were susceptible to bribes, and three months later, the SS officer charged with taking her to her execution by firing squad had knocked her unconscious on the way and left her lying on the side of the road.

Since then, she had been in hiding, returning only in January when the Soviet army declared Warsaw 'liberated'. And yet, to Zofia, she appeared as strong and resilient as ever, though Zofia knew she had scars – both physical and emotional – that would possibly never heal. As for the Warsaw Ghetto, it had been razed to the ground after the brave and desperate uprising in the spring of 1943, in which many thousands of men, women and children were killed, and of the remaining fifty thousand ghetto residents, almost all were captured and deported to the extermination camps of Treblinka and Majdanek.

'By the way, how is your sister?' Irena asked, straightening up to stretch her back again. 'Or is she still not speaking to you?'

'She's fine,' Zofia replied. 'She has her final examinations next week and she's scrambling to catch up with her school work, but I think she'll do well. She's strong-willed, if nothing else.'

After the attempted smuggling operation with Filip had failed so disastrously, Zofia had also gone into hiding, and Zuzanna had not quite forgiven her for leaving. It had never been established how the plan had been discovered, or even if Zofia and Filip had, indeed, been known to the Nazis, but she hadn't wanted to take any chances. In order to protect her family, she had fled to a small town outside the city of Bydgoszcz, some three hundred kilometres north-west of Warsaw, and cut off all contact with them overnight. It had been the hardest thing she had ever done, and even now, almost six months after her return, there remained a lot of work trying to re-establish their trust in her.

Of Filip there had been no news, neither of his arrest nor of any execution, though Zofia knew deep down that he mustn't have survived, otherwise he would have come for her. Even so, she had searched for him for a long time, desperate to see him again, to hold him, all the while pushing away a thought that troubled her in the dark of night – that he might believe she had betrayed him. But her searching had been in vain, so instead, she had channelled her grief and sadness into her work. From Bydgoszcz, she had become involved in finding foster homes for many of the children they had saved, and now they needed the children's real names, in the hope of reuniting them with their parents.

'And Zuzanna's heart?' Irena said. 'How is the new treatment going?'

'Dr Amosov is a real blessing,' Zofia replied. 'He has signed her up to a drug trial. Digoxin. It's derived from the purple foxglove, which my mother finds worrying – and my father doesn't trust the Soviets any further than he can throw them – but it seems to be doing Zuzanna the world of good. She has already put on some weight and is beginning to outgrow her clothes.'

Beside her, Irena dug up the final jar and held it aloft, triumphantly. 'This is it!' she exclaimed, smiling broadly. 'Now, let's take ourselves for a well-earned rest.'

Zofia wiped her damp forehead with a handkerchief and the two women joined Karolina at a small table beneath an awning on the terrace. Irena looked towards the apple tree, beneath which the jars had been buried.

'So many blossoms,' she said, smiling. 'You'll have a good apple harvest this year, Karolina.'

'I hope so,' Karolina replied. 'Perhaps you might bring a few of those many children around in September to help pick them.'

'Yes.' Irena nodded. 'Perhaps I might.'

Irena had never given up hope that one day, the children would be reunited with their parents. But Zofia suspected that might yield a whole new succession of sorrow and despair. The authorities were still collating lists of those who had perished in the death camps, those places of unspeakable, unthinkable evil. It was estimated that ninety percent of the Jewish population in Poland hadn't survived Nazi rule. Any child whose parents were still alive could consider themselves lucky.

Zofia thought of Julia and swallowed down her tears. All this time, she had been looking for Ola and Magda, but to no avail. Ola would now be eight years old, her sister Magda almost ten. For the last two years, she had contacted every orphanage, every youth welfare office, every foster organisation in the country. Every false lead, every dead-end had been heart-breaking, but to this day, she had refused to give up hope. That, she thought, was something she'd learned from Irena, even though she felt her optimism wearing thin. But just yesterday, she had received another fresh lead.

Irena touched her lightly on the arm.

'Penny for them,' she said.

Zofia shook her head. She wasn't really superstitious, but she didn't want to jinx anything by mentioning it out loud.

So, all she said was, 'I can't stay much longer, I'm afraid. I have a train to catch.'

Zofia stood outside the ramshackle house on the edge of a dusty road. She took out the slip of paper with the address to double check. Yes, she had come to the right place. The house was small and paint was peeling off the window frames. Against the side of the house was a pile of firewood, and from around the back, Zofia could hear children playing. The sound lifted her spirits a little. She might finally have come to the right place.

The six-hour train journey from Warsaw to Wrocław had left her with an aching back, and her feet were sore after a day of traipsing around the city. Her contact at the local welfare department had given her four possible addresses of families with a daughter named Magda who was around nine years old. Zofia had had no luck with the first two families; in fact, one man had slammed the door in her face when she had asked if he had taken in a Jewish child years ago. It had left Zofia angry and shaken that after all that had happened, after the cold-blooded, systematic murder of millions of Jews, some people still held such hatred in their hearts.

She stepped up to the front door and knocked, hoping to be greeted by someone kinder, even if it did turn out to be the wrong family. After only a moment, the door opened.

'Yes?'

The woman who opened the door looked to be in her early forties, with greying hair and dark rings under her eyes. She gave Zofia a wary look.

'Good day. My name is Zofia Szczęsny, and I'm looking for someone.'

The woman narrowed her eyes, not opening the door wider than a crack through which to look. Zofia was neither surprised nor offended. During the final stages of the war, when they knew they were losing, the Germans had inflicted as much damage as they could, to buildings and infrastructure, but also to people. It would take years, generations perhaps, before people trusted one another again. So it was no surprise that this woman would look suspiciously on an unannounced stranger arriving on her doorstep.

'What do you want?' she asked.

'I am a friend of Julia Zielińska.'

The woman opened the door a little wider, frowning. 'I've heard that name before.'

'Julia, she died, three years ago,' Zofia said quietly. Even after all this time, the grief was still fresh. 'She was in the ghetto and became very ill.'

'I'm sorry to hear that,' the woman said, gently now. 'I never knew Julia Zielińska. Only – the name is familiar somehow. But how can I help you? Who is it you're looking for?'

'I've been given to understand that Julia's daughter is living with you. Magda. You were kind enough to take her in when she escaped from the ghetto.'

The woman opened the door wide. 'I am Maria Dąbrowska. I think you'd better come in.'

Zofia sat on a wooden chair in the kitchen, while Maria made tea. The kitchen was small and cluttered; dozens of shoes piled haphazardly in a corner, a worn kitchen cabinet heaving with chipped crockery, a string suspended from one wall to the other with laundry hanging on it to dry.

'Don't look too closely,' Maria said with an embarrassed smile. 'Tidying up after children is like shovelling snow in a blizzard.'

Zofia smiled and shook her head. 'Please don't worry on my account. My house looks just as bad, and I don't even have any children.'

Maria gave a tired laugh, just as the kettle boiled. She turned to pour the water into the pot and then her shoulders seemed to sag.

'It's been hard,' she said quietly.

Zofia wasn't sure she had heard properly. 'I'm sorry?'

Maria turned back around, a grave look on her face. 'Magda has been with us for almost three years. When she first came here, we didn't think we had a choice. The woman who brought her – a colleague of my brother's and the former neighbours of the Zielińska family – told us they had been forced into the ghetto, and that one of their daughters had managed to escape. Magda was only six years old, but she was already deeply disturbed by what she had experienced there.'

She took a few deep breaths, then continued. 'You must understand that my husband and I have tried to love her like our own, but there is barely enough food to go around. I cannot work, as I have to take care of the children, and my husband was injured on the front. He can only work for a few hours at a time before he succumbs to terrible pain.'

'I'm so sorry,' Zofia said.

'And Magda is a lovely child, certainly,' Maria continued, smiling to herself. 'A little high-spirited, perhaps.' Her expression became serious again. 'But every time I have to give my own children a smaller portion of bread, of potatoes, of meat when we have it, there is a little part of me that resents having her here.'

She swallowed and lifted a hand to wipe away a tear. 'It is shameful, I know.'

Zofia got to her feet. 'No! It's not shameful at all, Maria.' She crossed the floor and put her hands on the woman's shoulders. 'You saved Magda's life. It if weren't for your family's kindness, Magda would never have survived this awful war. That is far from shameful. That is generous and brave and good.'

At that moment, five children stormed in, their cheeks flushed from playing outside. They took one look at Zofia and immediately started talking higgledy-piggledy. The oldest child, a tall and skinny boy, was about fourteen, the youngest girl looked about three. All the children had blonde hair, apart from one. It was a girl, who looked about the right age, with dark hair cut just below her chin, and a star-shaped mark on her left cheek. The children's chattering rose in volume as they jostled for space in the small kitchen.

'Quiet!' Maria said, raising her voice above the noise. She sounded tired, Zofia thought. No, not tired – weary.

The children fell silent instantly, and the girl with the dark hair pulled her lips into a pout. Zofia's pulse rose – the girl had the same round eyes as Ola, though they were slightly lighter, more hazel than chocolate. *It must be her*, Zofia thought excitedly, *this must be Magda*.

And indeed, a moment later, Maria called her over.

'Magda, sweetheart, this is Zofia. She was a good friend of your mother's.'

Magda pulled her brow into a frown and took a step closer.

'Hello,' Zofia said.

Magda didn't respond, she just stood there eyeing Zofia suspiciously.

'Well,' Maria said, somewhat impatiently. 'Have you nothing to say? Our guest will think you've been brought up without any manners.'

Magda sniffed. Then she held out her right hand to shake. 'Hello. I'm Magda.'

'Hello, Magda,' Zofia repeated and took the girl's hand. 'Like Maria said, I was a friend of your mother's. And I also knew your sister, Ola.'

At these words, Magda's eyes brightened, but a moment later she began to cry. Zofia opened her arms, tentatively at first, then wrapped them around the girl.

'Shh, don't cry,' she whispered. 'I've been looking for you for a long time, and now I've found you.'

The next morning, Zofia arrived at the Dąbrowski house with a bag containing apples, hard-boiled eggs and sandwiches for the journey, and an empty suitcase. Magda's farewell from her foster family was heart-wrenching and tearful, and promises to write regularly were exchanged.

'I hope you know I wouldn't let her go off with just anyone,' Maria said. 'But you knew her mother.' She hesitated for a moment, then added, 'We have taken good care of her, we really have.'

'I know,' Zofia said, even though she was convinced that Magda would never have received the love she deserved with this family. Giving a child room and board was one thing, albeit an important one, but every child deserved unconditional love. And from the moment she had seen Magda, that love had flooded through her. She hoped, over time, Magda would feel the same.

'We have to leave now,' she said now, 'otherwise we will miss our train.'

She picked up the suitcase Maria had packed for Magda – she only had a few belongings and the case was very light – and offered the girl her hand.

'Where are we going?' Magda asked as they turned the corner.

Zofia squeezed her hand. 'We're going home.'

35

Warsaw, Present Day

Please ensure that your seat back is straight up and your tray table is stowed. On behalf of the captain and our entire crew, it is our pleasure to have you aboard. Enjoy your flight.

Lizzie hadn't paid attention to the flight attendant's announcement. Her mind was buzzing. She looked out of the porthole window, watching as the luggage handlers stowed the final suitcases into the hold. She was still smiling, hadn't really stopped since she had spoken to Alex. She yawned; she'd had less than four hours sleep after spending most of the night on the phone.

In their hours-long conversation, it had almost been like when they were first dating and felt the need to get to know each other inside out. And at the same time, they were so familiar with one another, it was like two old souls being reunited. They had talked about anything and everything and nothing, about his day at the hospital and a particularly cranky patient, but also about how lost he had felt without her, and how painful it had been over the past year to feel her slipping away from him. Lizzie, in turn, told him all about her trip to

Warsaw, Ola and Magda, her new friendship with Roksana – but also how much of a failure she'd felt over the past few years and how impossible it had been for her to let Alex see it. There was a lot to talk about still, Lizzie knew that, but they had made a good start to finding their way back to one another.

She checked the time. It would be another fifteen hours before she landed, but Alex was coming to meet her and tomorrow, they would visit her grandmother together. In the aisle, the flight attendant was demonstrating how to put on an oxygen mask. 'And please secure your own mask before helping others,' she instructed. She was right, Lizzie thought suddenly. Sometimes it's important to look after yourself first. If you don't practice self-care and compassion, how can you possibly care for others? Coming here, finding out about who she really was, what it was she really needed, had put this into perspective.

She couldn't quite believe that this trip to Warsaw was all it had taken to get to a place of hope. Perhaps the city had magical powers? She chuckled to herself, imagining how Alex – the no-nonsense medical professional – would react if she shared this thought with him. But at the same time, coming here had given her an incredible sense of clarity that had managed to completely transform her life. Perhaps it had something to do with the 'cosmic equilibrium' Aliza Blumsztajn had talked about. She took a final glance out of the window. Whatever it was, she was ready, now, to tackle what lay ahead, and Alex was the only person she could imagine by her side.

The flight attendant walked down the aisle, checking seatbelts and tray tables. She stopped when she got to Lizzie's row and quietly asked the man sitting beside Lizzie to push his bag a little further under the seat in front. He was elderly and struggled to bend, so Lizzie helped him. When she sat up, settling in her seat, she bumped elbows with him when she put her arm on the rest. They both apologised to each other.

'Please, you take the armrest,' he said politely. He had a very wrinkled face, with bushy grey eyebrows and gentle eyes. He must have been a very handsome man in his prime. 'I have one on the right.'

Lizzie smiled and thanked him.

'Have you been visiting?' he asked.

'Yes,' she replied. 'I've been visiting family.'

He smiled widely, deepening the starburst wrinkles around his eyes. 'Me too! I left Poland decades ago, but I make sure to return whenever I can. I'm old now, so there aren't that many of my generation left, but still. Family is so important, is it not?'

Lizzie nodded, thinking of Magda and Ola. She was thrilled at the idea of reuniting them, even if it would only be virtually. And yet, she was beset by a deep sense of grief at their loss of each other for almost their entire lives and an aching sadness that she would never be able to speak to her great-grandmother Zofia, to get answers to her many questions. What, she wondered, could have happened that made Zofia find Magda, the one who hadn't been in the ghetto, and not Ola, the one who had?

36

Warsaw, February 1946

'Zofia!' Izabel called. 'A letter for you.'

Zofia dumped the laundry basket and ran into the hallway, where her mother stood holding out an envelope. She knew from painful experience not to get her hopes up, but it was instinctive, that little flutter of expectation that rose every time she thought she might have got closer to finding Ola. She ripped open the envelope just as Magda came in from the garden.

'Is it from her?' the girl asked, her eyes wide.

Zofia didn't answer; instead, she scanned the letter quickly, and as she did so, the flutter of expectation crashed to the ground in one harsh swoop.

'No,' she said quietly. 'It's a different child. This letter is from the aunt of a girl called Aleksandra. They call her "Ola" for short.'

'Oh,' Magda said, her gaze dropping to the floor.

Zofia leaned forward and hugged her. 'We will find her,' she whispered into her hair. 'And then we'll be a proper family.'

Magda hugged her back tightly, and after a while Zofia felt the girl relax. She released her and smiled.

'Now, have you done the maths tasks I set you?'

Magda nodded.

'Good girl. Would you like to help Grandma make the soup for supper?'

Magda pursed her lips. 'Can I go and play with Natalia next door instead?'

Izabel threw Zofia a worried glance, but Zofia nodded.

'Just make sure to be back for supper,' she said.

When Magda had left the room, Izabel gestured for Zofia to take a seat beside her at the kitchen table.

'Zofia, *kochanie*,' she said earnestly. 'You must come to a decision about Magda. Schooling her at home is one thing, but the neighbours are already talking. Just the other day, Mrs Kamińska from number twenty-four asked when the girl's mother would be back. I gave her the usual excuse, but someone is bound to report it sooner or later.'

Zofia sighed. Magda had been living with them for eight months now, ostensibly the child of a friend who was too ill to care for her. In that time, she had come out of her shell and the quiet, earnest little girl Zofia had found in Wrocław had turned into a lively, curious and happy child. Zofia couldn't imagine life without her.

Back in June, when she had fetched Magda from the Dąbrowski family, she had intended to adopt her as soon as possible, but had immediately run into a hurdle she hadn't anticipated: in this strictly Catholic country, the idea of a young, unmarried woman adopting a child was unthinkable. When she had enquired at the child welfare office, the clerk had looked at her as if she'd just asked if he might fly her to the moon.

'A young lady like you?' he had said, barely managing to suppress a smirk. 'Find yourself a husband, why don't you, and have your own babies. You're an attractive girl, it shouldn't be too difficult.'

Zofia had stormed out, red-faced and raging. Since then, the Szczęsny family had been looking after Magda, using the cover story that she was their temporary ward. Since the war had ended, the country had been in a state of upheaval and administrative confusion; there was still no functioning government and there was widespread fear and anger among many Poles at the Soviet annexation of some Polish regions and the permanent garrisoning of Red Army units on the country's territory. While Zofia was as troubled by these developments as many others, and the turmoil had made it near impossible to locate a nine-year-old girl named Maria Nowak, it had so far prevented the local authorities from looking too closely at her 'guardianship' of Magda. But things were gradually settling down, and her mother was right, she would have to take a decision soon about Magda's future. One option had come to mind already.

'Elżbieta has a visa for the United States,' she said after a long pause. 'She is leaving next month, and I … I was thinking it might be the right thing for Magda and me, too.'

Izabel's face crumpled. 'First Zuzanna, now you.'

Zuzanna had turned eighteen a few months ago and had immediately applied for a three-year nurses' training scheme with the Red Cross in Switzerland. Although her school grades hadn't been very good – largely due to the lengthy absences during her illness – she had so impressed the interview panel with her fierce dedication and enthusiasm that they offered her a place on the spot. Zofia and her parents now received postcards from Bern, and although they were usually brief and to the point, Zuzanna made sure to write regularly. The alpine air was doing her heart and lungs the world of good.

'But Zuzanna will be back soon, Mama,' Zofia replied, gently stroking Izabel's arm, hoping her mother wouldn't catch the insincerity in her voice. In light of political developments here in Poland, Zofia secretly hoped her sister would make Switzerland her permanent home. Perhaps, when the time came, their parents would go and live with her.

'But nothing is decided yet,' she continued, unable to bear the sorrow in her mother's face. 'Besides, Magda has no papers, so I'm not even sure it's an option at all.'

Izabel pressed her lips together in a tired smile. 'Well, something will have to be decided. If only for Magda's sake. The child needs to know where she belongs.'

Two weeks later, Zofia got off the tram at Kruszynki Square and took the slip of paper containing the address from her bag: *8 Falentyńska Road*. She looked around, unfamiliar with this part of the city. Across the road, a group of builders, white-faced with plaster dust, were busy sawing and hammering inside a building whose fourth wall had been completely destroyed. There had been so much destruction wreaked over the last seven years, it might take generations to repair. Thousands upon thousands of ruins were scattered all over the city, but beneath it all lay a fierce will to live, and Zofia knew that the Polish people would emerge proud and strong.

The men on the building site glanced over at her, but not in a way that made her want to go and ask for directions, so instead, she turned left along the main road.

She hadn't seen Marek for several years. She had found out from Elżbieta that he had survived the war, and that he was living in the west of the city. It had taken Elżbieta quite a lot of coaxing to give Zofia his address; apparently, Marek wanted nothing to do with anything that might cause painful memories of the past to resurface. Zofia understood this well. In fact, it seemed that most people had adopted one of two strategies – those who, like Marek, had put the past firmly in the past with the hope it remained buried there, and those who would be forever looking back, hoping for answers to questions that may never be answered, such as: how could this have happened? Where had our humanity gone? Could we, as human beings, ever recover fully from this collective trauma? As for Zofia, she was torn. As much as she understood the need to bury the past and all its wretchedness, she still longed to find the child to whom she had promised a new life and a family. Ola would always be Zofia's past and present and future.

The sky was steel-grey and heavy with clouds; it would start raining any moment now. Zofia paused for a moment, worried she might be lost, but when she came to a small junction the street sign read: **Falentyńska Road**. She didn't even know if Marek still had any of the contacts necessary for her to enact her plan, but she owed it to Magda to try. She quickened her pace, knowing that if she hesitated, she might not see it through.

A new birth certificate for Magda – that's what she was here for. Then she could apply for a passport, and visas for America.

She had been meaning to make the arrangements ever since she had found out it would be impossible to adopt Magda here in Poland. But the thought of Ola had kept her from doing it. The notion of leaving the girl behind was almost too much to bear. And yet, she thought as she knocked on the door to number eight, there was no future for her or Magda here in Poland. Perhaps, one day, they might all be reunited. Until then, she would keep Ola firmly in her prayers.

It had been a long and miserable journey from Warsaw in smoke-filled, overcrowded trains. Many, if not most, of the railway lines had suffered damage during the war, so Zofia and Magda had had to change trains several times, sometimes switching to a bus and then back onto a train to finally arrive in Hamburg.

When they had crossed the Polish-German border at Frankfurt-Oder, Zofia felt a moment's trepidation. For so long, this had been enemy territory, home to those who had inflicted so much harm and suffering on people they believed to be sub-human. For hours, the train travelled through war-ravaged towns and cities, many places reduced to heaps of rubble. Here and there Zofia saw people, some of them dressed in nothing but rags, clearing away debris with shovels or even their bare hands. It was a pitiful sight, yet it did little to soften her heart. Too many of these people had supported the barbaric war, right up to the end, and even now claimed they had known nothing of the atrocities committed within the walls of ghettos and concentration camps. Irena had always spoken about a reckoning with God – Zofia, by contrast, would have liked to see a reckoning with human justice.

From the train station in Hamburg they took a bus to the port, and when they finally arrived, Magda was almost asleep on her feet and it took all manner of coaxing and cajoling – and promises of chocolate – to get her to walk the few hundred metres from the bus stop to the emigration checkpoint. Dozens of people were already in line, many of them chattering with excitement about the journey ahead. As they joined the queue, Zofia felt an old familiar tension rise inside her, as though she were standing in line to enter the ghetto carrying some illicit contraband. But she didn't have any contraband sewn into her coat, or stuffed into her waistband. Instead, she carried two passports and two tickets for the ship in her bag, made out in the names of Zofia Chesney and her daughter, Magda.

Marek had refused to take her money, though she knew these papers were worth hundreds of złoty, if not thousands. When he had given her the documents though, he had irritably mumbled something about people leaving their homeland, something he claimed he could never do. Like Irena, he was thinking of joining the communist party, to work at rebuilding the country as a free and just place for all to live. Although Zofia had every understanding for his motives, she didn't have enough energy left for that kind of fight. Besides, she doubted whether the country would turn into a free and just place under the influence of the Soviet Union. In the recent referendum, held to test the popularity of the various political forces vying for control in post-war Poland, over seventy percent of the population had apparently voted yes to the communist position of nationalisation and agricultural reform according to the Soviet model. It was an open secret that the results had been falsified, but Zofia held out little hope that those in control would voluntarily give up any of their power. Nonetheless, she wished Marek and Irena all the best in their struggle for a free Poland. As for herself, she had to use the little fighting spirit she had left to create a better life for herself and Magda. And, she had realised sadly, that couldn't be in Poland.

When it was her turn at passport control, she took out her and Magda's papers and presented them to the guard, a young American soldier with hair cropped close to his skull and perfectly straight teeth. He checked the passports and handed them back.

'A new life?' he asked with a broad smile.

Zofia nodded. 'Yes,' she replied, mirroring his smile. 'A new life for myself and my daughter.'

'Good luck, then, Mrs Chesney.'

Quickly, before the soldier could ask her any more questions or change his mind about letting her through, she grabbed Magda's hand and led her up the long flight of steps to the ship's deck. They could feel the throb of the engines beneath their feet.

'It's huge,' Magda said in a reverent whisper. Then she looked around somewhat nervously at all the other passengers. 'Do we get our own room?'

'Yes, we do. It's called a cabin.'

'How long is the journey?'

'Two weeks,' Zofia said, adding, 'shall we find somewhere to stand to wave goodbye?'

'Who are we waving goodbye to?' Magda asked with a frown.

'To everyone.'

In an attempt to distract the girl from further questions, Zofia pointed towards a free spot close to the ship's railing.

'There, let's grab that spot before someone else does.'

They hurried over and pressed themselves against the railing. Much like Elżbieta, Zofia believed that she needed a new start. She and Elżbieta had exchanged a flurry of excited letters, and Elżbieta had promised she would meet them when they arrived in New York. She herself had found work as a secretary and said it should be easy for Zofia to find work, too.

The vibrations from the ship's engines intensified. *This is it then*, Zofia thought. She was leaving the country she'd called home all her life, and with it, almost everyone that had given her life meaning thus far – her family, Irena, Filip. She had no idea when she would be back in Poland, and her sorrow at the thought was momentarily overwhelming. But she knew she couldn't give in to such feelings or else they would weigh her down forever. She had Ola with her, which was worth more than she could say. And the faces of all those she'd had to bid farewell to would be imprinted in her mind forever. Instinctively, her hand went into her pocket and touched the music box Zuzanna had sent her from Switzerland last month. It was a tiny, pocket-sized box, and when she turned the little handle, it played a Swiss folk song: *Oh, My Homeland*. Zofia wrapped her hand around it, tight, feeling the corners of the box dig into her palm.

The ship's horn blared suddenly, tearing her out of her thoughts. She held Magda's hand tightly, terrified a sudden gust of wind might pick up the child and sweep her overboard.

'You're silly,' Magda said, smiling, when Zofia mentioned her fear. 'We haven't even left the port yet.'

At that moment, the ship's engines rumbled into life, drowning out further conversation. Beside them, the other passengers were whooping and calling out, waving hats and handkerchiefs at the people standing on the dock. Magda fished a handkerchief out of her own pocket and began waving at random strangers, jumping up and down and laughing.

Zofia slumped forward against the railing, her body suddenly impossibly heavy with grief. She was leaving Ola – and Filip – behind forever.

'Why are you sad?' Magda asked in a quiet voice.

Zofia wiped a tear away. 'I'm not sad, little one. I'm just thinking about the past, which is never a good thing to do.'

She stood up straight and held her hand out for Magda.

'Now, Magda Chesney, how about we go and unpack our suitcases and then explore the ship? I've heard they serve the most delicious chocolate cake in the dining room.'

37

Seattle, Present Day

'Is that an actual chicken run?' Alex said, as they walked up to path towards the main building of the Spring Valley Residential Care Home. It was another warm, humid day, made bearable by the cool, salty breeze that washed in from the coast.

Lizzie nodded. 'Sure thing. They get fresh eggs every day for breakfast.'

Behind the wire, a dozen chickens clucked and pecked at the ground.

'We should get ourselves a few chickens,' Alex said, grinning. 'What d'you say, hun? And we can have roast chicken for dinner on Sundays.'

Lizzie elbowed him gently in the ribs and took his hand. He had been amazing. They had signed up with an adoption agency a few days after Lizzie's return from Warsaw, and although the woman they had spoken to had been mindful not to give them any false hope, she had said that they would make wonderful adoptive parents – in a way that had led both Lizzie and Alex to believe they might not have to wait long. It was another round of waiting, true, but this time, Lizzie and Alex were waiting for good news, not for bad. It made a difference, somehow. And besides, there was so much to keep them distracted in the meantime. Hannah's wedding, for example. She was getting married to a young man she'd met at college, Dave, who was just as eccentric as she was. They had planned the wedding party to coincide with the Fourth of July celebrations, and it had been all hands on deck to organise the catering, hire a live band, and decorate the house, inside and out.

But it was the long-anticipated reunion of Magda and Ola that had occupied Lizzie's thoughts ever since her return. She'd spoken to Tomasz earlier and they'd set up a video call for eleven a.m. Seattle time, eight p.m. Warsaw time. Ola, Tomasz told her, had been on tenterhooks, unable to eat or sleep. She couldn't wait to see her sister again. It saddened Lizzie beyond belief that it had taken so long to find her. But better late than never, she knew. She and Alex walked up to reception and were told that Magda was in the common room. Lizzie squeezed her husband's hand.

'I'd better wait out here,' he said gently. 'This is a matter for Chesney women, don't you think?' He gave her a soft kiss on the lips.

Lizzie entered the common room uncertainly. She'd spoken with the nurses on the phone every day since she'd returned from Warsaw, but Magda had been having more bad days than good lately, days during which she didn't recognise anyone and even forgot her own name. This morning, though, the nurse had said she seemed fine.

Magda was sitting at the far end of the common room in a floral-patterned armchair, her eyes closed and her chest rising and falling in regular intervals. Lizzie hesitated; should she

322

leave her grandmother asleep and come back later? Perhaps she would be confused if Lizzie woke her – too confused to process what she had to tell her. But they had the time scheduled and Ola would be terribly disappointed if she rang to say they'd have to wait even longer.

'It's okay,' a voice behind her said.

Lizzie turned to see the friendly nurse she'd met on her last visit.

'Like I told you earlier on the phone, she's having a pretty good day so far. She's been playing Mah-jongg all morning, that's why she's a little tired. But you go right ahead and wake her, I'll go get her a coffee.'

'Can you make it a Coke?' Lizzie asked.

'Sure.' The nurse smiled and left.

Lizzie leaned down and gave her grandmother a light kiss on the cheek, then she crouched down and stroked her hand.

'*Babcia*,' she said softly.

Magda's eyelids fluttered. Her skin was thin, almost translucent, but the star-shaped birthmark was as discernible as ever.

'It's me, Lizzie.'

The old woman's eyes opened slowly and she looked at Lizzie. For a long moment, it seemed like she didn't recognise her, but then she smiled. 'Lizzie! How nice of you to come.'

Lizzie pulled up a chair.

'*Babcia*, I have something to tell you.'

Magda's eyes opened wider, making them appear even rounder. 'Is it good news, or bad? If it's bad, don't tell me. I'd rather not know.'

Lizzie smiled. 'No, it's good news. Very good news. Now, you know I've been on a trip to Warsaw?'

'Warsaw? The capital of Poland?'

'Yes.' Lizzie felt a lump forming in her throat. She had told her grandmother about the trip, and now she'd forgotten. She wasn't having a good day, after all.

But then a grin crept across Magda's face. 'I'm just teasing you, Lizzie. Of course I know you've been to Warsaw.'

Lizzie smiled and shook her head. 'Don't do that, *Babcia*! You had me worried.'

Magda shuffled forward in her chair. 'Sorry, dear. So anyway, you went to Warsaw…'

'Yes. I went to Warsaw and I … I found someone.' Lizzie felt her heart beating faster now. 'I found Ola. Your sister.'

Magda's face seemed to crumple. 'Ola?'

At that moment, the nurse approached. 'Here's your Coke, Magda,' she said, holding out the glass. Her eyes widened in alarm when she saw Magda's expression. 'What is it? Are you not feeling well? Should I call the doctor?'

For the longest moment, Magda sat there, silently. Then a tear rolled down her cheek, lightly grazing her birthmark. Finally, she whispered, 'Ola.'

Lizzie turned to the nurse. 'I think she's all right. I've just brought her some news about her sister. It's a bit … unexpected.'

The nurse tilted her head sympathetically. 'I never knew she had a sister,' she said quietly. 'Has she died?'

'No.' Lizzie smiled. 'Quite the opposite.'

Frowning, the nurse placed the Coke down. 'Well, if you need me, just call.'

Lizzie turned back to Magda. 'I found Ola,' she said again, softly. 'She's living in Warsaw with her grandson and his family. I told her all about you.'

Magda took out a handkerchief and wiped her face. Her hands were trembling. 'But how? I don't … I can't…'

As concisely as she could, Lizzie told her everything, about Tomasz and Maja and, of course, Roksana. When she was finished, Magda smiled sadly. 'I guess she's very old now, like me.'

Lizzie nodded. 'Listen, *Babcia*. Tomasz suggested a video call. You and Ola can speak, over the internet. Would you like that?'

Magda looked terrified for a moment, but then she said, 'When? When can I speak to her?'

Lizzie took the notebook out of the case. 'In about seven minutes,' she said. 'I just have to set everything up and dial you in. You think you're ready?'

Magda looked her straight in the eyes. 'I've waited my whole life for this. How can I not be ready?'

Lizzie switched the computer on, set it up so it would be at Magda's eye level, and clicked on the app. A few seconds later, she was looking at Tomasz on the screen.

'Hey, second cousin!' he said, grinning. 'I have an old woman here wants to see her sister. Are you all set?'

'All set,' Lizzie said. 'I also have an old woman here. She's been waiting her whole life to see her sister.'

'What are we waiting for, then?'

Lizzie turned the screen towards Magda, adjusting it so there was no light from the window reflecting on the screen.

'There you go,' she whispered to Magda. 'Now take all the time you want.'

As she got to her feet, she caught sight of Ola on the screen, her expression almost the exact copy of her sister's. She turned and headed out of the room, as Magda and Ola began a tearful conversation. Lizzie's own tears were suddenly close to the surface. She let them fall freely.

'Sweetie, are you okay?' Alex rushed towards her, a look of concern on his face.

Lizzie went and put her head on his chest, inhaled his familiar musky smell.

'Never better,' she said.

Acknowledgements

Huge thanks to Elisha Lundin at Avon, without whom this novel would never have been written.

Thanks also to Laura McCallen, for the super-valuable feedback on an earlier draft, and to Thorne Ryan for thinking of me.

I met some lovely people on a research trip to Warsaw; thanks in particular to Tomasz for the fascinating tour of the former Jewish Ghetto.

My agent, Jenny Brown, has been in my corner for over ten years now and will hopefully remain there for many years to come!

And special thanks – as always – to all those who have shown the patience, kindness and encouragement I rely on so heavily: my husband Christian and my children Jake, Fay, Amy and June.